HALLOWEEN CLASSICS

Graphic Classics® Volume 23

2012

AT HOME
THE VAULT KEEPER
THE OLD WITCH
THE CRYPT KEEPER
AL FELDSTEIN

ORIGINAL PAINTING © BY AL FELDSTEIN

Edited by Tom Pomplun

EUREKA PRODUCTIONS
8778 Oak Grove Road, Mount Horeb, Wisconsin 53572
www.graphicclassics.com

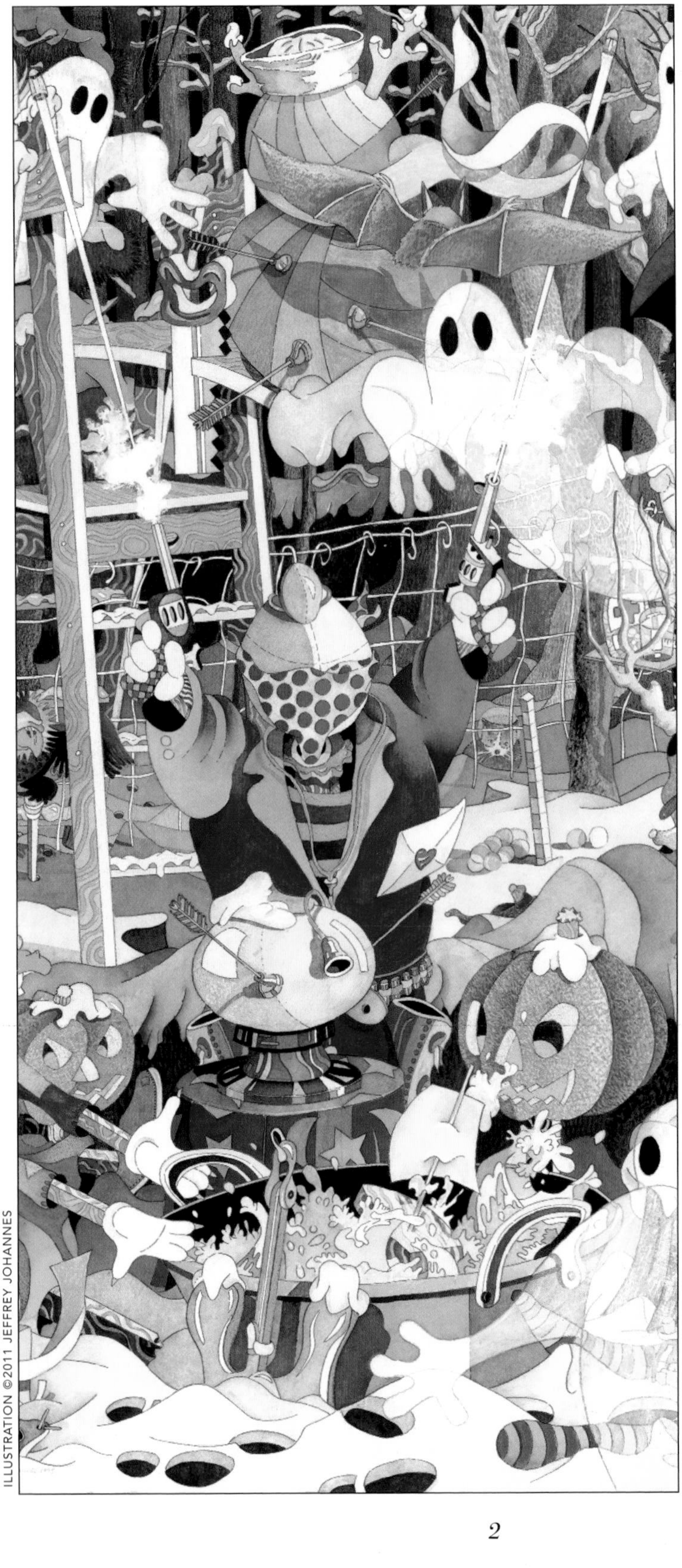

ILLUSTRATION ©2011 JEFFREY JOHANNES

Hallowe'en in a Suburb

by **H. P. LOVECRAFT**
illustrated by **JEFFREY JOHANNES**

The steeples are white in the wild moonlight,
And the trees have a silver glare;
Past the chimneys high see the vampires fly,
And the harpies of upper air,
That flutter and laugh and stare.

For the village dead to the moon outspread
Never shone in the sunset's gleam,
But grew out of the deep that the dead years keep
Where the rivers of madness stream
Down the gulfs to a pit of dream.

A chill wind blows through the rows of sheaves
In the meadows that shimmer pale,
And comes to twine where the headstones shine
And the ghouls of the churchyard wail
For harvests that fly and fail.

Not a breath of the strange grey gods of change
That tore from the past its own
Can quicken this hour, when a spectral power
Spreads sleep o'er the cosmic throne,
And looses the vast unknown.

So here again stretch the vale and plain
That moons long-forgotten saw,
And the dead leap gay in the pallid ray,
Sprung out of the tomb's black maw
To shake all the world with awe.

And all that the morn shall greet forlorn,
The ugliness and the pest
Of rows where thick rise the stones and brick,
Shall some day be with the rest,
And brood with the shades unblest.

Then wild in the dark let the lemurs bark,
And the leprous spires ascend;
For new and old alike in the fold
Of horror and death are penned,
For the hounds of Time to rend.

CONTENTS

HALLOWEEN CLASSICS

GRAPHIC CLASSICS® VOLUME 23

NERWIN THE DOCENT

THE HEADLESS HORSEMAN

THE SKELETON CORPSE

THE EGYPTIAN MUMMY

THE MAD SCIENTIST

THE SOMNAMBULIST

ILLUSTRATIONS BY KEVIN ATKINSON
COVER ILLUSTRATION BY SIMON GANE
TITLE PAGE ILLUSTRATION BY AL FELDSTEIN
BACK COVER ILLUSTRATION BY MATT HOWARTH

Halloween Classics: Graphic Classics Volume 23, ISBN 978-0-9825630-5-2 is published by Eureka Productions. Price US $17.95, CAN $20.95. Available from Eureka Productions, 8778 Oak Grove Road, Mount Horeb, WI 53572. Tom Pomplun, designer and publisher, tom@graphicclassics.com. Eileen Fitzgerald, editorial assistant. Permission to adapt "Hallowe'en in a Suburb" and "Cool Air" by H.P. Lovecraft in this volume has been granted by Lovecraft Holdings, LLC. Compilation and all original works ©2012 Eureka Productions. Graphic Classics is a registered trademark of Eureka Productions. For ordering information and previews of upcoming volumes visit the Graphic Classics website at http://www.graphicclassics.com. Printed in Canada.

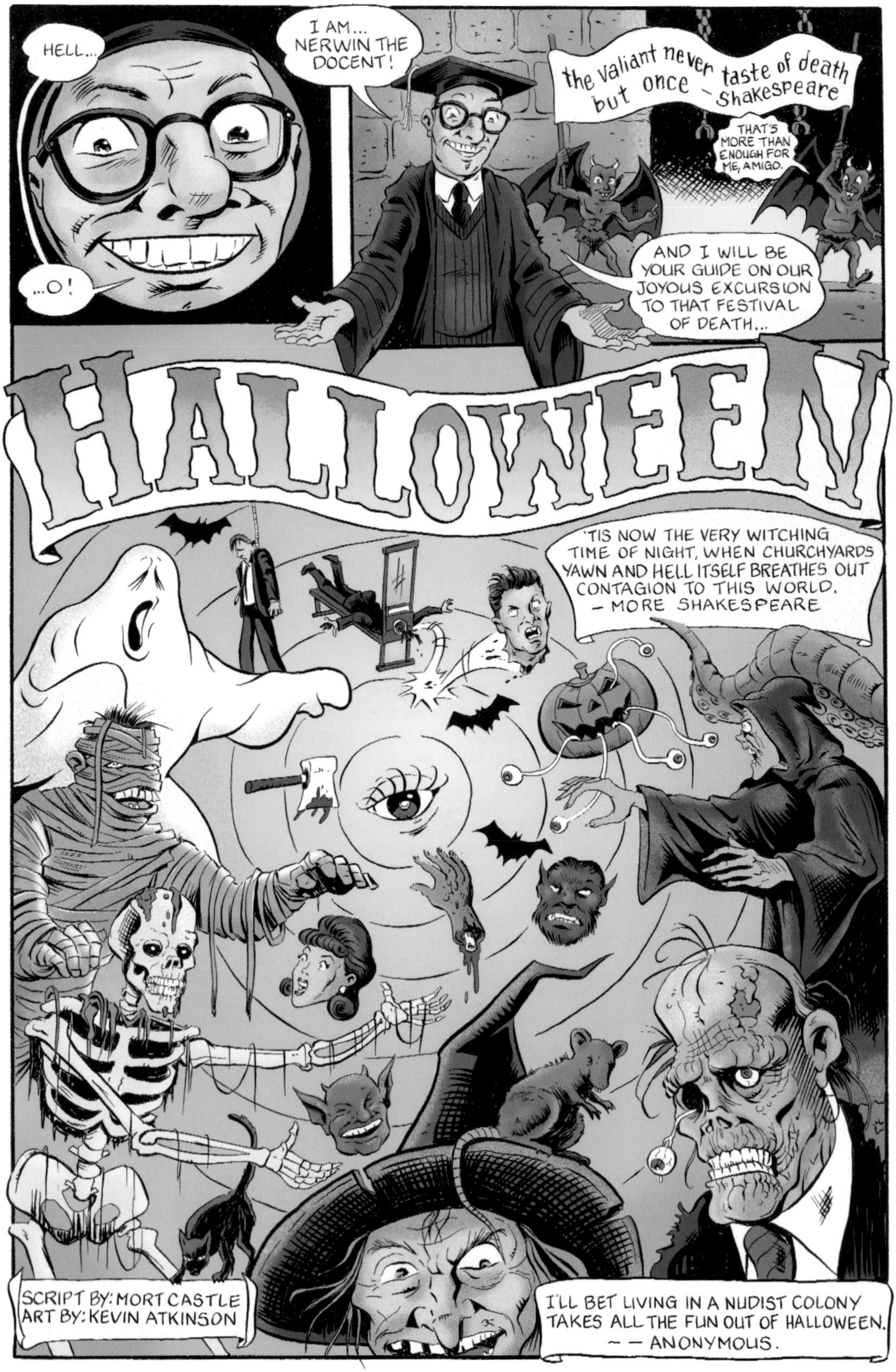
HELL...
...O!
I AM... NERWIN THE DOCENT!
the valiant never taste of death but once – Shakespeare
THAT'S MORE THAN ENOUGH FOR ME, AMIGO.
AND I WILL BE YOUR GUIDE ON OUR JOYOUS EXCURSION TO THAT FESTIVAL OF DEATH...
HALLOWEEN
'TIS NOW THE VERY WITCHING TIME OF NIGHT, WHEN CHURCHYARDS YAWN AND HELL ITSELF BREATHES OUT CONTAGION TO THIS WORLD. – MORE SHAKESPEARE
SCRIPT BY: MORT CASTLE
ART BY: KEVIN ATKINSON
I'LL BET LIVING IN A NUDIST COLONY TAKES ALL THE FUN OUT OF HALLOWEEN. – – ANONYMOUS.

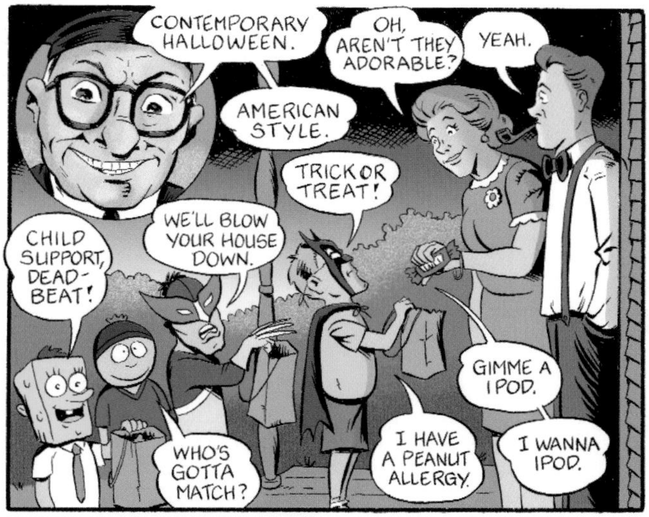
CONTEMPORARY HALLOWEEN.
AMERICAN STYLE.
OH, AREN'T THEY ADORABLE?
YEAH.
TRICK OR TREAT!
WE'LL BLOW YOUR HOUSE DOWN.
CHILD SUPPORT, DEAD-BEAT!
GIMME A IPOD.
WHO'S GOTTA MATCH?
I HAVE A PEANUT ALLERGY.
I WANNA IPOD.

"NO! THE REAL HALLOWEEN IS ABOUT THE **DEAD**! IT'S A DAY FOR THE DEAD.

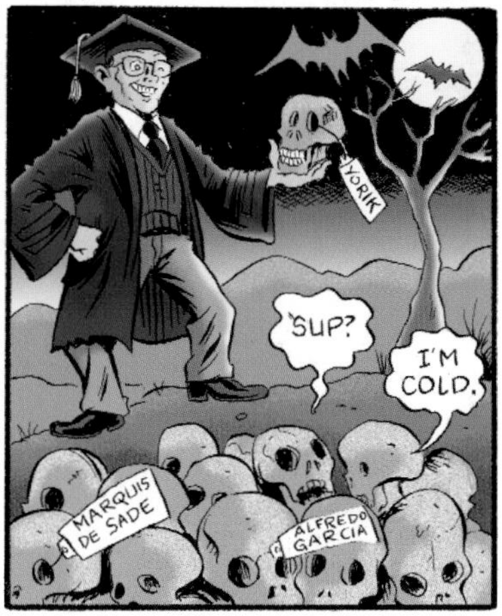
YORIK
'SUP?
I'M COLD.
MARQUIS DE SADE
ALFREDO GARCIA

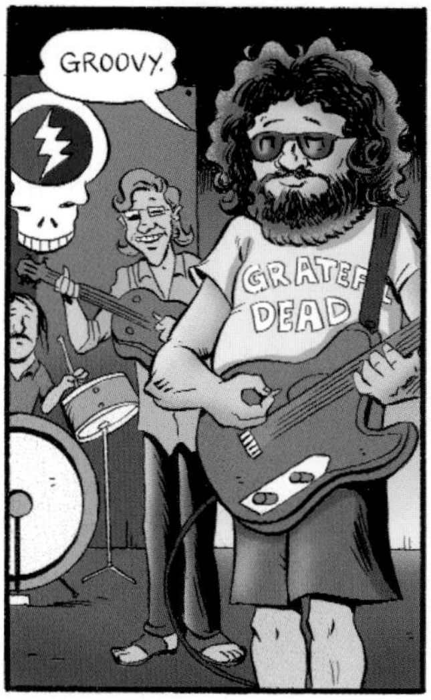
GROOVY.
GRATEFUL DEAD

"IN ANCIENT DAYS, BEFORE THE INTERNET OR ROLL-ON DEODORANT, HALLOWEEN BEGAN AS THE CELTIC FESTIVAL SAMHAIN. IT WAS A DEEPLY SPIRITUAL TIME MARKED BY A LOT OF JUMPING AROUND, PREFERABLY IN AN ANIMAL SKIN. SACRED FIRES KEPT AWAY EVIL SPIRITS.

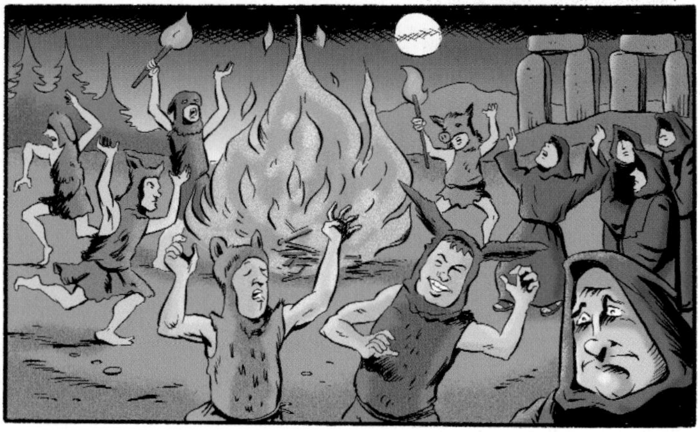

"DURING THE FIRST CENTURY, THE ROMANS INVADED BRITAIN, BRINGING WITH THEM THE FESTIVAL OF **POMONA DAY**, CELEBRATING THEIR GODDESS OF FRUITS.

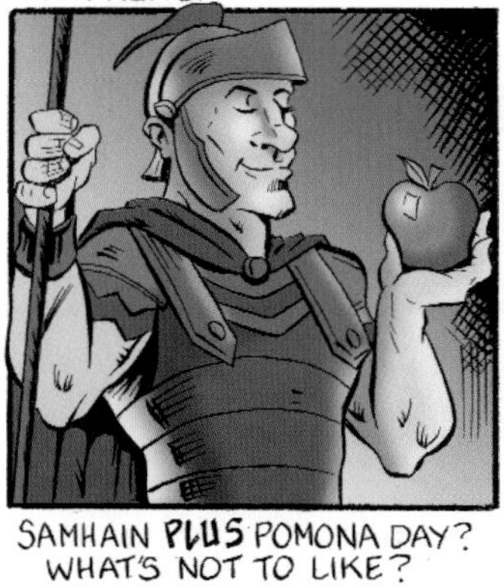

SAMHAIN **PLUS** POMONA DAY? WHAT'S NOT TO LIKE?

"THEN CHRISTIANITY SPREAD THROUGHOUT BRITAIN AND EUROPE, AND IN 835 A.D. (THERE WAS NO CHRISTIANITY IN 835 B.C.!) THE CHURCH DECLARED NOVEMBER 1 TO BE **ALL SAINTS DAY**-- WHICH HAD SO MUCH PIZZAZZ THAT, YEARS LATER, NOVEMBER 2 BECAME **ALL SOULS DAY**, A DAY TO HONOR THE DEAD-- AND TO MAKE NICE WITH THE SPIRITS OF THE DEPARTED THAT WERE BAD ON YOU."

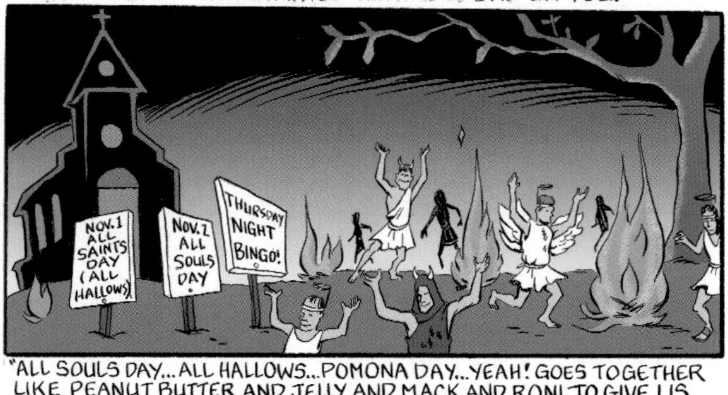
NOV. 1 ALL SAINTS DAY (ALL HALLOWS)
NOV. 2 ALL SOULS DAY
THURSDAY NIGHT BINGO!

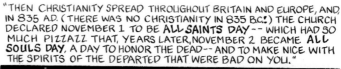

"ALL SOULS DAY... ALL HALLOWS... POMONA DAY... YEAH! GOES TOGETHER LIKE PEANUT BUTTER AND JELLY AND MACK AND RONI TO GIVE US THAT **FUN** DAY FOR THE DEAD: HALLOWEEN."

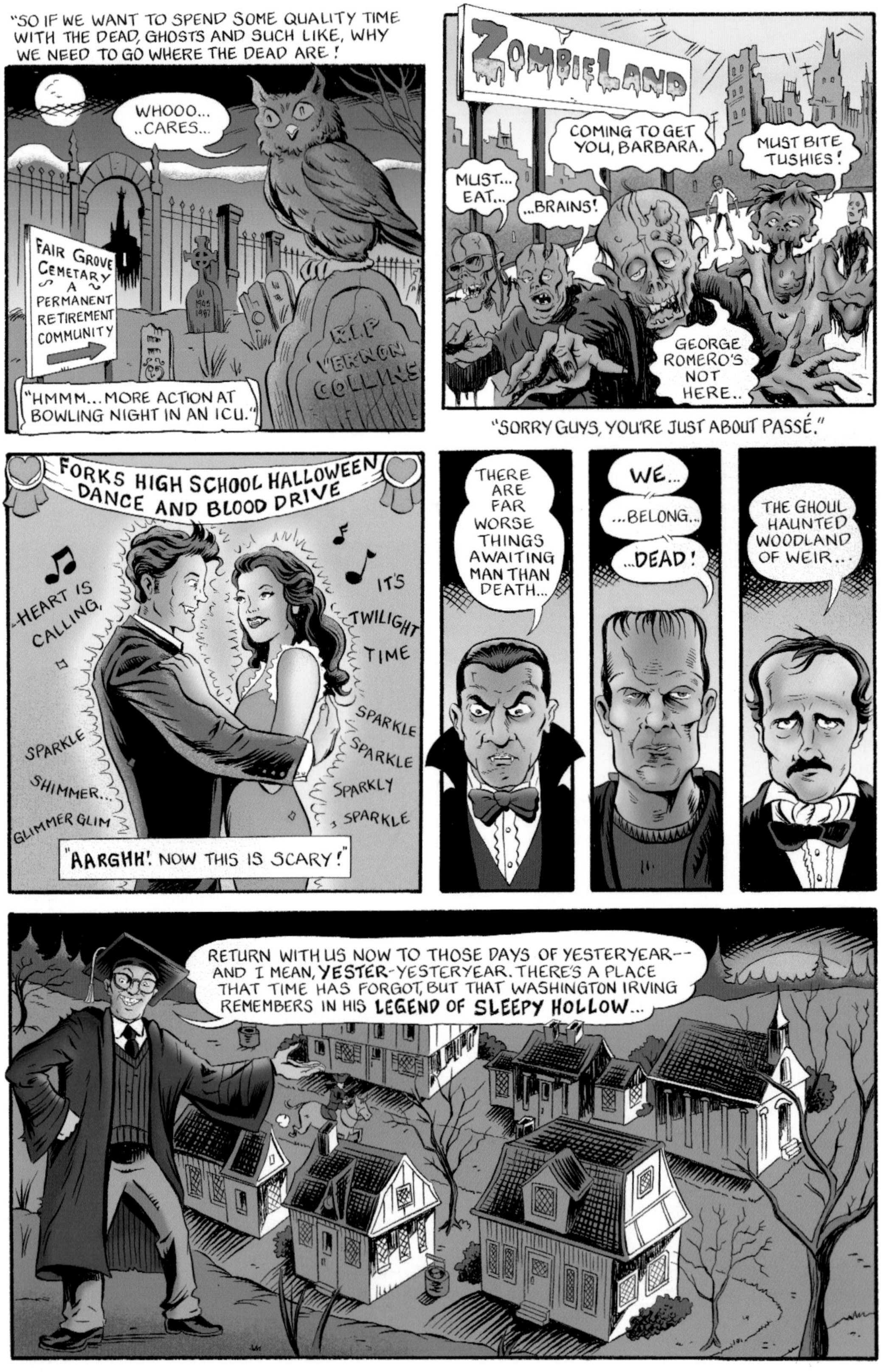
"SO IF WE WANT TO SPEND SOME QUALITY TIME WITH THE DEAD, GHOSTS AND SUCH LIKE, WHY WE NEED TO GO WHERE THE DEAD ARE!
WHOOO... ..CARES...
FAIR GROVE CEMETARY A PERMANENT RETIREMENT COMMUNITY
R.I.P. VERNON COLLINS
"HMMM... MORE ACTION AT BOWLING NIGHT IN AN ICU."
ZOMBIELAND
MUST... EAT...
...BRAINS!
COMING TO GET YOU, BARBARA.
MUST BITE TUSHIES!
GEORGE ROMERO'S NOT HERE..
"SORRY GUYS, YOU'RE JUST ABOUT PASSÉ."
FORKS HIGH SCHOOL HALLOWEEN DANCE AND BLOOD DRIVE
HEART IS CALLING,
IT'S TWILIGHT TIME
SPARKLE
SHIMMER...
GLIMMER GLIM
SPARKLE
SPARKLE
SPARKLY
SPARKLE
"AARGHH! NOW THIS IS SCARY!"
THERE ARE FAR WORSE THINGS AWAITING MAN THAN DEATH...
WE...
...BELONG...
...DEAD!
THE GHOUL HAUNTED WOODLAND OF WEIR...
RETURN WITH US NOW TO THOSE DAYS OF YESTERYEAR-- AND I MEAN, YESTER-YESTERYEAR. THERE'S A PLACE THAT TIME HAS FORGOT, BUT THAT WASHINGTON IRVING REMEMBERS IN HIS LEGEND OF SLEEPY HOLLOW...

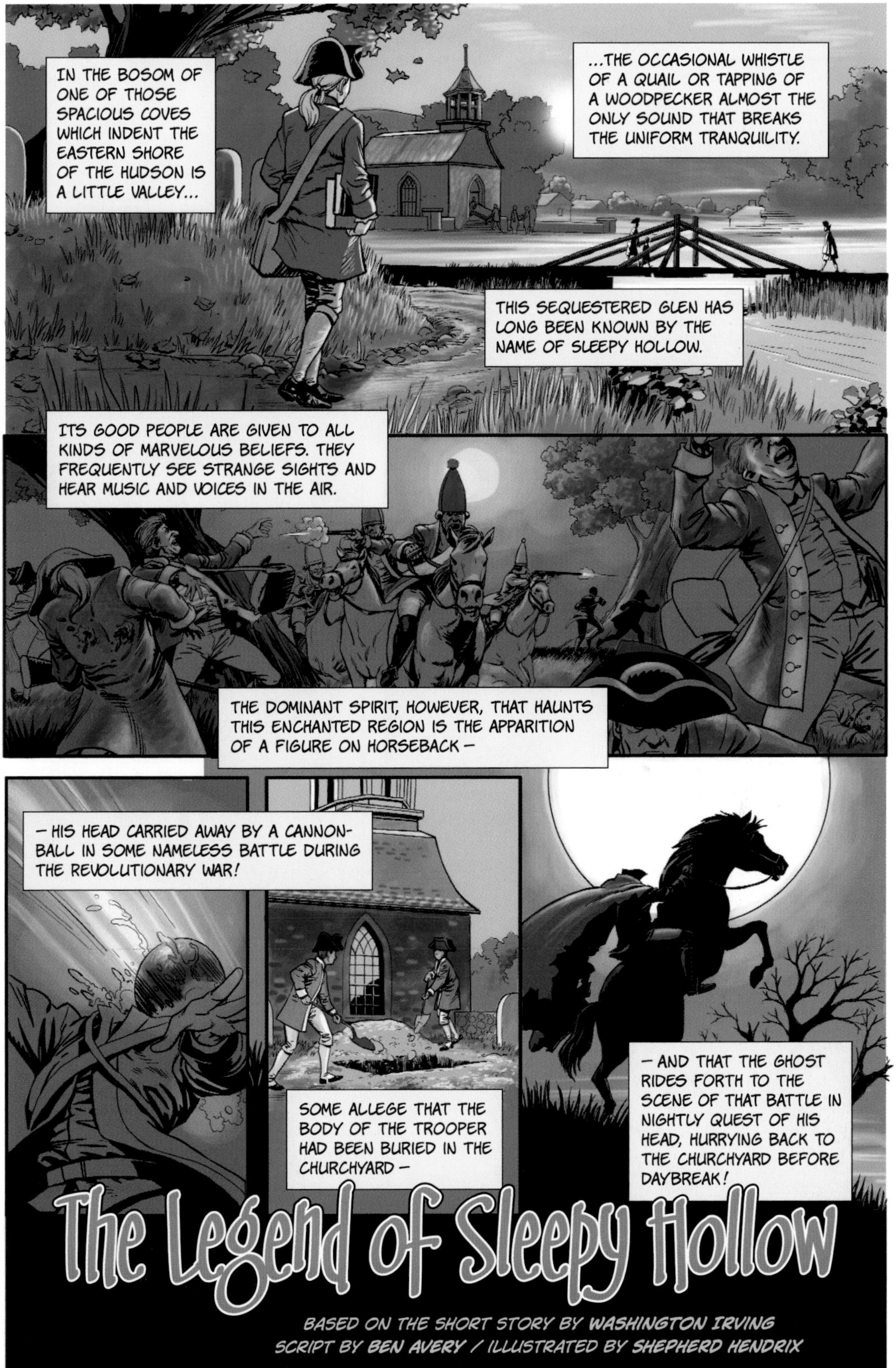
IN THE BOSOM OF ONE OF THOSE SPACIOUS COVES WHICH INDENT THE EASTERN SHORE OF THE HUDSON IS A LITTLE VALLEY...
...THE OCCASIONAL WHISTLE OF A QUAIL OR TAPPING OF A WOODPECKER ALMOST THE ONLY SOUND THAT BREAKS THE UNIFORM TRANQUILITY.
THIS SEQUESTERED GLEN HAS LONG BEEN KNOWN BY THE NAME OF SLEEPY HOLLOW.
ITS GOOD PEOPLE ARE GIVEN TO ALL KINDS OF MARVELOUS BELIEFS. THEY FREQUENTLY SEE STRANGE SIGHTS AND HEAR MUSIC AND VOICES IN THE AIR.
THE DOMINANT SPIRIT, HOWEVER, THAT HAUNTS THIS ENCHANTED REGION IS THE APPARITION OF A FIGURE ON HORSEBACK –
– HIS HEAD CARRIED AWAY BY A CANNON-BALL IN SOME NAMELESS BATTLE DURING THE REVOLUTIONARY WAR!
SOME ALLEGE THAT THE BODY OF THE TROOPER HAD BEEN BURIED IN THE CHURCHYARD –
– AND THAT THE GHOST RIDES FORTH TO THE SCENE OF THAT BATTLE IN NIGHTLY QUEST OF HIS HEAD, HURRYING BACK TO THE CHURCHYARD BEFORE DAYBREAK!
The Legend of Sleepy Hollow
BASED ON THE SHORT STORY BY WASHINGTON IRVING
SCRIPT BY BEN AVERY / ILLUSTRATED BY SHEPHERD HENDRIX

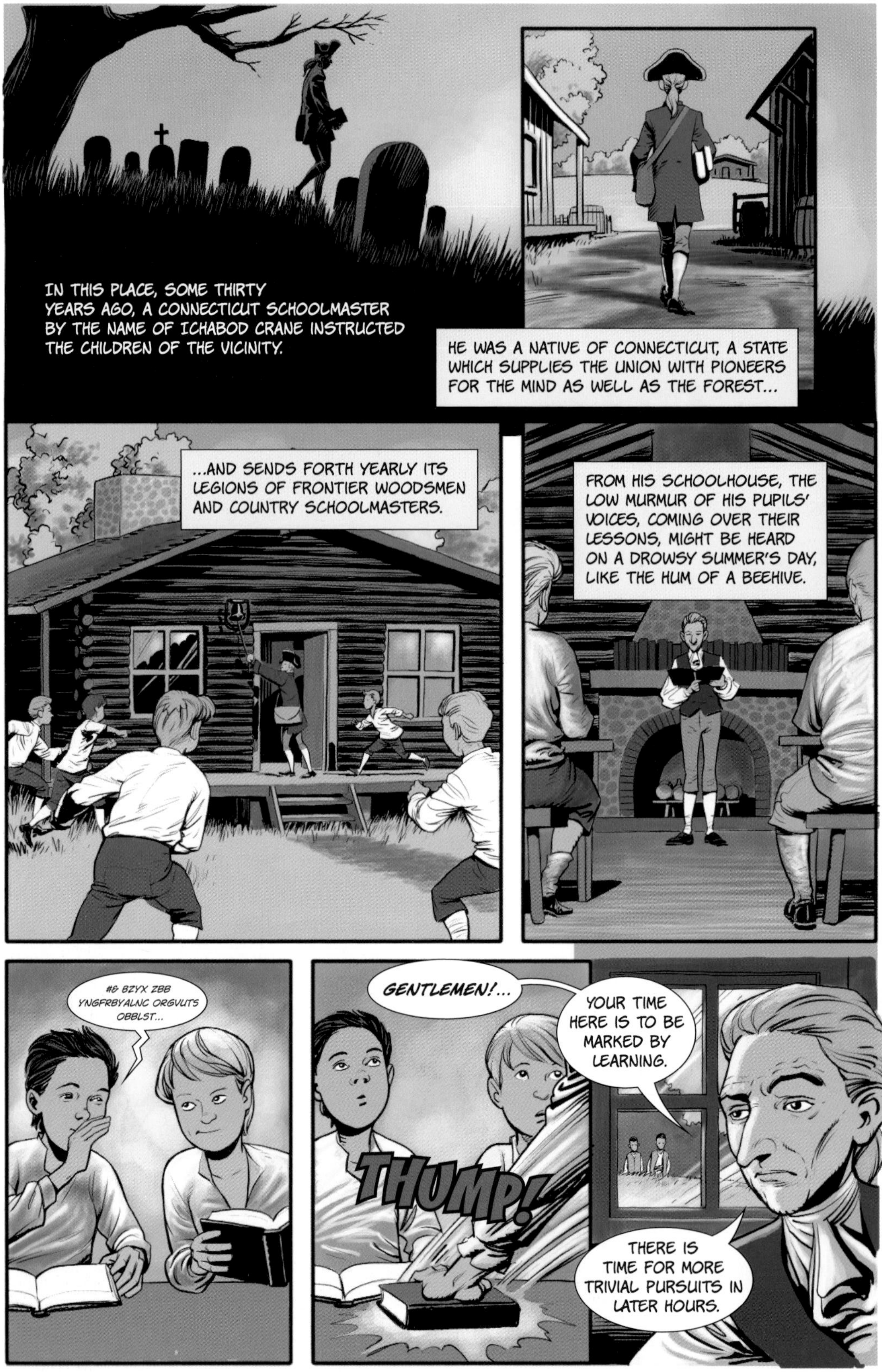
IN THIS PLACE, SOME THIRTY YEARS AGO, A CONNECTICUT SCHOOLMASTER BY THE NAME OF ICHABOD CRANE INSTRUCTED THE CHILDREN OF THE VICINITY.
HE WAS A NATIVE OF CONNECTICUT, A STATE WHICH SUPPLIES THE UNION WITH PIONEERS FOR THE MIND AS WELL AS THE FOREST...
...AND SENDS FORTH YEARLY ITS LEGIONS OF FRONTIER WOODSMEN AND COUNTRY SCHOOLMASTERS.
FROM HIS SCHOOLHOUSE, THE LOW MURMUR OF HIS PUPILS' VOICES, COMING OVER THEIR LESSONS, MIGHT BE HEARD ON A DROWSY SUMMER'S DAY, LIKE THE HUM OF A BEEHIVE.
#& BZYX ZBB YNGFRBYALNC ORGVUTS OBBLST...
GENTLEMEN!...
THUMP!
YOUR TIME HERE IS TO BE MARKED BY LEARNING.
THERE IS TIME FOR MORE TRIVIAL PURSUITS IN LATER HOURS.

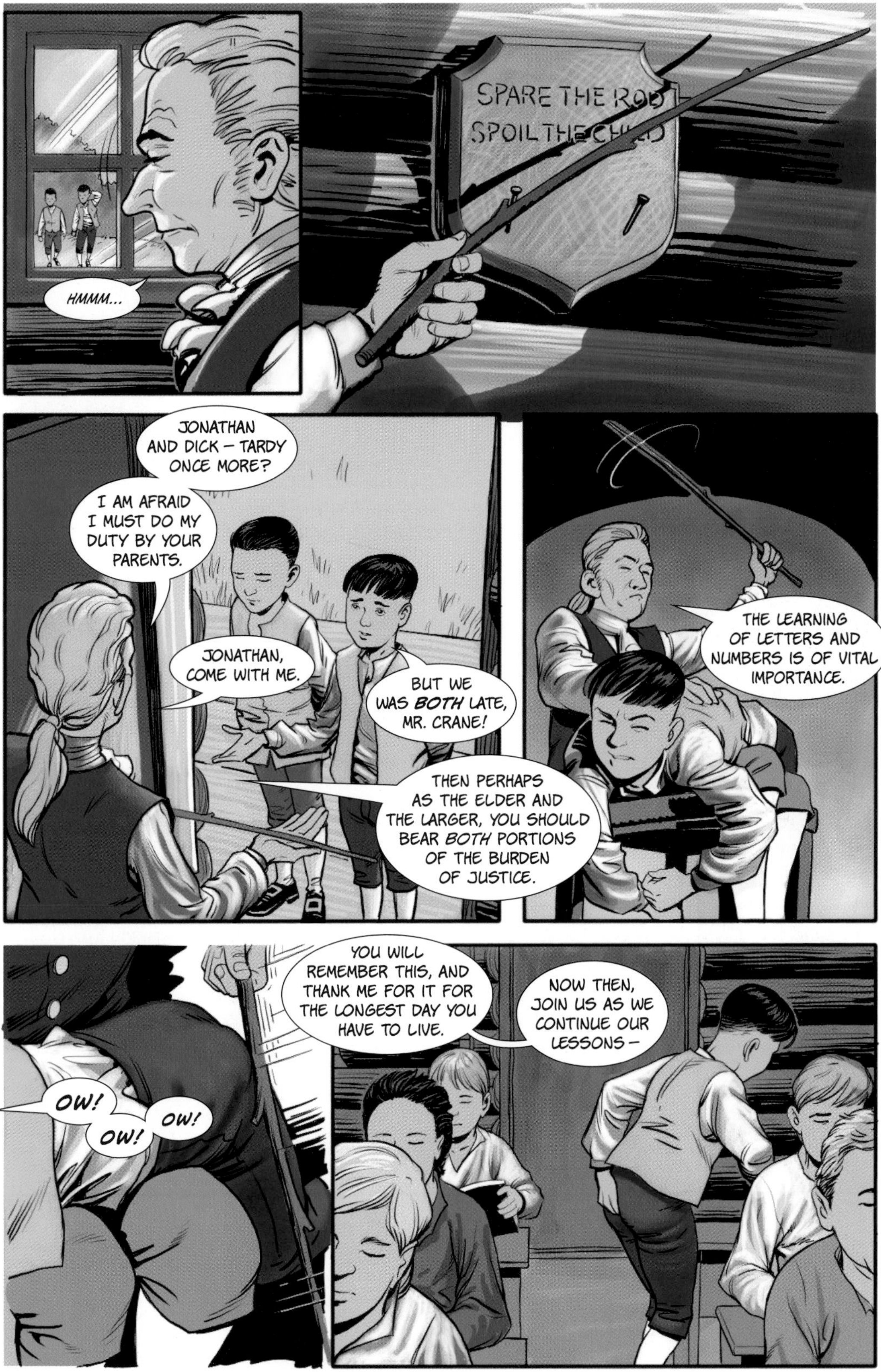
HMMM...
SPARE THE ROD
SPOIL THE CHILD
JONATHAN AND DICK – TARDY ONCE MORE?
I AM AFRAID I MUST DO MY DUTY BY YOUR PARENTS.
JONATHAN, COME WITH ME.
BUT WE WAS *BOTH* LATE, MR. CRANE!
THEN PERHAPS AS THE ELDER AND THE LARGER, YOU SHOULD BEAR *BOTH* PORTIONS OF THE BURDEN OF JUSTICE.
THE LEARNING OF LETTERS AND NUMBERS IS OF VITAL IMPORTANCE.
OW!
OW!
OW!
YOU WILL REMEMBER THIS, AND THANK ME FOR IT FOR THE LONGEST DAY YOU HAVE TO LIVE.
NOW THEN, JOIN US AS WE CONTINUE OUR LESSONS –

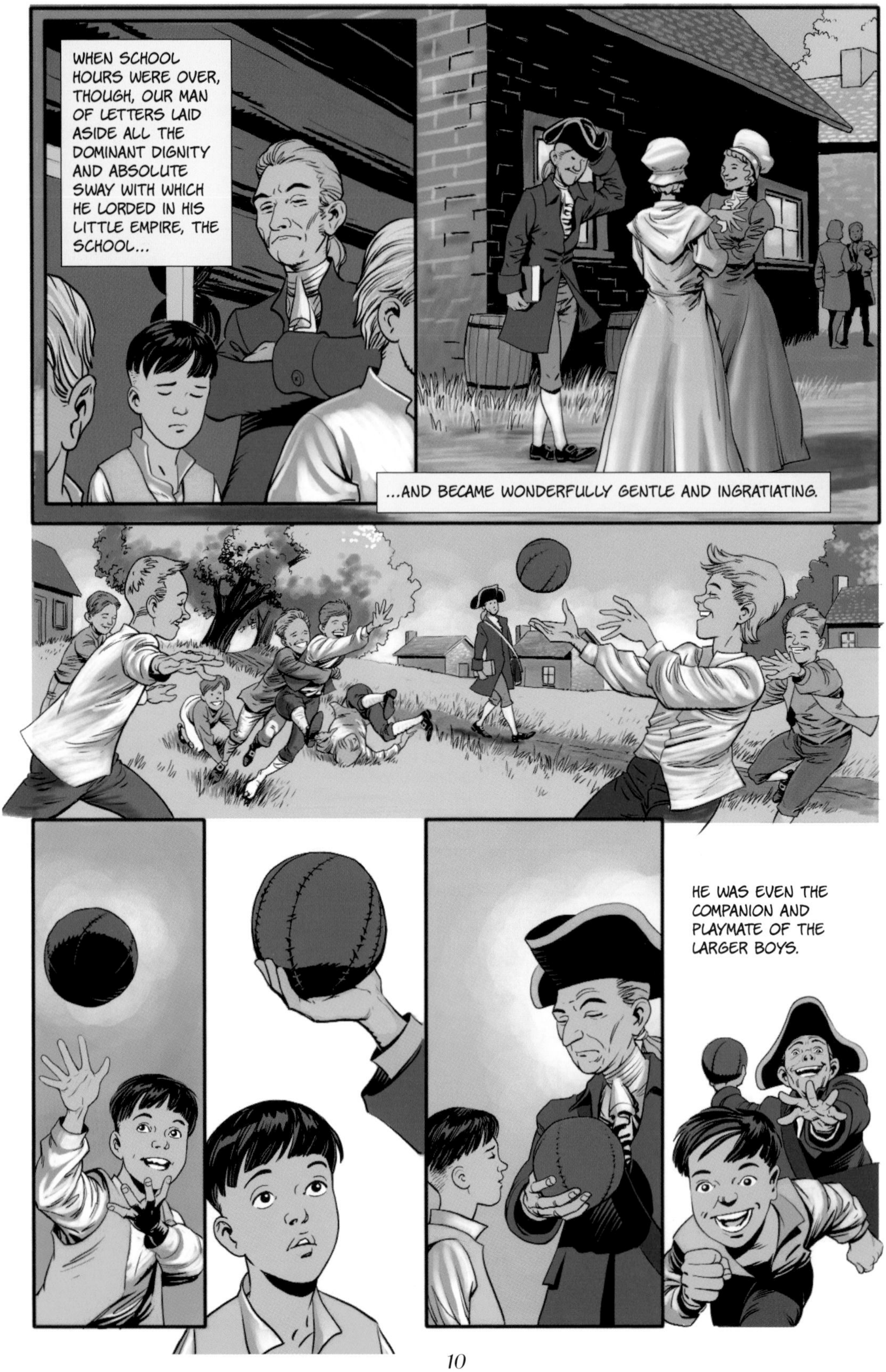
WHEN SCHOOL HOURS WERE OVER, THOUGH, OUR MAN OF LETTERS LAID ASIDE ALL THE DOMINANT DIGNITY AND ABSOLUTE SWAY WITH WHICH HE LORDED IN HIS LITTLE EMPIRE, THE SCHOOL...
...AND BECAME WONDERFULLY GENTLE AND INGRATIATING.
HE WAS EVEN THE COMPANION AND PLAYMATE OF THE LARGER BOYS.

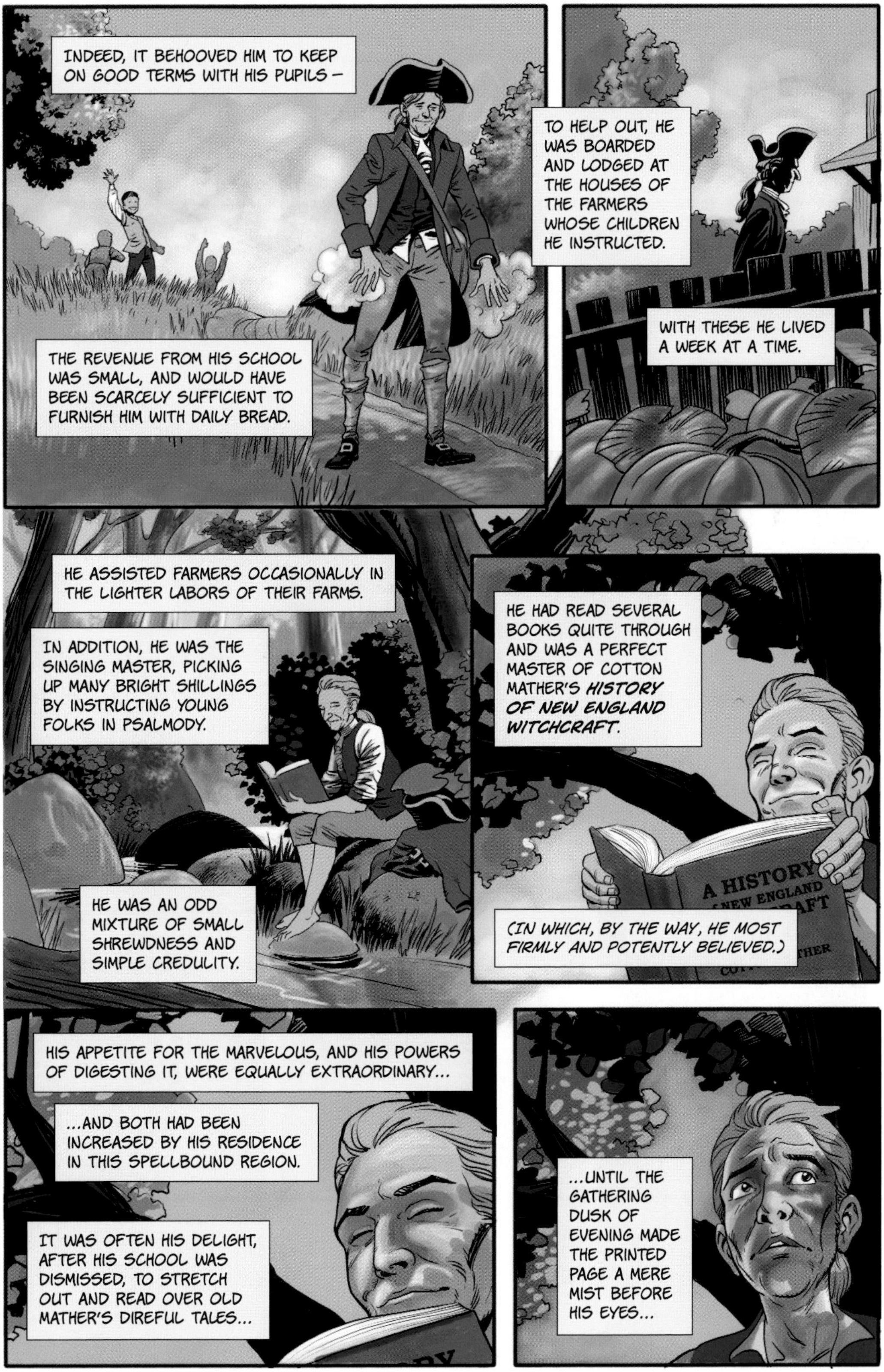
INDEED, IT BEHOOVED HIM TO KEEP ON GOOD TERMS WITH HIS PUPILS –
THE REVENUE FROM HIS SCHOOL WAS SMALL, AND WOULD HAVE BEEN SCARCELY SUFFICIENT TO FURNISH HIM WITH DAILY BREAD.
TO HELP OUT, HE WAS BOARDED AND LODGED AT THE HOUSES OF THE FARMERS WHOSE CHILDREN HE INSTRUCTED.
WITH THESE HE LIVED A WEEK AT A TIME.
HE ASSISTED FARMERS OCCASIONALLY IN THE LIGHTER LABORS OF THEIR FARMS.
IN ADDITION, HE WAS THE SINGING MASTER, PICKING UP MANY BRIGHT SHILLINGS BY INSTRUCTING YOUNG FOLKS IN PSALMODY.
HE WAS AN ODD MIXTURE OF SMALL SHREWDNESS AND SIMPLE CREDULITY.
HE HAD READ SEVERAL BOOKS QUITE THROUGH AND WAS A PERFECT MASTER OF COTTON MATHER'S *HISTORY OF NEW ENGLAND WITCHCRAFT*.
A HISTORY
(IN WHICH, BY THE WAY, HE MOST FIRMLY AND POTENTLY BELIEVED.)
HIS APPETITE FOR THE MARVELOUS, AND HIS POWERS OF DIGESTING IT, WERE EQUALLY EXTRAORDINARY...
...AND BOTH HAD BEEN INCREASED BY HIS RESIDENCE IN THIS SPELLBOUND REGION.
IT WAS OFTEN HIS DELIGHT, AFTER HIS SCHOOL WAS DISMISSED, TO STRETCH OUT AND READ OVER OLD MATHER'S DIREFUL TALES...
...UNTIL THE GATHERING DUSK OF EVENING MADE THE PRINTED PAGE A MERE MIST BEFORE HIS EYES...

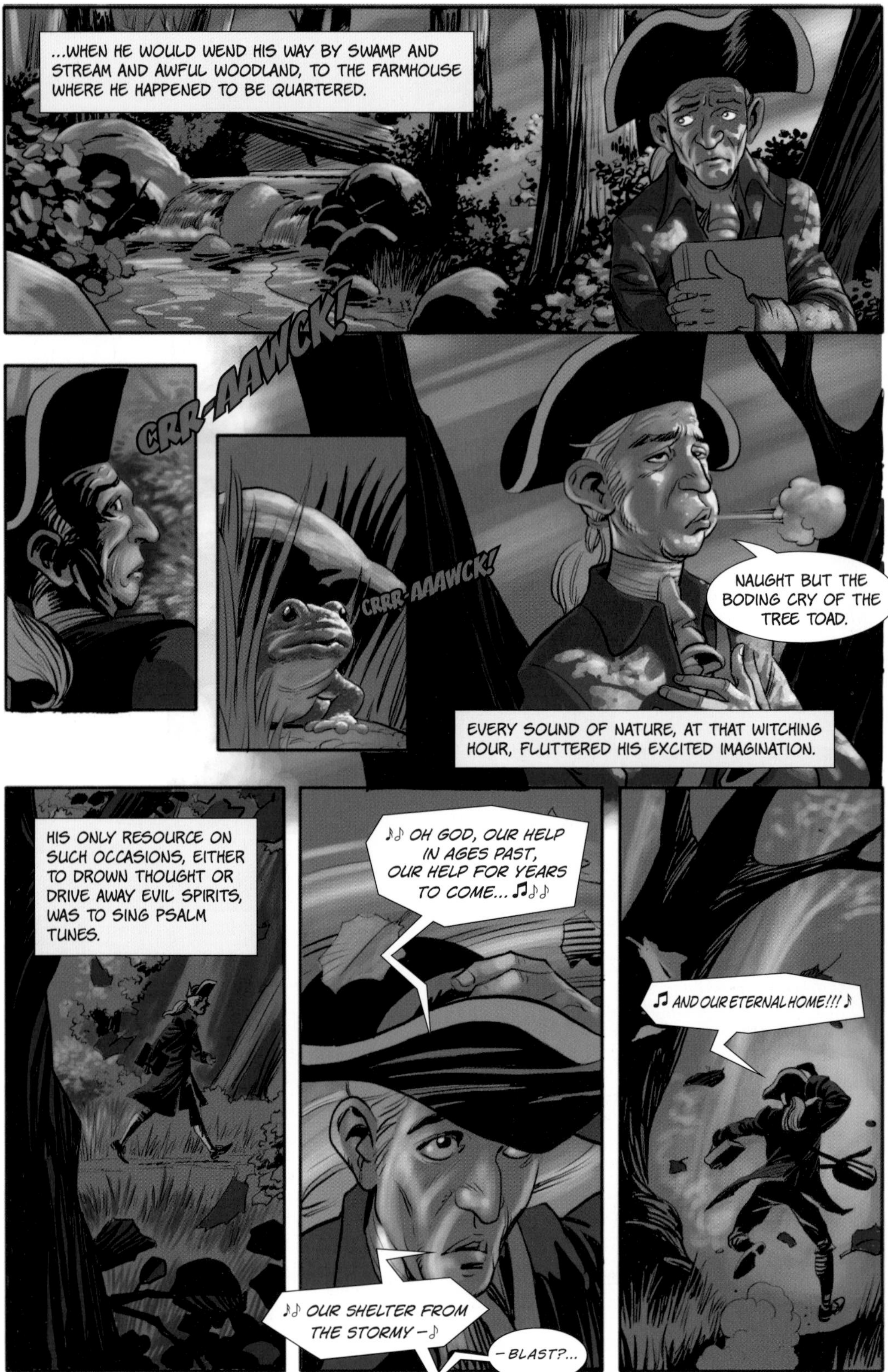
...WHEN HE WOULD WEND HIS WAY BY SWAMP AND STREAM AND AWFUL WOODLAND, TO THE FARMHOUSE WHERE HE HAPPENED TO BE QUARTERED.
CRR-AAWCK!
CRRR-AAAWCK!
NAUGHT BUT THE BODING CRY OF THE TREE TOAD.
EVERY SOUND OF NATURE, AT THAT WITCHING HOUR, FLUTTERED HIS EXCITED IMAGINATION.
HIS ONLY RESOURCE ON SUCH OCCASIONS, EITHER TO DROWN THOUGHT OR DRIVE AWAY EVIL SPIRITS, WAS TO SING PSALM TUNES.
♪♪ OH GOD, OUR HELP IN AGES PAST, OUR HELP FOR YEARS TO COME... ♫♪♪
♪♪ OUR SHELTER FROM THE STORMY –♪
– BLAST?...
♫ AND OUR ETERNAL HOME!!! ♪

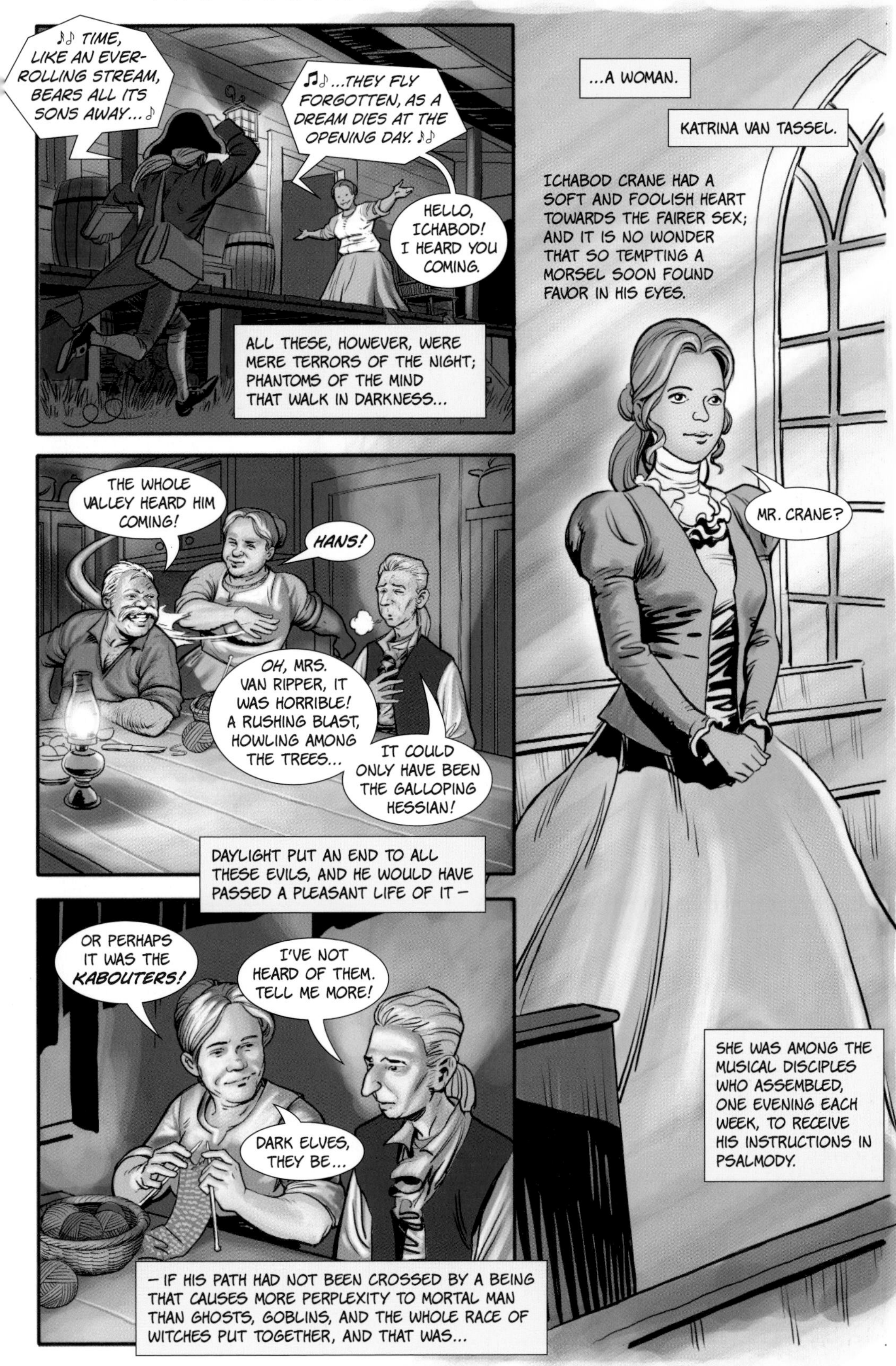
♪♪ TIME, LIKE AN EVER-ROLLING STREAM, BEARS ALL ITS SONS AWAY... ♪
♫♪ ...THEY FLY FORGOTTEN, AS A DREAM DIES AT THE OPENING DAY. ♪♪
HELLO, ICHABOD! I HEARD YOU COMING.
ALL THESE, HOWEVER, WERE MERE TERRORS OF THE NIGHT; PHANTOMS OF THE MIND THAT WALK IN DARKNESS...
THE WHOLE VALLEY HEARD HIM COMING!
HANS!
OH, MRS. VAN RIPPER, IT WAS HORRIBLE! A RUSHING BLAST, HOWLING AMONG THE TREES...
IT COULD ONLY HAVE BEEN THE GALLOPING HESSIAN!
DAYLIGHT PUT AN END TO ALL THESE EVILS, AND HE WOULD HAVE PASSED A PLEASANT LIFE OF IT –
OR PERHAPS IT WAS THE KABOUTERS!
I'VE NOT HEARD OF THEM. TELL ME MORE!
DARK ELVES, THEY BE...
– IF HIS PATH HAD NOT BEEN CROSSED BY A BEING THAT CAUSES MORE PERPLEXITY TO MORTAL MAN THAN GHOSTS, GOBLINS, AND THE WHOLE RACE OF WITCHES PUT TOGETHER, AND THAT WAS...
...A WOMAN.
KATRINA VAN TASSEL.
ICHABOD CRANE HAD A SOFT AND FOOLISH HEART TOWARDS THE FAIRER SEX; AND IT IS NO WONDER THAT SO TEMPTING A MORSEL SOON FOUND FAVOR IN HIS EYES.
MR. CRANE?
SHE WAS AMONG THE MUSICAL DISCIPLES WHO ASSEMBLED, ONE EVENING EACH WEEK, TO RECEIVE HIS INSTRUCTIONS IN PSALMODY.

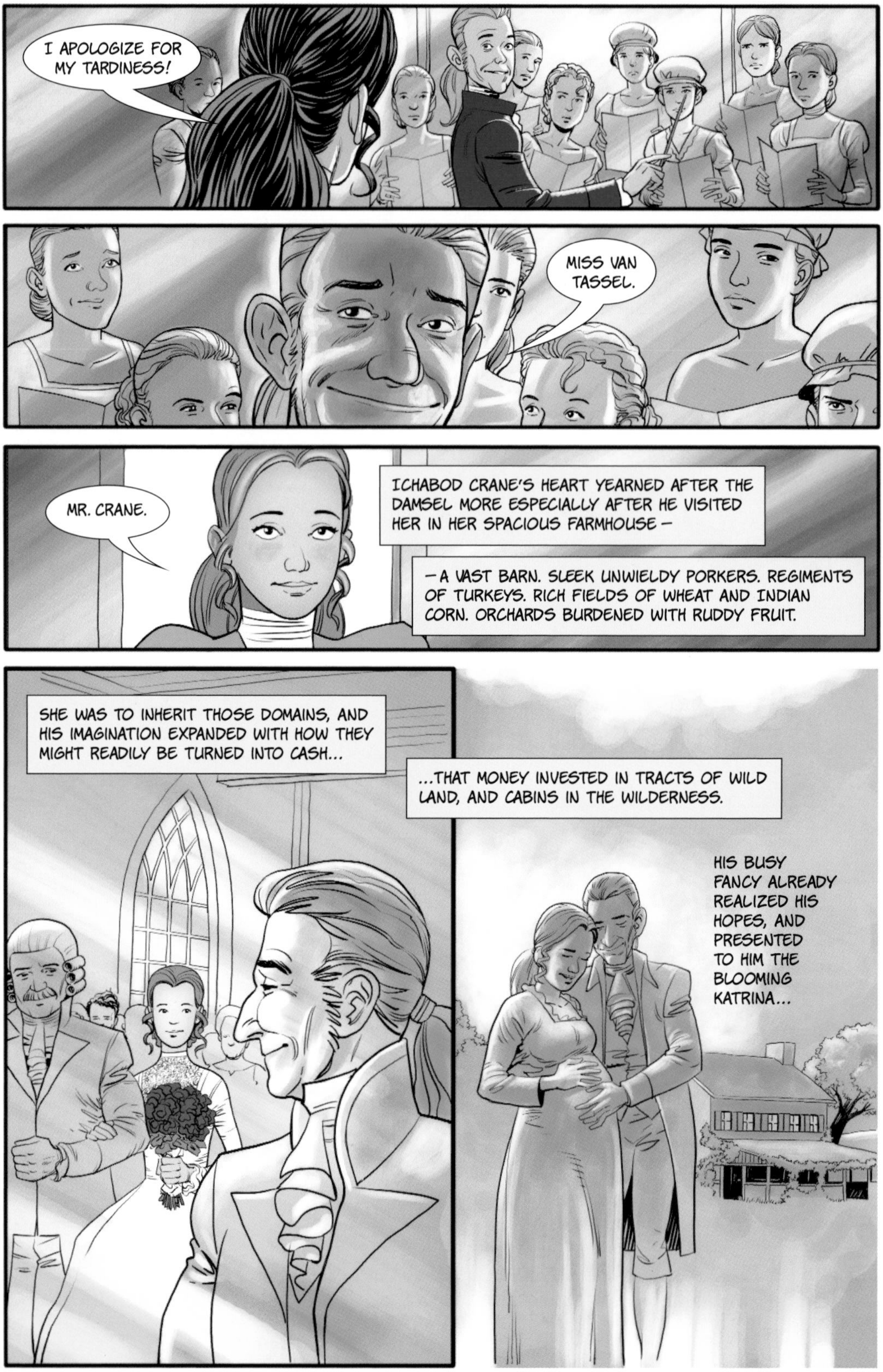
I APOLOGIZE FOR MY TARDINESS!
MISS VAN TASSEL.
MR. CRANE.
ICHABOD CRANE'S HEART YEARNED AFTER THE DAMSEL MORE ESPECIALLY AFTER HE VISITED HER IN HER SPACIOUS FARMHOUSE–
–A VAST BARN. SLEEK UNWIELDY PORKERS. REGIMENTS OF TURKEYS. RICH FIELDS OF WHEAT AND INDIAN CORN. ORCHARDS BURDENED WITH RUDDY FRUIT.
SHE WAS TO INHERIT THOSE DOMAINS, AND HIS IMAGINATION EXPANDED WITH HOW THEY MIGHT READILY BE TURNED INTO CASH...
...THAT MONEY INVESTED IN TRACTS OF WILD LAND, AND CABINS IN THE WILDERNESS.
HIS BUSY FANCY ALREADY REALIZED HIS HOPES, AND PRESENTED TO HIM THE BLOOMING KATRINA...

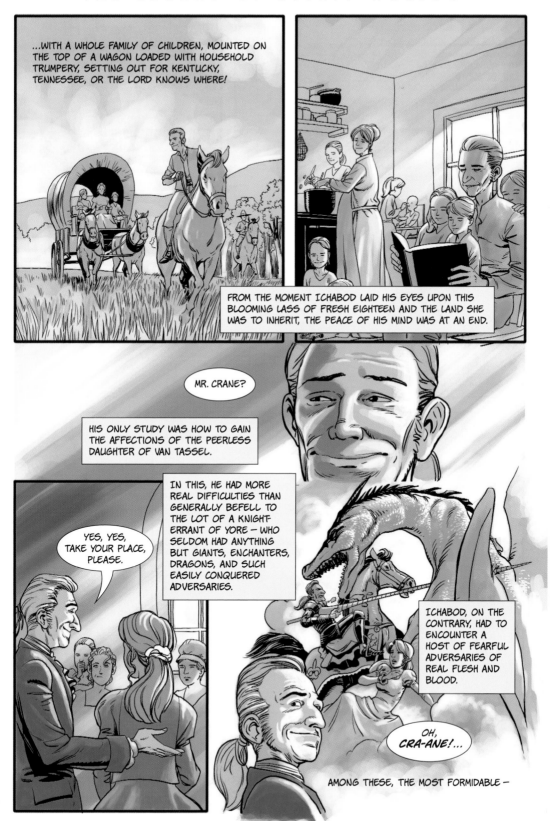

...WITH A WHOLE FAMILY OF CHILDREN, MOUNTED ON THE TOP OF A WAGON LOADED WITH HOUSEHOLD TRUMPERY, SETTING OUT FOR KENTUCKY, TENNESSEE, OR THE LORD KNOWS WHERE!

FROM THE MOMENT ICHABOD LAID HIS EYES UPON THIS BLOOMING LASS OF FRESH EIGHTEEN AND THE LAND SHE WAS TO INHERIT, THE PEACE OF HIS MIND WAS AT AN END.

MR. CRANE?

HIS ONLY STUDY WAS HOW TO GAIN THE AFFECTIONS OF THE PEERLESS DAUGHTER OF VAN TASSEL.

IN THIS, HE HAD MORE REAL DIFFICULTIES THAN GENERALLY BEFELL TO THE LOT OF A KNIGHT ERRANT OF YORE — WHO SELDOM HAD ANYTHING BUT GIANTS, ENCHANTERS, DRAGONS, AND SUCH EASILY CONQUERED ADVERSARIES.

YES, YES, TAKE YOUR PLACE, PLEASE.

ICHABOD, ON THE CONTRARY, HAD TO ENCOUNTER A HOST OF FEARFUL ADVERSARIES OF REAL FLESH AND BLOOD.

OH, CRA-ANE!...

AMONG THESE, THE MOST FORMIDABLE —

15

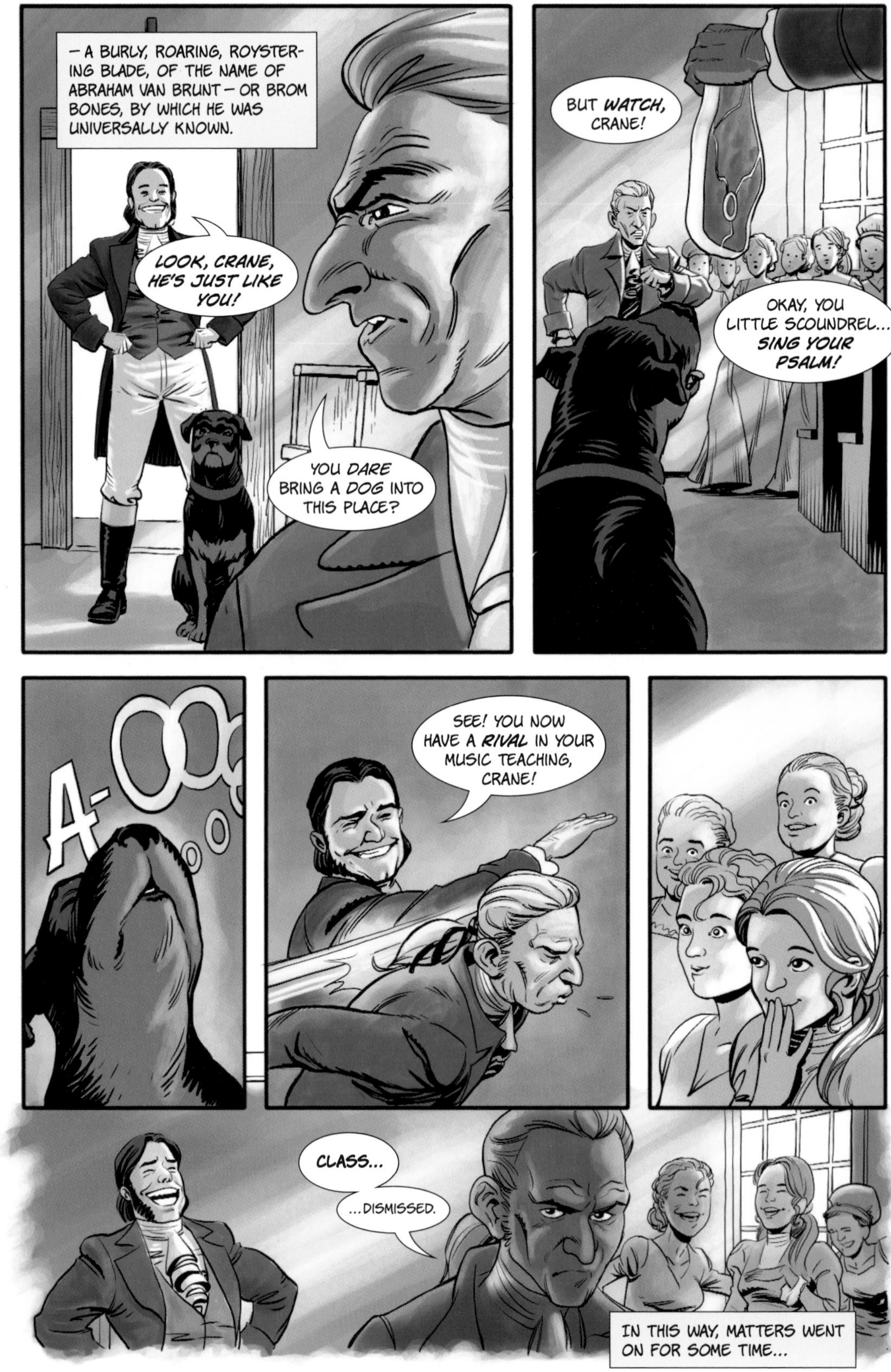
—A BURLY, ROARING, ROYSTERING BLADE, OF THE NAME OF ABRAHAM VAN BRUNT—OR BROM BONES, BY WHICH HE WAS UNIVERSALLY KNOWN.
LOOK, CRANE, HE'S JUST LIKE YOU!
YOU DARE BRING A DOG INTO THIS PLACE?
BUT WATCH, CRANE!
OKAY, YOU LITTLE SCOUNDREL... SING YOUR PSALM!
A-OOO
SEE! YOU NOW HAVE A RIVAL IN YOUR MUSIC TEACHING, CRANE!
CLASS...
...DISMISSED.
IN THIS WAY, MATTERS WENT ON FOR SOME TIME...

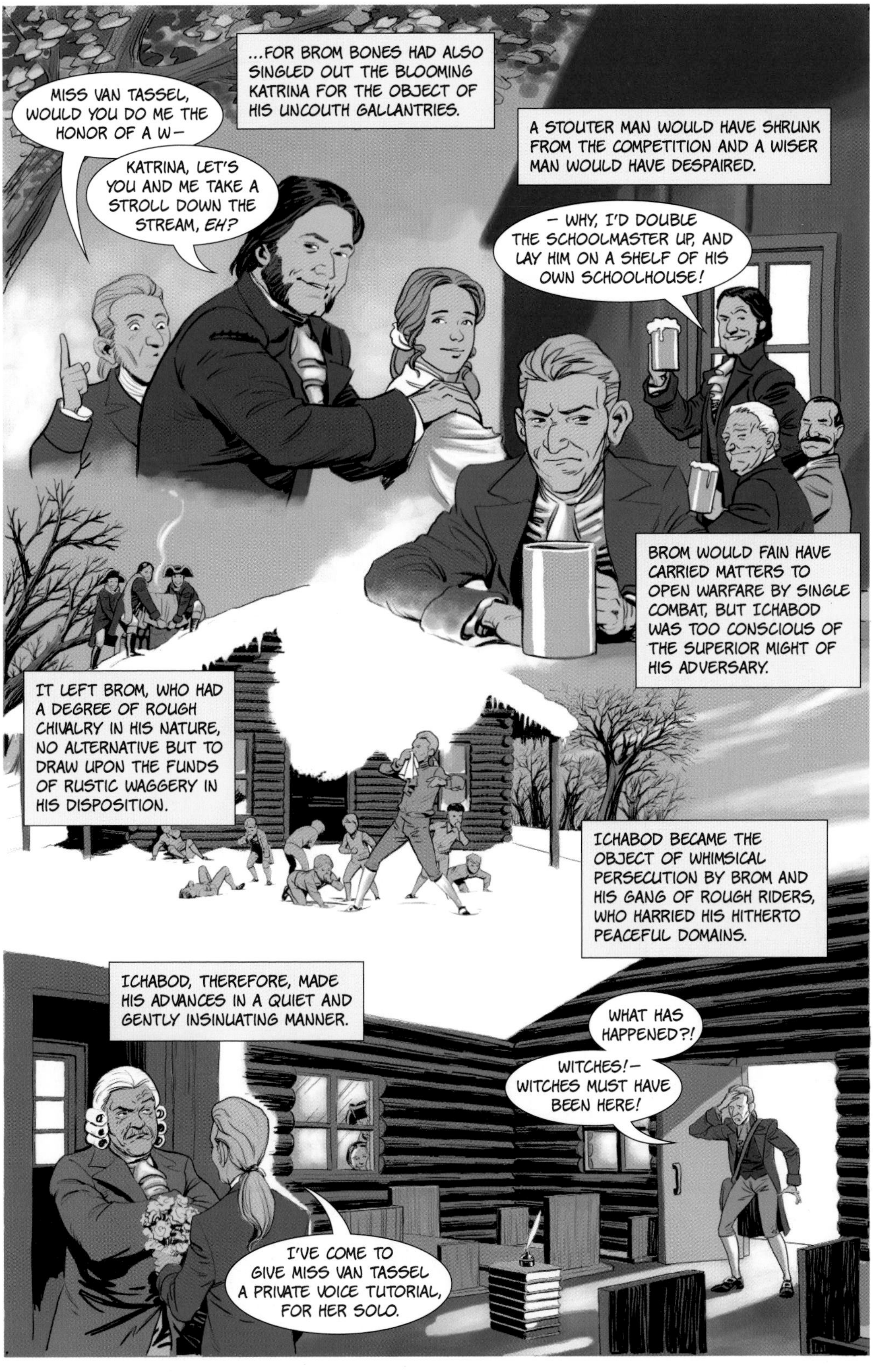
MISS VAN TASSEL, WOULD YOU DO ME THE HONOR OF A W—
...FOR BROM BONES HAD ALSO SINGLED OUT THE BLOOMING KATRINA FOR THE OBJECT OF HIS UNCOUTH GALLANTRIES.
KATRINA, LET'S YOU AND ME TAKE A STROLL DOWN THE STREAM, EH?
A STOUTER MAN WOULD HAVE SHRUNK FROM THE COMPETITION AND A WISER MAN WOULD HAVE DESPAIRED.
— WHY, I'D DOUBLE THE SCHOOLMASTER UP, AND LAY HIM ON A SHELF OF HIS OWN SCHOOLHOUSE!
BROM WOULD FAIN HAVE CARRIED MATTERS TO OPEN WARFARE BY SINGLE COMBAT, BUT ICHABOD WAS TOO CONSCIOUS OF THE SUPERIOR MIGHT OF HIS ADVERSARY.
IT LEFT BROM, WHO HAD A DEGREE OF ROUGH CHIVALRY IN HIS NATURE, NO ALTERNATIVE BUT TO DRAW UPON THE FUNDS OF RUSTIC WAGGERY IN HIS DISPOSITION.
ICHABOD BECAME THE OBJECT OF WHIMSICAL PERSECUTION BY BROM AND HIS GANG OF ROUGH RIDERS, WHO HARRIED HIS HITHERTO PEACEFUL DOMAINS.
ICHABOD, THEREFORE, MADE HIS ADVANCES IN A QUIET AND GENTLY INSINUATING MANNER.
WHAT HAS HAPPENED?!
WITCHES!— WITCHES MUST HAVE BEEN HERE!
I'VE COME TO GIVE MISS VAN TASSEL A PRIVATE VOICE TUTORIAL, FOR HER SOLO.

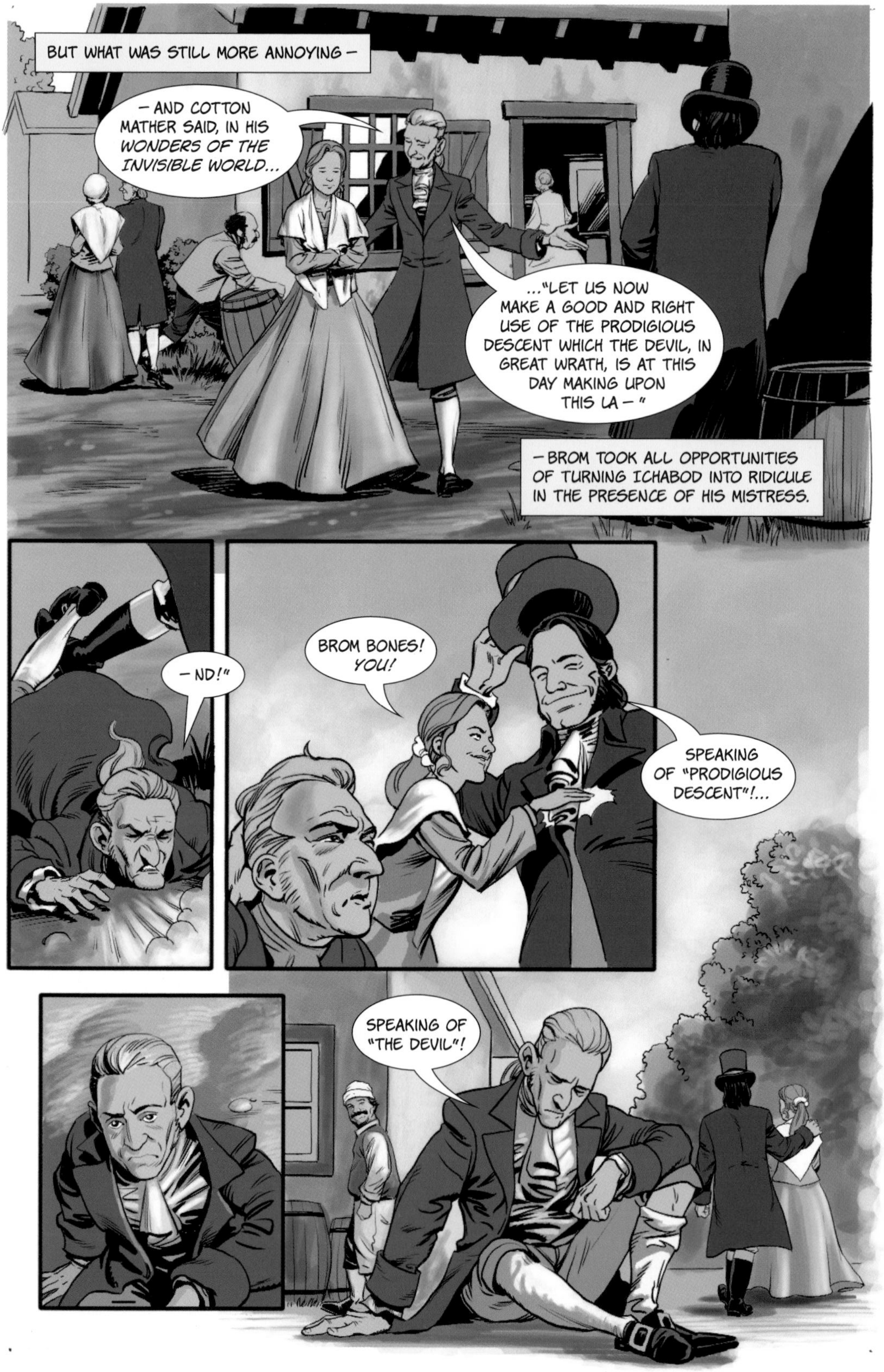
BUT WHAT WAS STILL MORE ANNOYING –
– AND COTTON MATHER SAID, IN HIS *WONDERS OF THE INVISIBLE WORLD*...
..."LET US NOW MAKE A GOOD AND RIGHT USE OF THE PRODIGIOUS DESCENT WHICH THE DEVIL, IN GREAT WRATH, IS AT THIS DAY MAKING UPON THIS LA – "
– BROM TOOK ALL OPPORTUNITIES OF TURNING ICHABOD INTO RIDICULE IN THE PRESENCE OF HIS MISTRESS.
– ND!"
BROM BONES! *YOU!*
SPEAKING OF "PRODIGIOUS DESCENT"!...
SPEAKING OF "THE DEVIL"!

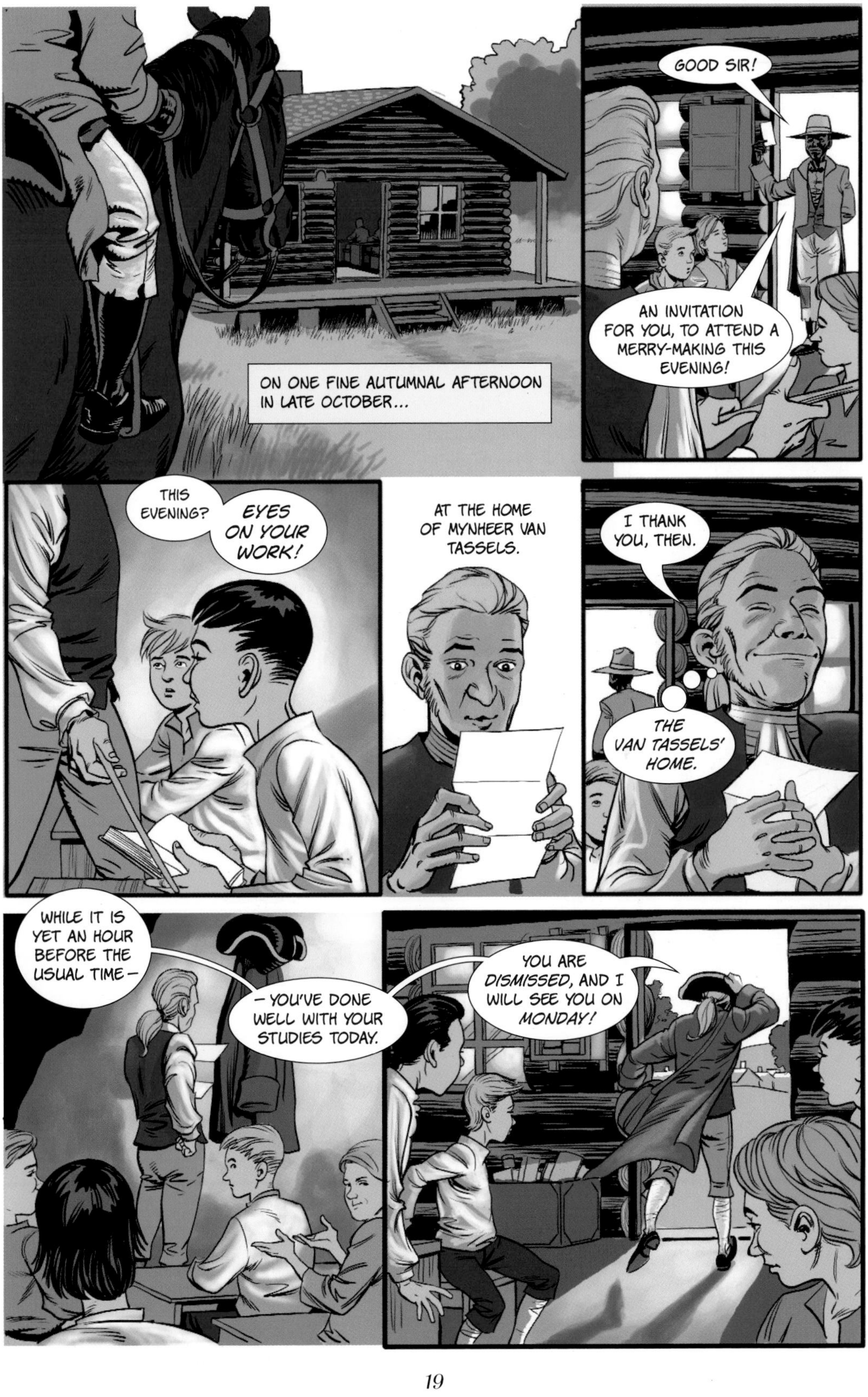

ON ONE FINE AUTUMNAL AFTERNOON IN LATE OCTOBER...
GOOD SIR!
AN INVITATION FOR YOU, TO ATTEND A MERRY-MAKING THIS EVENING!
THIS EVENING?
EYES ON YOUR WORK!
AT THE HOME OF MYNHEER VAN TASSELS.
I THANK YOU, THEN.
THE VAN TASSELS' HOME.
WHILE IT IS YET AN HOUR BEFORE THE USUAL TIME—
—YOU'VE DONE WELL WITH YOUR STUDIES TODAY.
YOU ARE *DISMISSED*, AND I WILL SEE YOU ON *MONDAY*!

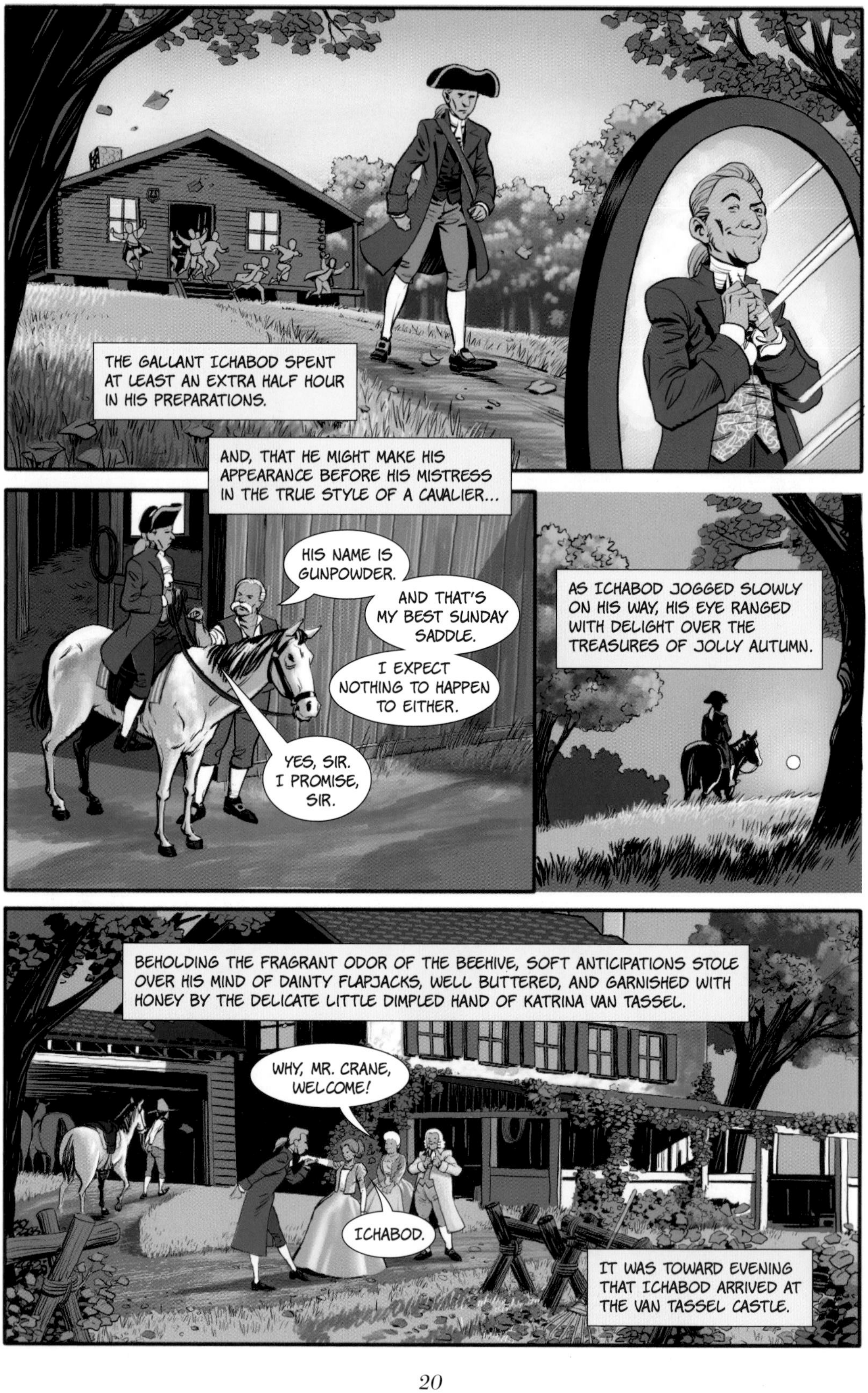
THE GALLANT ICHABOD SPENT AT LEAST AN EXTRA HALF HOUR IN HIS PREPARATIONS.
AND, THAT HE MIGHT MAKE HIS APPEARANCE BEFORE HIS MISTRESS IN THE TRUE STYLE OF A CAVALIER...
HIS NAME IS GUNPOWDER.
AND THAT'S MY BEST SUNDAY SADDLE.
I EXPECT NOTHING TO HAPPEN TO EITHER.
YES, SIR. I PROMISE, SIR.
AS ICHABOD JOGGED SLOWLY ON HIS WAY, HIS EYE RANGED WITH DELIGHT OVER THE TREASURES OF JOLLY AUTUMN.
BEHOLDING THE FRAGRANT ODOR OF THE BEEHIVE, SOFT ANTICIPATIONS STOLE OVER HIS MIND OF DAINTY FLAPJACKS, WELL BUTTERED, AND GARNISHED WITH HONEY BY THE DELICATE LITTLE DIMPLED HAND OF KATRINA VAN TASSEL.
WHY, MR. CRANE, WELCOME!
ICHABOD.
IT WAS TOWARD EVENING THAT ICHABOD ARRIVED AT THE VAN TASSEL CASTLE.

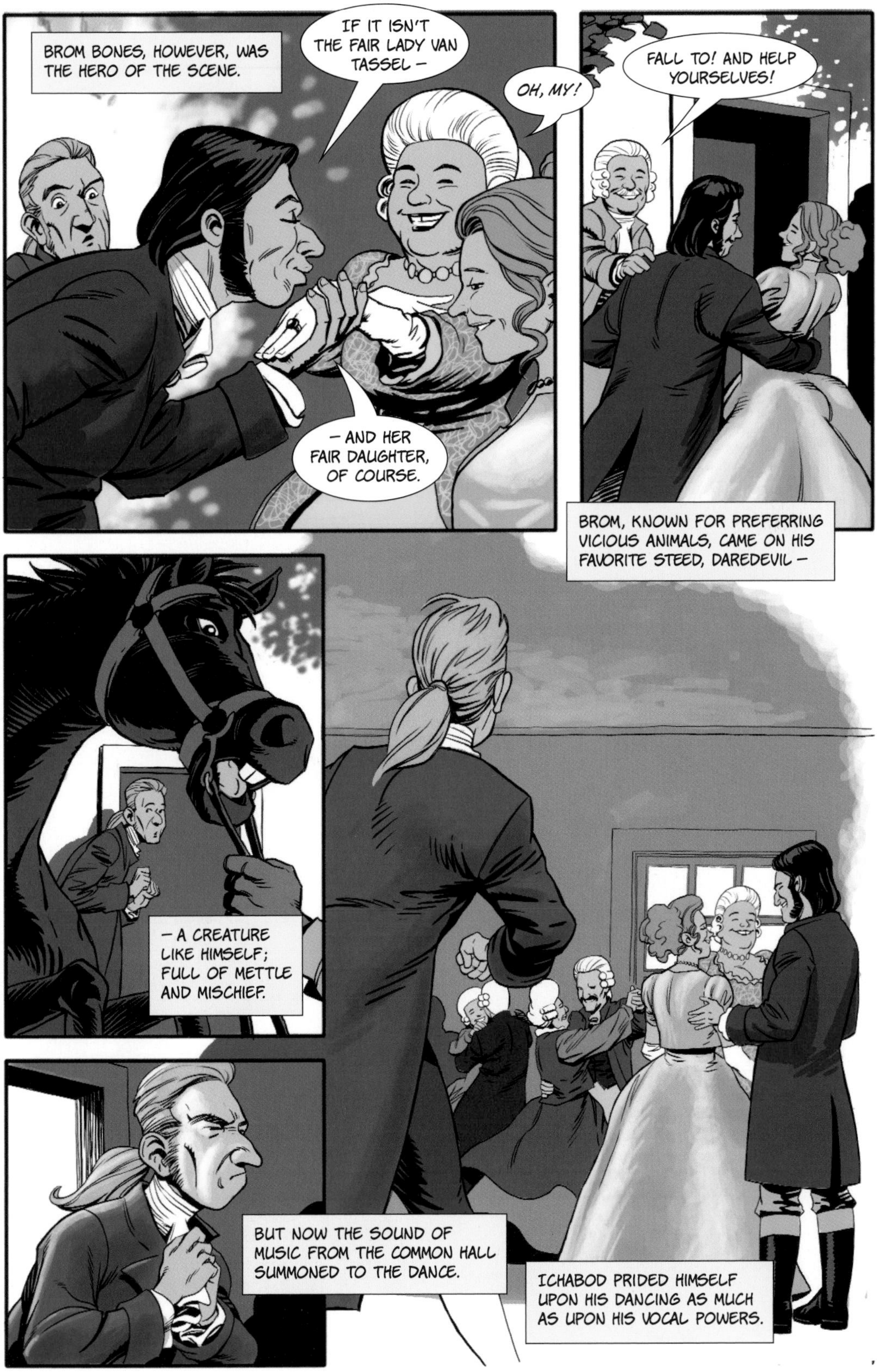
BROM BONES, HOWEVER, WAS THE HERO OF THE SCENE.
IF IT ISN'T THE FAIR LADY VAN TASSEL –
OH, MY!
– AND HER FAIR DAUGHTER, OF COURSE.
FALL TO! AND HELP YOURSELVES!
BROM, KNOWN FOR PREFERRING VICIOUS ANIMALS, CAME ON HIS FAVORITE STEED, DAREDEVIL –
– A CREATURE LIKE HIMSELF; FULL OF METTLE AND MISCHIEF.
BUT NOW THE SOUND OF MUSIC FROM THE COMMON HALL SUMMONED TO THE DANCE.
ICHABOD PRIDED HIMSELF UPON HIS DANCING AS MUCH AS UPON HIS VOCAL POWERS.

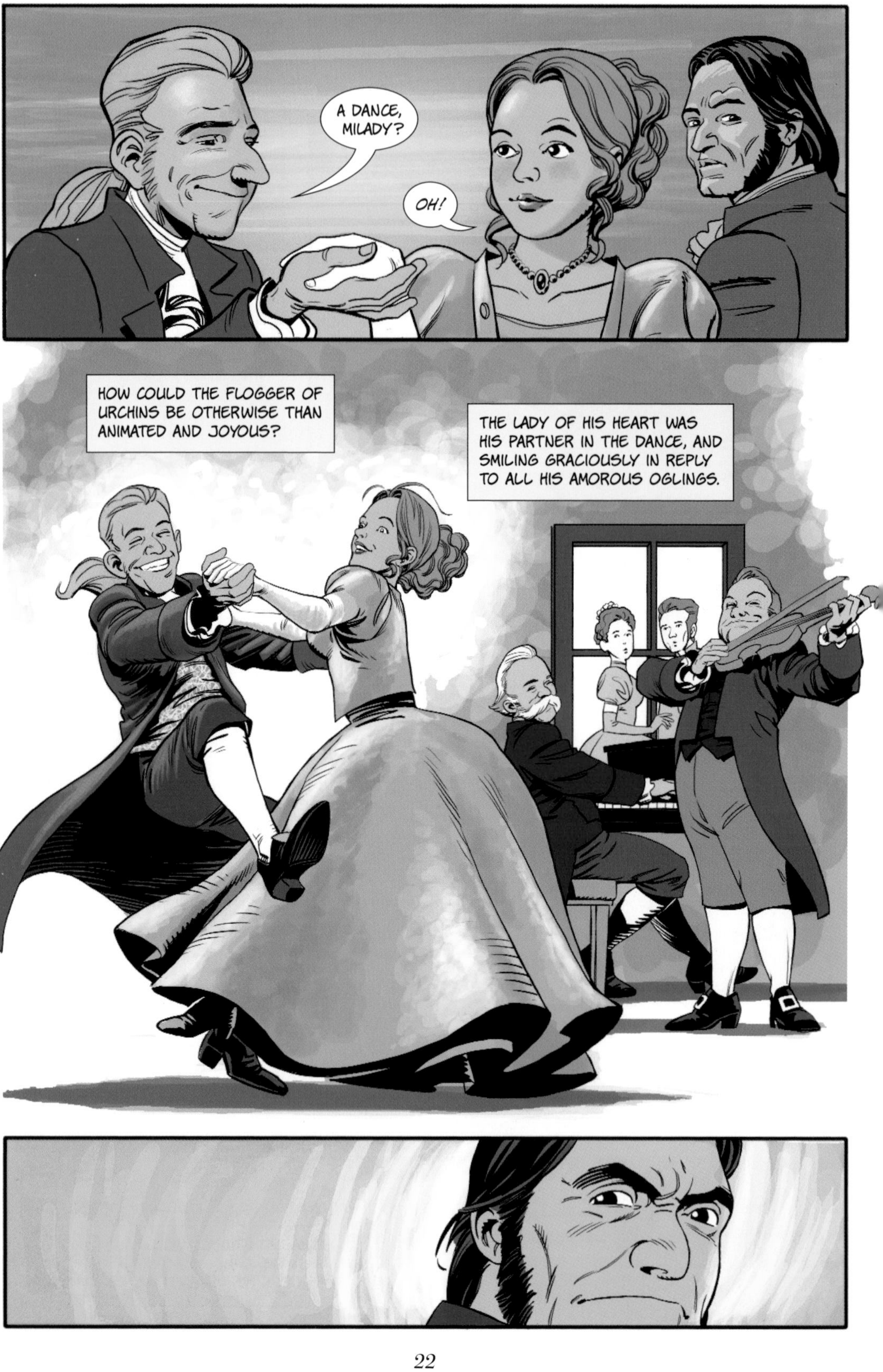
A DANCE, MILADY?
OH!
HOW COULD THE FLOGGER OF URCHINS BE OTHERWISE THAN ANIMATED AND JOYOUS?
THE LADY OF HIS HEART WAS HIS PARTNER IN THE DANCE, AND SMILING GRACIOUSLY IN REPLY TO ALL HIS AMOROUS OGLINGS.

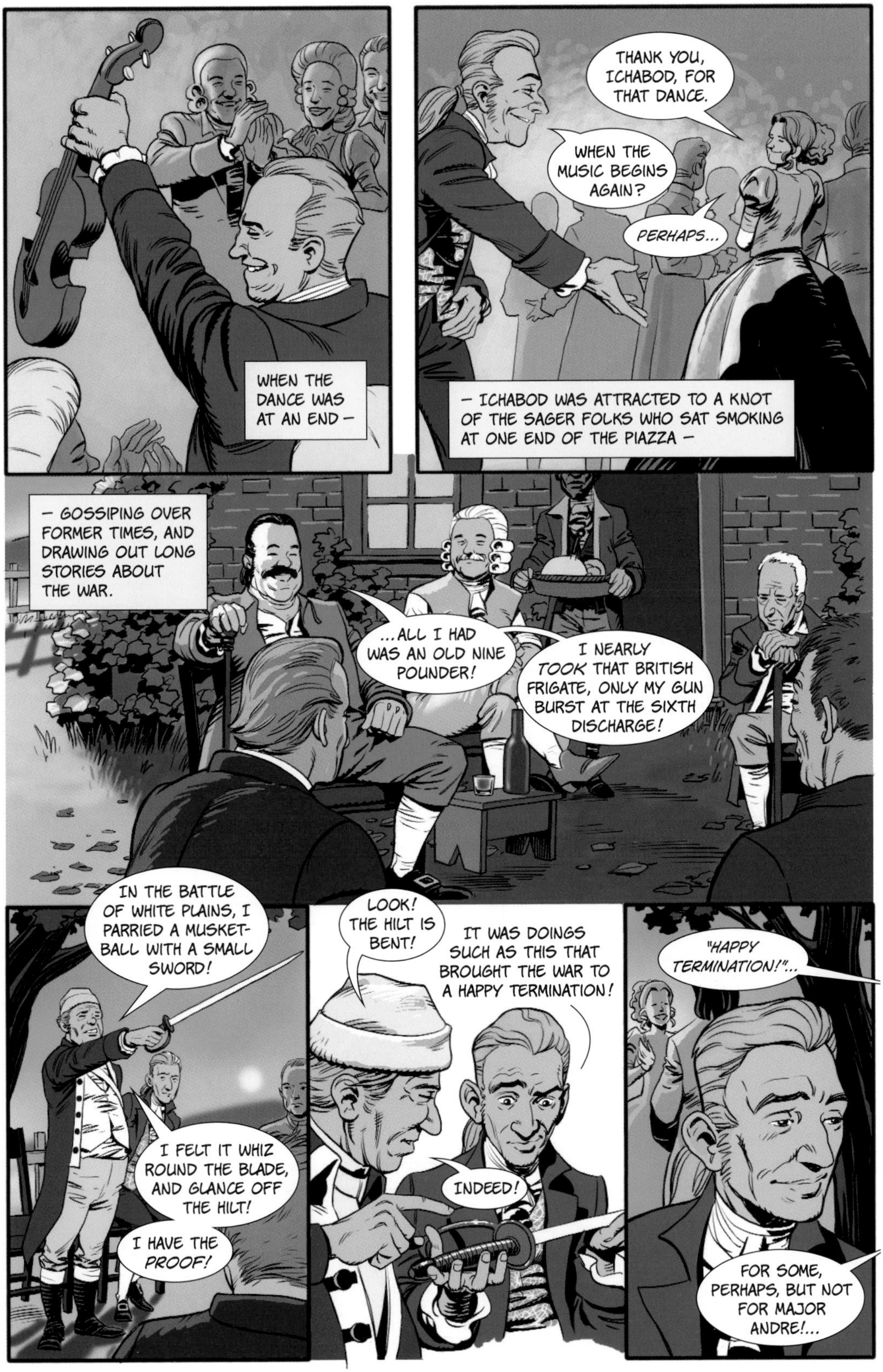
WHEN THE DANCE WAS AT AN END –
THANK YOU, ICHABOD, FOR THAT DANCE.
WHEN THE MUSIC BEGINS AGAIN?
PERHAPS...
– ICHABOD WAS ATTRACTED TO A KNOT OF THE SAGER FOLKS WHO SAT SMOKING AT ONE END OF THE PIAZZA –
– GOSSIPING OVER FORMER TIMES, AND DRAWING OUT LONG STORIES ABOUT THE WAR.
...ALL I HAD WAS AN OLD NINE POUNDER!
I NEARLY *TOOK* THAT BRITISH FRIGATE, ONLY MY GUN BURST AT THE SIXTH DISCHARGE!
IN THE BATTLE OF WHITE PLAINS, I PARRIED A MUSKET-BALL WITH A SMALL SWORD!
I FELT IT WHIZ ROUND THE BLADE, AND GLANCE OFF THE HILT!
I HAVE THE *PROOF!*
LOOK! THE HILT IS BENT!
IT WAS DOINGS SUCH AS THIS THAT BROUGHT THE WAR TO A HAPPY TERMINATION!
INDEED!
"HAPPY TERMINATION!"...
FOR SOME, PERHAPS, BUT NOT FOR MAJOR ANDRE!...

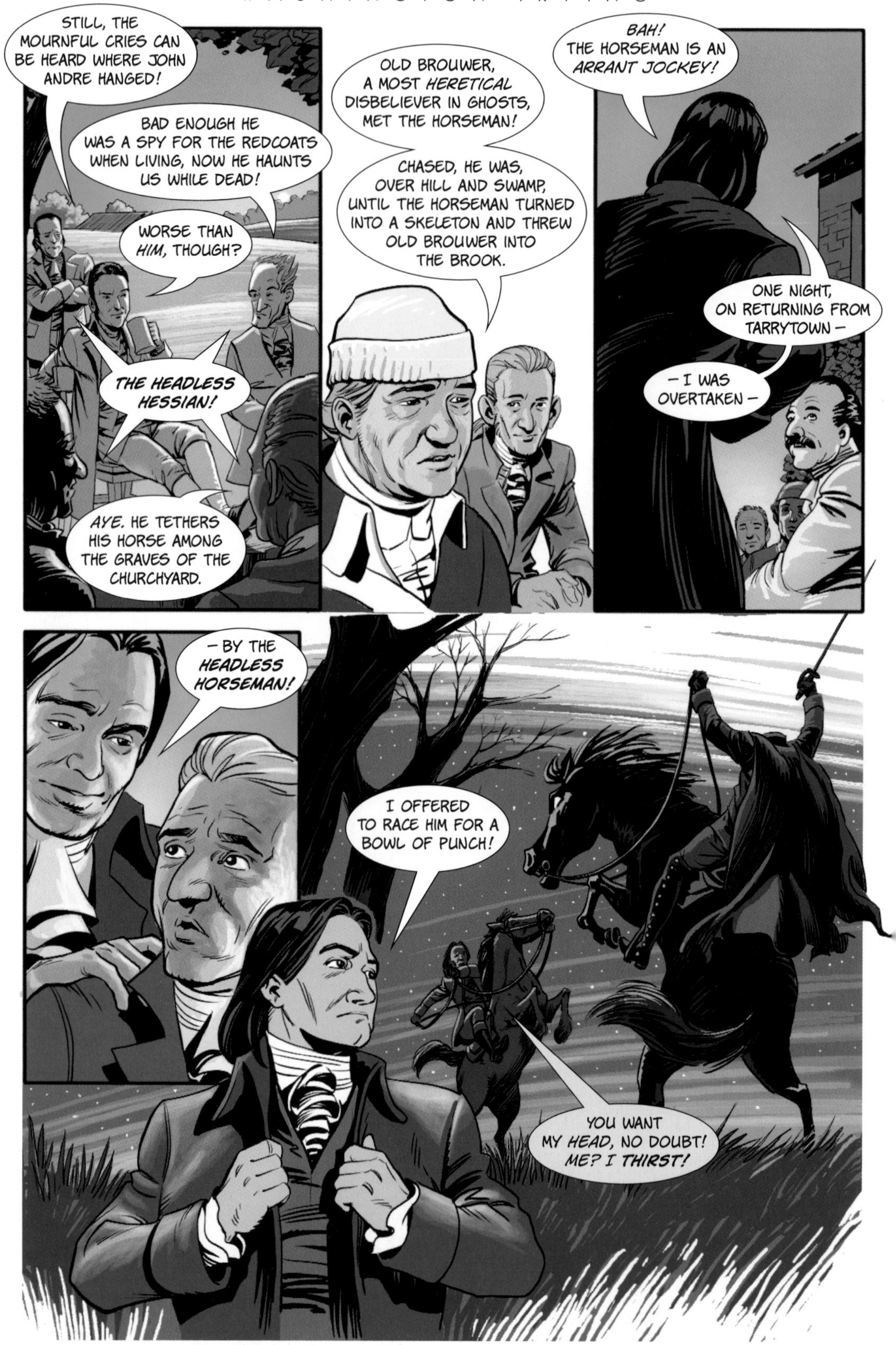
STILL, THE MOURNFUL CRIES CAN BE HEARD WHERE JOHN ANDRE HANGED!
BAD ENOUGH HE WAS A SPY FOR THE REDCOATS WHEN LIVING, NOW HE HAUNTS US WHILE DEAD!
WORSE THAN *HIM*, THOUGH?
THE HEADLESS HESSIAN!
AYE. HE TETHERS HIS HORSE AMONG THE GRAVES OF THE CHURCHYARD.
OLD BROUWER, A MOST *HERETICAL* DISBELIEVER IN GHOSTS, MET THE HORSEMAN!
CHASED, HE WAS, OVER HILL AND SWAMP, UNTIL THE HORSEMAN TURNED INTO A SKELETON AND THREW OLD BROUWER INTO THE BROOK.
BAH! THE HORSEMAN IS AN *ARRANT JOCKEY!*
ONE NIGHT, ON RETURNING FROM TARRYTOWN –
– I WAS OVERTAKEN –
– BY THE ***HEADLESS HORSEMAN!***
I OFFERED TO RACE HIM FOR A BOWL OF PUNCH!
YOU WANT MY *HEAD*, NO DOUBT! *ME?* I ***THIRST!***

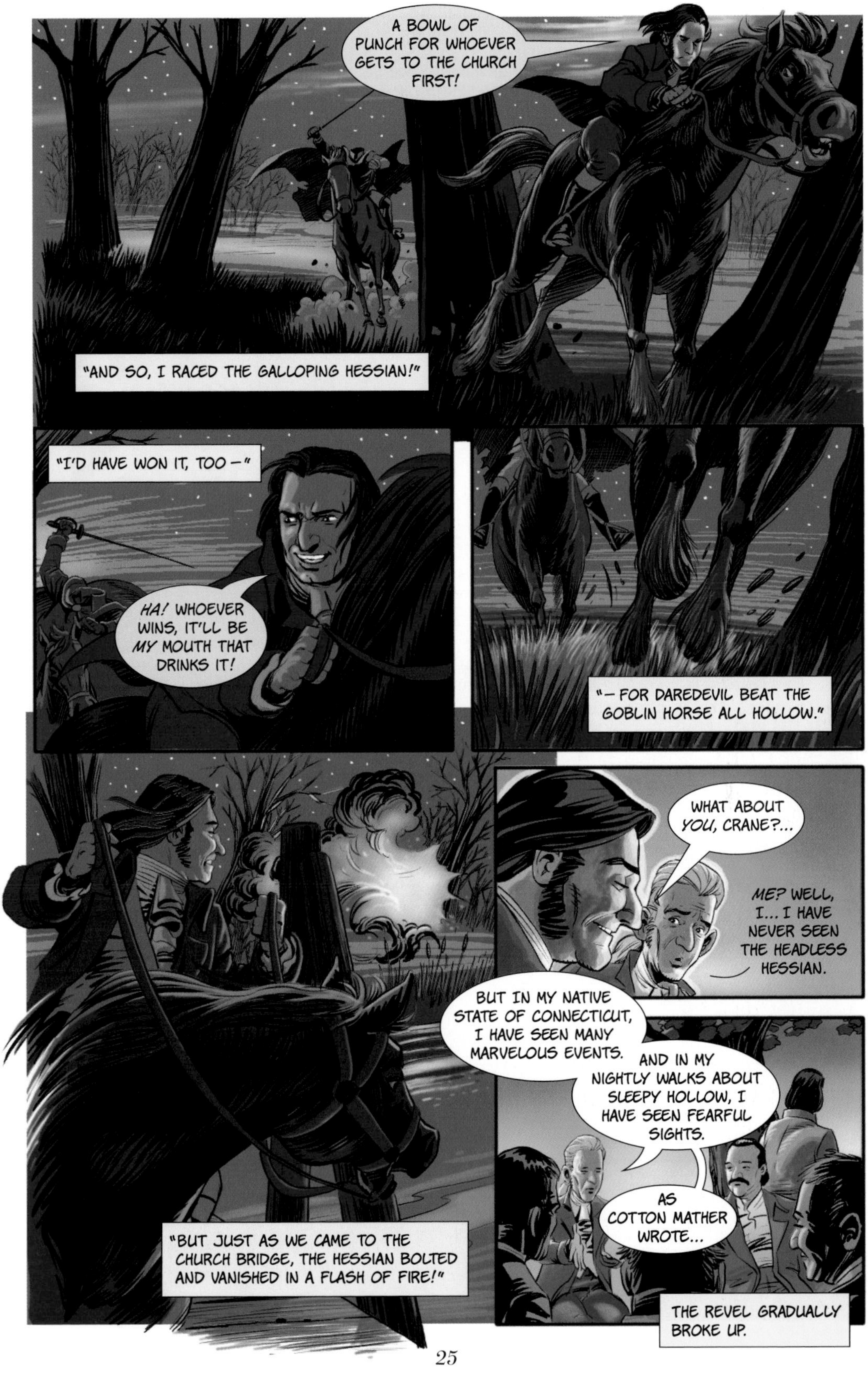
A BOWL OF PUNCH FOR WHOEVER GETS TO THE CHURCH FIRST!
"AND SO, I RACED THE GALLOPING HESSIAN!"
"I'D HAVE WON IT, TOO –"
HA! WHOEVER WINS, IT'LL BE MY MOUTH THAT DRINKS IT!
"– FOR DAREDEVIL BEAT THE GOBLIN HORSE ALL HOLLOW."
"BUT JUST AS WE CAME TO THE CHURCH BRIDGE, THE HESSIAN BOLTED AND VANISHED IN A FLASH OF FIRE!"
WHAT ABOUT YOU, CRANE?...
ME? WELL, I... I HAVE NEVER SEEN THE HEADLESS HESSIAN.
BUT IN MY NATIVE STATE OF CONNECTICUT, I HAVE SEEN MANY MARVELOUS EVENTS.
AND IN MY NIGHTLY WALKS ABOUT SLEEPY HOLLOW, I HAVE SEEN FEARFUL SIGHTS.
AS COTTON MATHER WROTE...
THE REVEL GRADUALLY BROKE UP.

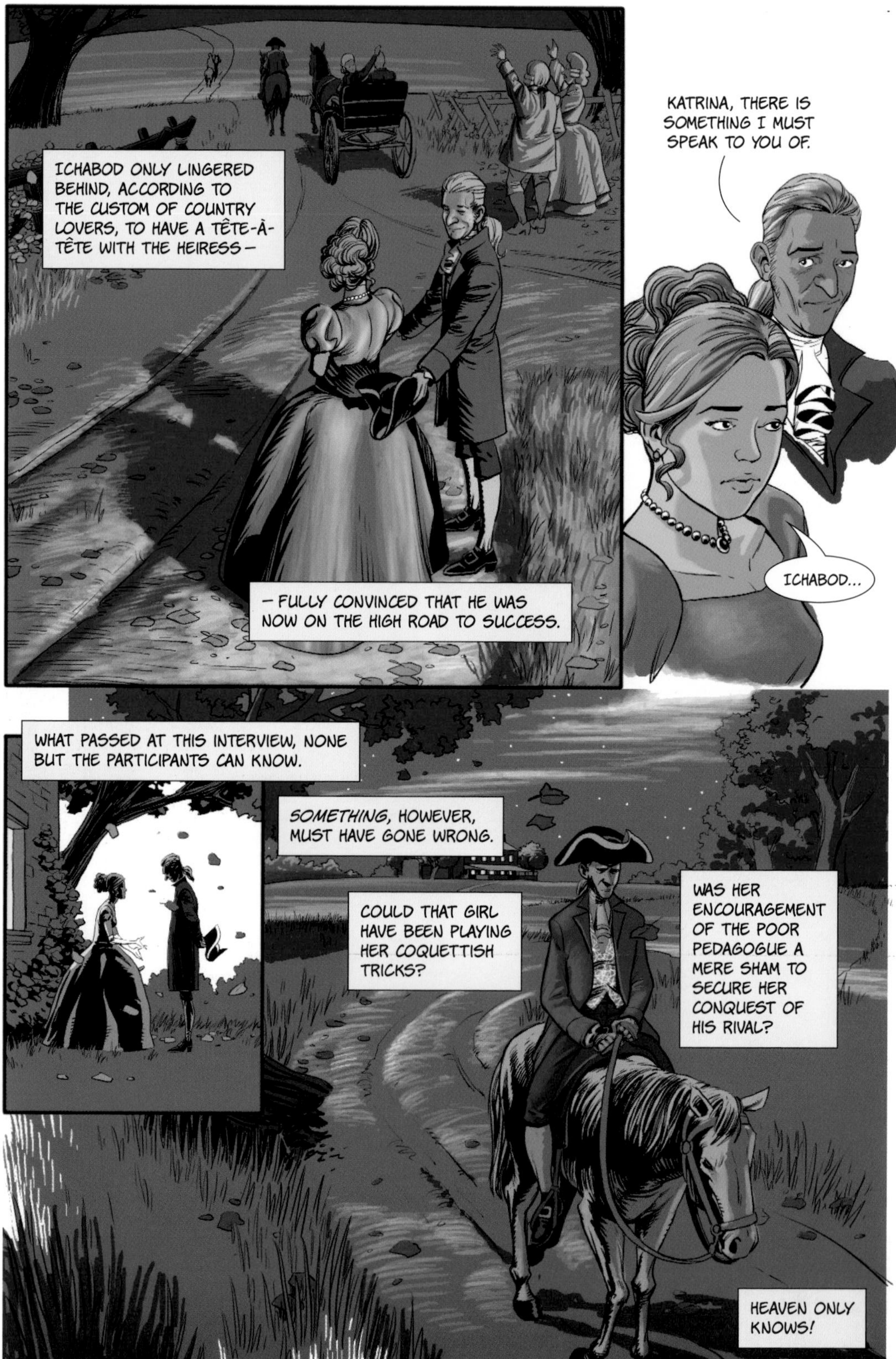
ICHABOD ONLY LINGERED BEHIND, ACCORDING TO THE CUSTOM OF COUNTRY LOVERS, TO HAVE A TÊTE-À-TÊTE WITH THE HEIRESS—
—FULLY CONVINCED THAT HE WAS NOW ON THE HIGH ROAD TO SUCCESS.
KATRINA, THERE IS SOMETHING I MUST SPEAK TO YOU OF.
ICHABOD...
WHAT PASSED AT THIS INTERVIEW, NONE BUT THE PARTICIPANTS CAN KNOW.
SOMETHING, HOWEVER, MUST HAVE GONE WRONG.
COULD THAT GIRL HAVE BEEN PLAYING HER COQUETTISH TRICKS?
WAS HER ENCOURAGEMENT OF THE POOR PEDAGOGUE A MERE SHAM TO SECURE HER CONQUEST OF HIS RIVAL?
HEAVEN ONLY KNOWS!

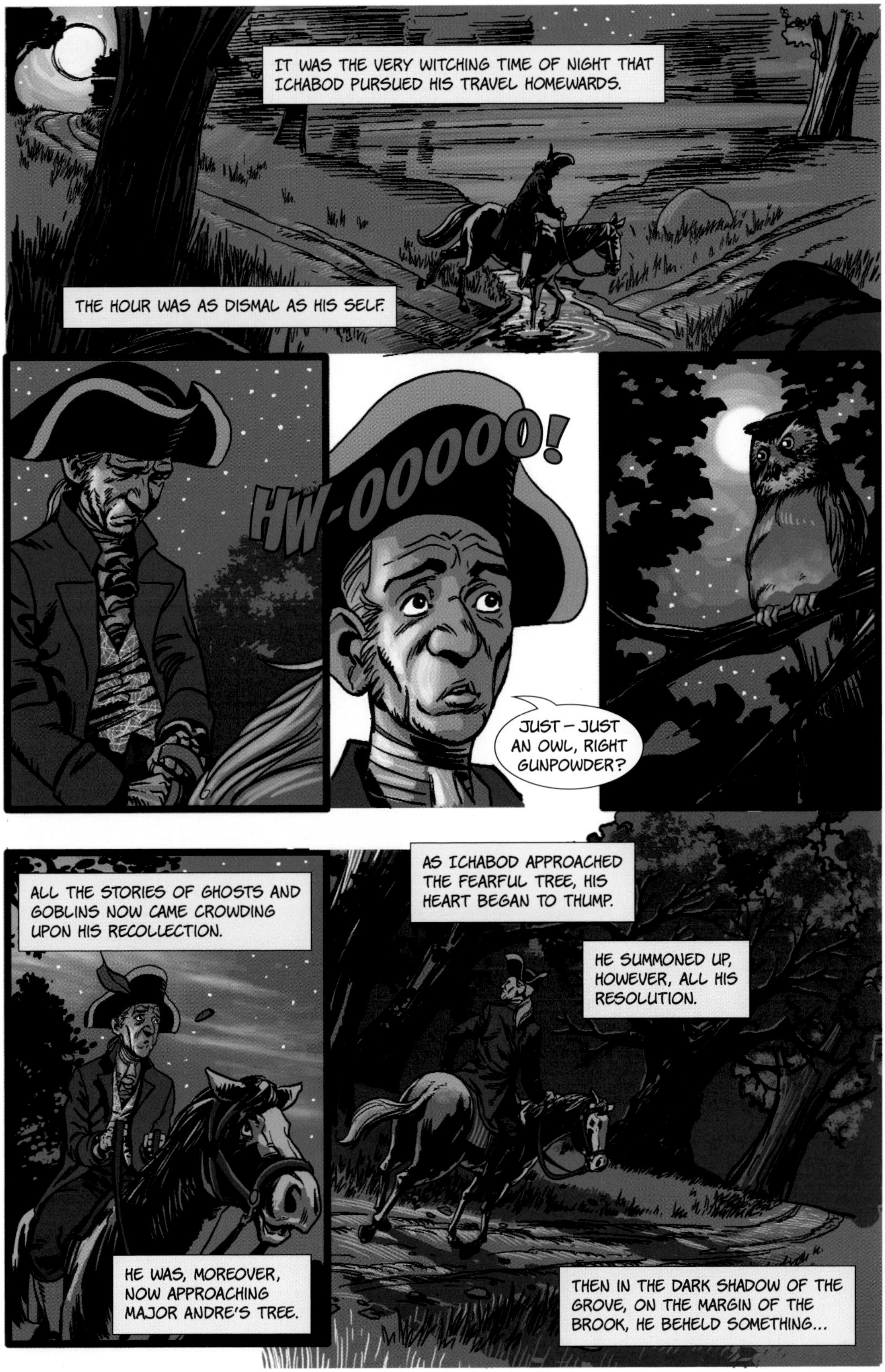
IT WAS THE VERY WITCHING TIME OF NIGHT THAT ICHABOD PURSUED HIS TRAVEL HOMEWARDS.
THE HOUR WAS AS DISMAL AS HIS SELF.
HW-OOOOOO!
JUST—JUST AN OWL, RIGHT GUNPOWDER?
ALL THE STORIES OF GHOSTS AND GOBLINS NOW CAME CROWDING UPON HIS RECOLLECTION.
HE WAS, MOREOVER, NOW APPROACHING MAJOR ANDRE'S TREE.
AS ICHABOD APPROACHED THE FEARFUL TREE, HIS HEART BEGAN TO THUMP.
HE SUMMONED UP, HOWEVER, ALL HIS RESOLUTION.
THEN IN THE DARK SHADOW OF THE GROVE, ON THE MARGIN OF THE BROOK, HE BEHELD SOMETHING...

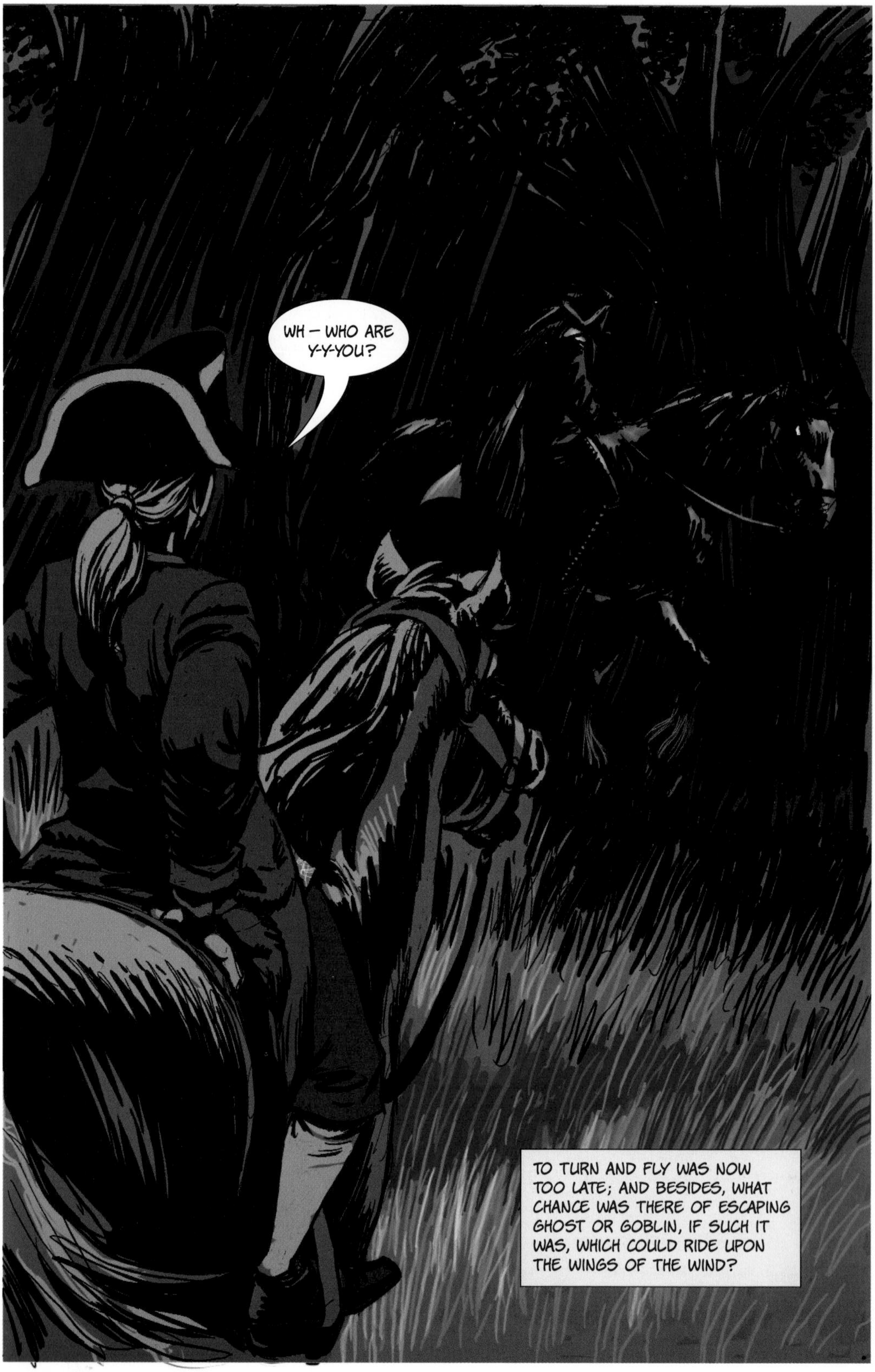
WH – WHO ARE Y-Y-YOU?
TO TURN AND FLY WAS NOW TOO LATE; AND BESIDES, WHAT CHANCE WAS THERE OF ESCAPING GHOST OR GOBLIN, IF SUCH IT WAS, WHICH COULD RIDE UPON THE WINGS OF THE WIND?

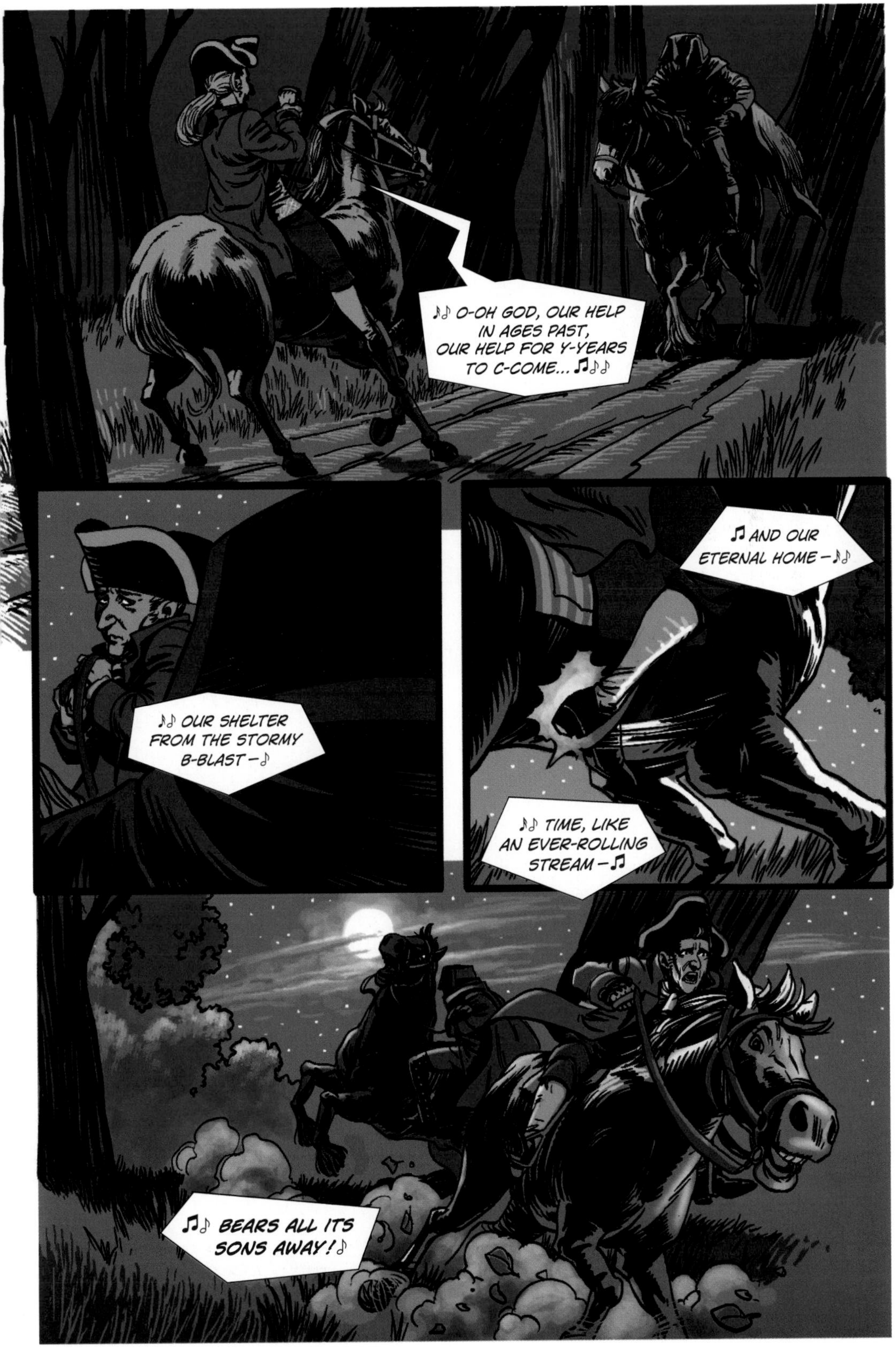
♪♪ O-OH GOD, OUR HELP IN AGES PAST, OUR HELP FOR Y-YEARS TO C-COME... ♫♪♪
♪♪ OUR SHELTER FROM THE STORMY B-BLAST –♪
♫ AND OUR ETERNAL HOME –♪♪
♪♪ TIME, LIKE AN EVER-ROLLING STREAM –♫
♫♪ BEARS ALL ITS SONS AWAY! ♪

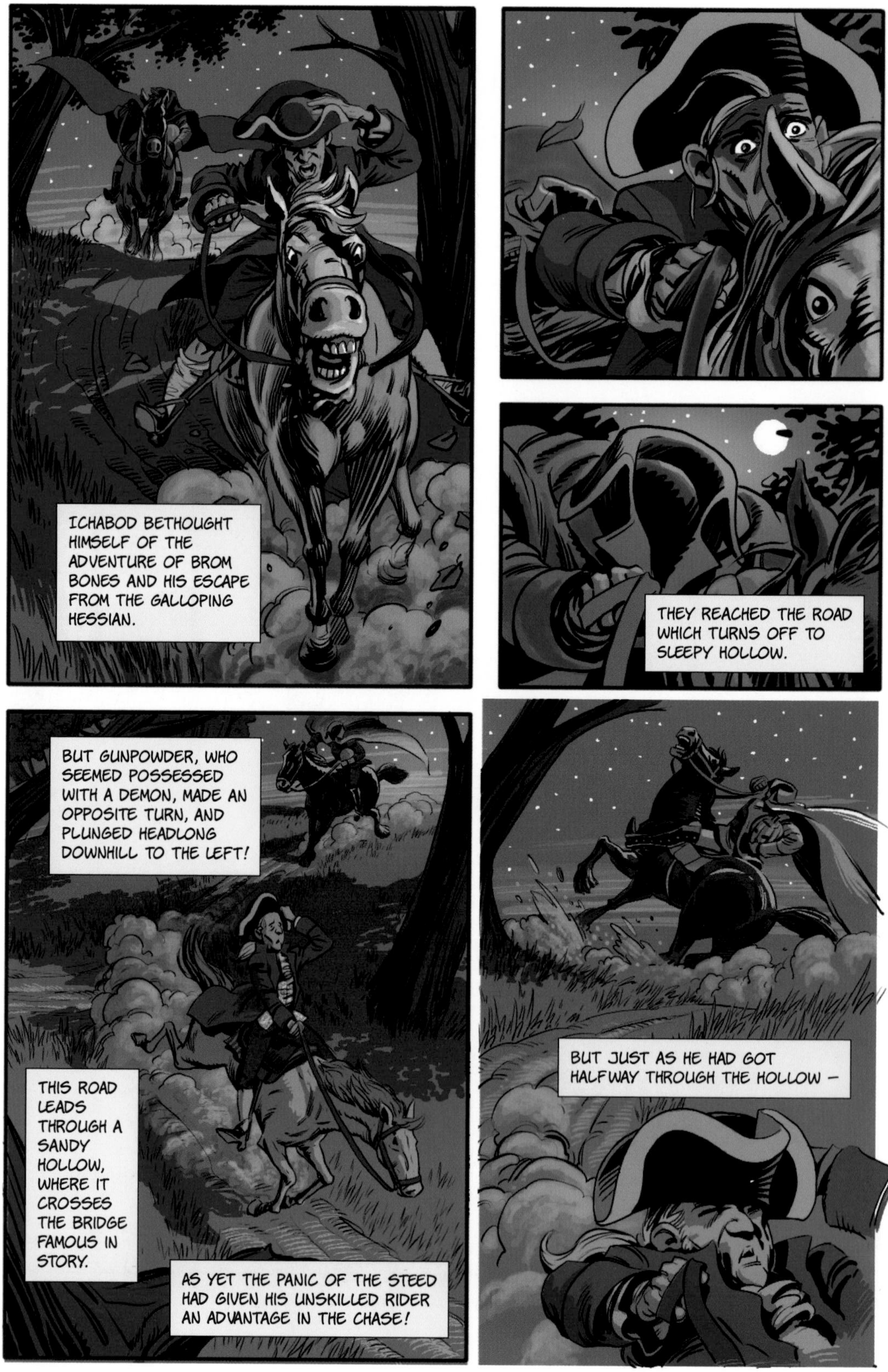
ICHABOD BETHOUGHT HIMSELF OF THE ADVENTURE OF BROM BONES AND HIS ESCAPE FROM THE GALLOPING HESSIAN.
THEY REACHED THE ROAD WHICH TURNS OFF TO SLEEPY HOLLOW.
BUT GUNPOWDER, WHO SEEMED POSSESSED WITH A DEMON, MADE AN OPPOSITE TURN, AND PLUNGED HEADLONG DOWNHILL TO THE LEFT!
THIS ROAD LEADS THROUGH A SANDY HOLLOW, WHERE IT CROSSES THE BRIDGE FAMOUS IN STORY.
AS YET THE PANIC OF THE STEED HAD GIVEN HIS UNSKILLED RIDER AN ADVANTAGE IN THE CHASE!
BUT JUST AS HE HAD GOT HALFWAY THROUGH THE HOLLOW –

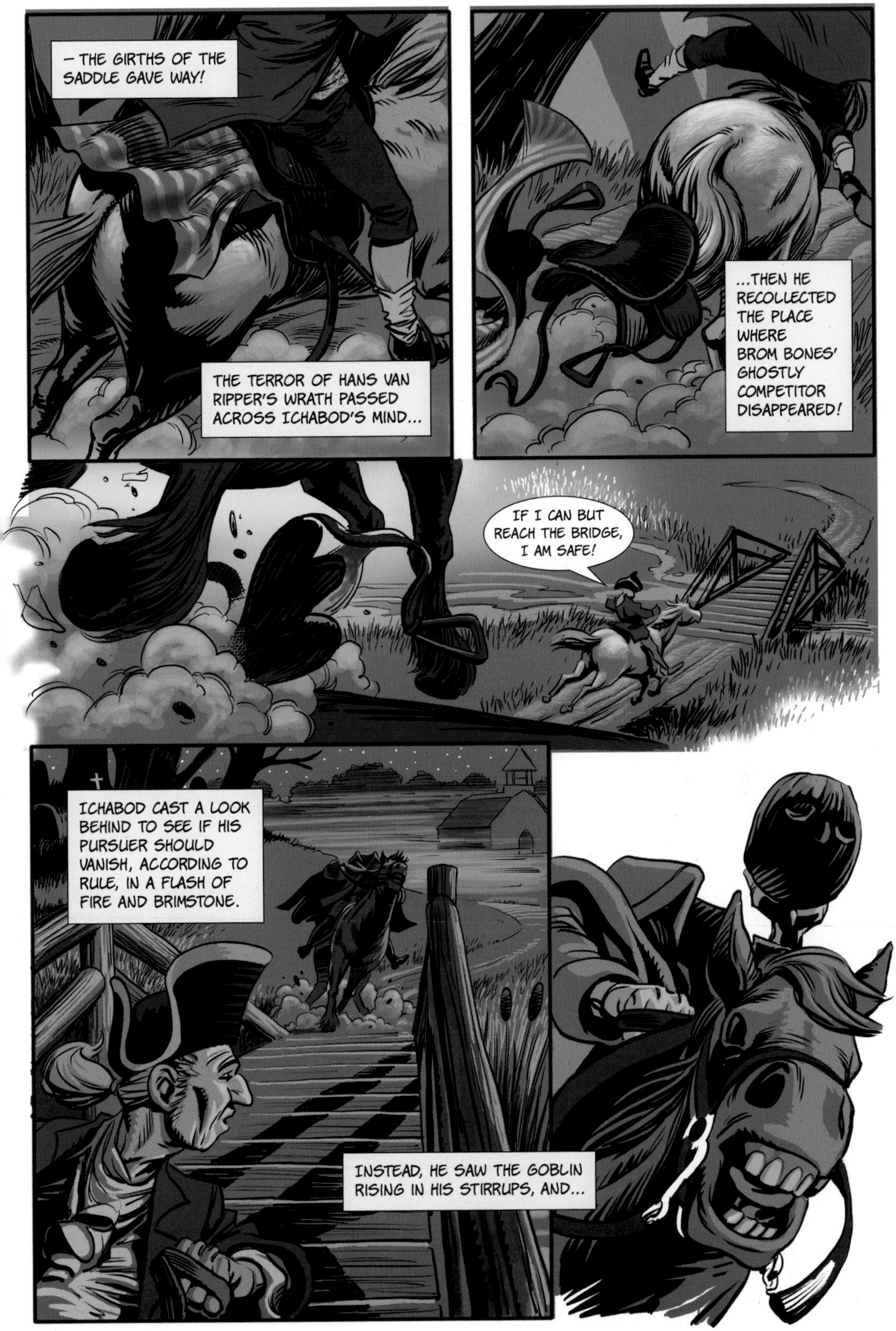
–THE GIRTHS OF THE SADDLE GAVE WAY!
THE TERROR OF HANS VAN RIPPER'S WRATH PASSED ACROSS ICHABOD'S MIND...
...THEN HE RECOLLECTED THE PLACE WHERE BROM BONES' GHOSTLY COMPETITOR DISAPPEARED!
IF I CAN BUT REACH THE BRIDGE, I AM SAFE!
ICHABOD CAST A LOOK BEHIND TO SEE IF HIS PURSUER SHOULD VANISH, ACCORDING TO RULE, IN A FLASH OF FIRE AND BRIMSTONE.
INSTEAD, HE SAW THE GOBLIN RISING IN HIS STIRRUPS, AND...

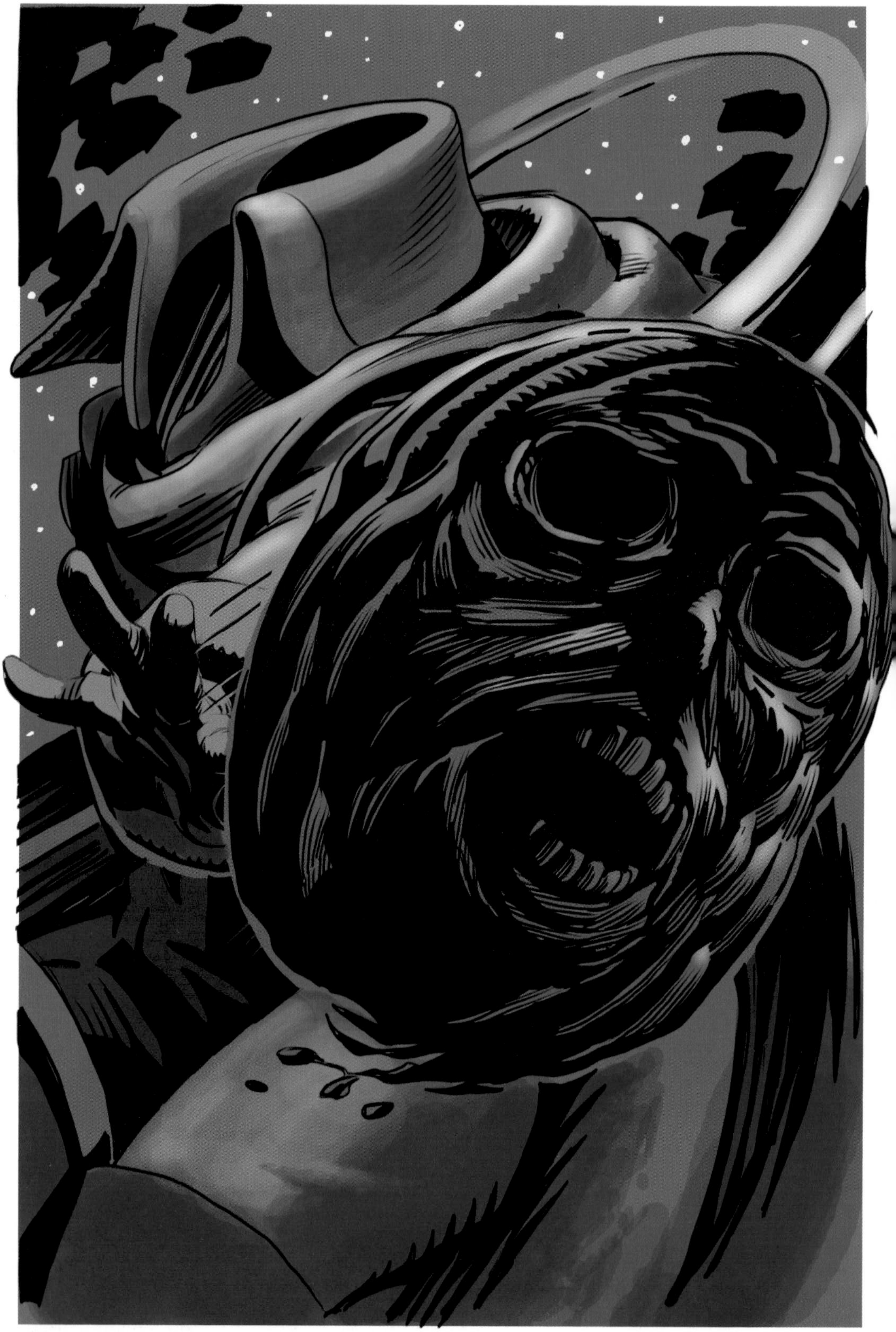

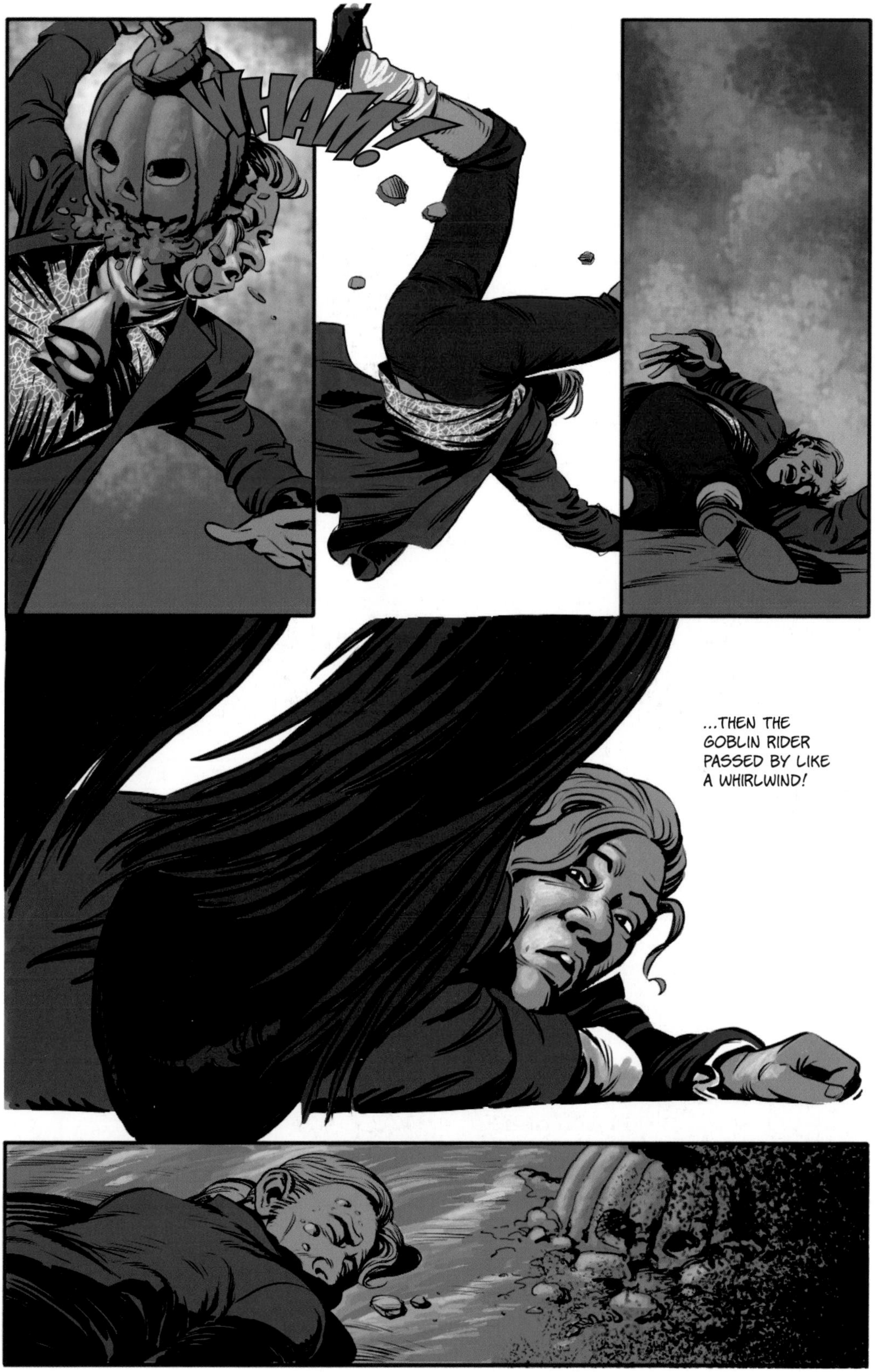
WHAM!
...THEN THE GOBLIN RIDER PASSED BY LIKE A WHIRLWIND!

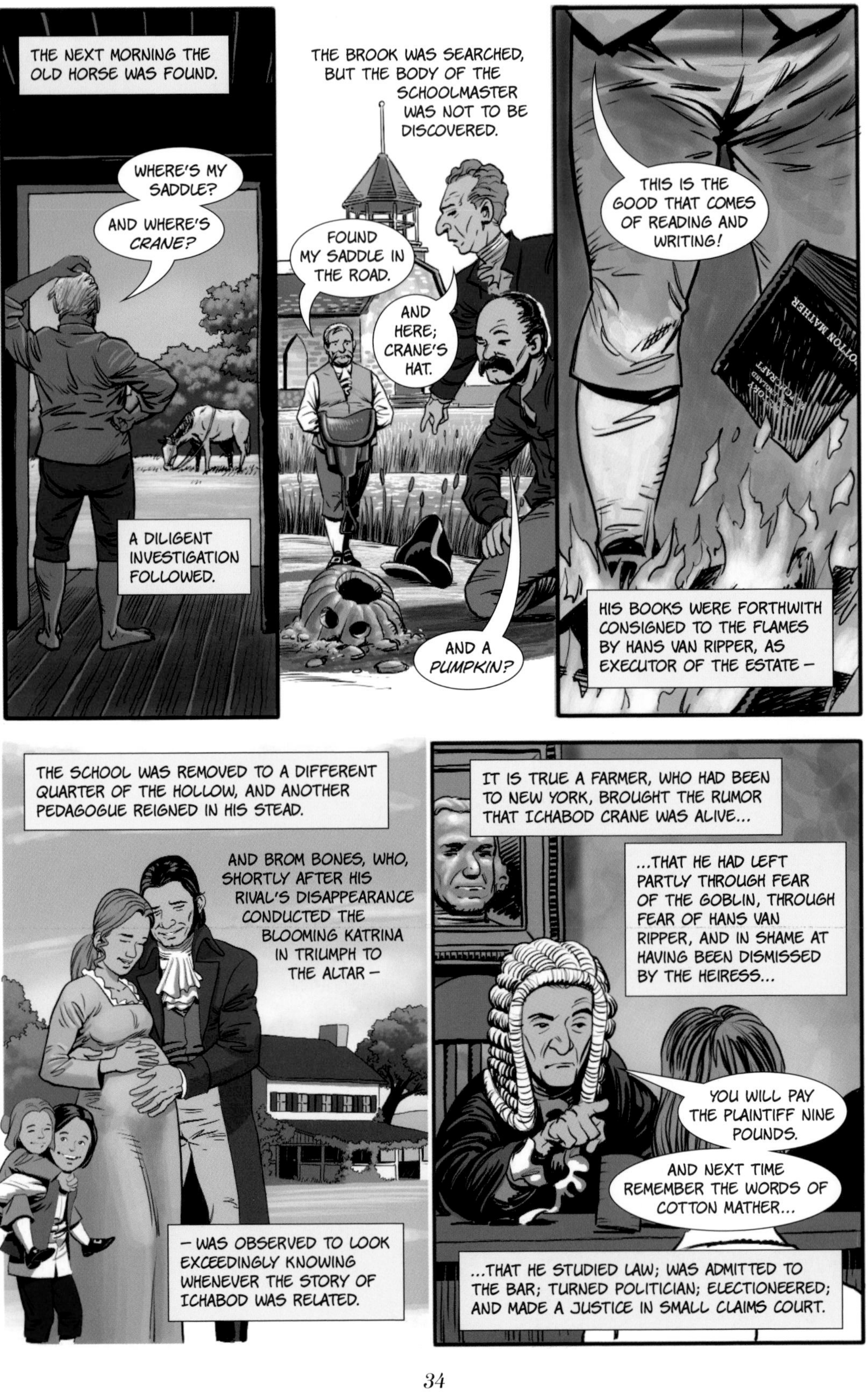
THE NEXT MORNING THE OLD HORSE WAS FOUND.
WHERE'S MY SADDLE?
AND WHERE'S *CRANE?*
A DILIGENT INVESTIGATION FOLLOWED.
THE BROOK WAS SEARCHED, BUT THE BODY OF THE SCHOOLMASTER WAS NOT TO BE DISCOVERED.
FOUND MY SADDLE IN THE ROAD.
AND HERE; CRANE'S HAT.
AND A *PUMPKIN?*
THIS IS THE GOOD THAT COMES OF READING AND WRITING!
HIS BOOKS WERE FORTHWITH CONSIGNED TO THE FLAMES BY HANS VAN RIPPER, AS EXECUTOR OF THE ESTATE –
THE SCHOOL WAS REMOVED TO A DIFFERENT QUARTER OF THE HOLLOW, AND ANOTHER PEDAGOGUE REIGNED IN HIS STEAD.
AND BROM BONES, WHO, SHORTLY AFTER HIS RIVAL'S DISAPPEARANCE CONDUCTED THE BLOOMING KATRINA IN TRIUMPH TO THE ALTAR –
– WAS OBSERVED TO LOOK EXCEEDINGLY KNOWING WHENEVER THE STORY OF ICHABOD WAS RELATED.
IT IS TRUE A FARMER, WHO HAD BEEN TO NEW YORK, BROUGHT THE RUMOR THAT ICHABOD CRANE WAS ALIVE...
...THAT HE HAD LEFT PARTLY THROUGH FEAR OF THE GOBLIN, THROUGH FEAR OF HANS VAN RIPPER, AND IN SHAME AT HAVING BEEN DISMISSED BY THE HEIRESS...
YOU WILL PAY THE PLAINTIFF NINE POUNDS.
AND NEXT TIME REMEMBER THE WORDS OF COTTON MATHER...
...THAT HE STUDIED LAW; WAS ADMITTED TO THE BAR; TURNED POLITICIAN; ELECTIONEERED; AND MADE A JUSTICE IN SMALL CLAIMS COURT.

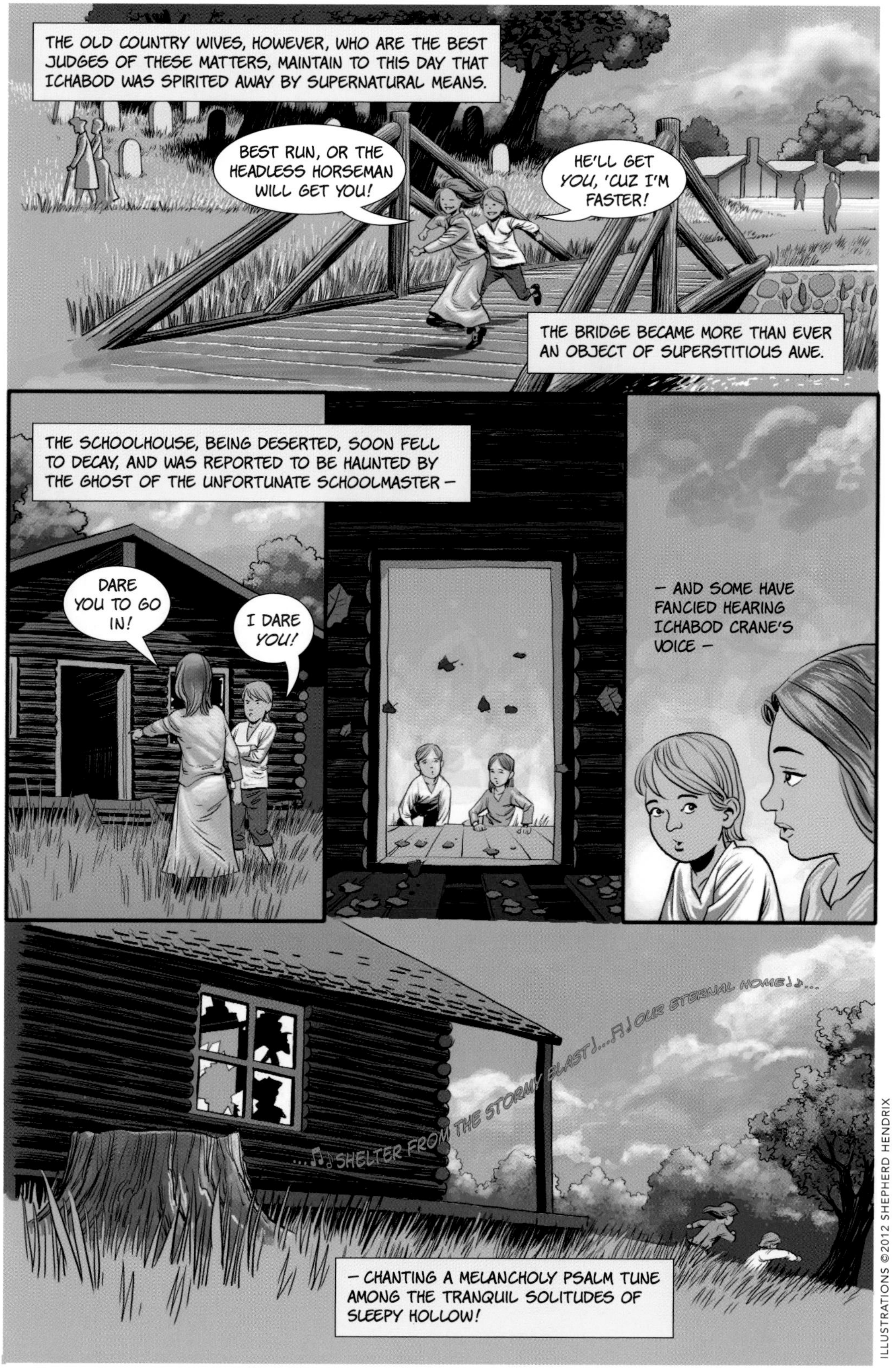
THE OLD COUNTRY WIVES, HOWEVER, WHO ARE THE BEST JUDGES OF THESE MATTERS, MAINTAIN TO THIS DAY THAT ICHABOD WAS SPIRITED AWAY BY SUPERNATURAL MEANS.
BEST RUN, OR THE HEADLESS HORSEMAN WILL GET YOU!
HE'LL GET YOU, 'CUZ I'M FASTER!
THE BRIDGE BECAME MORE THAN EVER AN OBJECT OF SUPERSTITIOUS AWE.
THE SCHOOLHOUSE, BEING DESERTED, SOON FELL TO DECAY, AND WAS REPORTED TO BE HAUNTED BY THE GHOST OF THE UNFORTUNATE SCHOOLMASTER –
DARE YOU TO GO IN!
I DARE YOU!
– AND SOME HAVE FANCIED HEARING ICHABOD CRANE'S VOICE –
...♫♪SHELTER FROM THE STORMY BLAST♪...♫♪OUR ETERNAL HOME♪♪...
– CHANTING A MELANCHOLY PSALM TUNE AMONG THE TRANQUIL SOLITUDES OF SLEEPY HOLLOW!

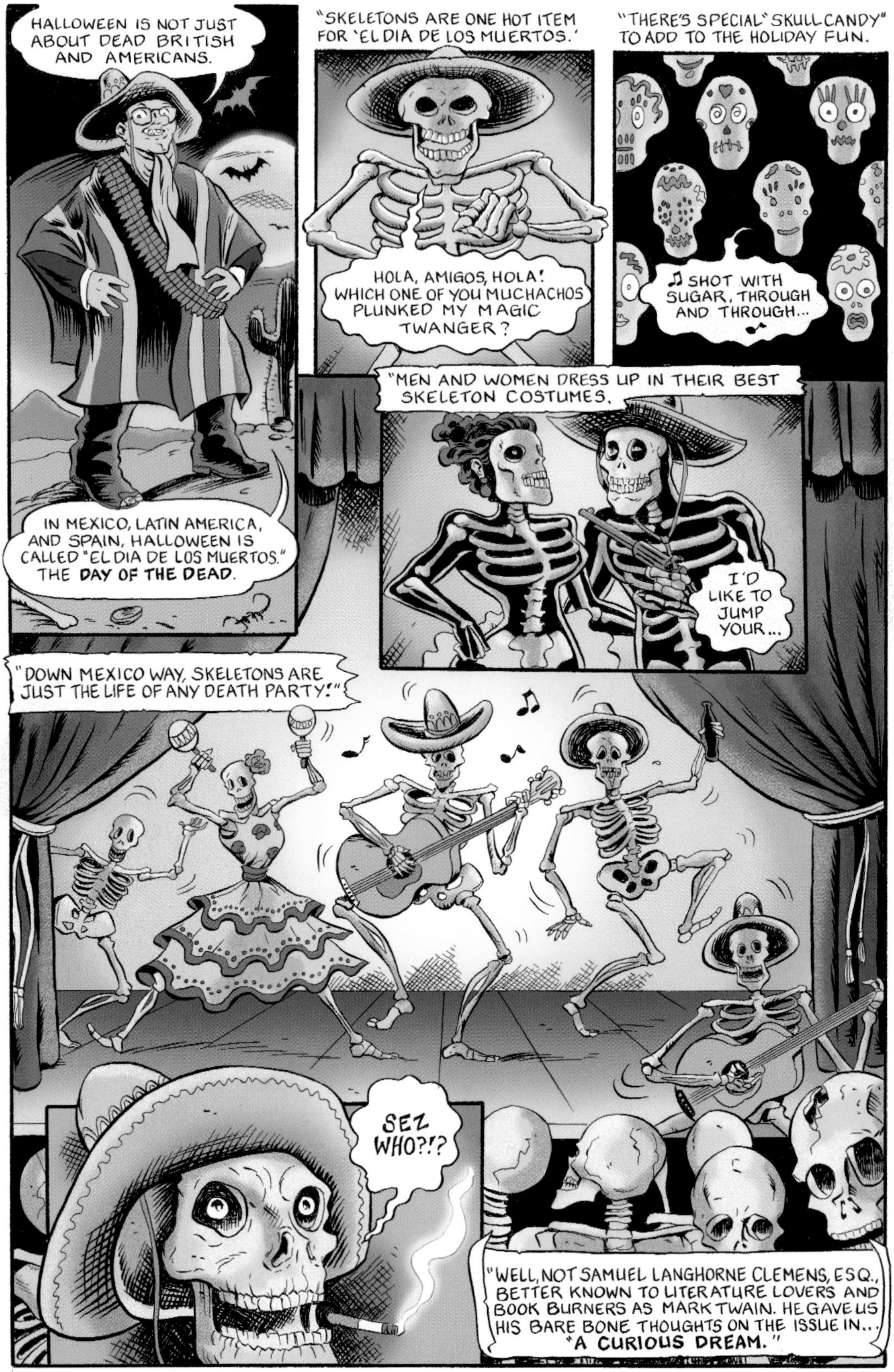
HALLOWEEN IS NOT JUST ABOUT DEAD BRITISH AND AMERICANS.
IN MEXICO, LATIN AMERICA, AND SPAIN, HALLOWEEN IS CALLED "EL DIA DE LOS MUERTOS." THE DAY OF THE DEAD.
"SKELETONS ARE ONE HOT ITEM FOR 'EL DIA DE LOS MUERTOS.'
HOLA, AMIGOS, HOLA! WHICH ONE OF YOU MUCHACHOS PLUNKED MY MAGIC TWANGER?
"THERE'S SPECIAL 'SKULL CANDY" TO ADD TO THE HOLIDAY FUN.
♫ SHOT WITH SUGAR, THROUGH AND THROUGH...
"MEN AND WOMEN DRESS UP IN THEIR BEST SKELETON COSTUMES.
I'D LIKE TO JUMP YOUR...
"DOWN MEXICO WAY, SKELETONS ARE JUST THE LIFE OF ANY DEATH PARTY!"
SEZ WHO?!?
"WELL, NOT SAMUEL LANGHORNE CLEMENS, ESQ., BETTER KNOWN TO LITERATURE LOVERS AND BOOK BURNERS AS MARK TWAIN. HE GAVE US HIS BARE BONE THOUGHTS ON THE ISSUE IN... "A CURIOUS DREAM."

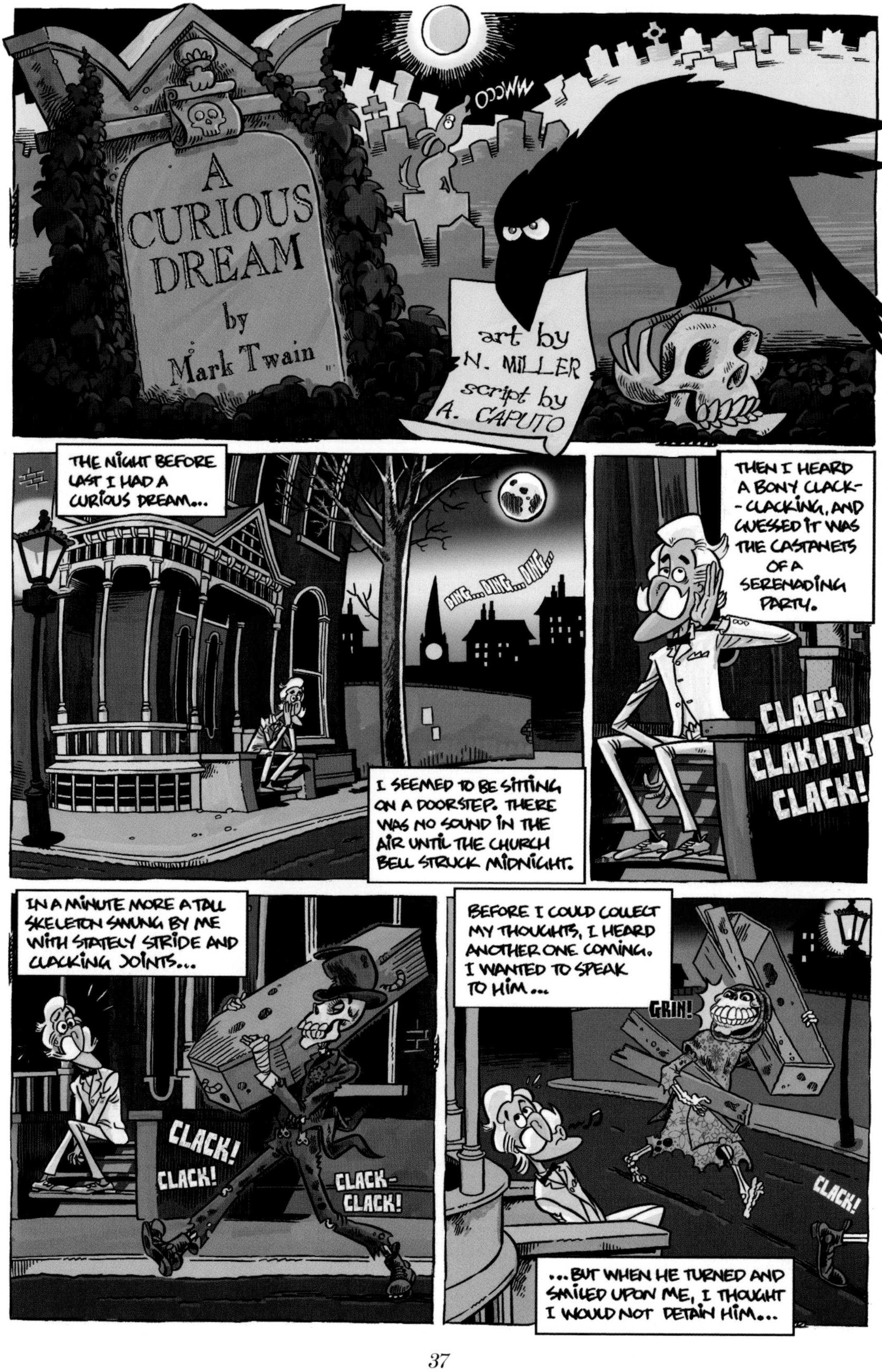
A CURIOUS DREAM
by
Mark Twain
art by
N. MILLER
script by
A. CAPUTO
THE NIGHT BEFORE LAST I HAD A CURIOUS DREAM...
DING...DING...DING...
I SEEMED TO BE SITTING ON A DOORSTEP. THERE WAS NO SOUND IN THE AIR UNTIL THE CHURCH BELL STRUCK MIDNIGHT.
THEN I HEARD A BONY CLACK-CLACKING, AND GUESSED IT WAS THE CASTANETS OF A SERENADING PARTY.
CLACK
CLAKITTY
CLACK!
IN A MINUTE MORE A TALL SKELETON SWUNG BY ME WITH STATELY STRIDE AND CLACKING JOINTS...
CLACK!
CLACK!
CLACK-CLACK!
BEFORE I COULD COLLECT MY THOUGHTS, I HEARD ANOTHER ONE COMING. I WANTED TO SPEAK TO HIM...
GRIN!
CLACK!
...BUT WHEN HE TURNED AND SMILED UPON ME, I THOUGHT I WOULD NOT DETAIN HIM...

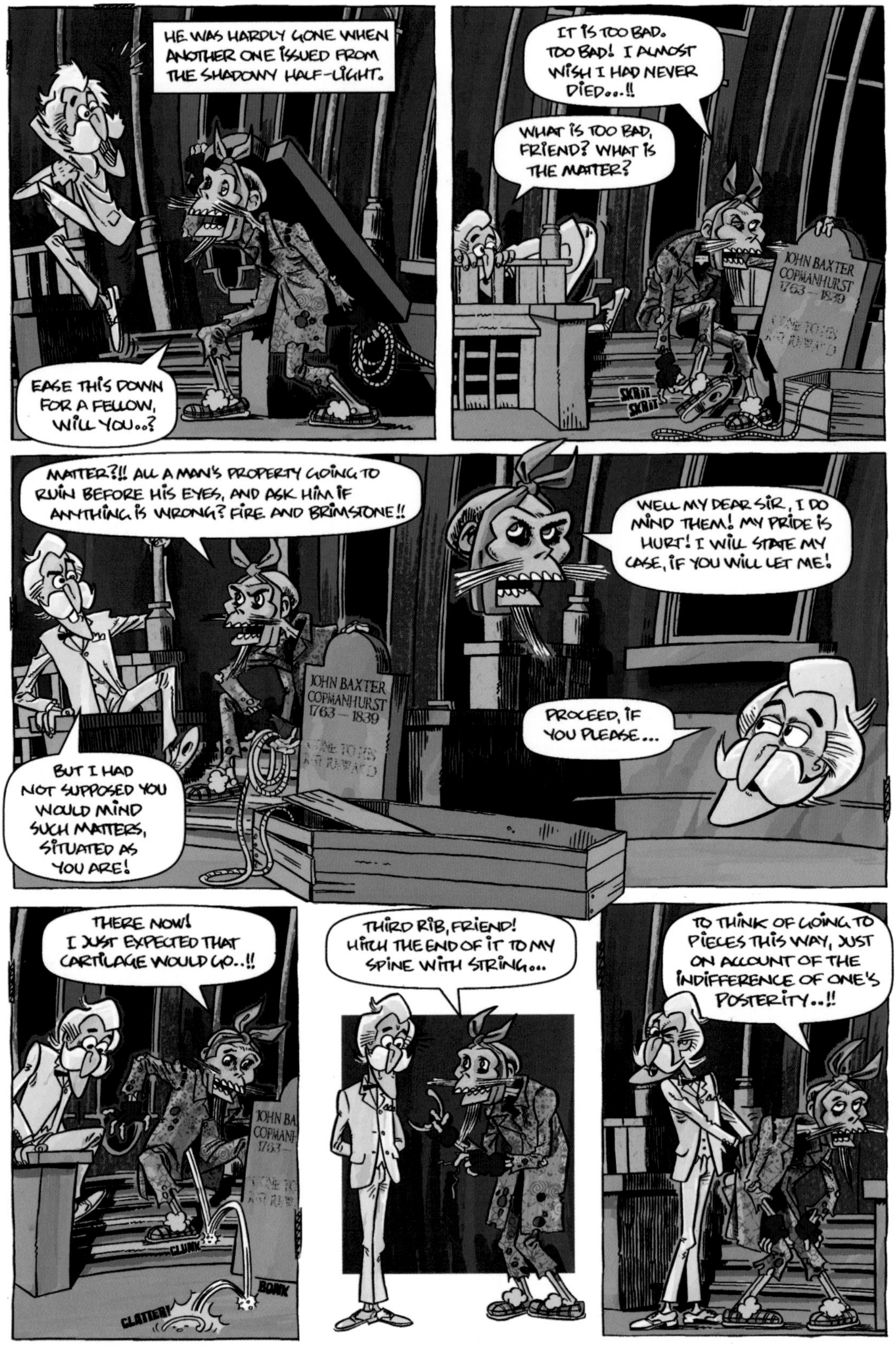
HE WAS HARDLY GONE WHEN ANOTHER ONE ISSUED FROM THE SHADOWY HALF-LIGHT.
EASE THIS DOWN FOR A FELLOW, WILL YOU..?
IT IS TOO BAD. TOO BAD! I ALMOST WISH I HAD NEVER DIED...!!
WHAT IS TOO BAD, FRIEND? WHAT IS THE MATTER?
JOHN BAXTER COPMANHURST 1763 — 1839
SKRIT SKRIT
MATTER?!! ALL A MAN'S PROPERTY GOING TO RUIN BEFORE HIS EYES, AND ASK HIM IF ANYTHING IS WRONG? FIRE AND BRIMSTONE!!
BUT I HAD NOT SUPPOSED YOU WOULD MIND SUCH MATTERS, SITUATED AS YOU ARE!
WELL MY DEAR SIR, I DO MIND THEM! MY PRIDE IS HURT! I WILL STATE MY CASE, IF YOU WILL LET ME!
PROCEED, IF YOU PLEASE...
THERE NOW! I JUST EXPECTED THAT CARTILAGE WOULD GO..!!
CLUNK
BONK
CLATTER!
THIRD RIB, FRIEND! HITCH THE END OF IT TO MY SPINE WITH STRING...
TO THINK OF GOING TO PIECES THIS WAY, JUST ON ACCOUNT OF THE INDIFFERENCE OF ONE'S POSTERITY..!!

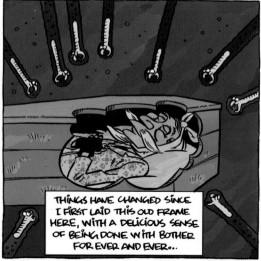

I RESIDE IN THAT SHAMEFUL OLD GRAVEYARD A BLOCK OR TWO ABOVE THIS STREET, AND HAVE FOR THESE THIRTY YEARS...

THINGS HAVE CHANGED SINCE I FIRST LAID THIS OLD FRAME HERE, WITH A DELICIOUS SENSE OF BEING DONE WITH BOTHER FOR EVER AND EVER...

IT'S A GRAND JOB Y'DOIN' THERE, LAD...

JOHN BAXTER COPMANHURST 1763 — 1839

GO TUMP! JUST TUMP! IT TUMP!

...LISTENING WITH SATISFACTION TO THE SEXTON DO THE WORK THAT SHAPED THE ROOF OF MY NEW HOME!

COUGH!

I WISH YOU COULD TRY IT TONIGHT..!!

YES, SIR, THIRTY YEARS AGO I LAID ME DOWN THERE AND WAS HAPPY. IT WAS OUT IN THE COUNTRY THEN, AND EVERYTHING WAS PLEASANT...

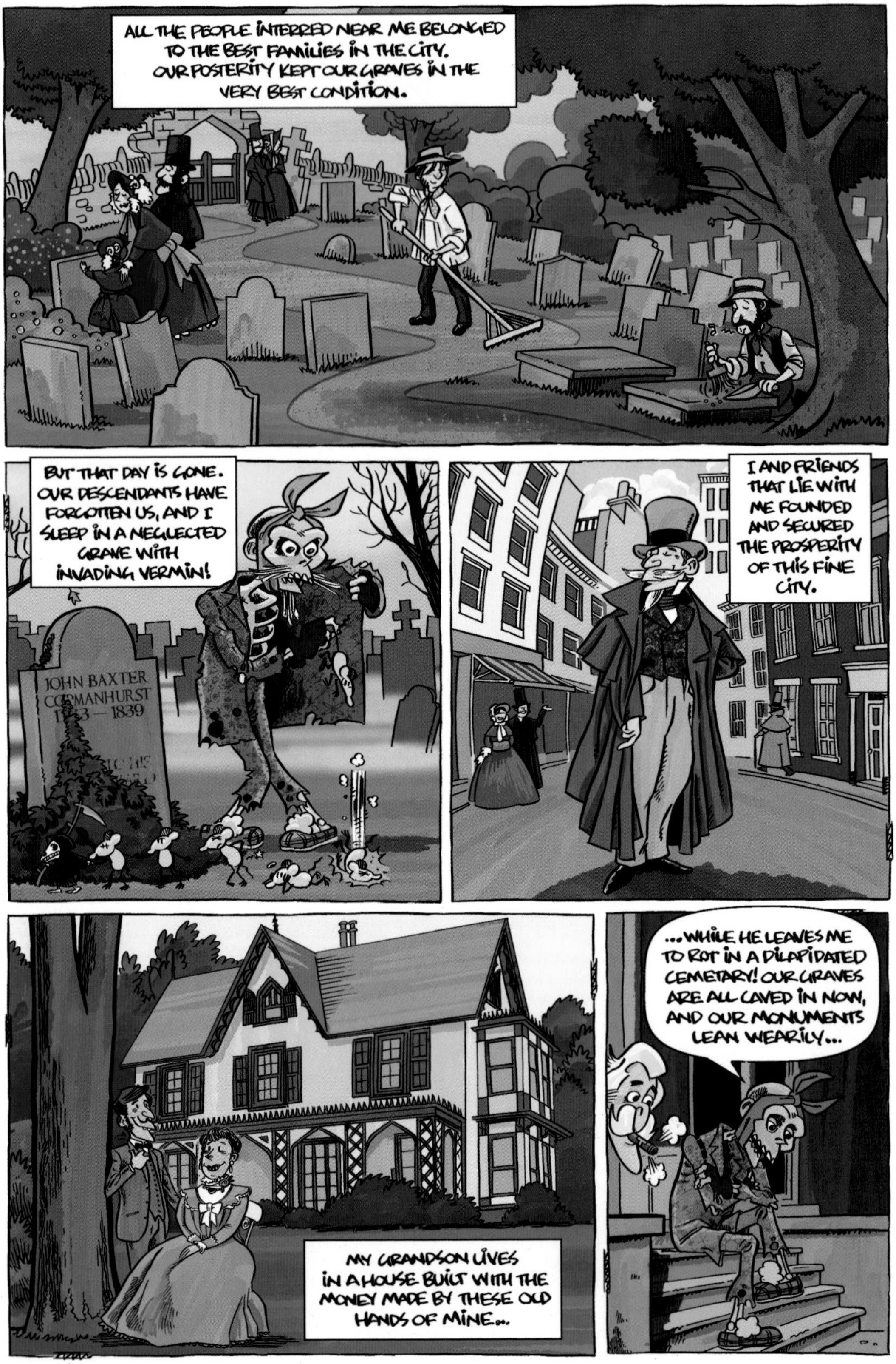
ALL THE PEOPLE INTERRED NEAR ME BELONGED TO THE BEST FAMILIES IN THE CITY. OUR POSTERITY KEPT OUR GRAVES IN THE VERY BEST CONDITION.
BUT THAT DAY IS GONE. OUR DESCENDANTS HAVE FORGOTTEN US, AND I SLEEP IN A NEGLECTED GRAVE WITH INVADING VERMIN!
JOHN BAXTER
I AND FRIENDS THAT LIE WITH ME FOUNDED AND SECURED THE PROSPERITY OF THIS FINE CITY.
MY GRANDSON LIVES IN A HOUSE BUILT WITH THE MONEY MADE BY THESE OLD HANDS OF MINE...
...WHILE HE LEAVES ME TO ROT IN A DILAPIDATED CEMETARY! OUR GRAVES ARE ALL CAVED IN NOW, AND OUR MONUMENTS LEAN WEARILY...

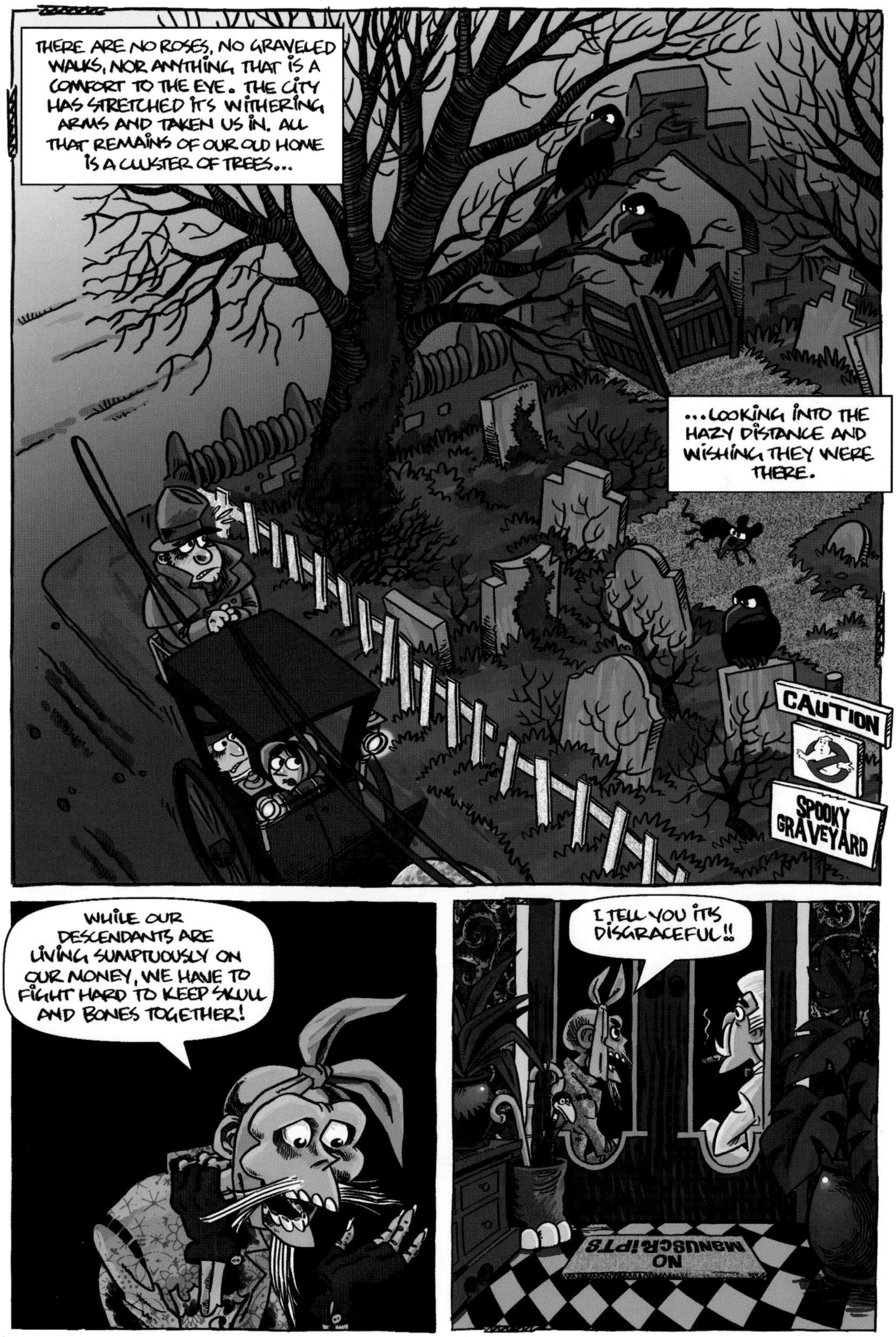
THERE ARE NO ROSES, NO GRAVELED WALKS, NOR ANYTHING THAT IS A COMFORT TO THE EYE. THE CITY HAS STRETCHED IT'S WITHERING ARMS AND TAKEN US IN. ALL THAT REMAINS OF OUR OLD HOME IS A CLUSTER OF TREES...
...LOOKING INTO THE HAZY DISTANCE AND WISHING THEY WERE THERE.
CAUTION
SPOOKY GRAVEYARD
WHILE OUR DESCENDANTS ARE LIVING SUMPTUOUSLY ON OUR MONEY, WE HAVE TO FIGHT HARD TO KEEP SKULL AND BONES TOGETHER!
I TELL YOU ITS DISGRACEFUL!!
NO MANUSCRIPTS

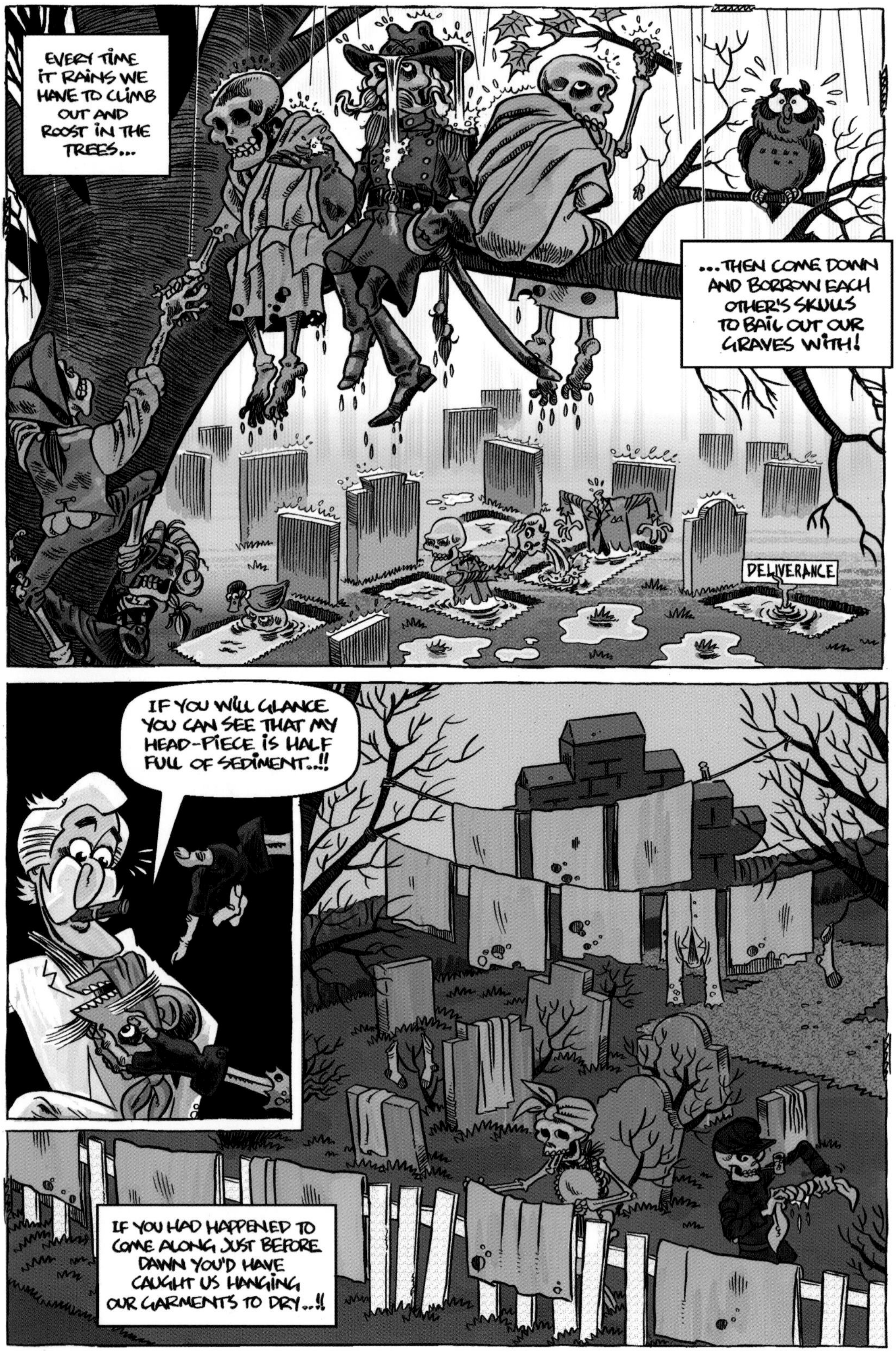
EVERY TIME IT RAINS WE HAVE TO CLIMB OUT AND ROOST IN THE TREES...
...THEN COME DOWN AND BORROW EACH OTHER'S SKULLS TO BAIL OUT OUR GRAVES WITH!
DELIVERANCE
IF YOU WILL GLANCE YOU CAN SEE THAT MY HEAD-PIECE IS HALF FULL OF SEDIMENT..!!
IF YOU HAD HAPPENED TO COME ALONG JUST BEFORE DAWN YOU'D HAVE CAUGHT US HANGING OUR GARMENTS TO DRY...!!

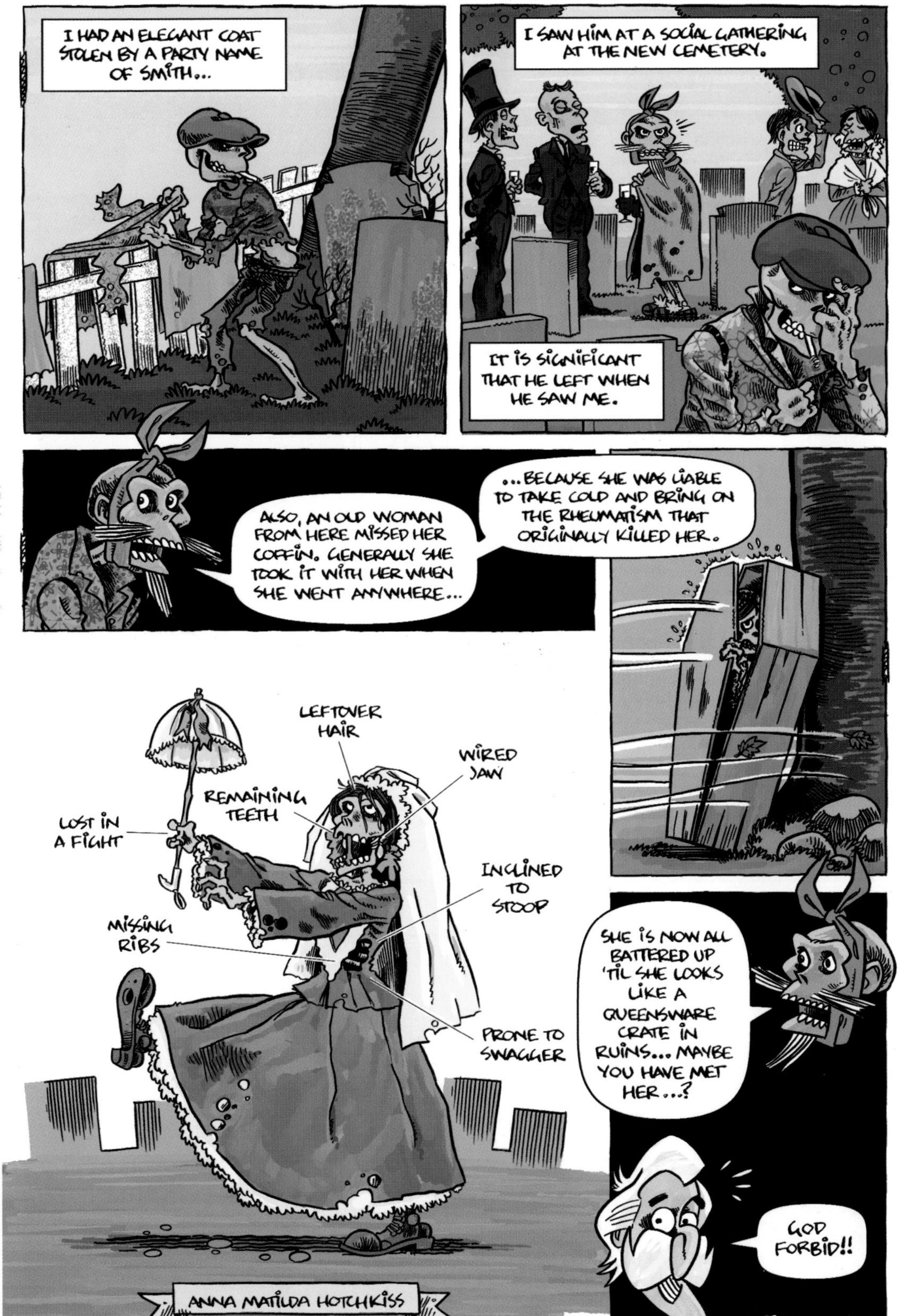
I HAD AN ELEGANT COAT STOLEN BY A PARTY NAME OF SMITH...
I SAW HIM AT A SOCIAL GATHERING AT THE NEW CEMETERY.
IT IS SIGNIFICANT THAT HE LEFT WHEN HE SAW ME.
ALSO, AN OLD WOMAN FROM HERE MISSED HER COFFIN. GENERALLY SHE TOOK IT WITH HER WHEN SHE WENT ANYWHERE...
...BECAUSE SHE WAS LIABLE TO TAKE COLD AND BRING ON THE RHEUMATISM THAT ORIGINALLY KILLED HER.
LEFTOVER HAIR
WIRED JAW
REMAINING TEETH
LOST IN A FIGHT
INCLINED TO STOOP
MISSING RIBS
PRONE TO SWAGGER
ANNA MATILDA HOTCHKISS
SHE IS NOW ALL BATTERED UP 'TIL SHE LOOKS LIKE A QUEENSWARE CRATE IN RUINS... MAYBE YOU HAVE MET HER...?
GOD FORBID!!

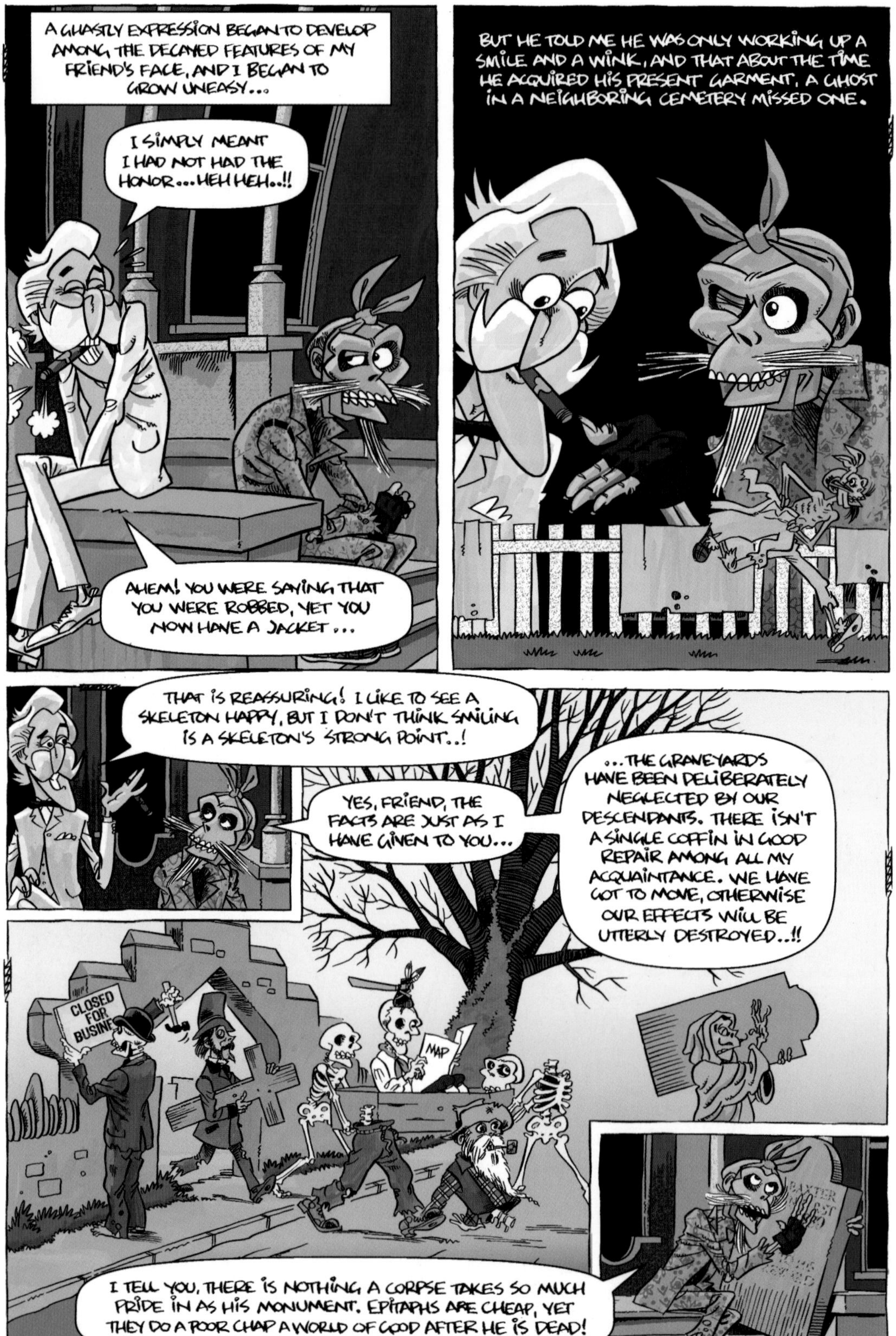
A GHASTLY EXPRESSION BEGAN TO DEVELOP AMONG THE DECAYED FEATURES OF MY FRIEND'S FACE, AND I BEGAN TO GROW UNEASY...
I SIMPLY MEANT I HAD NOT HAD THE HONOR...HEH HEH..!!
AHEM! YOU WERE SAYING THAT YOU WERE ROBBED, YET YOU NOW HAVE A JACKET...
BUT HE TOLD ME HE WAS ONLY WORKING UP A SMILE AND A WINK, AND THAT ABOUT THE TIME HE ACQUIRED HIS PRESENT GARMENT, A GHOST IN A NEIGHBORING CEMETERY MISSED ONE.
THAT IS REASSURING! I LIKE TO SEE A SKELETON HAPPY, BUT I DON'T THINK SMILING IS A SKELETON'S STRONG POINT..!
YES, FRIEND, THE FACTS ARE JUST AS I HAVE GIVEN TO YOU...
...THE GRAVEYARDS HAVE BEEN DELIBERATELY NEGLECTED BY OUR DESCENDANTS. THERE ISN'T A SINGLE COFFIN IN GOOD REPAIR AMONG ALL MY ACQUAINTANCE. WE HAVE GOT TO MOVE, OTHERWISE OUR EFFECTS WILL BE UTTERLY DESTROYED..!!
CLOSED FOR BUSINE
MAP
I TELL YOU, THERE IS NOTHING A CORPSE TAKES SO MUCH PRIDE IN AS HIS MONUMENT. EPITAPHS ARE CHEAP, YET THEY DO A POOR CHAP A WORLD OF GOOD AFTER HE IS DEAD!

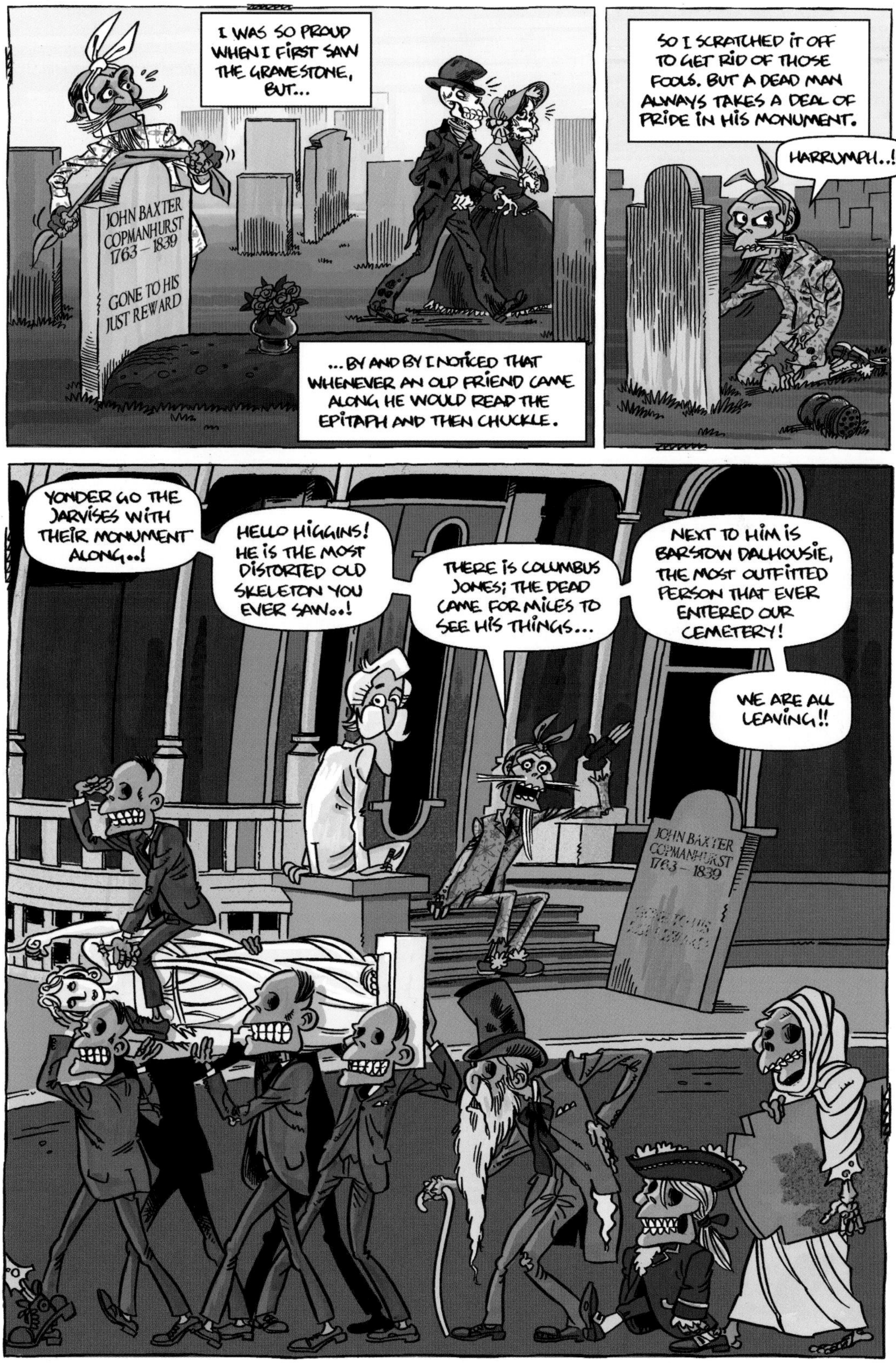

I WAS SO PROUD WHEN I FIRST SAW THE GRAVESTONE, BUT...
JOHN BAXTER COPMANHURST 1763 – 1839 GONE TO HIS JUST REWARD
...BY AND BY I NOTICED THAT WHENEVER AN OLD FRIEND CAME ALONG HE WOULD READ THE EPITAPH AND THEN CHUCKLE.
SO I SCRATCHED IT OFF TO GET RID OF THOSE FOOLS. BUT A DEAD MAN ALWAYS TAKES A DEAL OF PRIDE IN HIS MONUMENT.
HARRUMPH..!!
YONDER GO THE JARVISES WITH THEIR MONUMENT ALONG..!
HELLO HIGGINS! HE IS THE MOST DISTORTED OLD SKELETON YOU EVER SAW..!
THERE IS COLUMBUS JONES; THE DEAD CAME FOR MILES TO SEE HIS THINGS...
NEXT TO HIM IS BARSTOW DALHOUSIE, THE MOST OUTFITTED PERSON THAT EVER ENTERED OUR CEMETERY!
WE ARE ALL LEAVING!!
JOHN BAXTER COPMANHURST 1763 – 1839

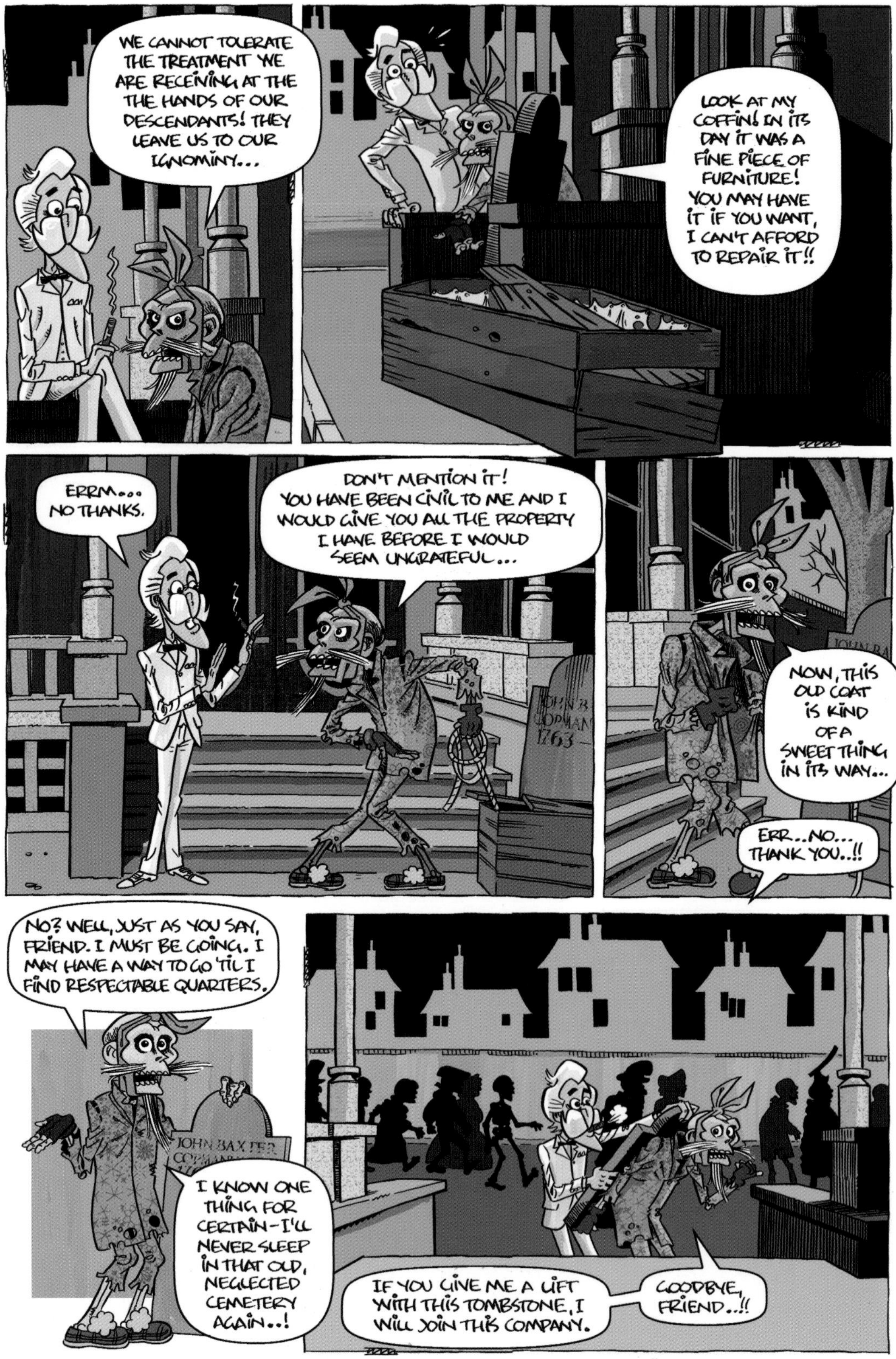
WE CANNOT TOLERATE THE TREATMENT WE ARE RECEIVING AT THE THE HANDS OF OUR DESCENDANTS! THEY LEAVE US TO OUR IGNOMINY...
LOOK AT MY COFFIN! IN ITS DAY IT WAS A FINE PIECE OF FURNITURE! YOU MAY HAVE IT IF YOU WANT, I CAN'T AFFORD TO REPAIR IT!!
ERRM... NO THANKS.
DON'T MENTION IT! YOU HAVE BEEN CIVIL TO ME AND I WOULD GIVE YOU ALL THE PROPERTY I HAVE BEFORE I WOULD SEEM UNGRATEFUL...
JOHN B COPMAN 1763
NOW, THIS OLD COAT IS KIND OF A SWEET THING IN ITS WAY...
ERR...NO... THANK YOU..!!
NO? WELL, JUST AS YOU SAY, FRIEND. I MUST BE GOING. I MAY HAVE A WAY TO GO 'TIL I FIND RESPECTABLE QUARTERS.
I KNOW ONE THING FOR CERTAIN - I'LL NEVER SLEEP IN THAT OLD, NEGLECTED CEMETERY AGAIN..!
IF YOU GIVE ME A LIFT WITH THIS TOMBSTONE, I WILL JOIN THIS COMPANY.
GOODBYE, FRIEND..!!

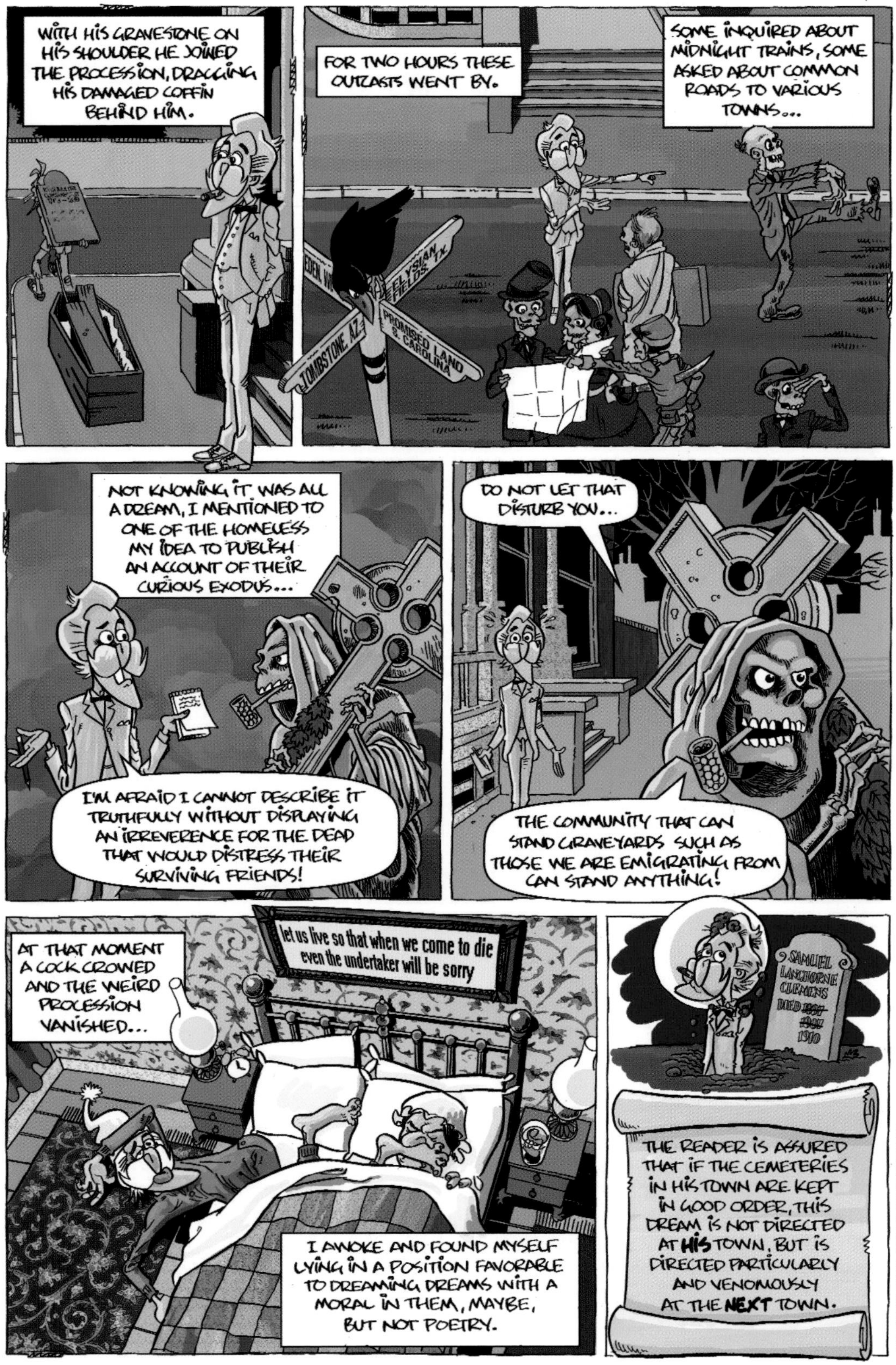
WITH HIS GRAVESTONE ON HIS SHOULDER HE JOINED THE PROCESSION, DRAGGING HIS DAMAGED COFFIN BEHIND HIM.
FOR TWO HOURS THESE OUTCASTS WENT BY.
SOME INQUIRED ABOUT MIDNIGHT TRAINS, SOME ASKED ABOUT COMMON ROADS TO VARIOUS TOWNS...
ELYSIAN FIELDS, TX.
TOMBSTONE, AZ
PROMISED LAND S. CAROLINA
NOT KNOWING IT WAS ALL A DREAM, I MENTIONED TO ONE OF THE HOMELESS MY IDEA TO PUBLISH AN ACCOUNT OF THEIR CURIOUS EXODUS...
I'M AFRAID I CANNOT DESCRIBE IT TRUTHFULLY WITHOUT DISPLAYING AN IRREVERENCE FOR THE DEAD THAT WOULD DISTRESS THEIR SURVIVING FRIENDS!
DO NOT LET THAT DISTURB YOU...
THE COMMUNITY THAT CAN STAND GRAVEYARDS SUCH AS THOSE WE ARE EMIGRATING FROM CAN STAND ANYTHING!
AT THAT MOMENT A COCK CROWED AND THE WEIRD PROCESSION VANISHED...
let us live so that when we come to die even the undertaker will be sorry
I AWOKE AND FOUND MYSELF LYING IN A POSITION FAVORABLE TO DREAMING DREAMS WITH A MORAL IN THEM, MAYBE, BUT NOT POETRY.
SAMUEL LANGHORNE CLEMENS
DIED
1910
THE READER IS ASSURED THAT IF THE CEMETERIES IN HIS TOWN ARE KEPT IN GOOD ORDER, THIS DREAM IS NOT DIRECTED AT **HIS** TOWN, BUT IS DIRECTED PARTICULARLY AND VENOMOUSLY AT THE **NEXT** TOWN.

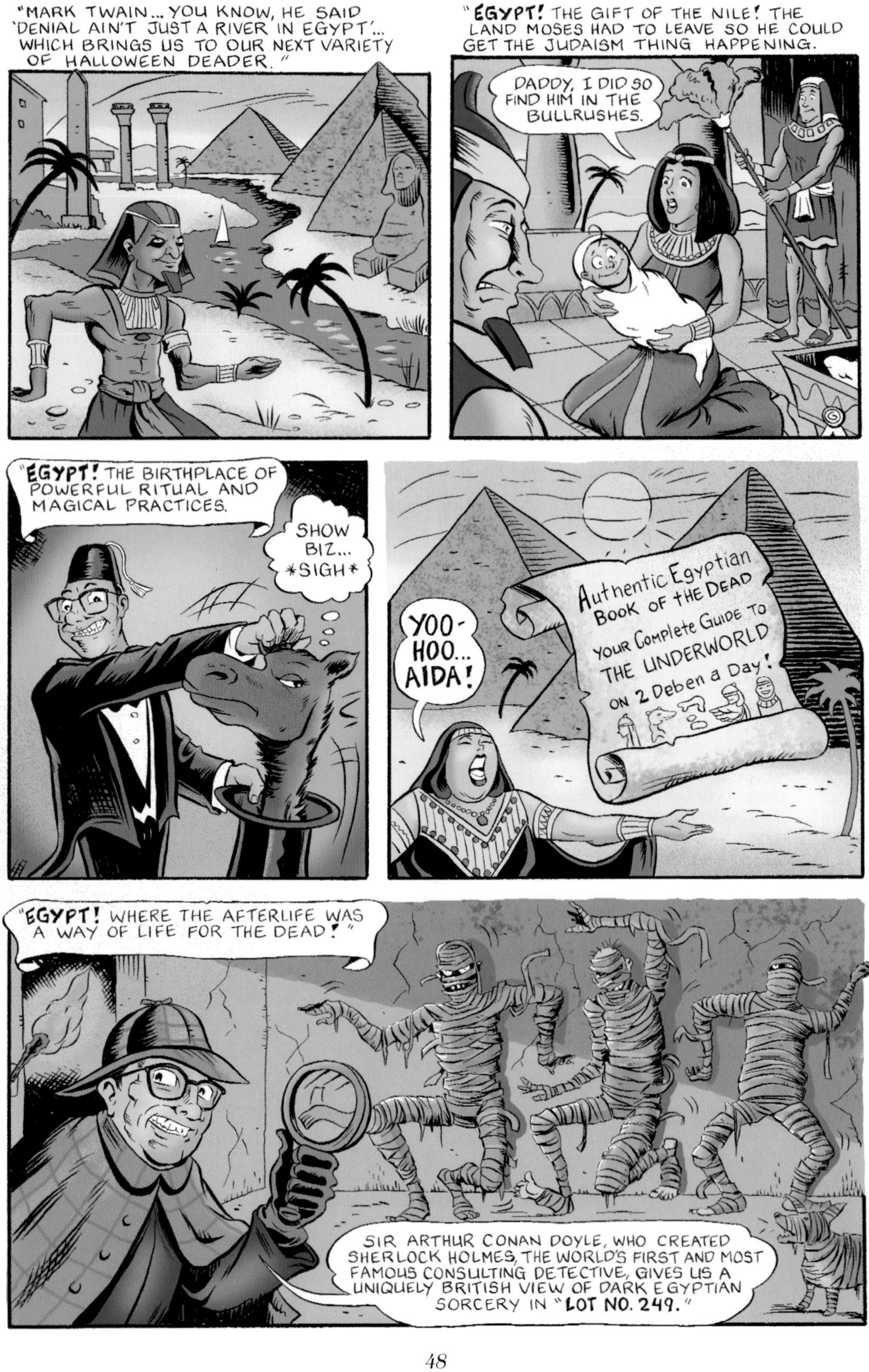
"MARK TWAIN... YOU KNOW, HE SAID 'DENIAL AIN'T JUST A RIVER IN EGYPT'... WHICH BRINGS US TO OUR NEXT VARIETY OF HALLOWEEN DEADER."
"EGYPT! THE GIFT OF THE NILE! THE LAND MOSES HAD TO LEAVE SO HE COULD GET THE JUDAISM THING HAPPENING.
DADDY, I DID SO FIND HIM IN THE BULLRUSHES.
"EGYPT! THE BIRTHPLACE OF POWERFUL RITUAL AND MAGICAL PRACTICES.
SHOW BIZ... *SIGH*
YOO-HOO... AIDA!
Authentic Egyptian Book of the Dead
Your Complete Guide to THE UNDERWORLD on 2 Deben a Day!
"EGYPT! WHERE THE AFTERLIFE WAS A WAY OF LIFE FOR THE DEAD!"
SIR ARTHUR CONAN DOYLE, WHO CREATED SHERLOCK HOLMES, THE WORLD'S FIRST AND MOST FAMOUS CONSULTING DETECTIVE, GIVES US A UNIQUELY BRITISH VIEW OF DARK EGYPTIAN SORCERY IN "LOT NO. 249."

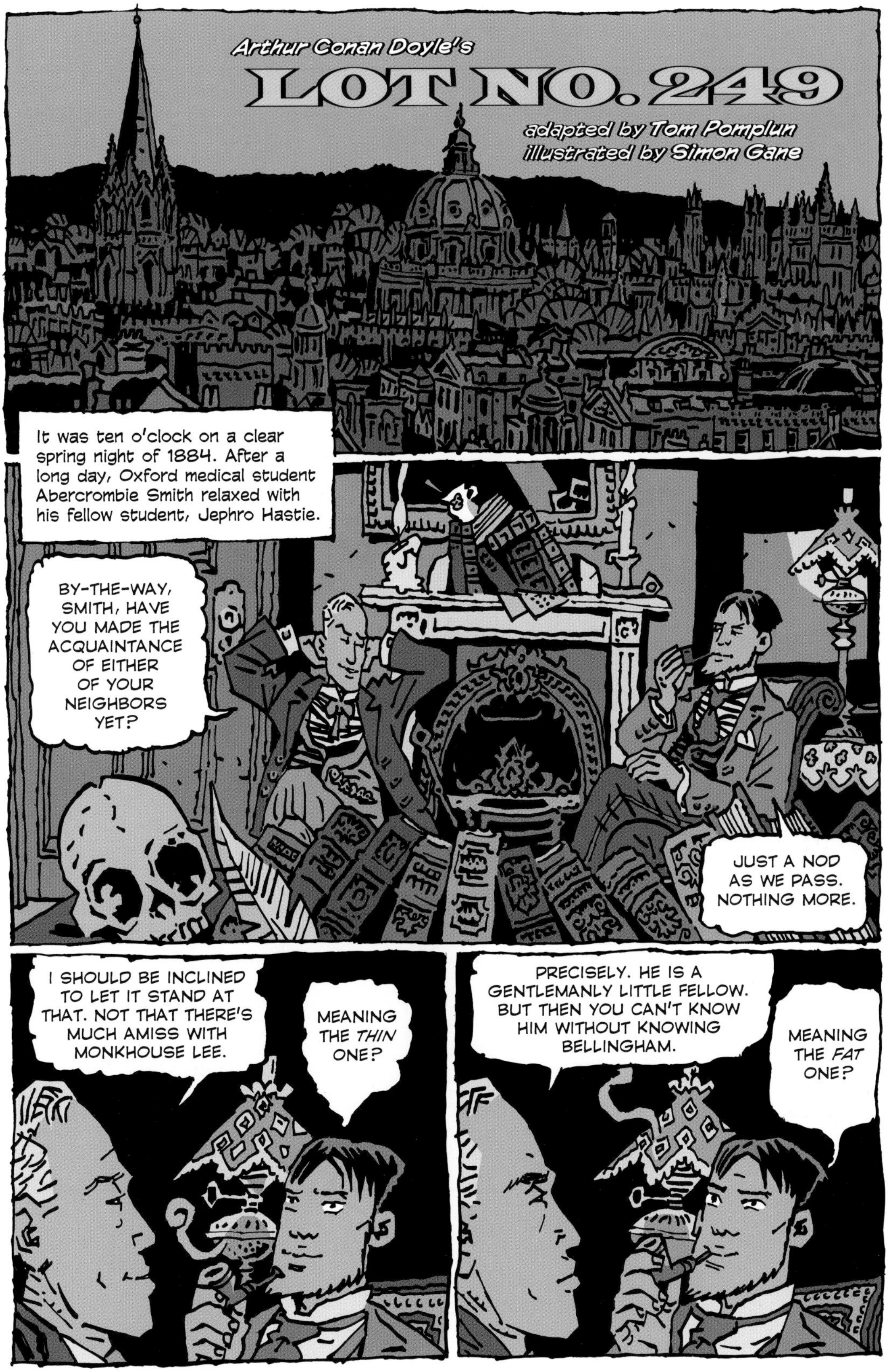
Arthur Conan Doyle's
LOT NO. 249
adapted by Tom Pomplun
illustrated by Simon Gane
It was ten o'clock on a clear spring night of 1884. After a long day, Oxford medical student Abercrombie Smith relaxed with his fellow student, Jephro Hastie.
BY-THE-WAY, SMITH, HAVE YOU MADE THE ACQUAINTANCE OF EITHER OF YOUR NEIGHBORS YET?
JUST A NOD AS WE PASS. NOTHING MORE.
I SHOULD BE INCLINED TO LET IT STAND AT THAT. NOT THAT THERE'S MUCH AMISS WITH MONKHOUSE LEE.
MEANING THE *THIN* ONE?
PRECISELY. HE IS A GENTLEMANLY LITTLE FELLOW. BUT THEN YOU CAN'T KNOW HIM WITHOUT KNOWING BELLINGHAM.
MEANING THE *FAT* ONE?

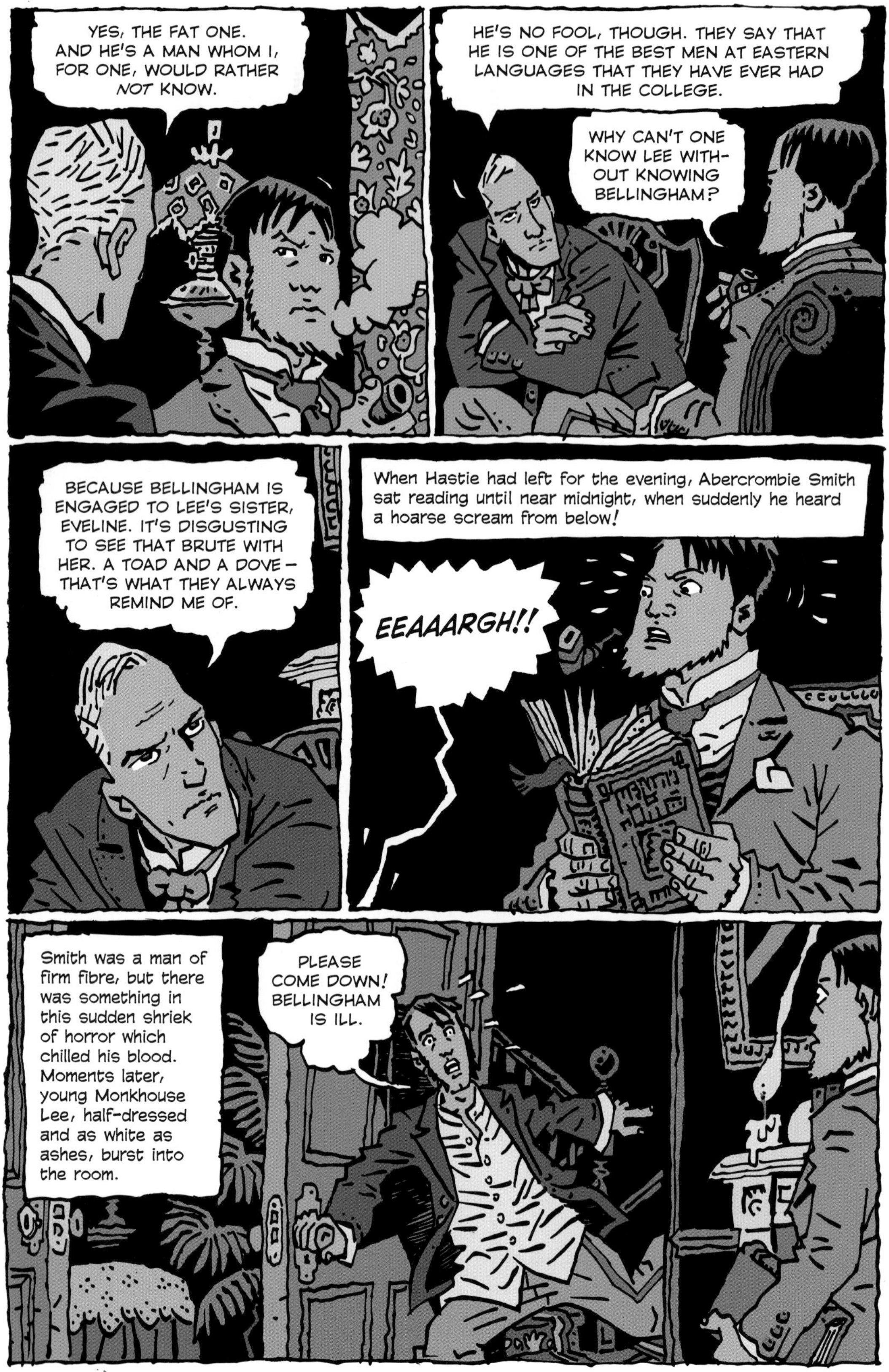

YES, THE FAT ONE. AND HE'S A MAN WHOM I, FOR ONE, WOULD RATHER *NOT* KNOW.
HE'S NO FOOL, THOUGH. THEY SAY THAT HE IS ONE OF THE BEST MEN AT EASTERN LANGUAGES THAT THEY HAVE EVER HAD IN THE COLLEGE.
WHY CAN'T ONE KNOW LEE WITHOUT KNOWING BELLINGHAM?
BECAUSE BELLINGHAM IS ENGAGED TO LEE'S SISTER, EVELINE. IT'S DISGUSTING TO SEE THAT BRUTE WITH HER. A TOAD AND A DOVE – THAT'S WHAT THEY ALWAYS REMIND ME OF.
When Hastie had left for the evening, Abercrombie Smith sat reading until near midnight, when suddenly he heard a hoarse scream from below!
EEAAARGH!!
Smith was a man of firm fibre, but there was something in this sudden shriek of horror which chilled his blood. Moments later, young Monkhouse Lee, half-dressed and as white as ashes, burst into the room.
PLEASE COME DOWN! BELLINGHAM IS ILL.

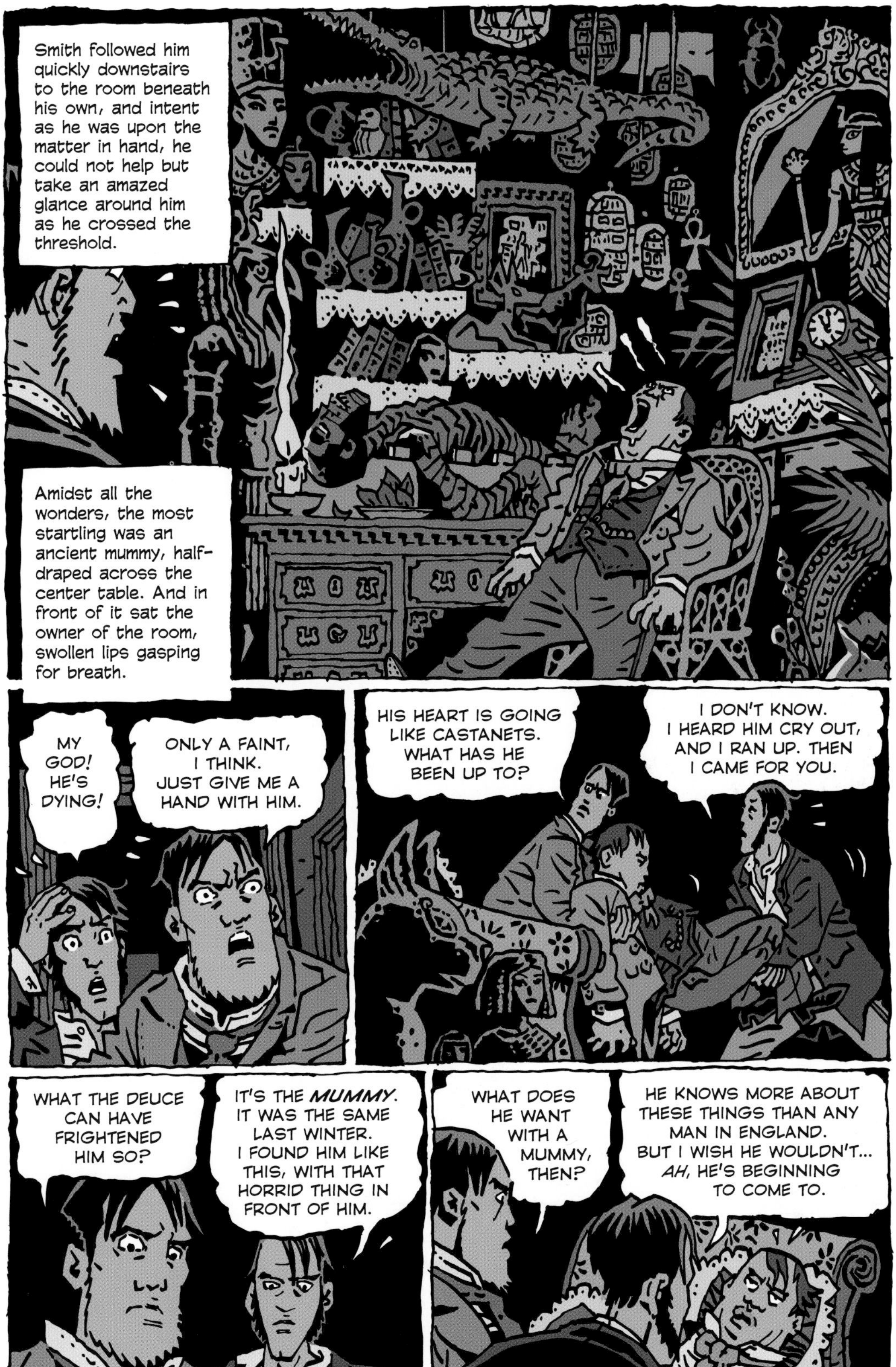
Smith followed him quickly downstairs to the room beneath his own, and intent as he was upon the matter in hand, he could not help but take an amazed glance around him as he crossed the threshold.
Amidst all the wonders, the most startling was an ancient mummy, half-draped across the center table. And in front of it sat the owner of the room, swollen lips gasping for breath.
MY GOD! HE'S DYING!
ONLY A FAINT, I THINK. JUST GIVE ME A HAND WITH HIM.
HIS HEART IS GOING LIKE CASTANETS. WHAT HAS HE BEEN UP TO?
I DON'T KNOW. I HEARD HIM CRY OUT, AND I RAN UP. THEN I CAME FOR YOU.
WHAT THE DEUCE CAN HAVE FRIGHTENED HIM SO?
IT'S THE *MUMMY*. IT WAS THE SAME LAST WINTER. I FOUND HIM LIKE THIS, WITH THAT HORRID THING IN FRONT OF HIM.
WHAT DOES HE WANT WITH A MUMMY, THEN?
HE KNOWS MORE ABOUT THESE THINGS THAN ANY MAN IN ENGLAND. BUT I WISH HE WOULDN'T... *AH*, HE'S BEGINNING TO COME TO.

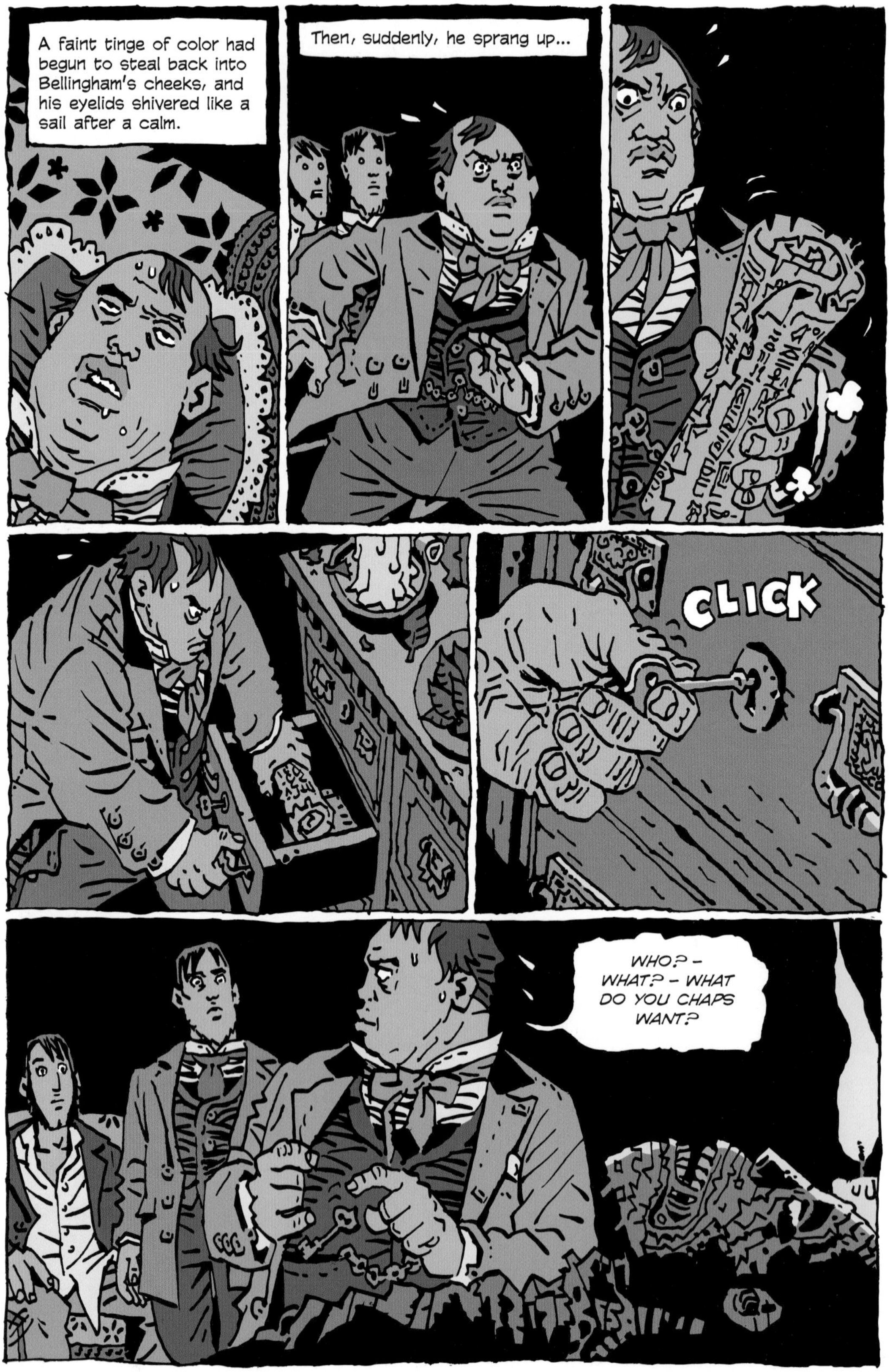
A faint tinge of color had begun to steal back into Bellingham's cheeks, and his eyelids shivered like a sail after a calm.
Then, suddenly, he sprang up...
CLICK
WHO? - WHAT? - WHAT DO YOU CHAPS WANT?

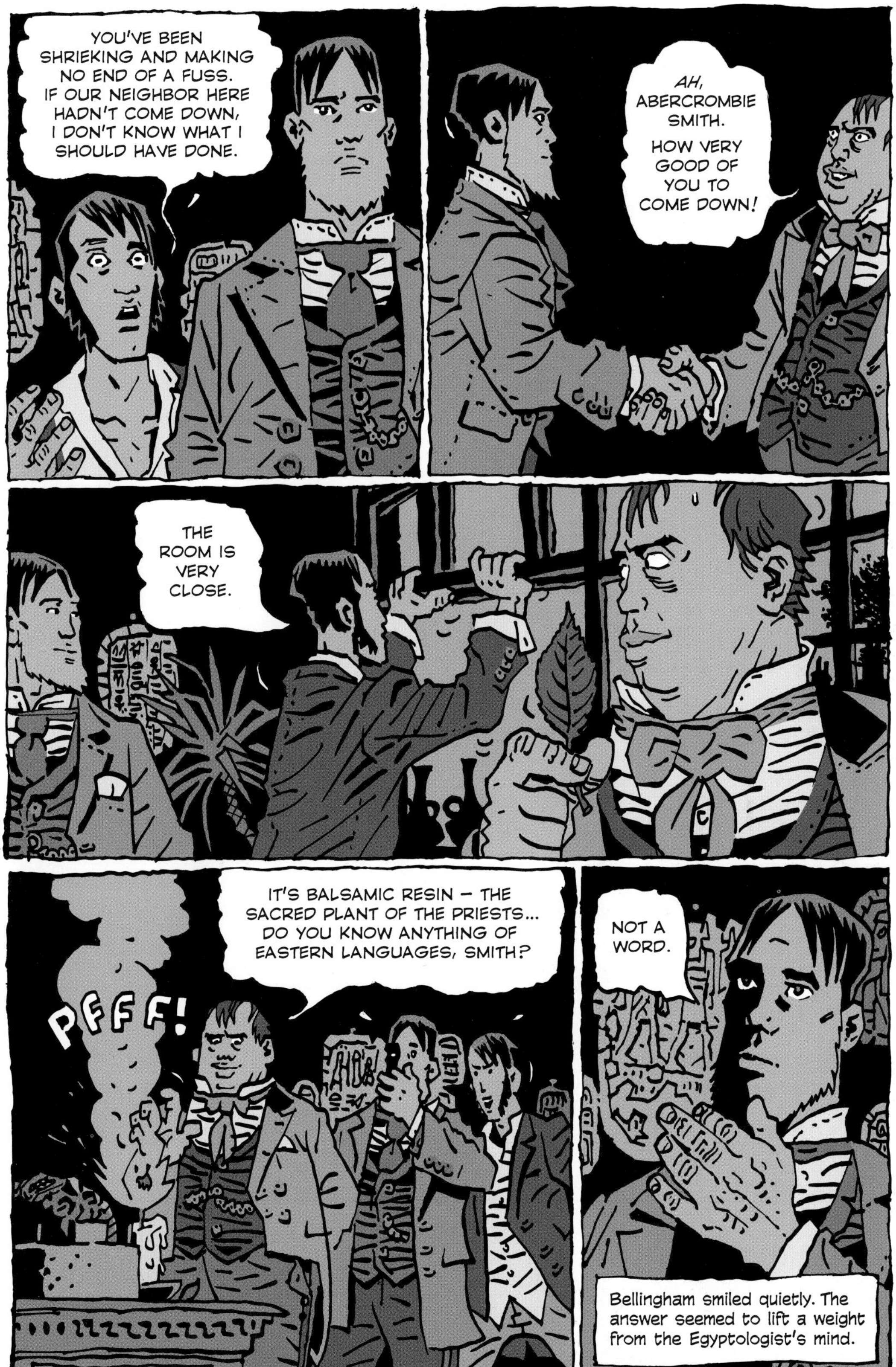
YOU'VE BEEN SHRIEKING AND MAKING NO END OF A FUSS. IF OUR NEIGHBOR HERE HADN'T COME DOWN, I DON'T KNOW WHAT I SHOULD HAVE DONE.
AH, ABERCROMBIE SMITH.
HOW VERY GOOD OF YOU TO COME DOWN!
THE ROOM IS VERY CLOSE.
PFFF!
IT'S BALSAMIC RESIN – THE SACRED PLANT OF THE PRIESTS... DO YOU KNOW ANYTHING OF EASTERN LANGUAGES, SMITH?
NOT A WORD.
Bellingham smiled quietly. The answer seemed to lift a weight from the Egyptologist's mind.

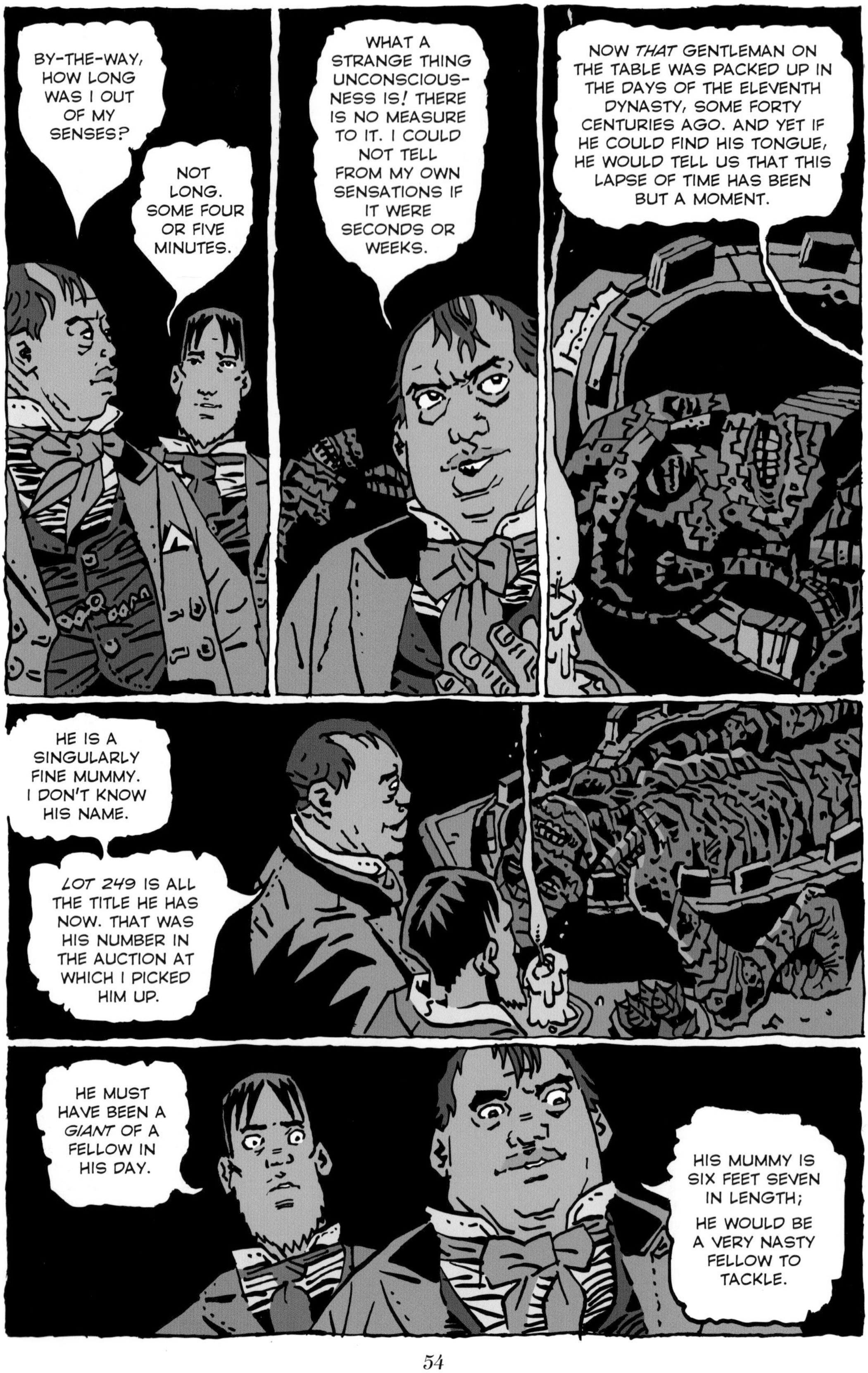
BY-THE-WAY, HOW LONG WAS I OUT OF MY SENSES?
NOT LONG. SOME FOUR OR FIVE MINUTES.
WHAT A STRANGE THING UNCONSCIOUSNESS IS! THERE IS NO MEASURE TO IT. I COULD NOT TELL FROM MY OWN SENSATIONS IF IT WERE SECONDS OR WEEKS.
NOW *THAT* GENTLEMAN ON THE TABLE WAS PACKED UP IN THE DAYS OF THE ELEVENTH DYNASTY, SOME FORTY CENTURIES AGO. AND YET IF HE COULD FIND HIS TONGUE, HE WOULD TELL US THAT THIS LAPSE OF TIME HAS BEEN BUT A MOMENT.
HE IS A SINGULARLY FINE MUMMY. I DON'T KNOW HIS NAME.
LOT 249 IS ALL THE TITLE HE HAS NOW. THAT WAS HIS NUMBER IN THE AUCTION AT WHICH I PICKED HIM UP.
HE MUST HAVE BEEN A *GIANT* OF A FELLOW IN HIS DAY.
HIS MUMMY IS SIX FEET SEVEN IN LENGTH;
HE WOULD BE A VERY NASTY FELLOW TO TACKLE.

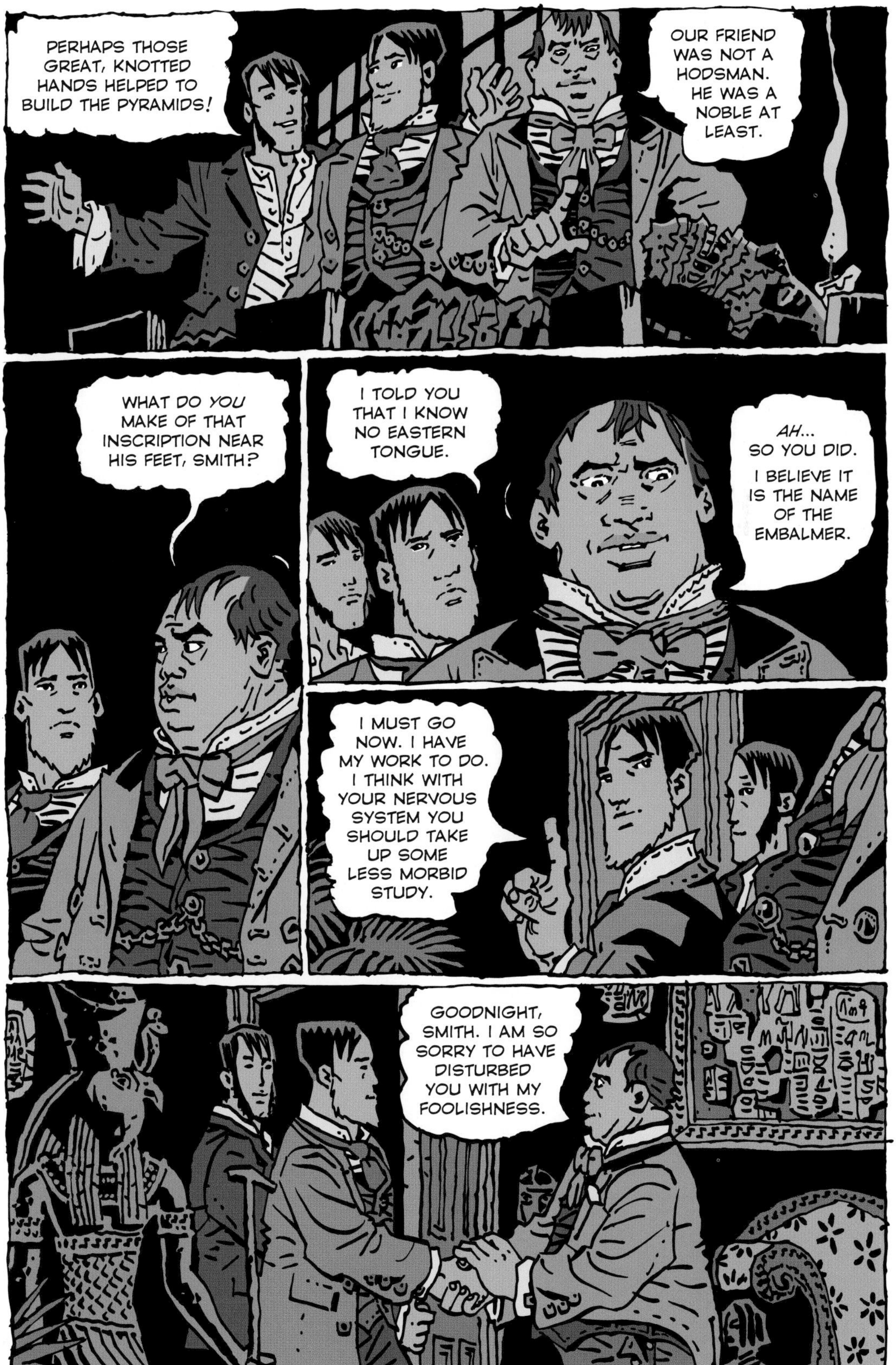
PERHAPS THOSE GREAT, KNOTTED HANDS HELPED TO BUILD THE PYRAMIDS!
OUR FRIEND WAS NOT A HODSMAN. HE WAS A NOBLE AT LEAST.
WHAT DO *YOU* MAKE OF THAT INSCRIPTION NEAR HIS FEET, SMITH?
I TOLD YOU THAT I KNOW NO EASTERN TONGUE.
AH... SO YOU DID.
I BELIEVE IT IS THE NAME OF THE EMBALMER.
I MUST GO NOW. I HAVE MY WORK TO DO. I THINK WITH YOUR NERVOUS SYSTEM YOU SHOULD TAKE UP SOME LESS MORBID STUDY.
GOODNIGHT, SMITH. I AM SO SORRY TO HAVE DISTURBED YOU WITH MY FOOLISHNESS.

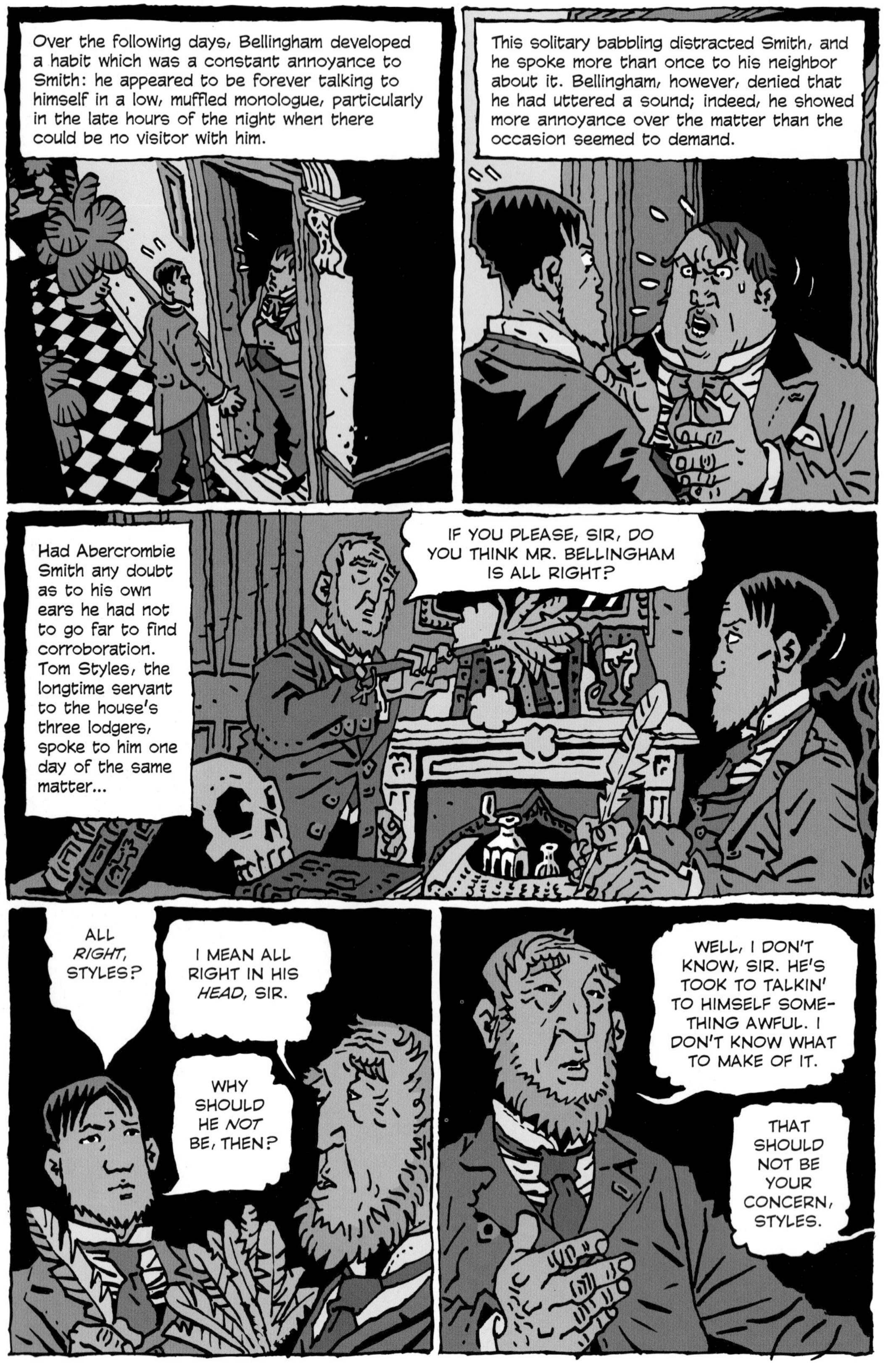
Over the following days, Bellingham developed a habit which was a constant annoyance to Smith: he appeared to be forever talking to himself in a low, muffled monologue, particularly in the late hours of the night when there could be no visitor with him.
This solitary babbling distracted Smith, and he spoke more than once to his neighbor about it. Bellingham, however, denied that he had uttered a sound; indeed, he showed more annoyance over the matter than the occasion seemed to demand.
Had Abercrombie Smith any doubt as to his own ears he had not to go far to find corroboration. Tom Styles, the longtime servant to the house's three lodgers, spoke to him one day of the same matter...
IF YOU PLEASE, SIR, DO YOU THINK MR. BELLINGHAM IS ALL RIGHT?
ALL *RIGHT*, STYLES?
I MEAN ALL RIGHT IN HIS *HEAD*, SIR.
WHY SHOULD HE *NOT* BE, THEN?
WELL, I DON'T KNOW, SIR. HE'S TOOK TO TALKIN' TO HIMSELF SOMETHING AWFUL. I DON'T KNOW WHAT TO MAKE OF IT.
THAT SHOULD NOT BE YOUR CONCERN, STYLES.

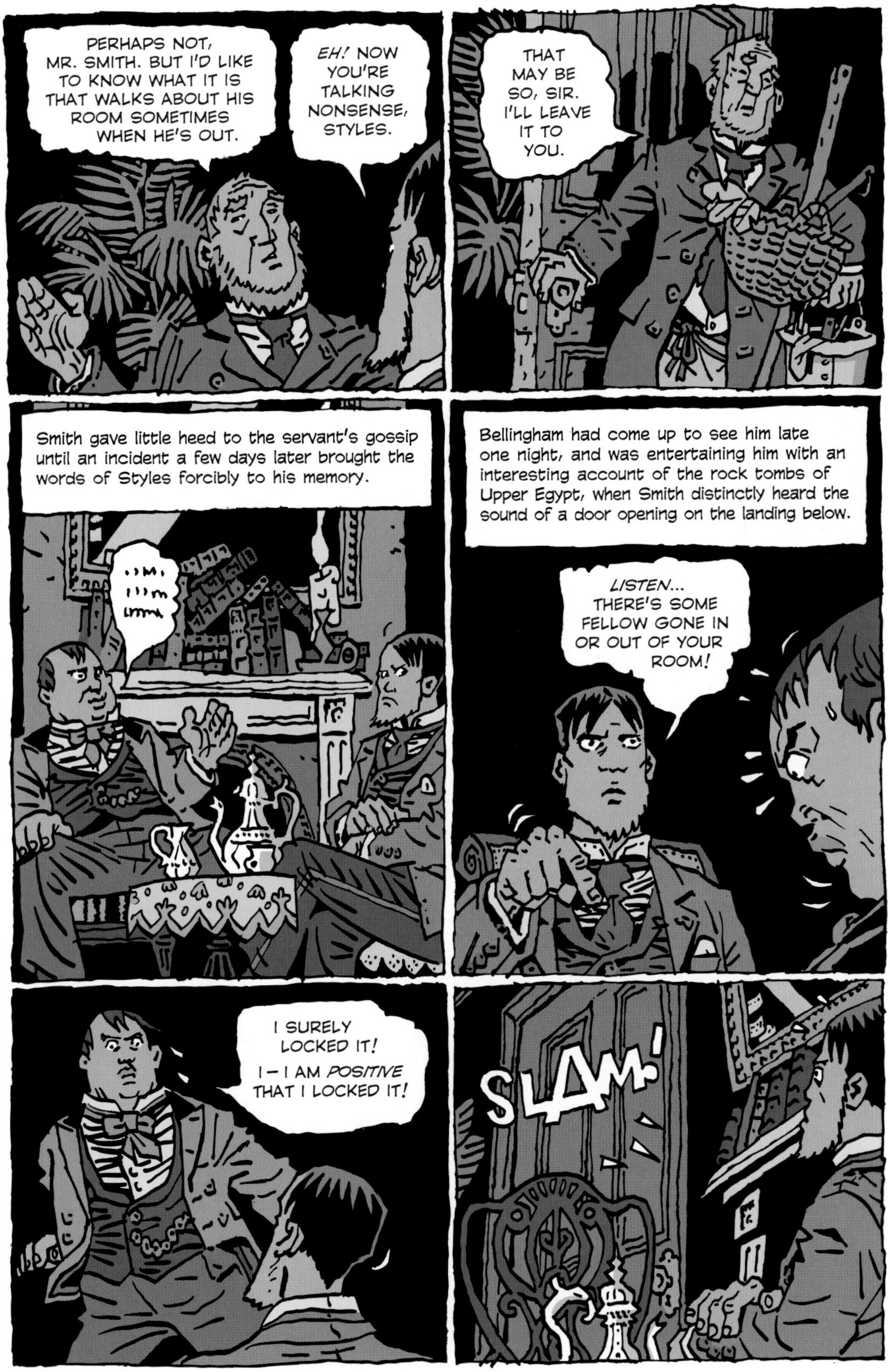
PERHAPS NOT, MR. SMITH. BUT I'D LIKE TO KNOW WHAT IT IS THAT WALKS ABOUT HIS ROOM SOMETIMES WHEN HE'S OUT.
EH! NOW YOU'RE TALKING NONSENSE, STYLES.
THAT MAY BE SO, SIR. I'LL LEAVE IT TO YOU.
Smith gave little heed to the servant's gossip until an incident a few days later brought the words of Styles forcibly to his memory.
Bellingham had come up to see him late one night, and was entertaining him with an interesting account of the rock tombs of Upper Egypt, when Smith distinctly heard the sound of a door opening on the landing below.
LISTEN... THERE'S SOME FELLOW GONE IN OR OUT OF YOUR ROOM*!*
I SURELY LOCKED IT*!* I — I AM *POSITIVE* THAT I LOCKED IT*!*
SLAM!

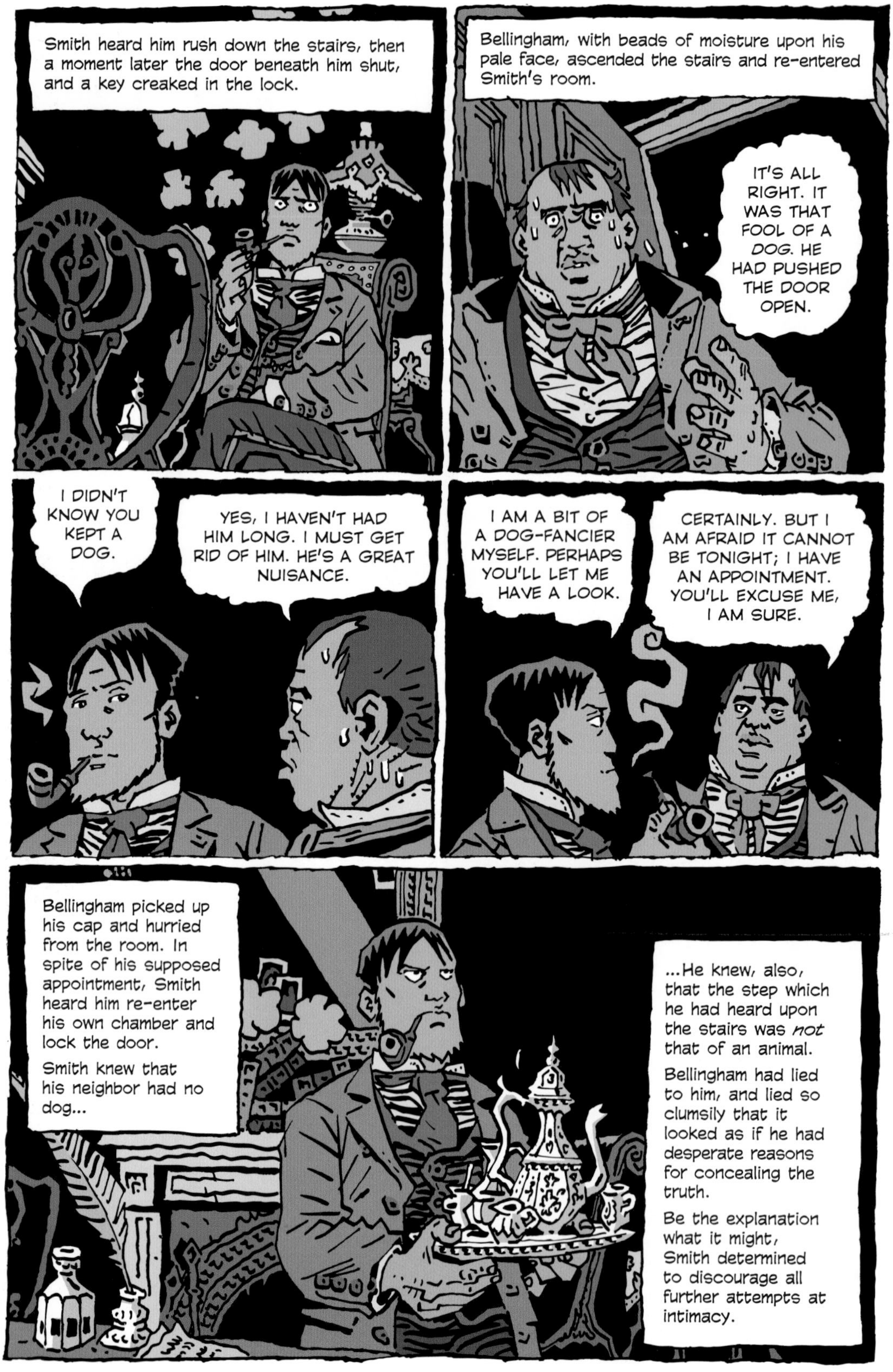
Smith heard him rush down the stairs, then a moment later the door beneath him shut, and a key creaked in the lock.
Bellingham, with beads of moisture upon his pale face, ascended the stairs and re-entered Smith's room.
IT'S ALL RIGHT. IT WAS THAT FOOL OF A *DOG*. HE HAD PUSHED THE DOOR OPEN.
I DIDN'T KNOW YOU KEPT A DOG.
YES, I HAVEN'T HAD HIM LONG. I MUST GET RID OF HIM. HE'S A GREAT NUISANCE.
I AM A BIT OF A DOG-FANCIER MYSELF. PERHAPS YOU'LL LET ME HAVE A LOOK.
CERTAINLY. BUT I AM AFRAID IT CANNOT BE TONIGHT; I HAVE AN APPOINTMENT. YOU'LL EXCUSE ME, I AM SURE.
Bellingham picked up his cap and hurried from the room. In spite of his supposed appointment, Smith heard him re-enter his own chamber and lock the door.
Smith knew that his neighbor had no dog...
...He knew, also, that the step which he had heard upon the stairs was *not* that of an animal.
Bellingham had lied to him, and lied so clumsily that it looked as if he had desperate reasons for concealing the truth.
Be the explanation what it might, Smith determined to discourage all further attempts at intimacy.

Smith attempted to resume his studies, but soon a heavy footfall came rushing up from below, and Hastie burst into the room.

HAVE YOU HEARD ABOUT LONG NORTON? HE'S BEEN ATTACKED!

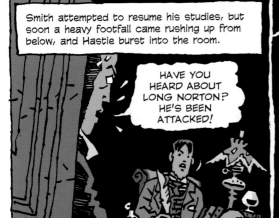

BY WHO?

NOT 'WHO,' BUT 'WHAT.' NORTON SWEARS THAT IT WAS NOT HUMAN, AND, FROM THE SCRATCHES ON HIS THROAT, I AM INCLINED TO AGREE WITH HIM.

"He says the thing dropped on him out of a tree that hangs low over the path he takes each night. He never got a fair sight of it, but he was nearly strangled by arms, which, he says, were as strong as steel bands."

"He yelled, and a couple chaps came running, and the thing went over the wall like a cat. It gave Norton a shake-up, I can tell you."

A MUGGER, MOST LIKELY.

POSSIBLY. BUT YOUR NEIGHBOR MIGHT JUST BE PLEASED TO HEAR ABOUT IT.

HE HAD AN ARGUMENT WITH NORTON, AND HE'S NOT ONE TO FORGET HIS DEBTS.

Smith returned to his books, but he found it hard to keep his mind upon his work that evening. The dim suspicions rising in his mind were yet so vague that they could not be put down in words.

59

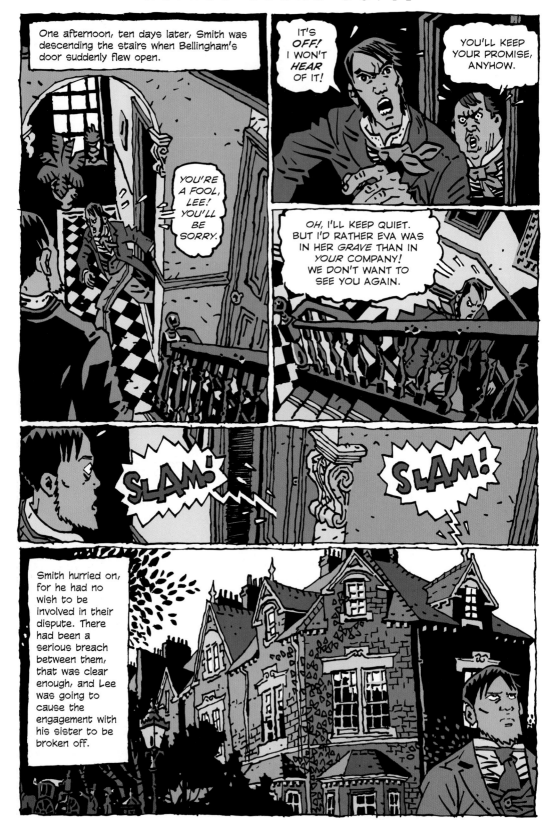

One afternoon, ten days later, Smith was descending the stairs when Bellingham's door suddenly flew open.

IT'S *OFF!* I WON'T *HEAR* OF IT!

YOU'LL KEEP YOUR PROMISE, ANYHOW.

YOU'RE A FOOL, LEE! YOU'LL BE SORRY.

OH, I'LL KEEP QUIET. BUT I'D RATHER EVA WAS IN HER *GRAVE* THAN IN *YOUR* COMPANY! WE DON'T WANT TO SEE YOU AGAIN.

SLAM!

SLAM!

Smith hurried on, for he had no wish to be involved in their dispute. There had been a serious breach between them, that was clear enough, and Lee was going to cause the engagement with his sister to be broken off.

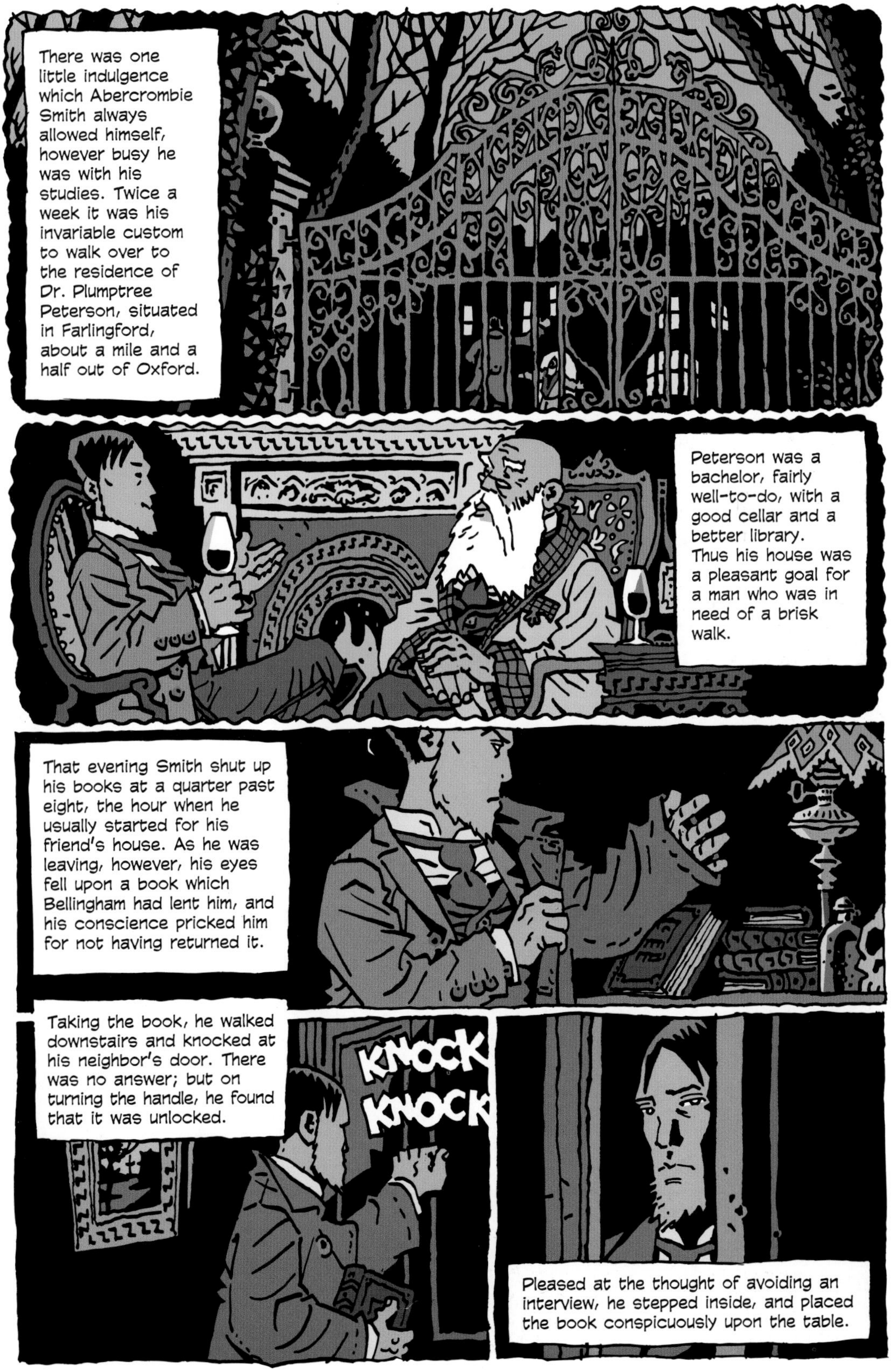
There was one little indulgence which Abercrombie Smith always allowed himself, however busy he was with his studies. Twice a week it was his invariable custom to walk over to the residence of Dr. Plumptree Peterson, situated in Farlingford, about a mile and a half out of Oxford.
Peterson was a bachelor, fairly well-to-do, with a good cellar and a better library. Thus his house was a pleasant goal for a man who was in need of a brisk walk.
That evening Smith shut up his books at a quarter past eight, the hour when he usually started for his friend's house. As he was leaving, however, his eyes fell upon a book which Bellingham had lent him, and his conscience pricked him for not having returned it.
Taking the book, he walked downstairs and knocked at his neighbor's door. There was no answer; but on turning the handle, he found that it was unlocked.
KNOCK
KNOCK
Pleased at the thought of avoiding an interview, he stepped inside, and placed the book conspicuously upon the table.

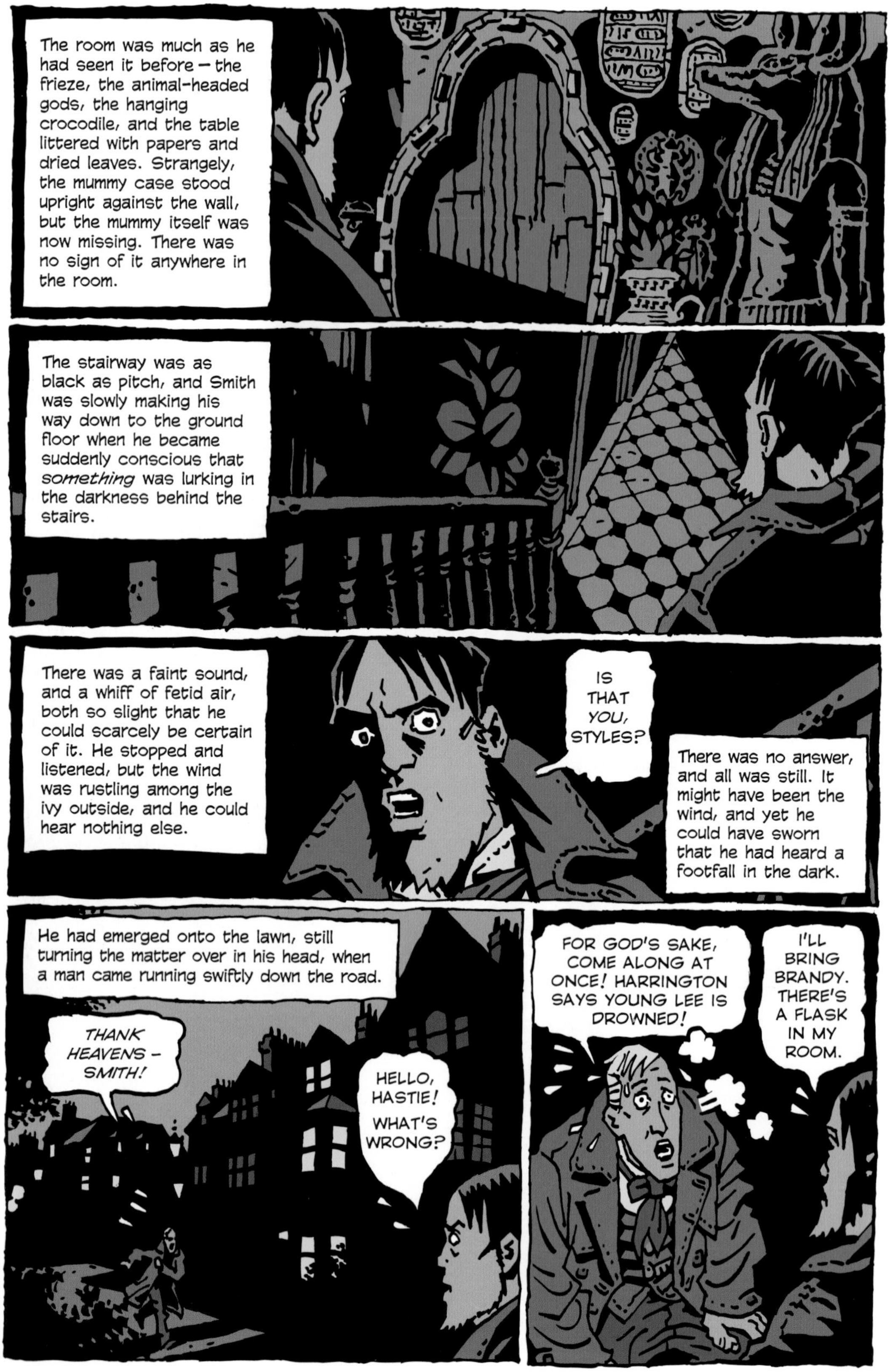
The room was much as he had seen it before — the frieze, the animal-headed gods, the hanging crocodile, and the table littered with papers and dried leaves. Strangely, the mummy case stood upright against the wall, but the mummy itself was now missing. There was no sign of it anywhere in the room.
The stairway was as black as pitch, and Smith was slowly making his way down to the ground floor when he became suddenly conscious that *something* was lurking in the darkness behind the stairs.
There was a faint sound, and a whiff of fetid air, both so slight that he could scarcely be certain of it. He stopped and listened, but the wind was rustling among the ivy outside, and he could hear nothing else.
IS THAT *YOU,* STYLES?
There was no answer, and all was still. It might have been the wind, and yet he could have sworn that he had heard a footfall in the dark.
He had emerged onto the lawn, still turning the matter over in his head, when a man came running swiftly down the road.
THANK HEAVENS — SMITH!
HELLO, HASTIE! WHAT'S WRONG?
FOR GOD'S SAKE, COME ALONG AT ONCE! HARRINGTON SAYS YOUNG LEE IS DROWNED!
I'LL BRING BRANDY. THERE'S A FLASK IN MY ROOM.

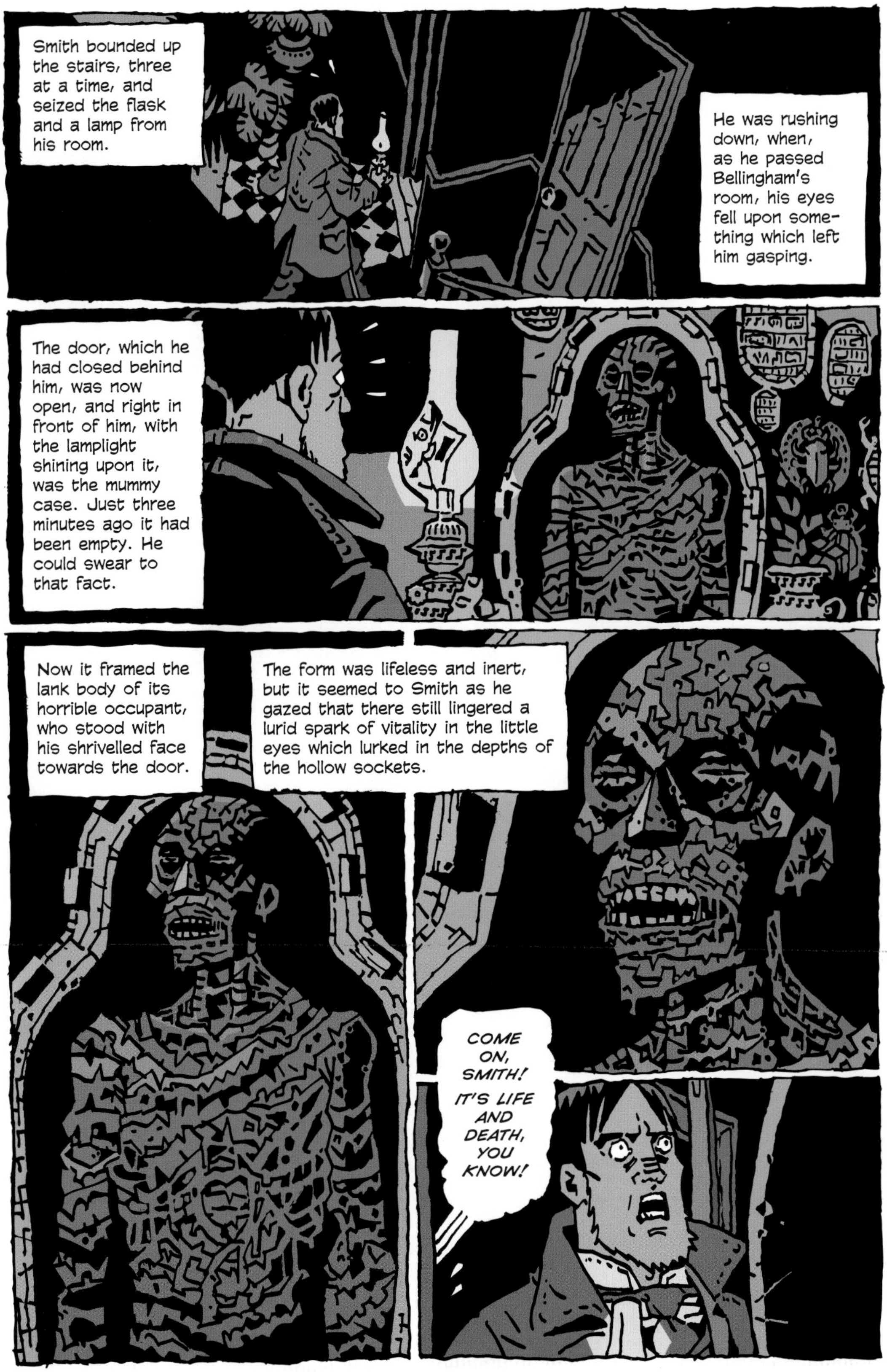
Smith bounded up the stairs, three at a time, and seized the flask and a lamp from his room.
He was rushing down, when, as he passed Bellingham's room, his eyes fell upon something which left him gasping.
The door, which he had closed behind him, was now open, and right in front of him, with the lamplight shining upon it, was the mummy case. Just three minutes ago it had been empty. He could swear to that fact.
Now it framed the lank body of its horrible occupant, who stood with his shrivelled face towards the door.
The form was lifeless and inert, but it seemed to Smith as he gazed that there still lingered a lurid spark of vitality in the little eyes which lurked in the depths of the hollow sockets.
COME ON, SMITH! IT'S LIFE AND DEATH, YOU KNOW!

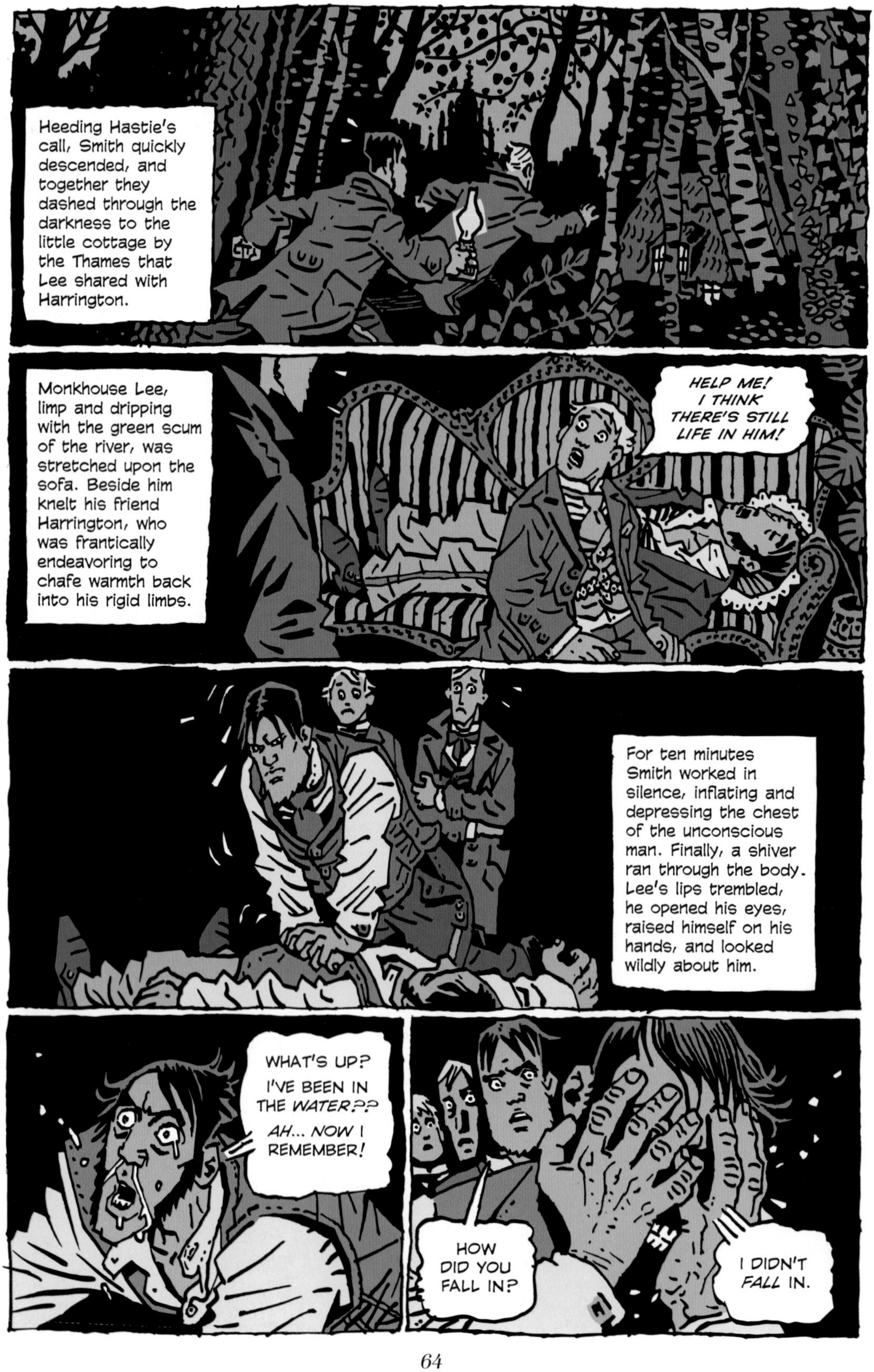
Heeding Hastie's call, Smith quickly descended, and together they dashed through the darkness to the little cottage by the Thames that Lee shared with Harrington.
Monkhouse Lee, limp and dripping with the green scum of the river, was stretched upon the sofa. Beside him knelt his friend Harrington, who was frantically endeavoring to chafe warmth back into his rigid limbs.
HELP ME! I THINK THERE'S STILL LIFE IN HIM!
For ten minutes Smith worked in silence, inflating and depressing the chest of the unconscious man. Finally, a shiver ran through the body. Lee's lips trembled, he opened his eyes, raised himself on his hands, and looked wildly about him.
WHAT'S UP? I'VE BEEN IN THE *WATER*?? *AH... NOW* I REMEMBER!
HOW DID YOU FALL IN?
I DIDN'T *FALL* IN.

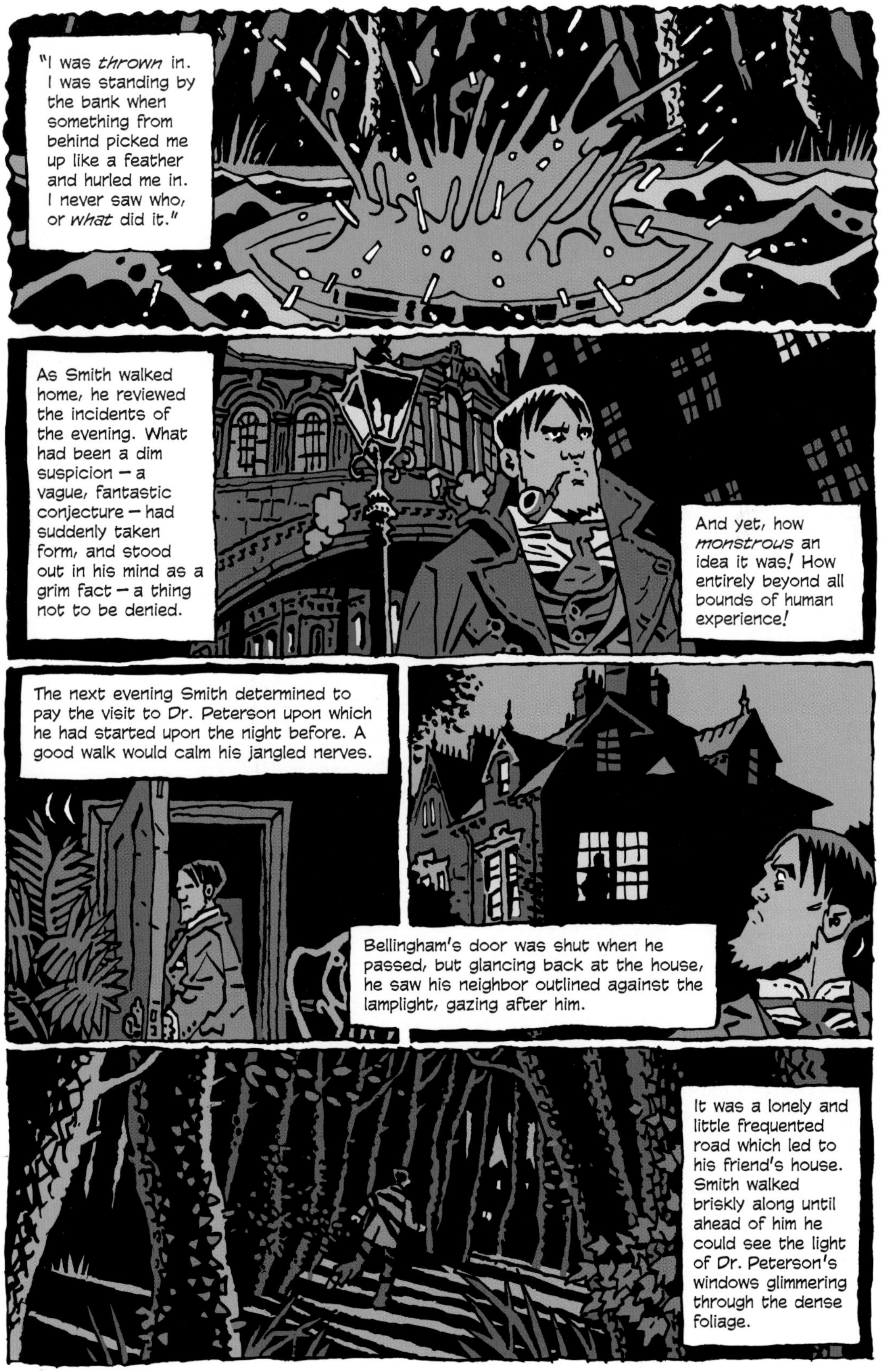
"I was *thrown* in. I was standing by the bank when something from behind picked me up like a feather and hurled me in. I never saw who, or *what* did it."
As Smith walked home, he reviewed the incidents of the evening. What had been a dim suspicion — a vague, fantastic conjecture — had suddenly taken form, and stood out in his mind as a grim fact — a thing not to be denied.
And yet, how *monstrous* an idea it was! How entirely beyond all bounds of human experience!
The next evening Smith determined to pay the visit to Dr. Peterson upon which he had started upon the night before. A good walk would calm his jangled nerves.
Bellingham's door was shut when he passed, but glancing back at the house, he saw his neighbor outlined against the lamplight, gazing after him.
It was a lonely and little frequented road which led to his friend's house. Smith walked briskly along until ahead of him he could see the light of Dr. Peterson's windows glimmering through the dense foliage.

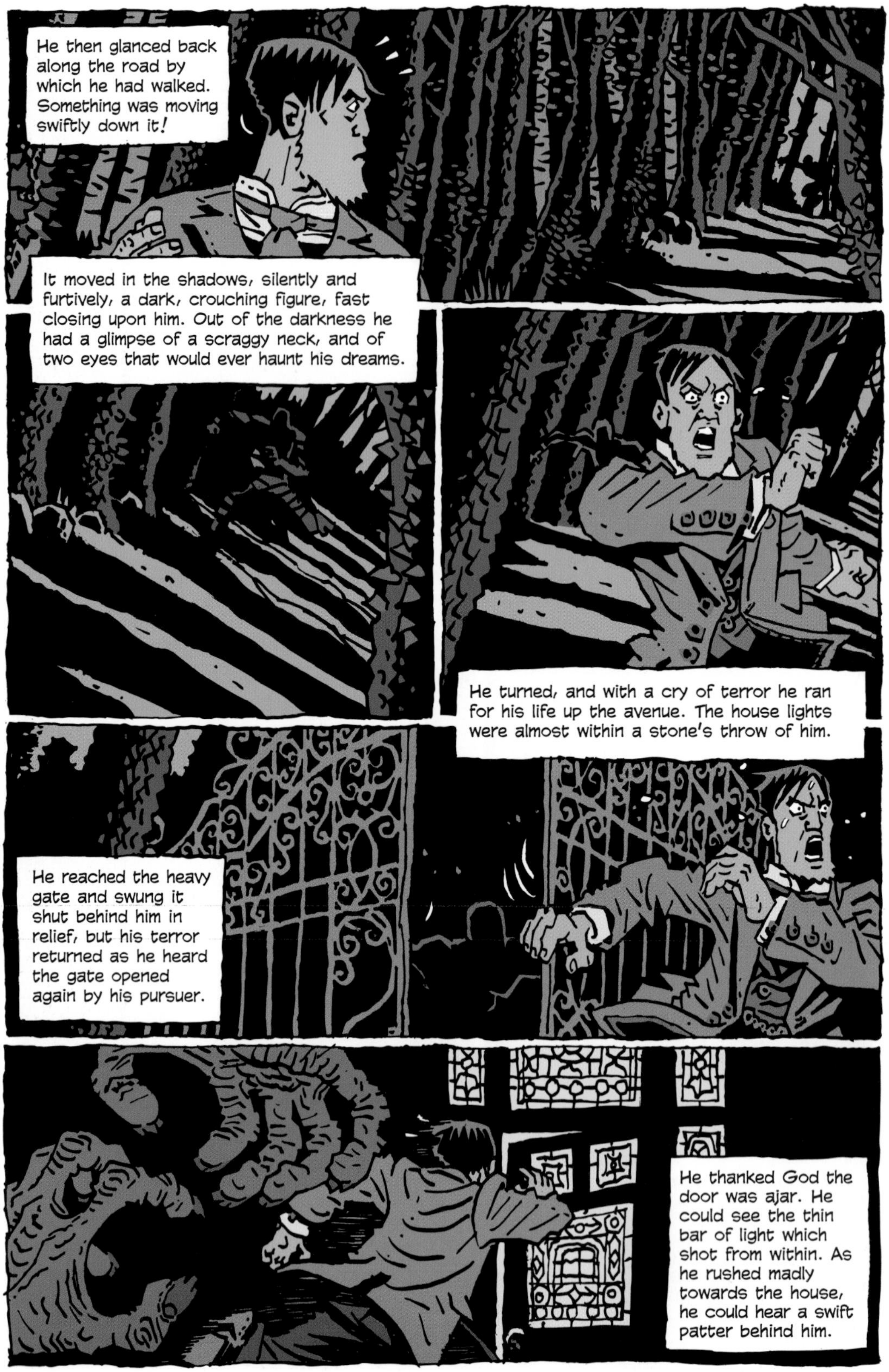
He then glanced back along the road by which he had walked. Something was moving swiftly down it!
It moved in the shadows, silently and furtively, a dark, crouching figure, fast closing upon him. Out of the darkness he had a glimpse of a scraggy neck, and of two eyes that would ever haunt his dreams.
He turned, and with a cry of terror he ran for his life up the avenue. The house lights were almost within a stone's throw of him.
He reached the heavy gate and swung it shut behind him in relief, but his terror returned as he heard the gate opened again by his pursuer.
He thanked God the door was ajar. He could see the thin bar of light which shot from within. As he rushed madly towards the house, he could hear a swift patter behind him.

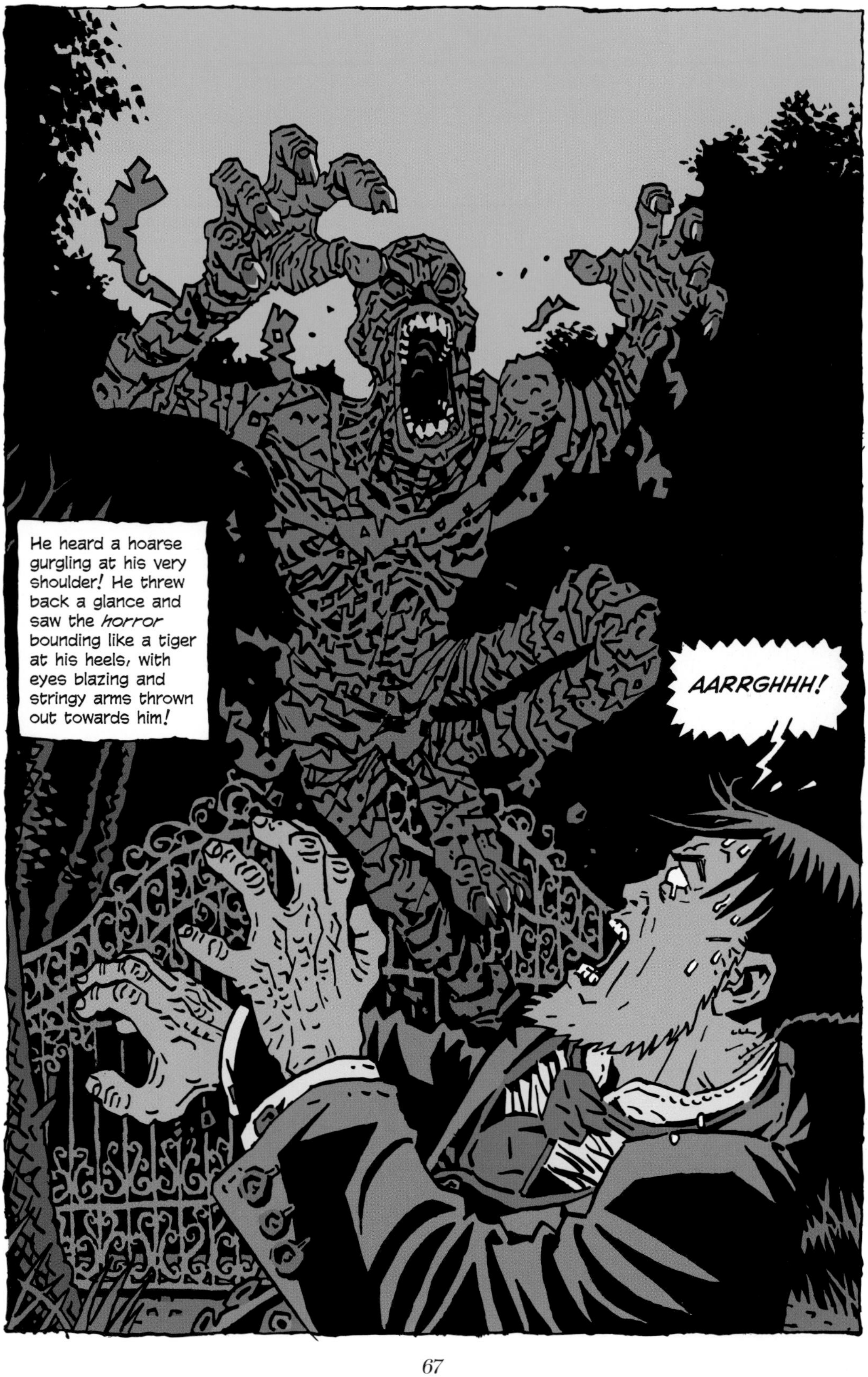
He heard a hoarse gurgling at his very shoulder! He threw back a glance and saw the *horror* bounding like a tiger at his heels, with eyes blazing and stringy arms thrown out towards him!
AARRGHHH!

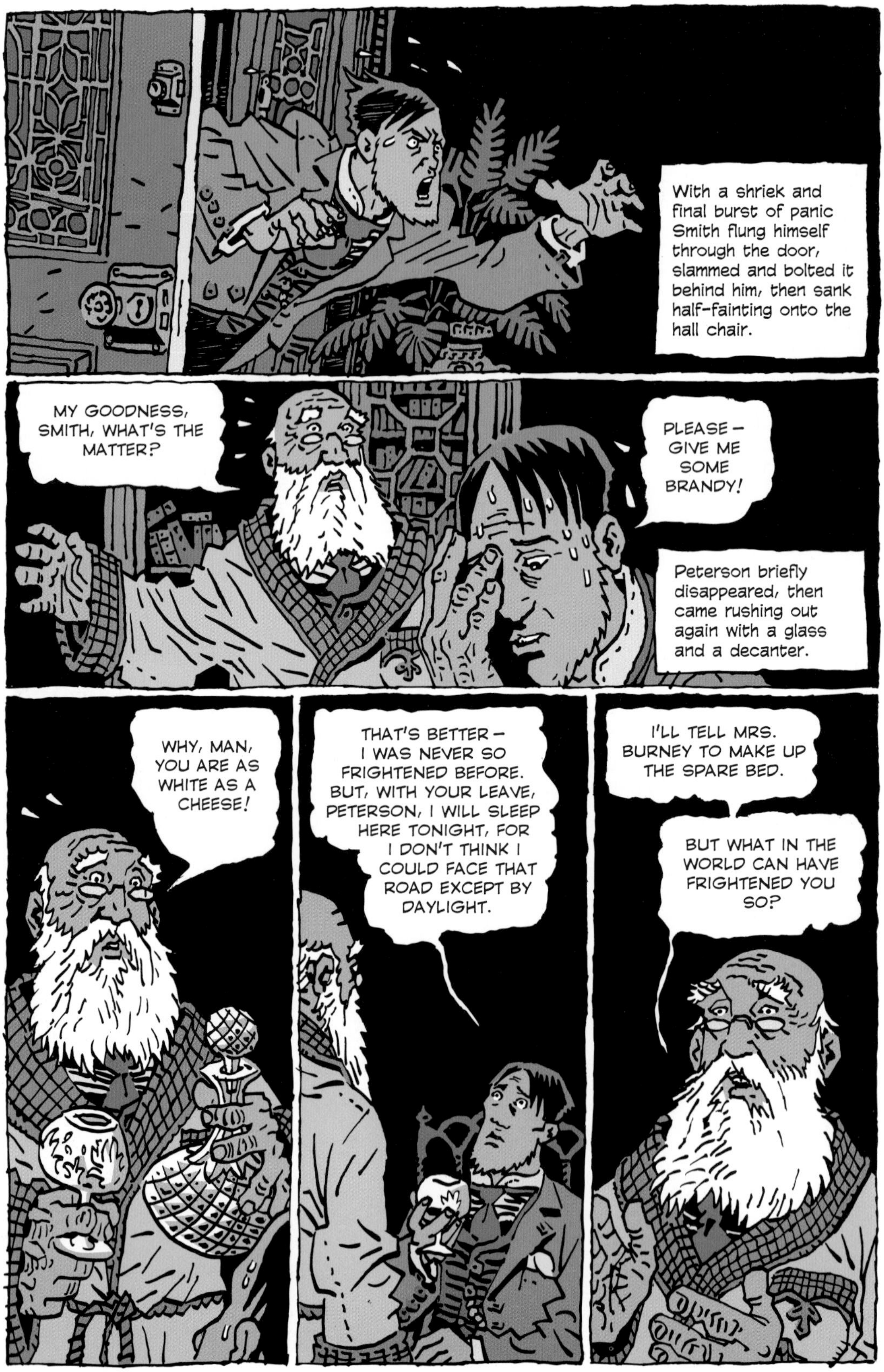
With a shriek and final burst of panic Smith flung himself through the door, slammed and bolted it behind him, then sank half-fainting onto the hall chair.
MY GOODNESS, SMITH, WHAT'S THE MATTER?
PLEASE – GIVE ME SOME BRANDY!
Peterson briefly disappeared, then came rushing out again with a glass and a decanter.
WHY, MAN, YOU ARE AS WHITE AS A CHEESE!
THAT'S BETTER – I WAS NEVER SO FRIGHTENED BEFORE. BUT, WITH YOUR LEAVE, PETERSON, I WILL SLEEP HERE TONIGHT, FOR I DON'T THINK I COULD FACE THAT ROAD EXCEPT BY DAYLIGHT.
I'LL TELL MRS. BURNEY TO MAKE UP THE SPARE BED.
BUT WHAT IN THE WORLD CAN HAVE FRIGHTENED YOU SO?

I HAVE BEEN WITHIN HAND-GRIP OF THE DEVIL! LET US GO TO YOUR STUDY, AND I SHALL TELL YOU THE WHOLE STORY...

...THAT'S THE WHOLE BLACK BUSINESS. IT IS MONSTROUS AND INCREDIBLE, BUT IT IS TRUE.

"This fellow Bellingham has got hold of some infernal secret by which a mummy can be temporarily brought to life. He was trying this disgusting business on the night when he fainted."

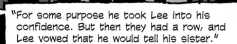

"For some purpose he took Lee into his confidence. But then they had a row, and Lee vowed that he would tell his sister."

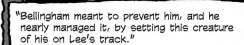

"Bellingham meant to prevent him, and he nearly managed it, by setting this creature of his on Lee's track."

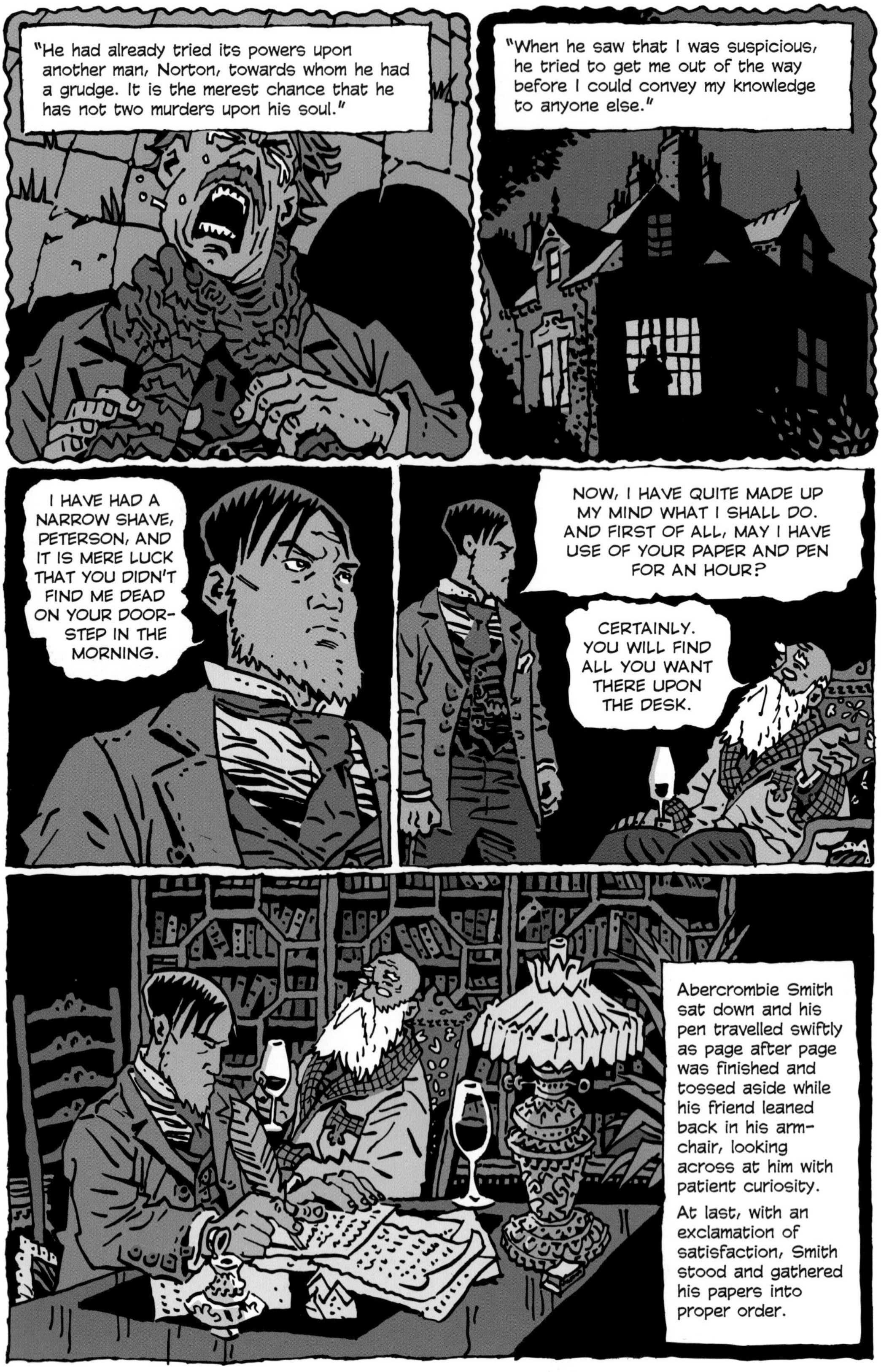
"He had already tried its powers upon another man, Norton, towards whom he had a grudge. It is the merest chance that he has not two murders upon his soul."
"When he saw that I was suspicious, he tried to get me out of the way before I could convey my knowledge to anyone else."
I HAVE HAD A NARROW SHAVE, PETERSON, AND IT IS MERE LUCK THAT YOU DIDN'T FIND ME DEAD ON YOUR DOOR-STEP IN THE MORNING.
NOW, I HAVE QUITE MADE UP MY MIND WHAT I SHALL DO. AND FIRST OF ALL, MAY I HAVE USE OF YOUR PAPER AND PEN FOR AN HOUR?
CERTAINLY. YOU WILL FIND ALL YOU WANT THERE UPON THE DESK.
Abercrombie Smith sat down and his pen travelled swiftly as page after page was finished and tossed aside while his friend leaned back in his arm-chair, looking across at him with patient curiosity.
At last, with an exclamation of satisfaction, Smith stood and gathered his papers into proper order.

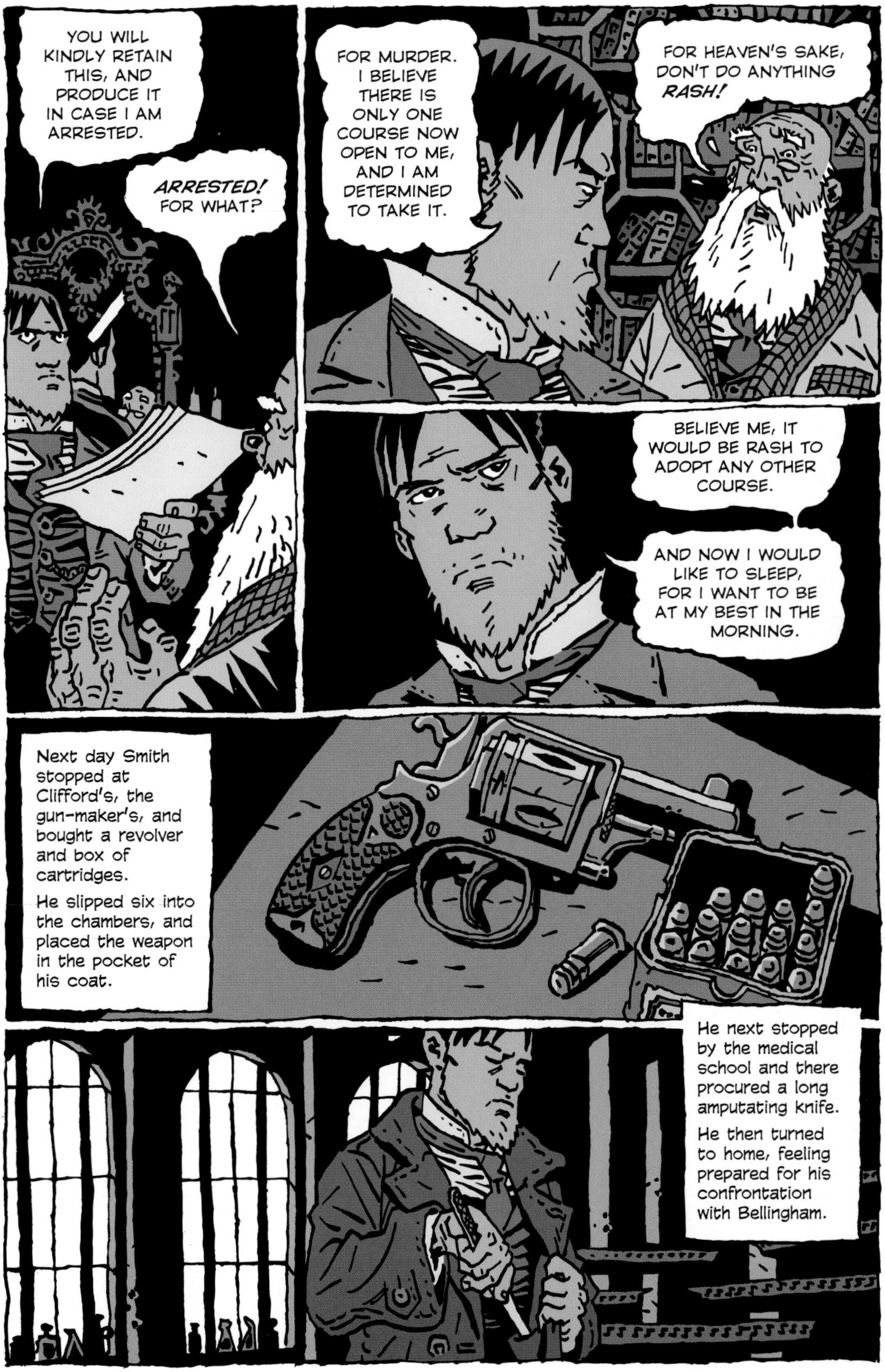
YOU WILL KINDLY RETAIN THIS, AND PRODUCE IT IN CASE I AM ARRESTED.
ARRESTED! FOR WHAT?
FOR MURDER. I BELIEVE THERE IS ONLY ONE COURSE NOW OPEN TO ME, AND I AM DETERMINED TO TAKE IT.
FOR HEAVEN'S SAKE, DON'T DO ANYTHING RASH!
BELIEVE ME, IT WOULD BE RASH TO ADOPT ANY OTHER COURSE.
AND NOW I WOULD LIKE TO SLEEP, FOR I WANT TO BE AT MY BEST IN THE MORNING.
Next day Smith stopped at Clifford's, the gun-maker's, and bought a revolver and box of cartridges.
He slipped six into the chambers, and placed the weapon in the pocket of his coat.
He next stopped by the medical school and there procured a long amputating knife.
He then turned to home, feeling prepared for his confrontation with Bellingham.

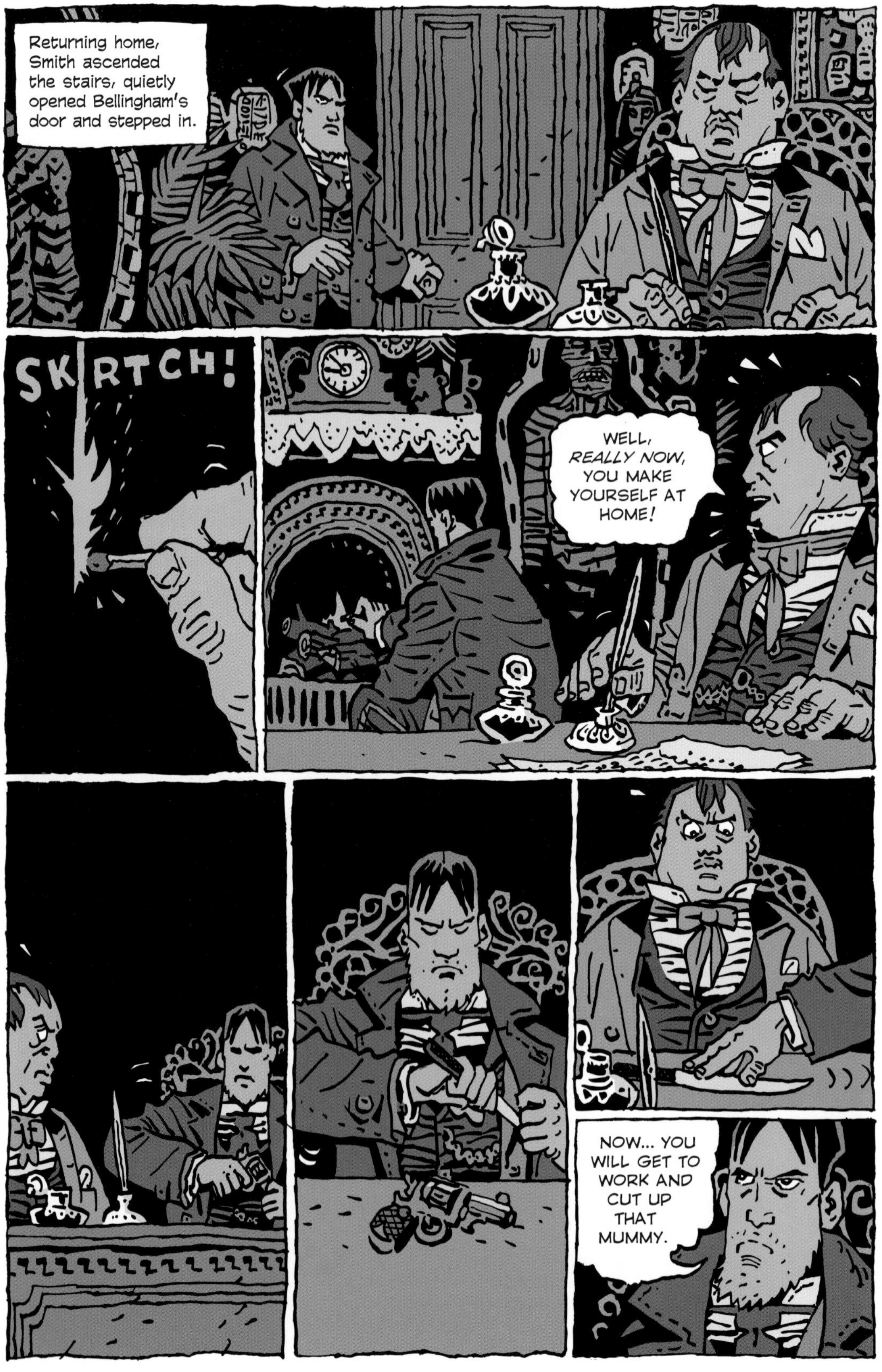
Returning home, Smith ascended the stairs, quietly opened Bellingham's door and stepped in.
SKRTCH!
WELL, *REALLY NOW*, YOU MAKE YOURSELF AT HOME!
NOW... YOU WILL GET TO WORK AND CUT UP THAT MUMMY.

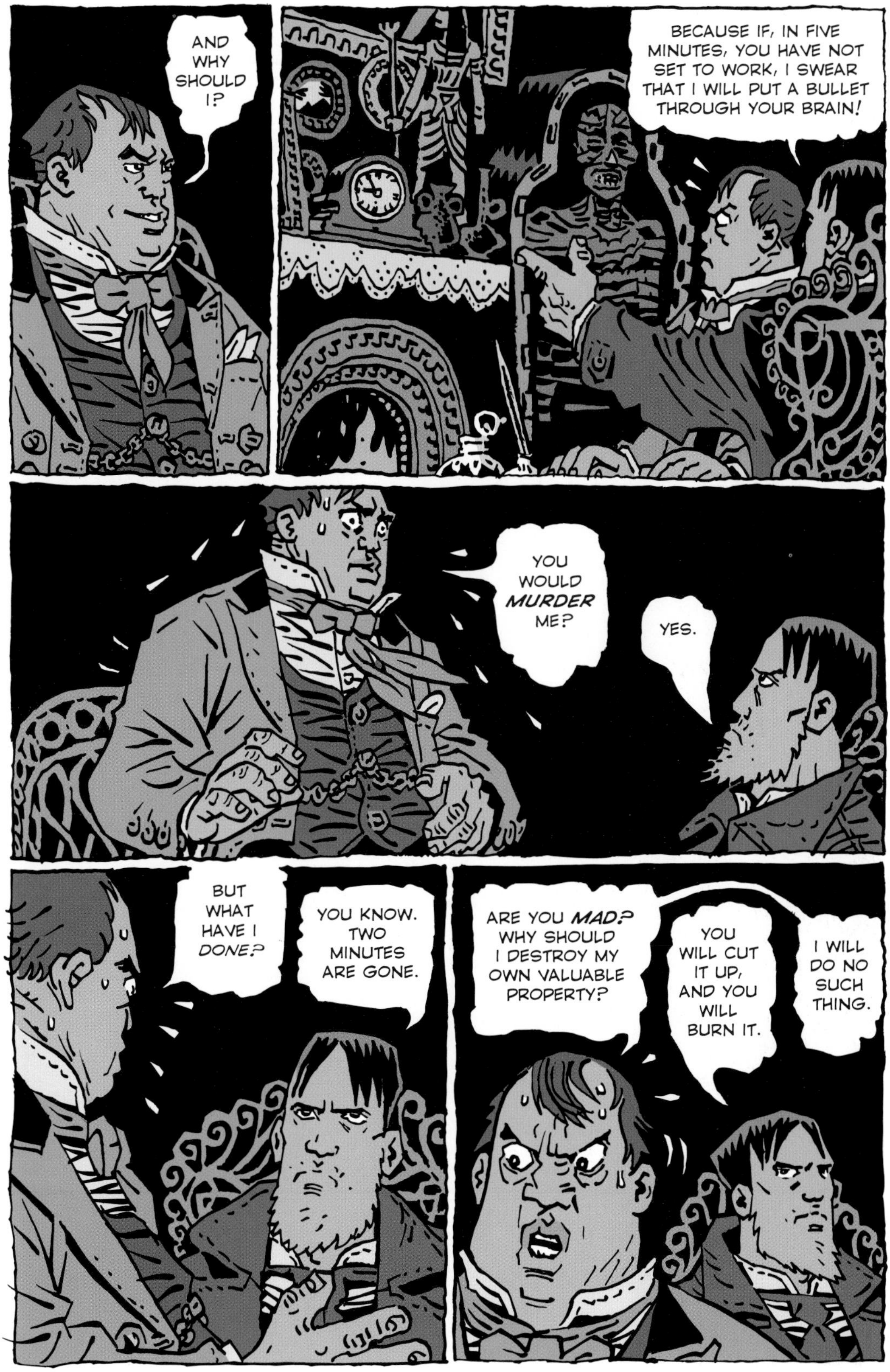
AND WHY SHOULD I?
BECAUSE IF, IN FIVE MINUTES, YOU HAVE NOT SET TO WORK, I SWEAR THAT I WILL PUT A BULLET THROUGH YOUR BRAIN!
YOU WOULD *MURDER* ME?
YES.
BUT WHAT HAVE I *DONE?*
YOU KNOW. TWO MINUTES ARE GONE.
ARE YOU *MAD?* WHY SHOULD I DESTROY MY OWN VALUABLE PROPERTY?
YOU WILL CUT IT UP, AND YOU WILL BURN IT.
I WILL DO NO SUCH THING.

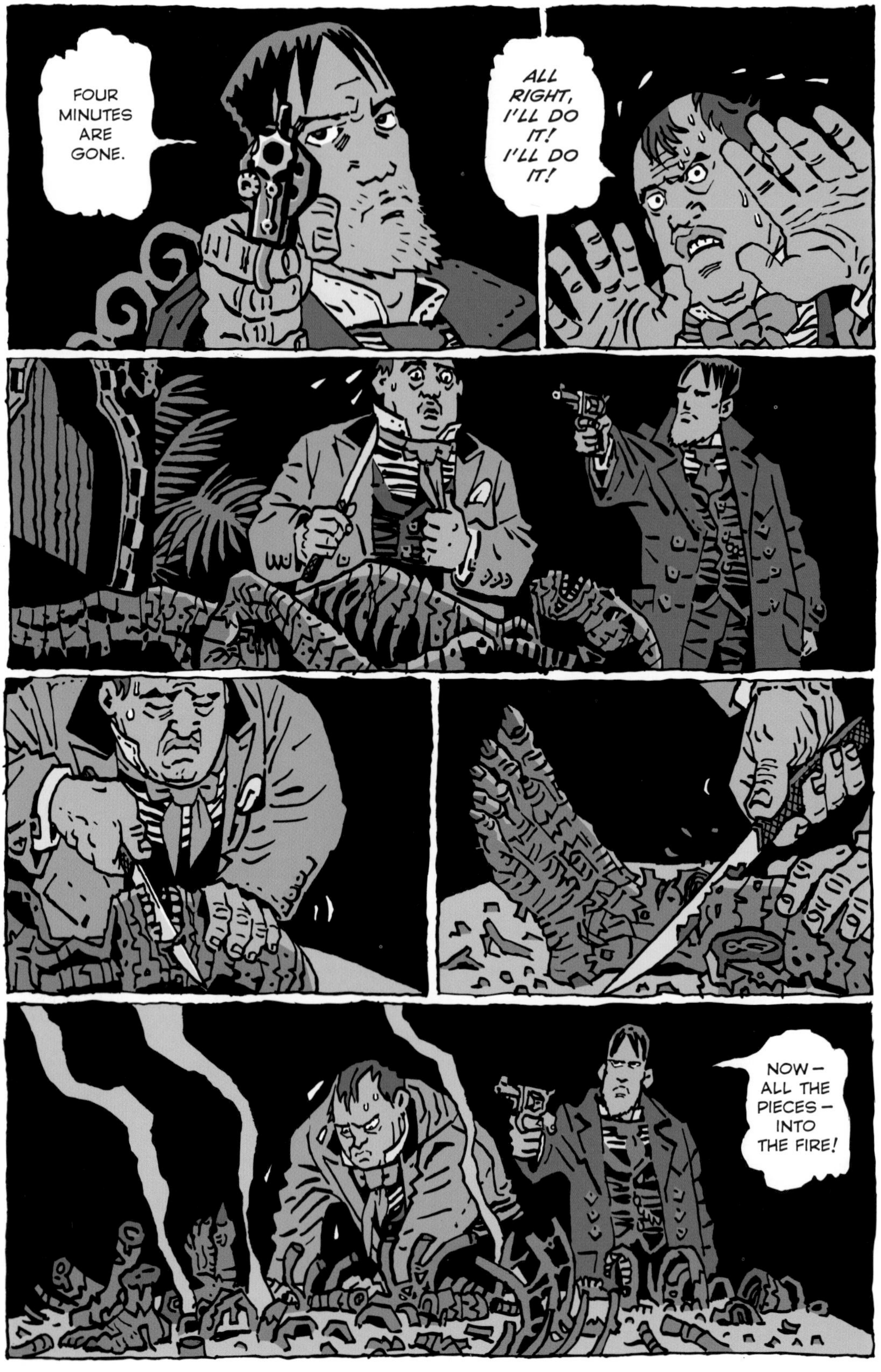
FOUR MINUTES ARE GONE.
ALL RIGHT, I'LL DO IT! I'LL DO IT!
NOW— ALL THE PIECES— INTO THE FIRE!

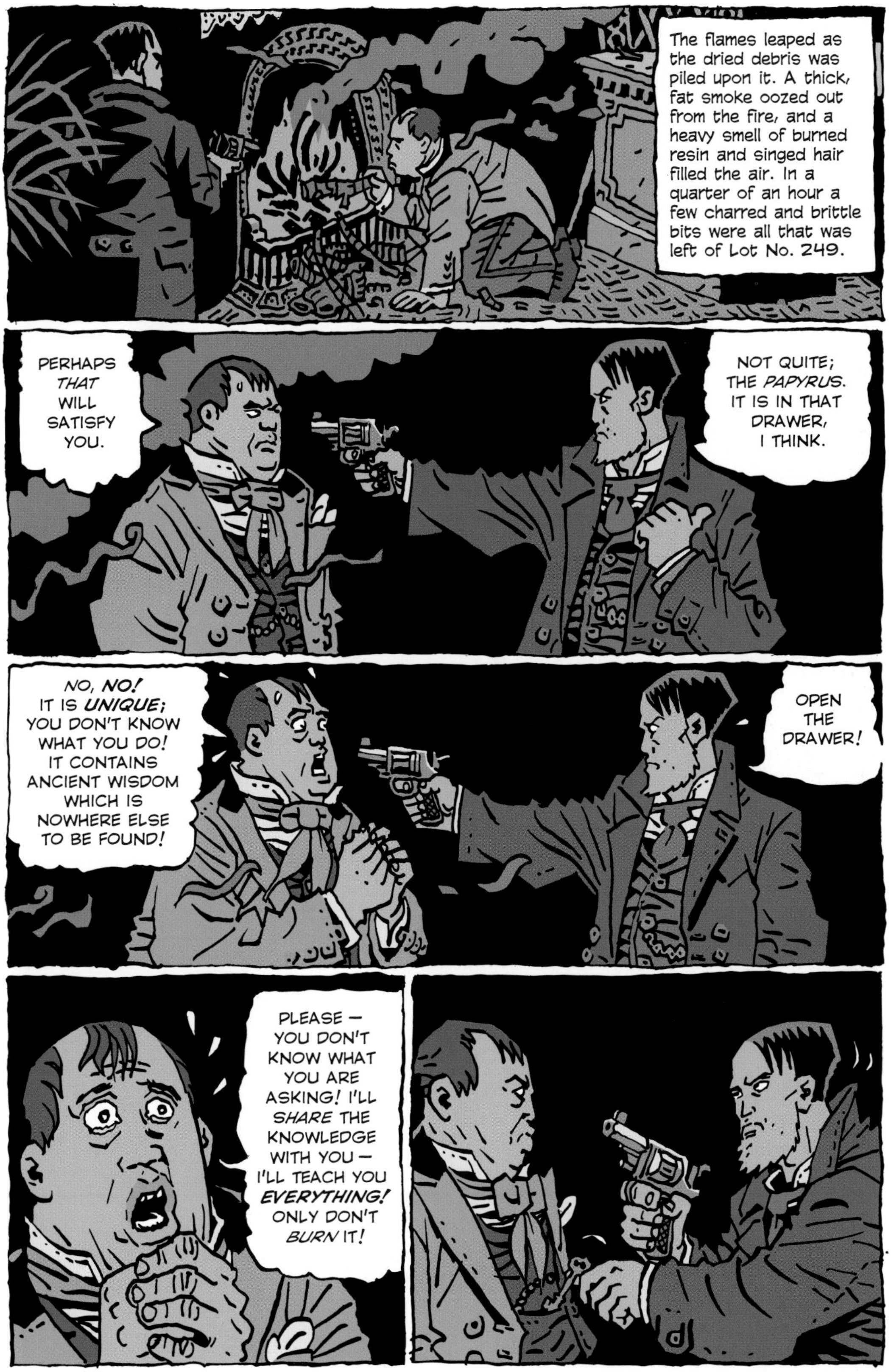
The flames leaped as the dried debris was piled upon it. A thick, fat smoke oozed out from the fire, and a heavy smell of burned resin and singed hair filled the air. In a quarter of an hour a few charred and brittle bits were all that was left of Lot No. 249.
PERHAPS THAT WILL SATISFY YOU.
NOT QUITE; THE PAPYRUS. IT IS IN THAT DRAWER, I THINK.
NO, NO! IT IS UNIQUE; YOU DON'T KNOW WHAT YOU DO! IT CONTAINS ANCIENT WISDOM WHICH IS NOWHERE ELSE TO BE FOUND!
OPEN THE DRAWER!
PLEASE — YOU DON'T KNOW WHAT YOU ARE ASKING! I'LL SHARE THE KNOWLEDGE WITH YOU — I'LL TEACH YOU EVERYTHING! ONLY DON'T BURN IT!

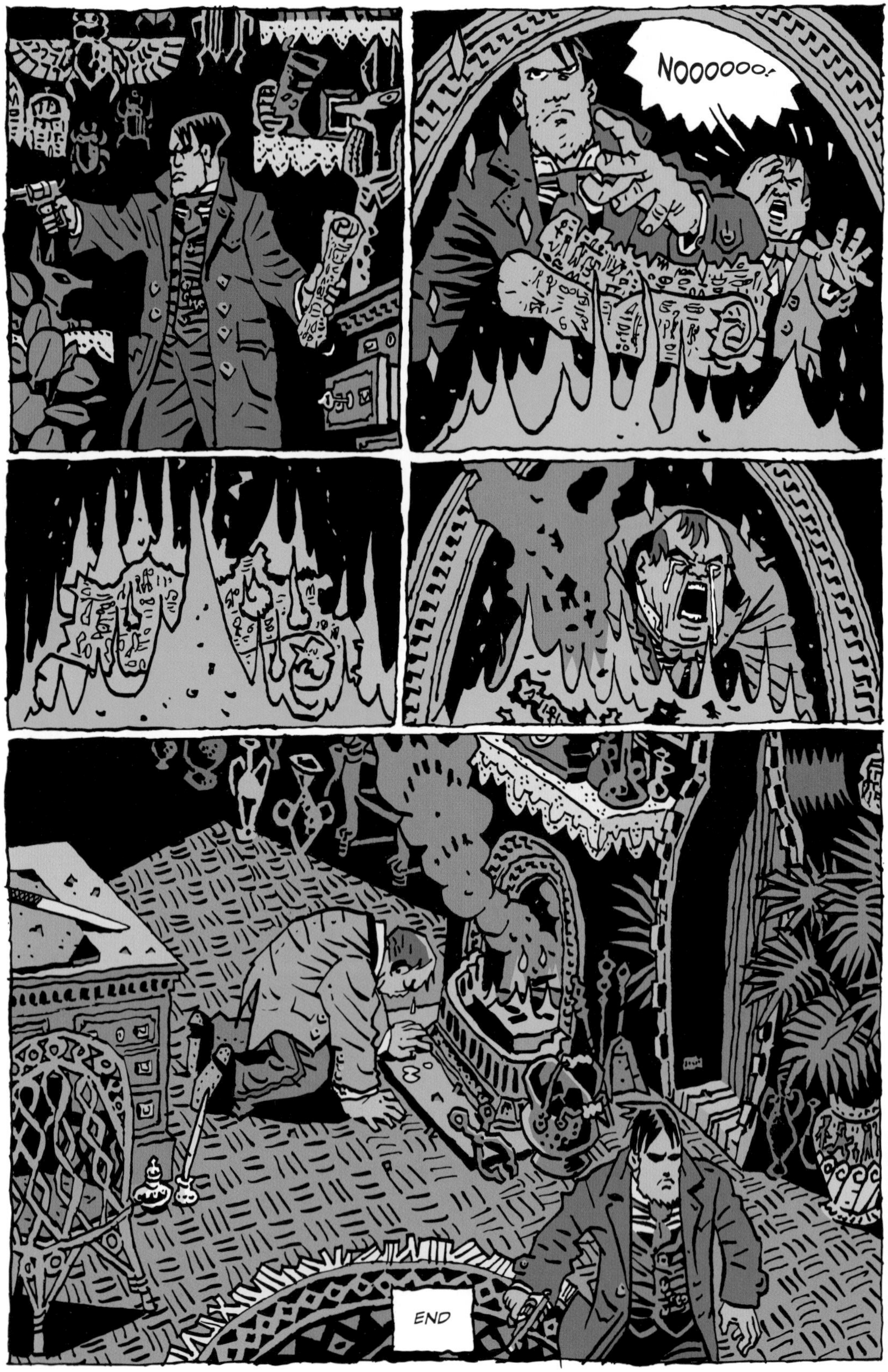
NOOOOOO!
END

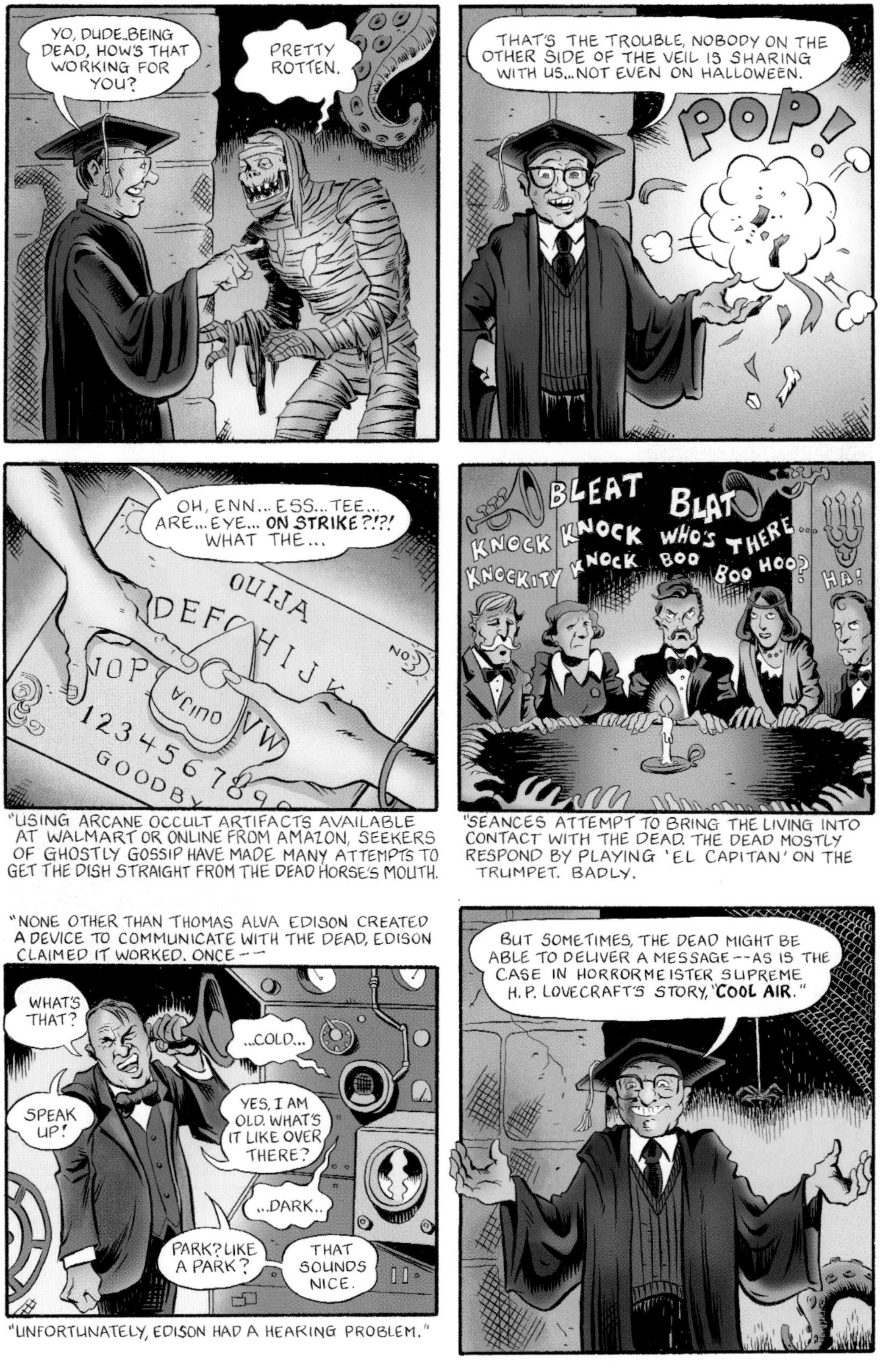
YO, DUDE..BEING DEAD, HOW'S THAT WORKING FOR YOU?
PRETTY ROTTEN.
THAT'S THE TROUBLE, NOBODY ON THE OTHER SIDE OF THE VEIL IS SHARING WITH US...NOT EVEN ON HALLOWEEN.
POP!
OH, ENN... ESS... TEE... ARE... EYE... ON STRIKE?!?! WHAT THE...
OUIJA
DEF HIJK
NOP VW
NO
1234567890
GOODBY
OUIJA
"USING ARCANE OCCULT ARTIFACTS AVAILABLE AT WALMART OR ONLINE FROM AMAZON, SEEKERS OF GHOSTLY GOSSIP HAVE MADE MANY ATTEMPTS TO GET THE DISH STRAIGHT FROM THE DEAD HORSE'S MOUTH.
BLEAT BLAT
KNOCK KNOCK WHO'S THERE...
KNOCKITY KNOCK BOO BOO HOO?
HA!
"SEANCES ATTEMPT TO BRING THE LIVING INTO CONTACT WITH THE DEAD. THE DEAD MOSTLY RESPOND BY PLAYING 'EL CAPITAN' ON THE TRUMPET. BADLY.
"NONE OTHER THAN THOMAS ALVA EDISON CREATED A DEVICE TO COMMUNICATE WITH THE DEAD. EDISON CLAIMED IT WORKED. ONCE--
WHAT'S THAT?
...COLD...
SPEAK UP!
YES, I AM OLD. WHAT'S IT LIKE OVER THERE?
...DARK...
PARK? LIKE A PARK?
THAT SOUNDS NICE.
"UNFORTUNATELY, EDISON HAD A HEARING PROBLEM."
BUT SOMETIMES, THE DEAD MIGHT BE ABLE TO DELIVER A MESSAGE--AS IS THE CASE IN HORRORMEISTER SUPREME H.P. LOVECRAFT'S STORY, "COOL AIR."

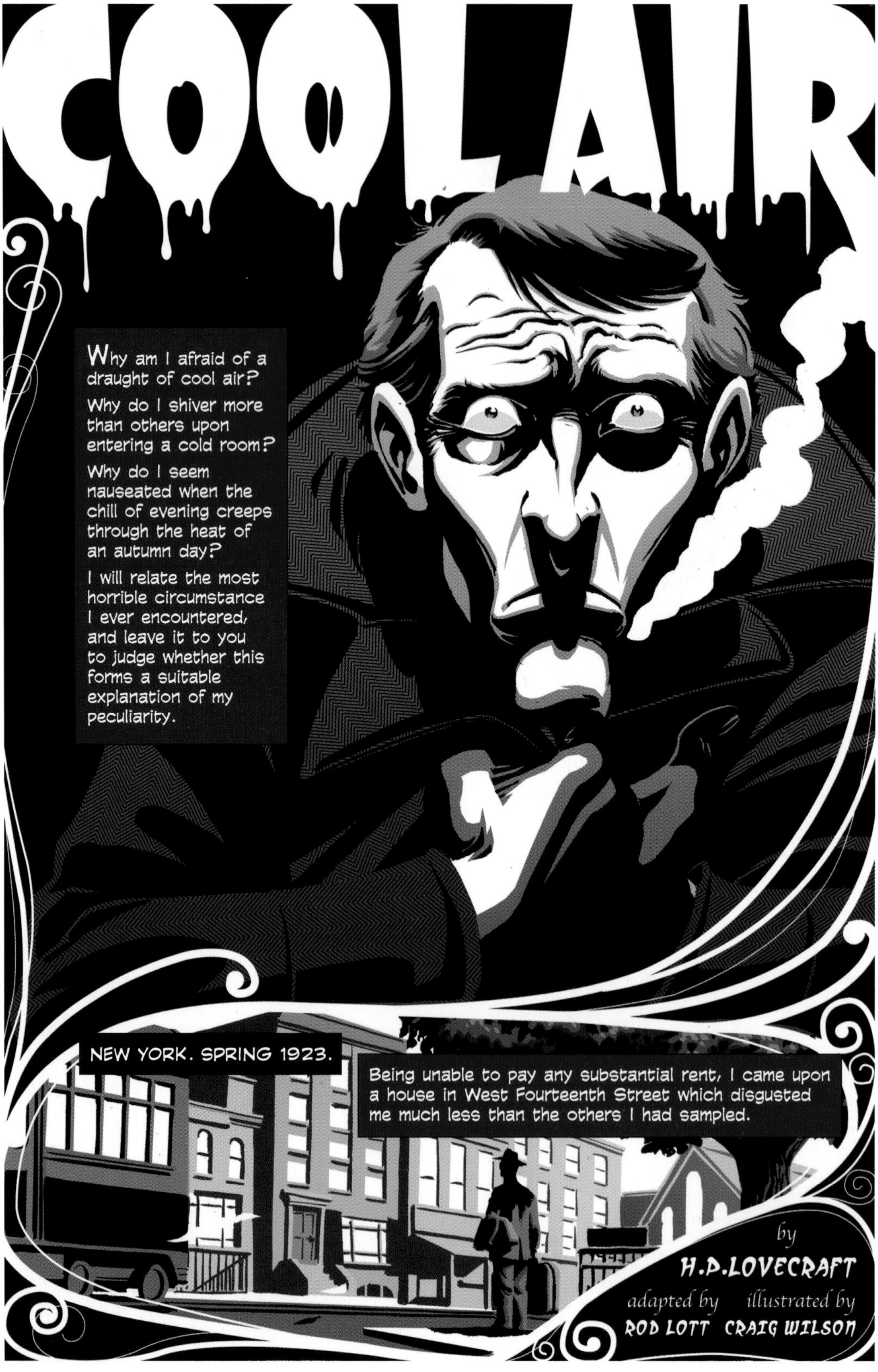
COOL AIR
Why am I afraid of a draught of cool air?
Why do I shiver more than others upon entering a cold room?
Why do I seem nauseated when the chill of evening creeps through the heat of an autumn day?
I will relate the most horrible circumstance I ever encountered, and leave it to you to judge whether this forms a suitable explanation of my peculiarity.
NEW YORK. SPRING 1923.
Being unable to pay any substantial rent, I came upon a house in West Fourteenth Street which disgusted me much less than the others I had sampled.
by H.P.LOVECRAFT
adapted by ROD LOTT
illustrated by CRAIG WILSON

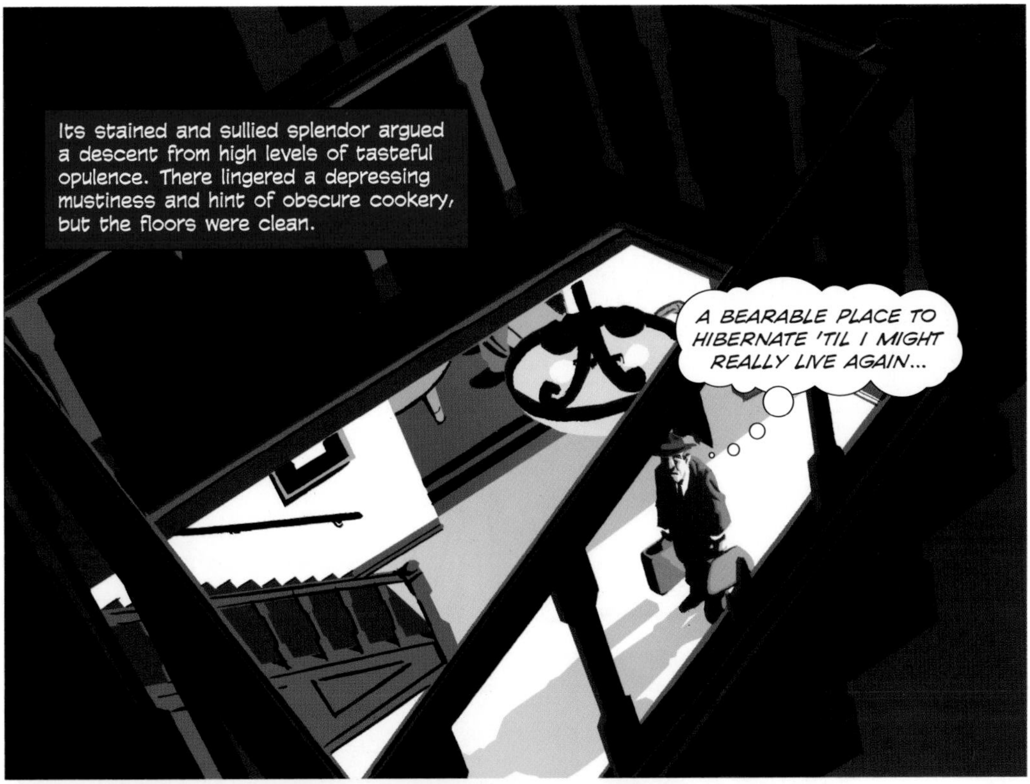
Its stained and sullied splendor argued a descent from high levels of tasteful opulence. There lingered a depressing mustiness and hint of obscure cookery, but the floors were clean.
A BEARABLE PLACE TO HIBERNATE 'TIL I MIGHT REALLY LIVE AGAIN...

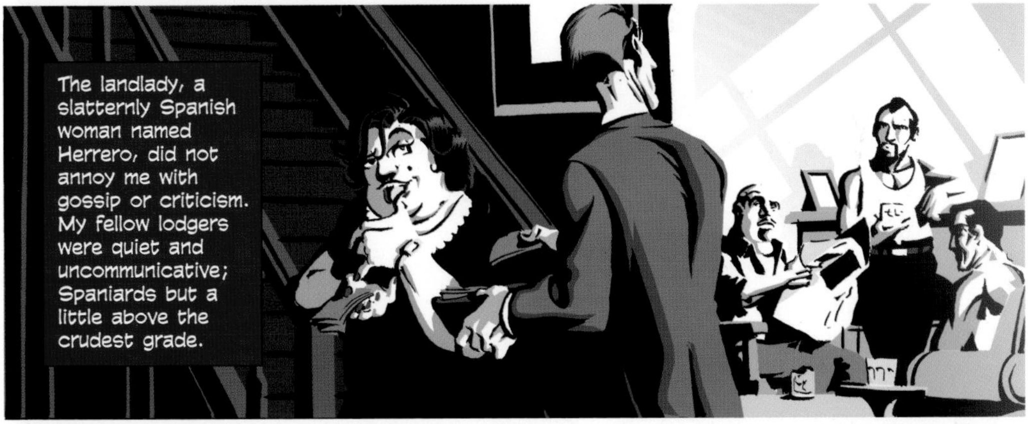
The landlady, a slatternly Spanish woman named Herrero, did not annoy me with gossip or criticism. My fellow lodgers were quiet and uncommunicative; Spaniards but a little above the crudest grade.

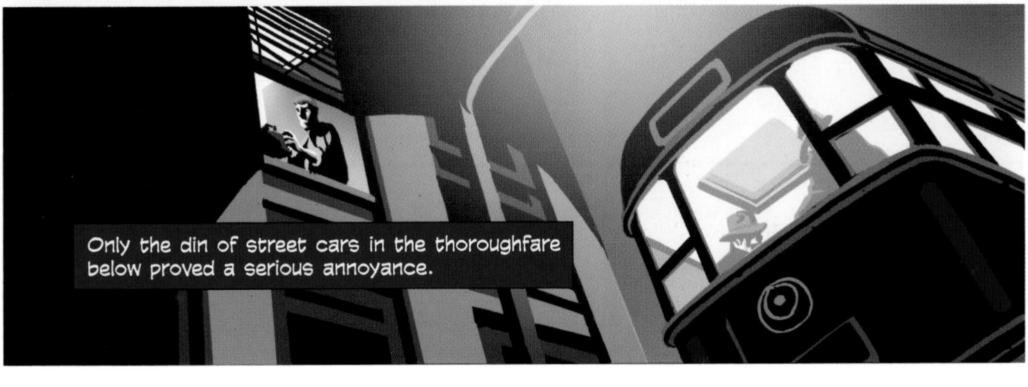
Only the din of street cars in the thoroughfare below proved a serious annoyance.

I had been there about three weeks when the first odd incident occurred.

SNIFF
SNIFF

I suddenly became aware of the pungent odor of ammonia.

I saw that the ceiling was wet and dripping; the soaking apparently proceeding from a corner on the side toward the street.

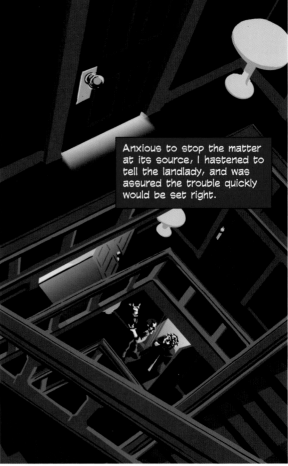

Anxious to stop the matter at its source, I hastened to tell the landlady, and was assured the trouble quickly would be set right.

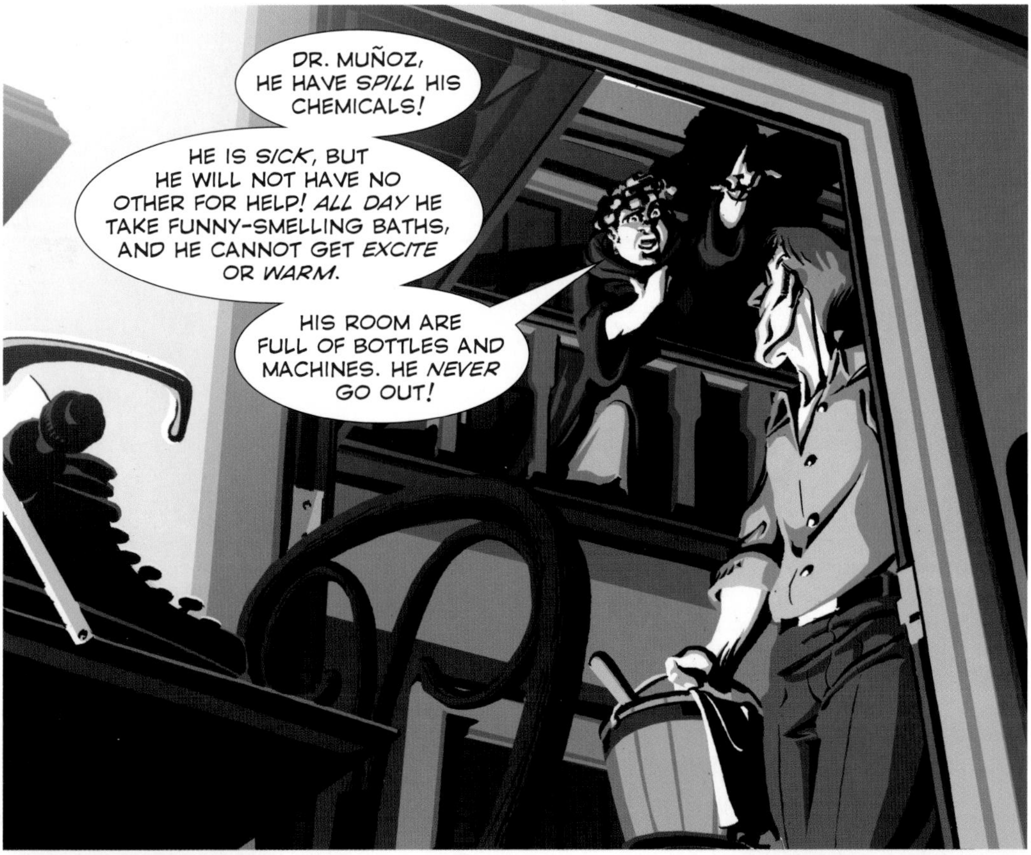
DR. MUÑOZ, HE HAVE *SPILL* HIS CHEMICALS!
HE IS *SICK*, BUT HE WILL NOT HAVE NO OTHER FOR HELP! *ALL DAY* HE TAKE FUNNY-SMELLING BATHS, AND HE CANNOT GET *EXCITE* OR *WARM*.
HIS ROOM ARE FULL OF BOTTLES AND MACHINES. HE *NEVER* GO OUT!

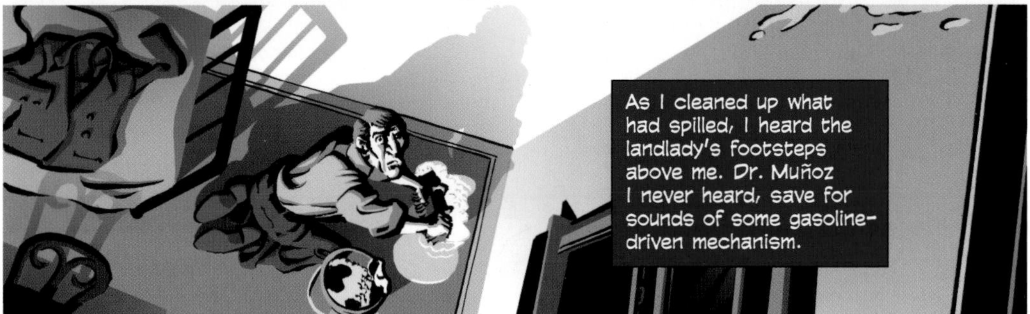
As I cleaned up what had spilled, I heard the landlady's footsteps above me. Dr. Muñoz I never heard, save for sounds of some gasoline-driven mechanism.

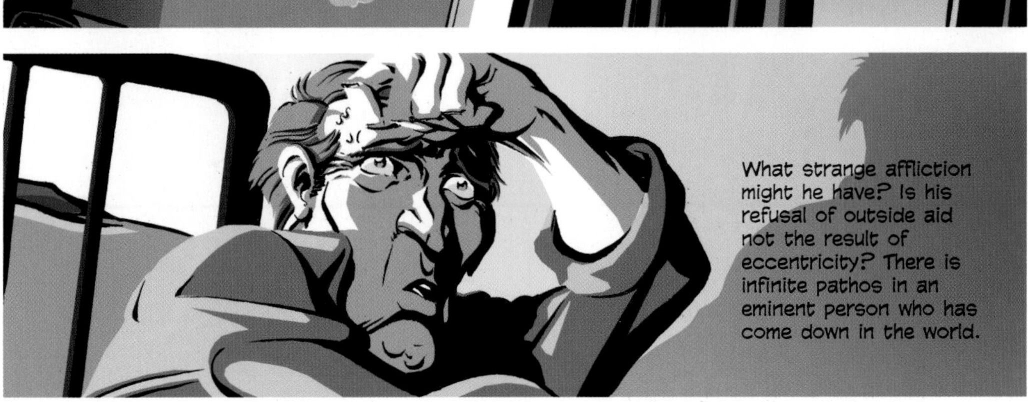
What strange affliction might he have? Is his refusal of outside aid not the result of eccentricity? There is infinite pathos in an eminent person who has come down in the world.

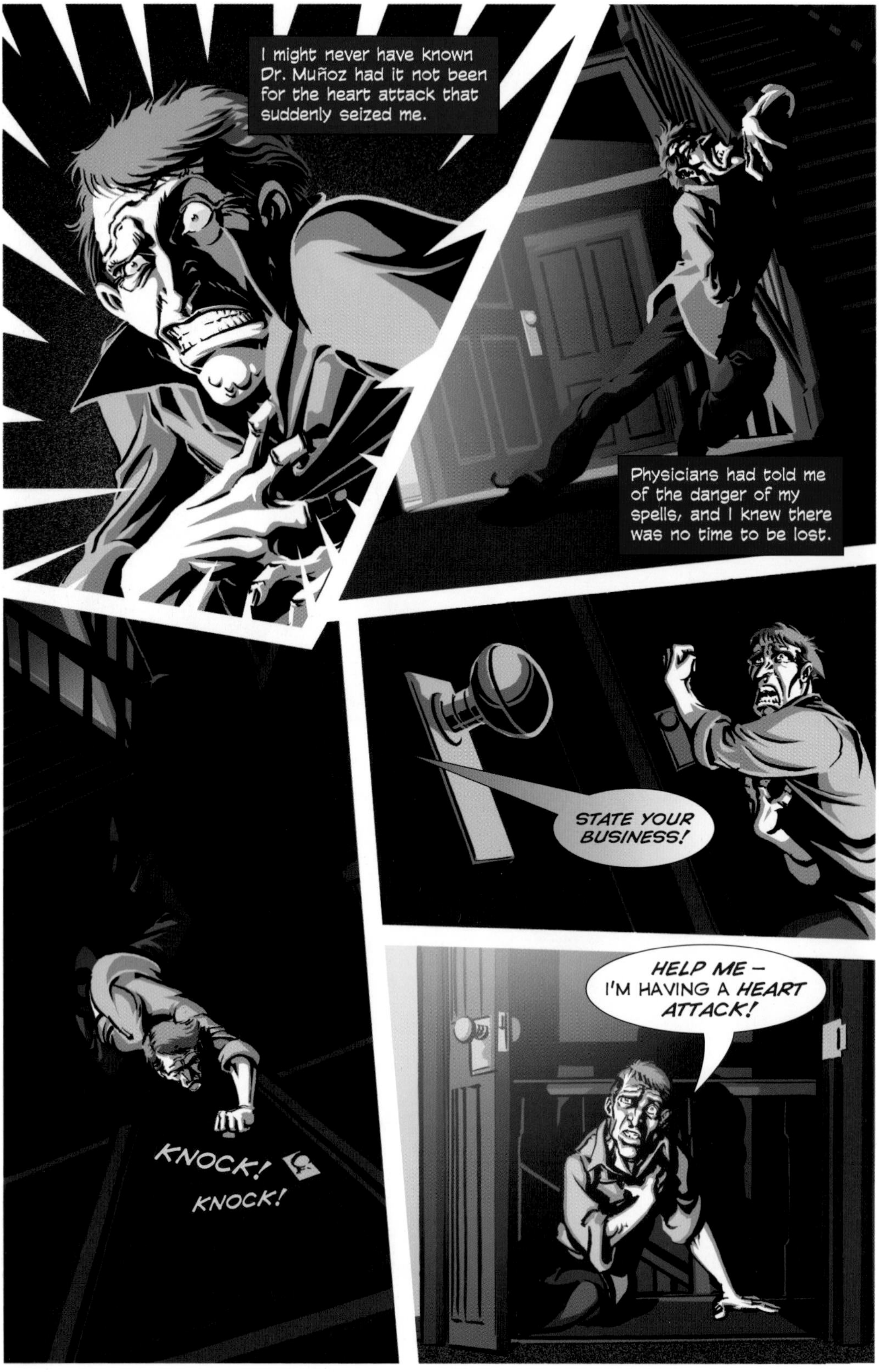
I might never have known Dr. Muñoz had it not been for the heart attack that suddenly seized me.
Physicians had told me of the danger of my spells, and I knew there was no time to be lost.
KNOCK!
KNOCK!
STATE YOUR BUSINESS!
HELP ME – I'M HAVING A HEART ATTACK!

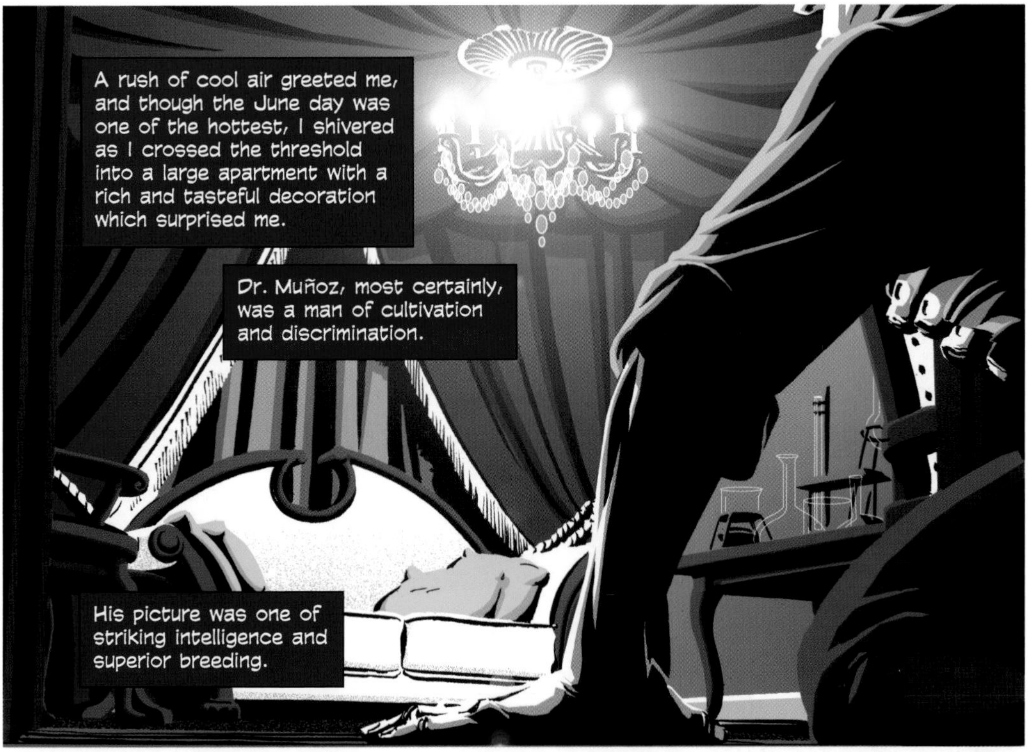
A rush of cool air greeted me, and though the June day was one of the hottest, I shivered as I crossed the threshold into a large apartment with a rich and tasteful decoration which surprised me.
Dr. Muñoz, most certainly, was a man of cultivation and discrimination.
His picture was one of striking intelligence and superior breeding.

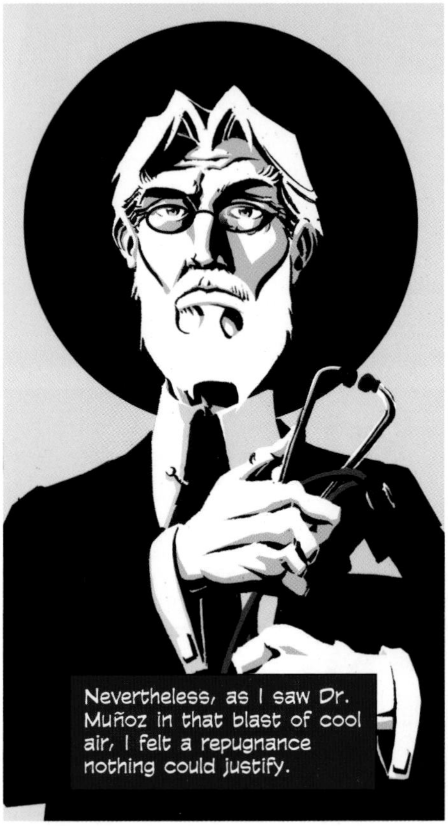
Nevertheless, as I saw Dr. Muñoz in that blast of cool air, I felt a repugnance nothing could justify.

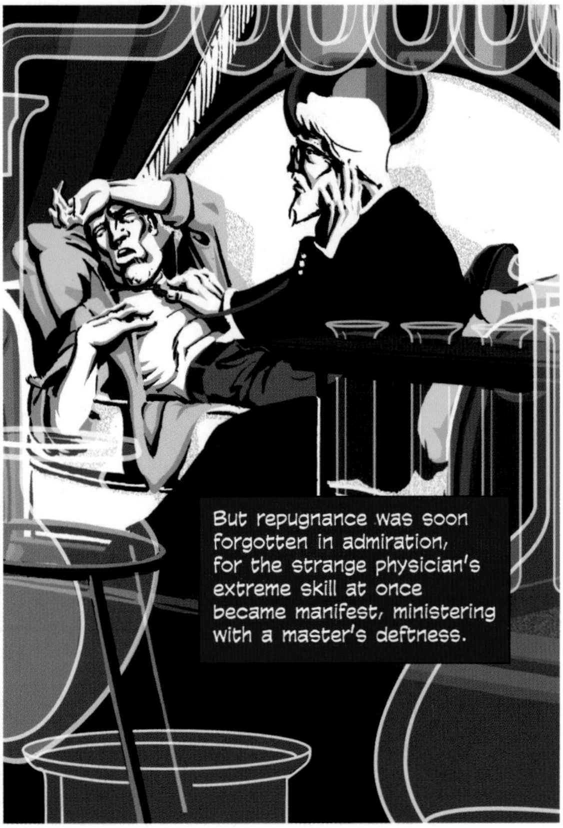
But repugnance was soon forgotten in admiration, for the strange physician's extreme skill at once became manifest, ministering with a master's deftness.

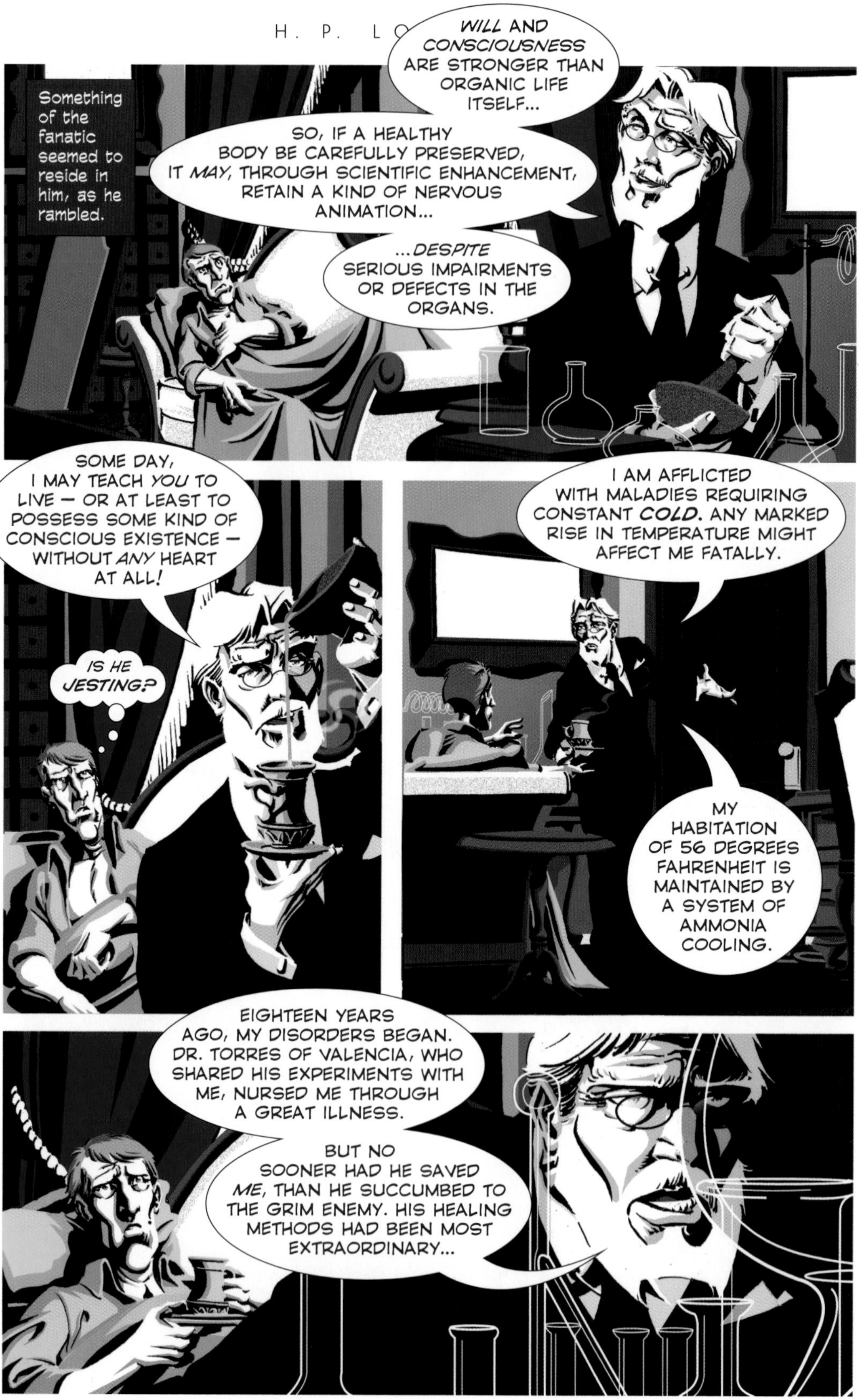
Something of the fanatic seemed to reside in him, as he rambled.
WILL AND CONSCIOUSNESS ARE STRONGER THAN ORGANIC LIFE ITSELF...
SO, IF A HEALTHY BODY BE CAREFULLY PRESERVED, IT MAY, THROUGH SCIENTIFIC ENHANCEMENT, RETAIN A KIND OF NERVOUS ANIMATION...
...DESPITE SERIOUS IMPAIRMENTS OR DEFECTS IN THE ORGANS.
SOME DAY, I MAY TEACH YOU TO LIVE — OR AT LEAST TO POSSESS SOME KIND OF CONSCIOUS EXISTENCE — WITHOUT ANY HEART AT ALL!
IS HE JESTING?
I AM AFFLICTED WITH MALADIES REQUIRING CONSTANT COLD. ANY MARKED RISE IN TEMPERATURE MIGHT AFFECT ME FATALLY.
MY HABITATION OF 56 DEGREES FAHRENHEIT IS MAINTAINED BY A SYSTEM OF AMMONIA COOLING.
EIGHTEEN YEARS AGO, MY DISORDERS BEGAN. DR. TORRES OF VALENCIA, WHO SHARED HIS EXPERIMENTS WITH ME, NURSED ME THROUGH A GREAT ILLNESS.
BUT NO SOONER HAD HE SAVED ME, THAN HE SUCCUMBED TO THE GRIM ENEMY. HIS HEALING METHODS HAD BEEN MOST EXTRAORDINARY...

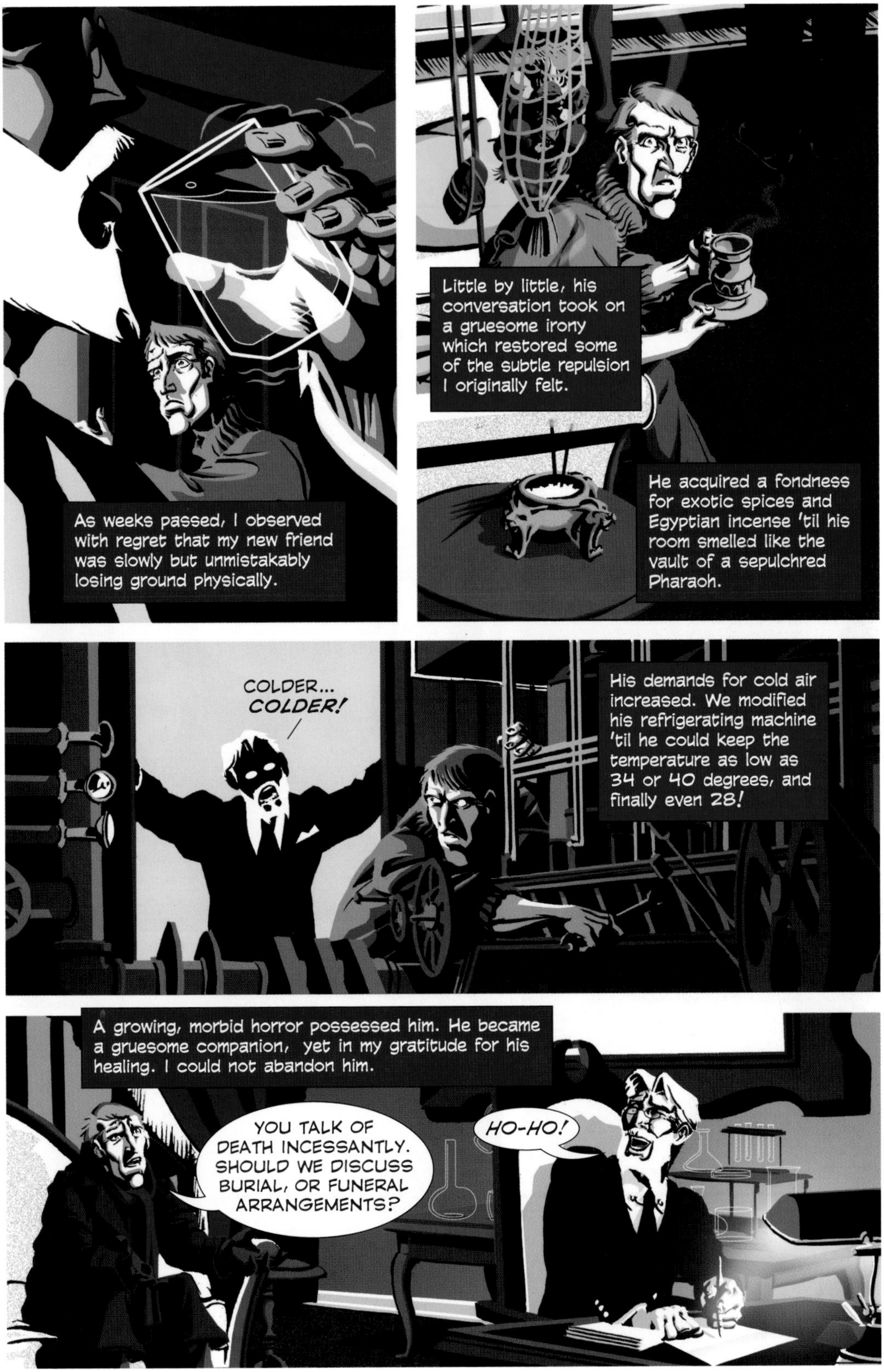
As weeks passed, I observed with regret that my new friend was slowly but unmistakably losing ground physically.
Little by little, his conversation took on a gruesome irony which restored some of the subtle repulsion I originally felt.
He acquired a fondness for exotic spices and Egyptian incense 'til his room smelled like the vault of a sepulchred Pharaoh.
COLDER... COLDER!
His demands for cold air increased. We modified his refrigerating machine 'til he could keep the temperature as low as 34 or 40 degrees, and finally even 28!
A growing, morbid horror possessed him. He became a gruesome companion, yet in my gratitude for his healing. I could not abandon him.
YOU TALK OF DEATH INCESSANTLY. SHOULD WE DISCUSS BURIAL, OR FUNERAL ARRANGEMENTS?
HO-HO!

Panic rose around his apartment. The whole house had a musty odor, but the smell in his room was worse, in spite of the spices and incense.

When I suggested other physicians, he flew into a rage. He refused to be confined to bed, yet the pretence of eating, he virtually abandoned. Mental power alone kept him from total collapse.

IT MUST BE CONNECTED WITH HIS AILMENT, BUT I SHUDDER AT WHAT THAT MIGHT BE.

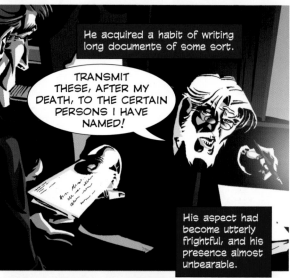

He acquired a habit of writing long documents of some sort.

TRANSMIT THESE, AFTER MY DEATH, TO THE CERTAIN PERSONS I HAVE NAMED!

His aspect had become utterly frightful, and his presence almost unbearable.

The addressees were, for the most part, lettered East Indians, but included a once-celebrated French physician about whom the most inconceivable things had been whispered.

Dr. Pierre Laison
24 Rue de Ville
Paris France

In the end, I burned all these papers — undelivered and unopened.

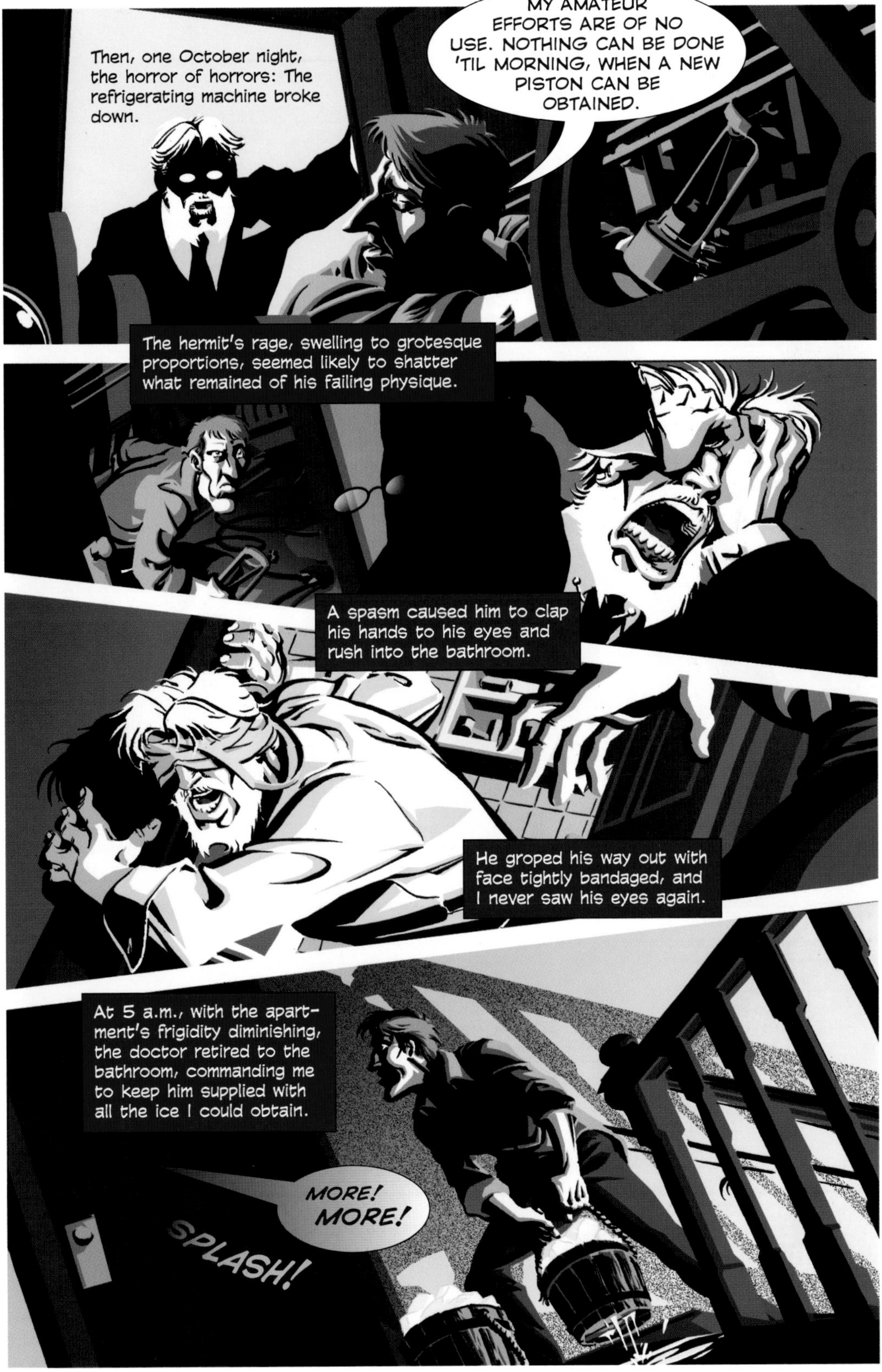
Then, one October night, the horror of horrors: The refrigerating machine broke down.
MY AMATEUR EFFORTS ARE OF NO USE. NOTHING CAN BE DONE 'TIL MORNING, WHEN A NEW PISTON CAN BE OBTAINED.
The hermit's rage, swelling to grotesque proportions, seemed likely to shatter what remained of his failing physique.
A spasm caused him to clap his hands to his eyes and rush into the bathroom.
He groped his way out with face tightly bandaged, and I never saw his eyes again.
At 5 a.m., with the apartment's frigidity diminishing, the doctor retired to the bathroom, commanding me to keep him supplied with all the ice I could obtain.
MORE! MORE!
SPLASH!

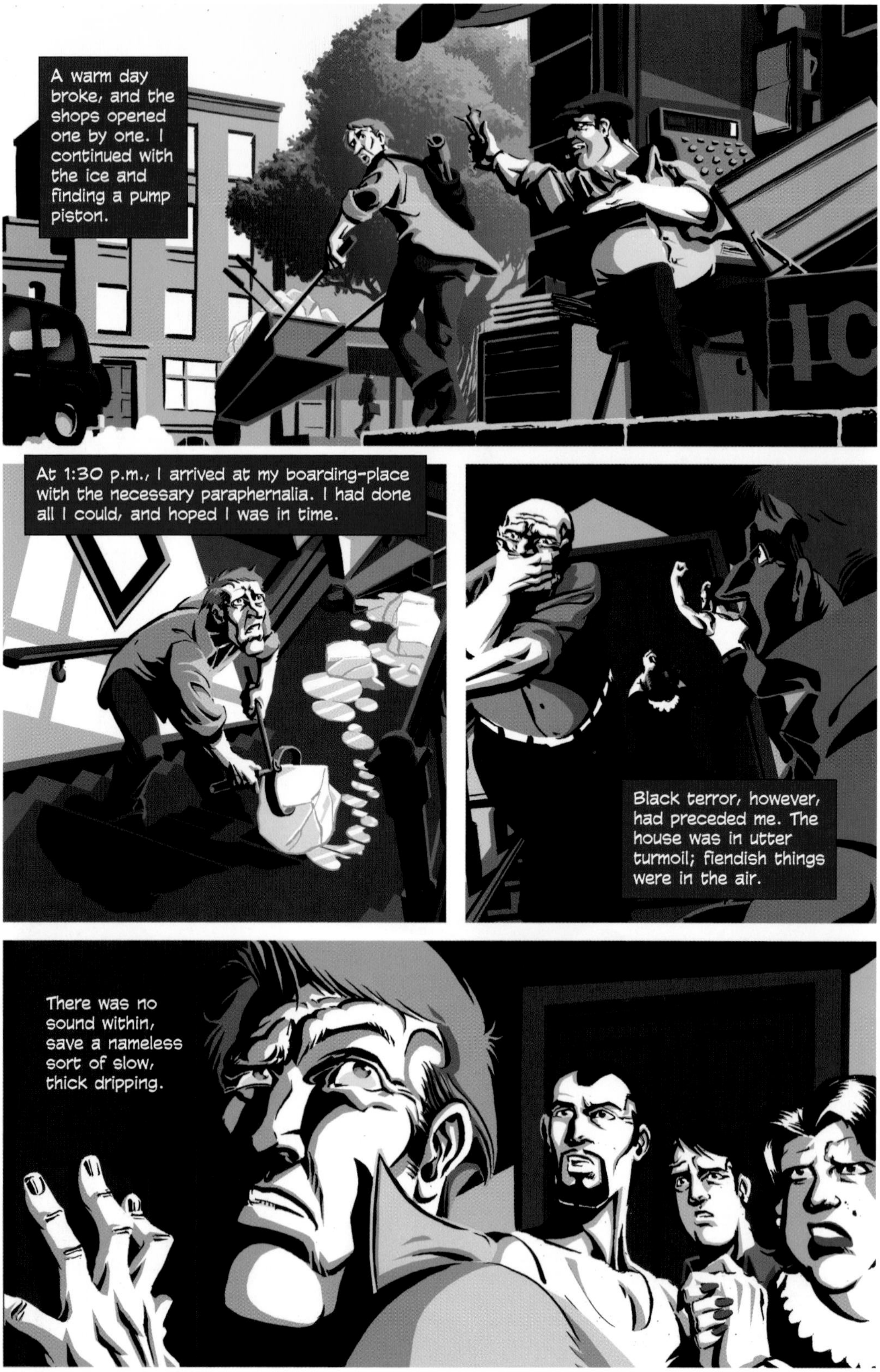
A warm day broke, and the shops opened one by one. I continued with the ice and finding a pump piston.
At 1:30 p.m., I arrived at my boarding-place with the necessary paraphernalia. I had done all I could, and hoped I was in time.
Black terror, however, had preceded me. The house was in utter turmoil; fiendish things were in the air.
There was no sound within, save a nameless sort of slow, thick dripping.

Gathering our courage, we tremblingly invaded the room, which blazed with the afternoon sun.

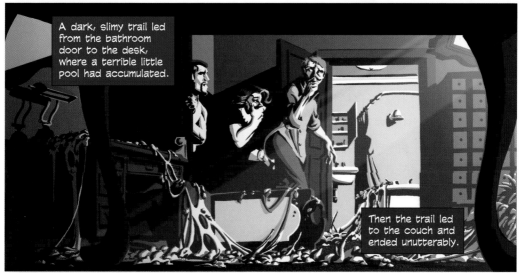

A dark, slimy trail led from the bathroom door to the desk, where a terrible little pool had accumulated.

Then the trail led to the couch and ended unutterably.

Something was scrawled there in an awful, blind hand on a piece of paper hideously smeared, as though by the very claws that traced the hurried last words.

What had been on the couch, I dare not say. But the nauseous words seemed well-nigh incredible.

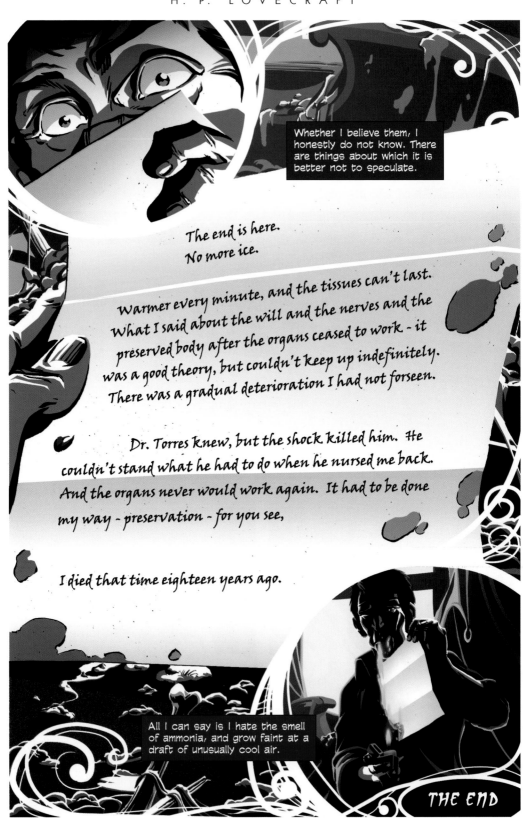

Whether I believe them, I honestly do not know. There are things about which it is better not to speculate.

The end is here.
No more ice.

Warmer every minute, and the tissues can't last. What I said about the will and the nerves and the preserved body after the organs ceased to work - it was a good theory, but couldn't keep up indefinitely. There was a gradual deterioration I had not forseen.

Dr. Torres knew, but the shock killed him. He couldn't stand what he had to do when he nursed me back. And the organs never would work again. It had to be done my way - preservation - for you see,

I died that time eighteen years ago.

All I can say is I hate the smell of ammonia, and grow faint at a draft of unusually cool air.

THE END

"WASN'T THAT A COOL STORY... ADIEU, THEN TO H.P. LOVECRAFT--

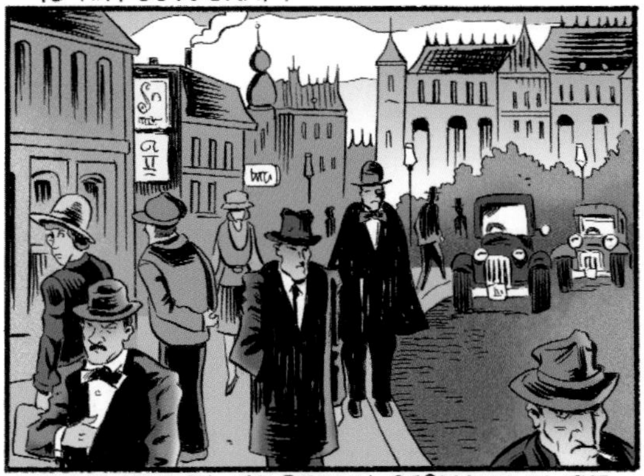

"AS WE TRAVEL TO BERLIN, GERMANY, IN THE YEARS AFTER THE **GREAT WAR**. BERLIN WAS A GREAT CITY, THE EPICENTER FOR EXPERIMENTATION IN THE ARTS'.

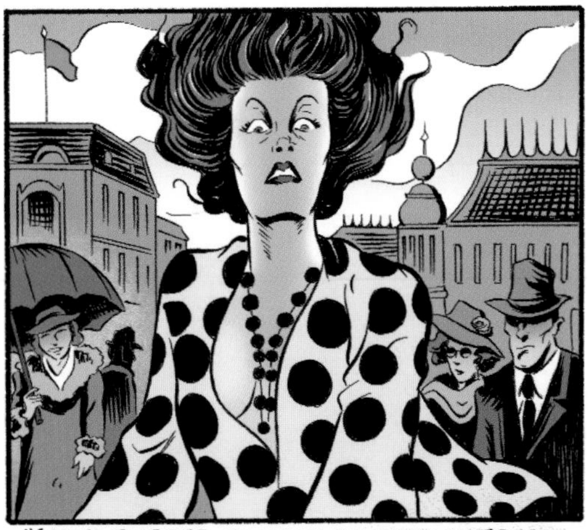

"**ANITA BERBER**, FAMOUS DANCER, ACTRESS, WRITER, AND LADY OF THE NIGHT. SHE DIED OF HER ADDICTIONS AT AGE 29.

"**CARL GUSTAV JUNG** WAS INTERPRETING DREAMS AND BREAKING WITH FREUD--

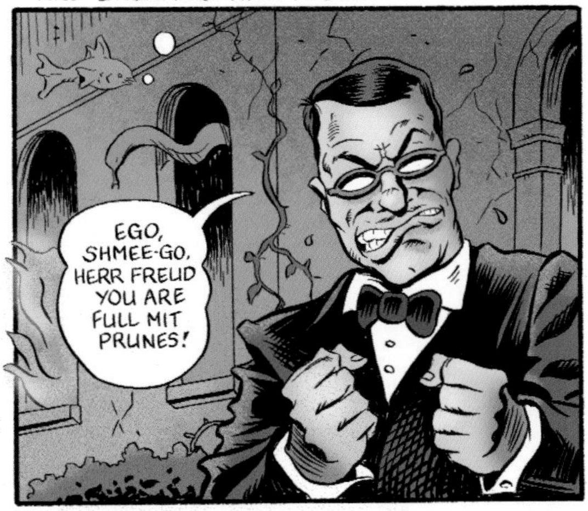
EGO, SHMEE-GO. HERR FREUD YOU ARE FULL MIT PRUNES!

"**ALBERT EINSTEIN** SERVED AS DIRECTOR OF THE KAISER WILHELM INSTITUTE FOR PHYSICS IN BERLIN.

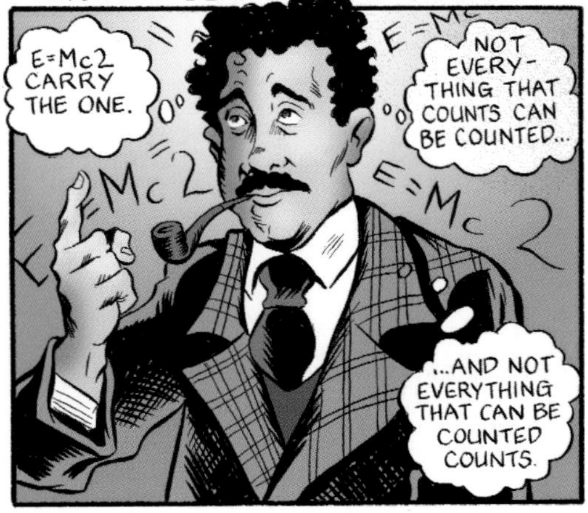
E=Mc2 CARRY THE ONE.
NOT EVERY-THING THAT COUNTS CAN BE COUNTED...
...AND NOT EVERYTHING THAT CAN BE COUNTED COUNTS.

"SEEKERS OF TRUTH PRACTICED "THE MYSTICAL ARTS" IN BERLIN: ALCHEMY, ASTROLOGY, CLAIRVOYANCE, TELEPATHY, AND ALL MANNER OF OCCULT ENDEAVOR."

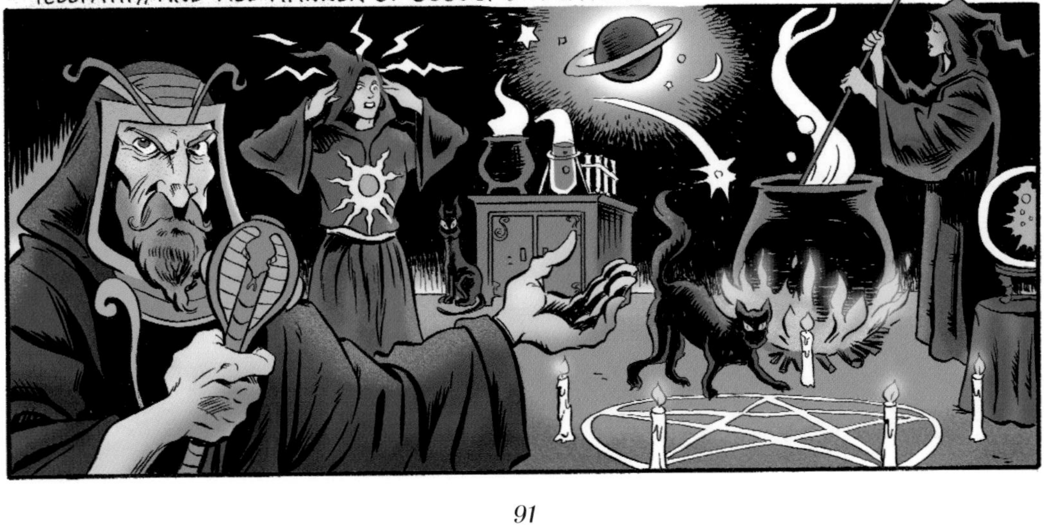

BERLIN WAS A **WILD** AND **CRAZY** PLACE. JUST LIKE *CABARET*, ONLY WITHOUT LIZA MINNELLI!

EVERY DAY WAS HALLOWEEN-- WEIMAR STYLE!

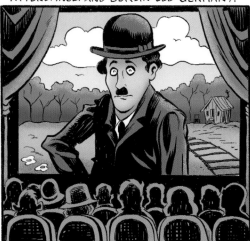

"GERMANY LED THE WORLD IN MOTION PICTURE ATTENDANCE. AND BERLIN LED GERMANY.

UND DZEY ARE ALWAYS MISHTOOKEN MIR FUR DER VERDAMMTE SCHWEINEHUND **CHARLIE CHAPLIN!**

"HERR HITLER HAD OTHER CONCERNS. HE'D JUST BECOME DIRECTOR OF PROPAGANDA FOR THE GERMAN WORKERS PARTY AND HAD DECIDED THE NAME HAD TO GO. SOMETHING SNAPPIER WAS NEEDED..."

"IT WAS IN BERLIN THAT TWO FRIENDS, **HANS JANOWITZ** AND **CARL MAYER**, DEVELOPED THEIR CONCEPT FOR A UNIQUE FILM."

JA, I'LL BRING YOU THE WURST.

AND THAT IS OUR CHARACTER CESARE. HE IS NOT ALIVE. HE IS NOT DEAD.

GUT, GUT! AND IT IS FILMED IN THE EXPRESSIONISTIC STYLE! JA, THAT IS SO GERMAN!

AND WE CALL IT...

GONE WITH THE WIND!

THANKFULLY, THEY CHOSE A MORE SUITABLE NAME FOR THEIR MOVIE, A HALLOWEEN NIGHTMARE OF DEATH IMAGES ENTITLED... **THE CABINET OF DR. CALIGARI!**

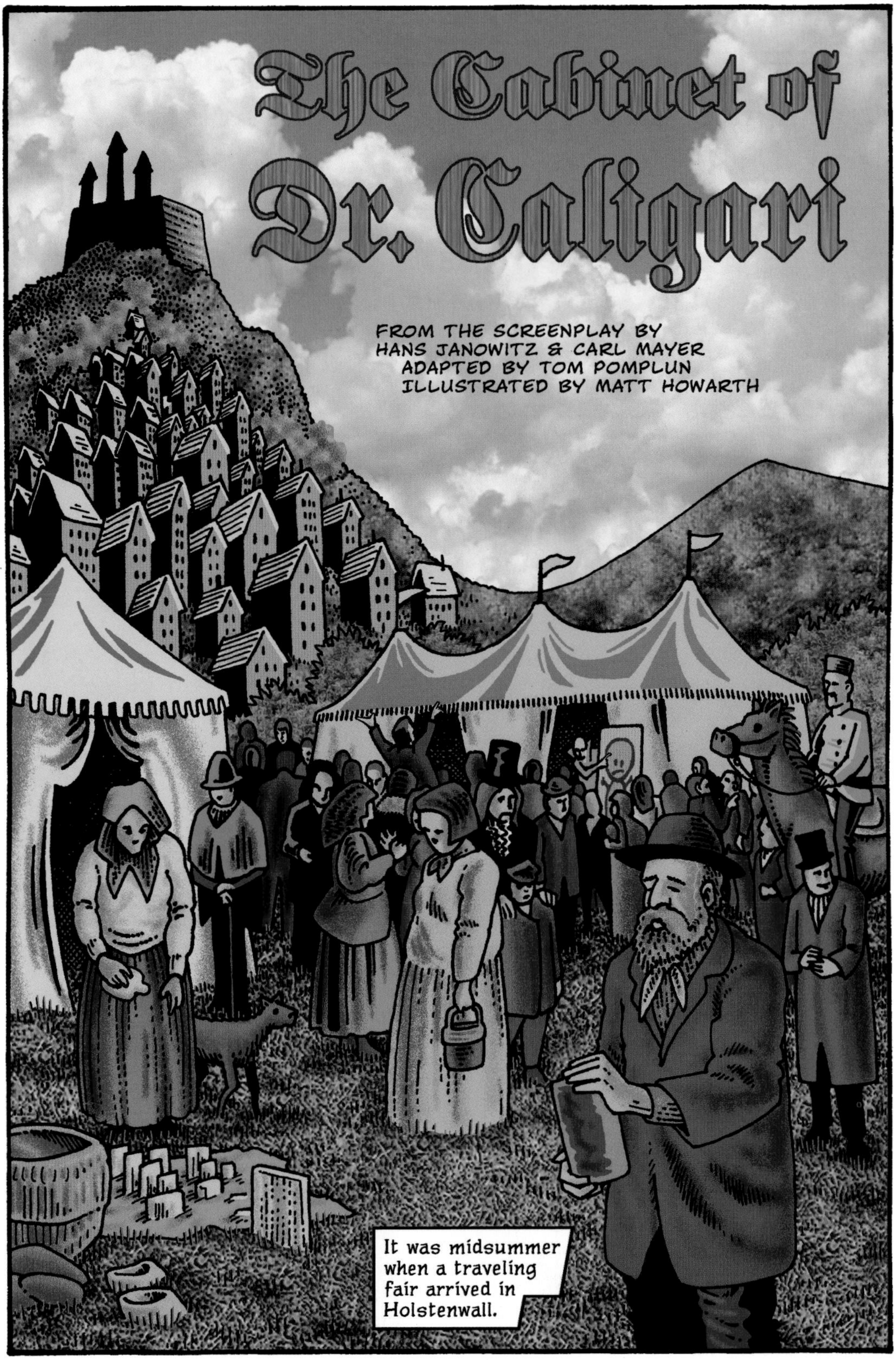
The Cabinet of Dr. Caligari
FROM THE SCREENPLAY BY
HANS JANOWITZ & CARL MAYER
ADAPTED BY TOM POMPLUN
ILLUSTRATED BY MATT HOWARTH
It was midsummer when a traveling fair arrived in Holstenwall.

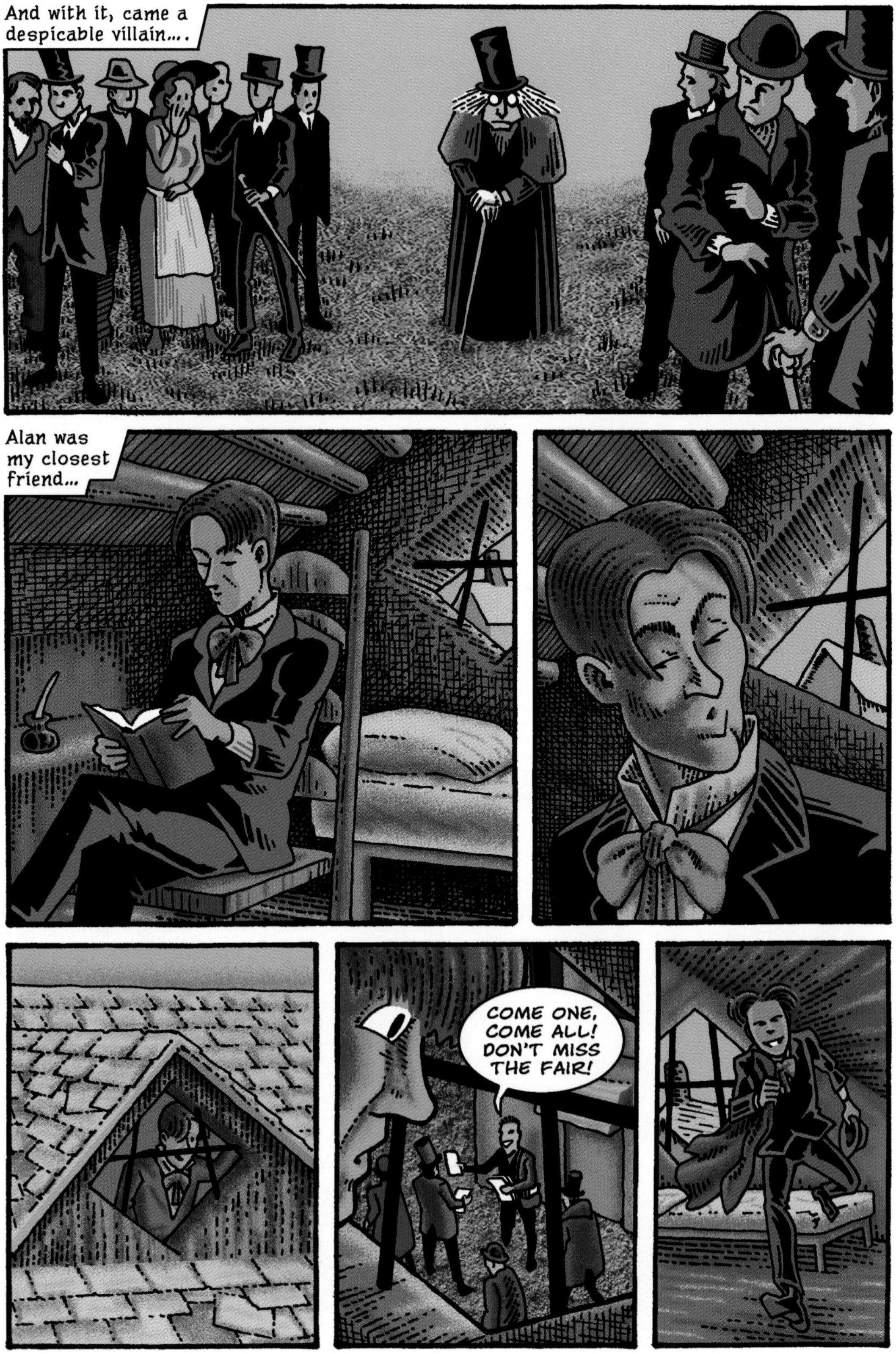
And with it, came a despicable villain....
Alan was my closest friend...
COME ONE, COME ALL! DON'T MISS THE FAIR!

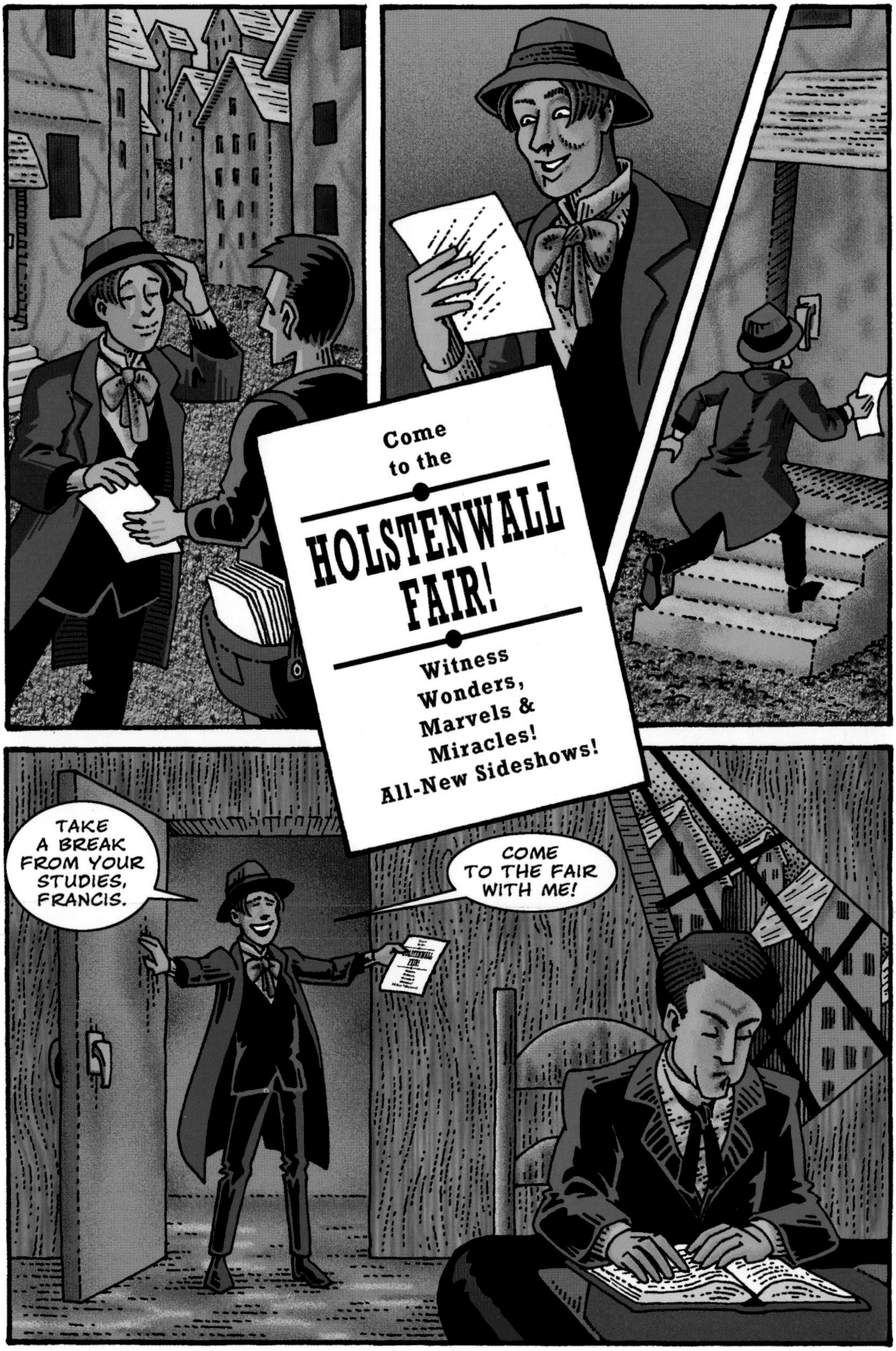
Come
to the
HOLSTENWALL
FAIR!
Witness
Wonders,
Marvels &
Miracles!
All-New Sideshows!
TAKE A BREAK FROM YOUR STUDIES, FRANCIS.
COME TO THE FAIR WITH ME!

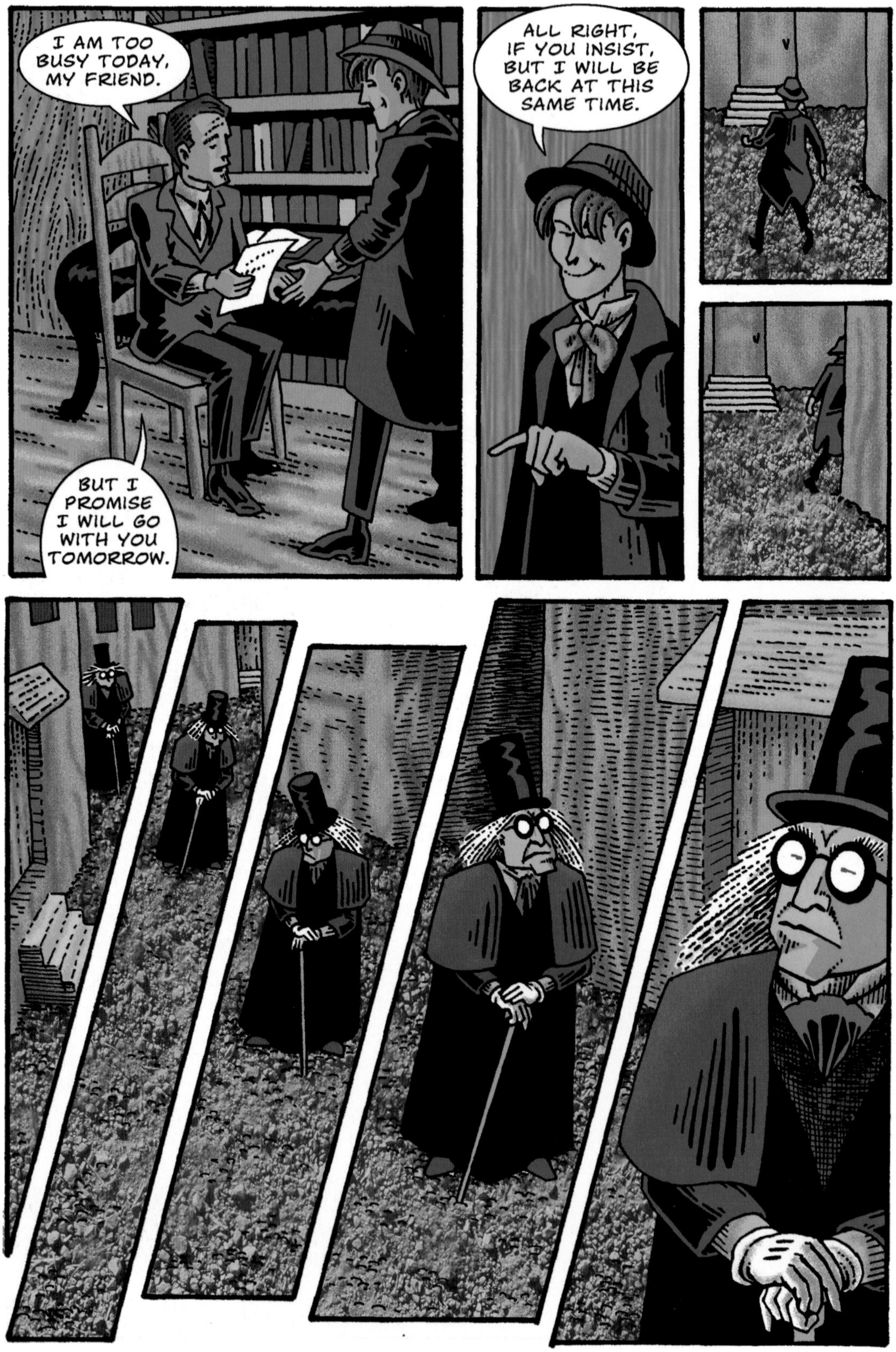
I AM TOO BUSY TODAY, MY FRIEND.
BUT I PROMISE I WILL GO WITH YOU TOMORROW.
ALL RIGHT, IF YOU INSIST, BUT I WILL BE BACK AT THIS SAME TIME.

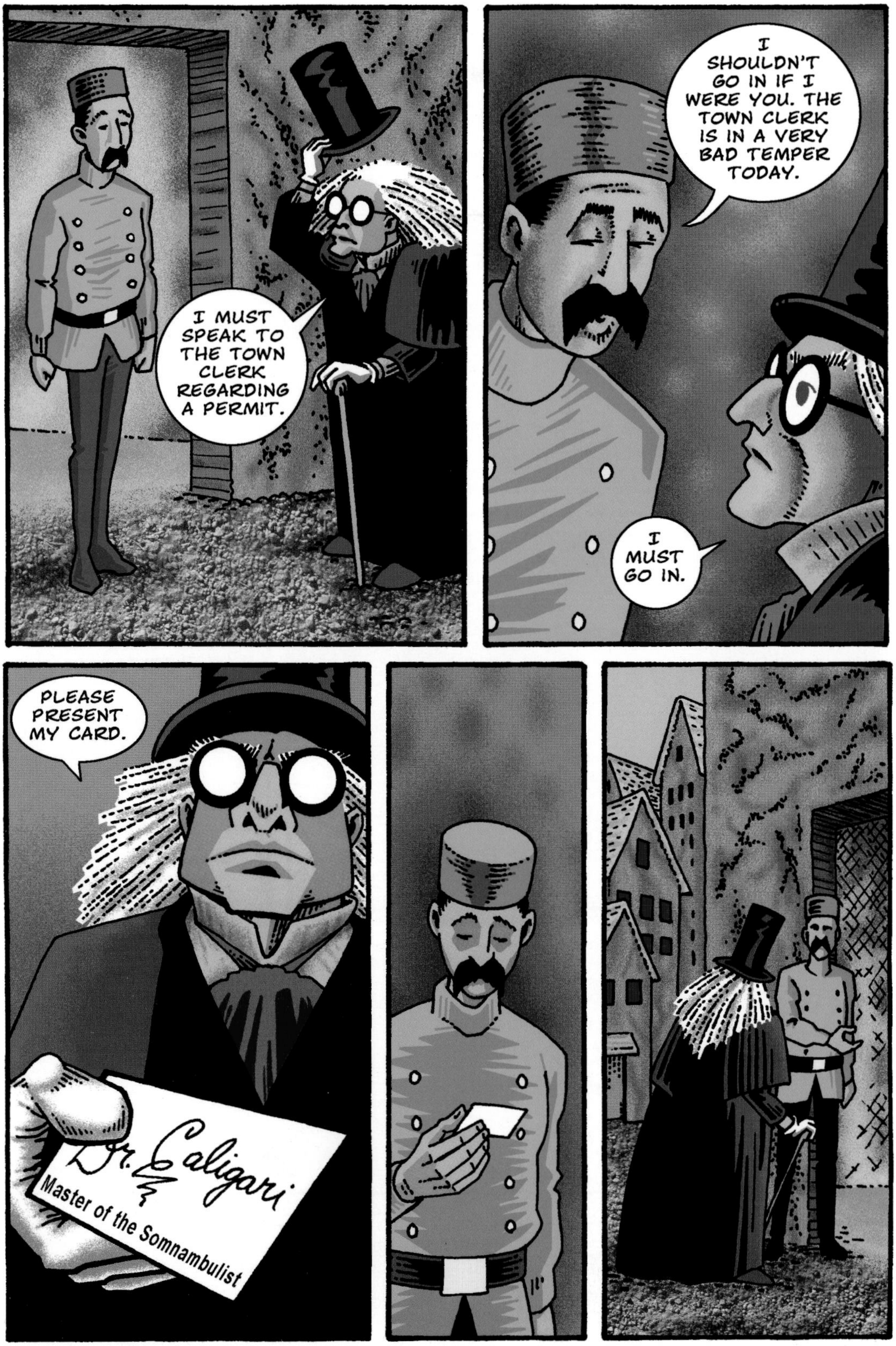
I MUST SPEAK TO THE TOWN CLERK REGARDING A PERMIT.
I SHOULDN'T GO IN IF I WERE YOU. THE TOWN CLERK IS IN A VERY BAD TEMPER TODAY.
I MUST GO IN.
PLEASE PRESENT MY CARD.
Dr. Caligari
Master of the Somnambulist

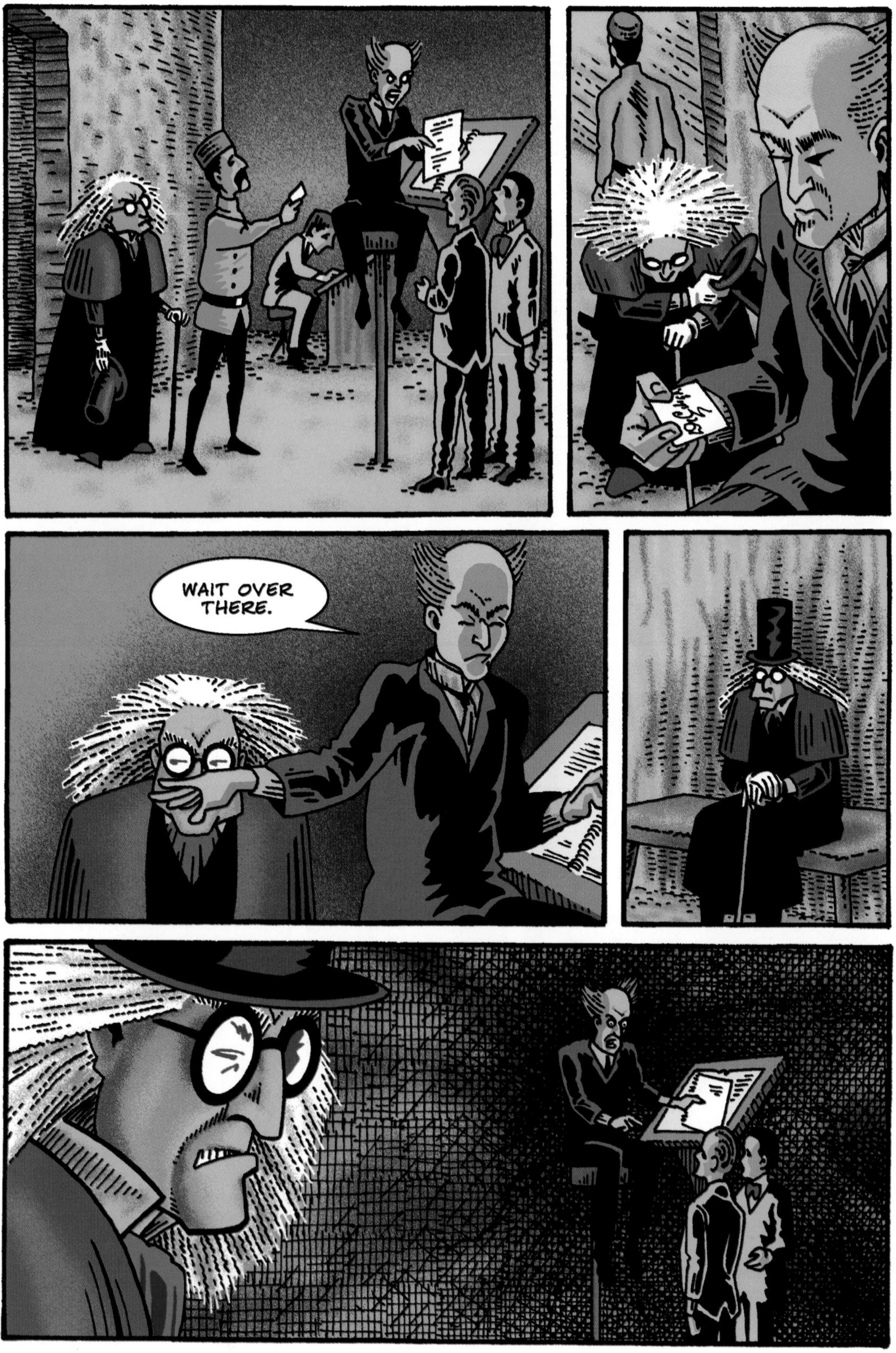
WAIT OVER THERE.

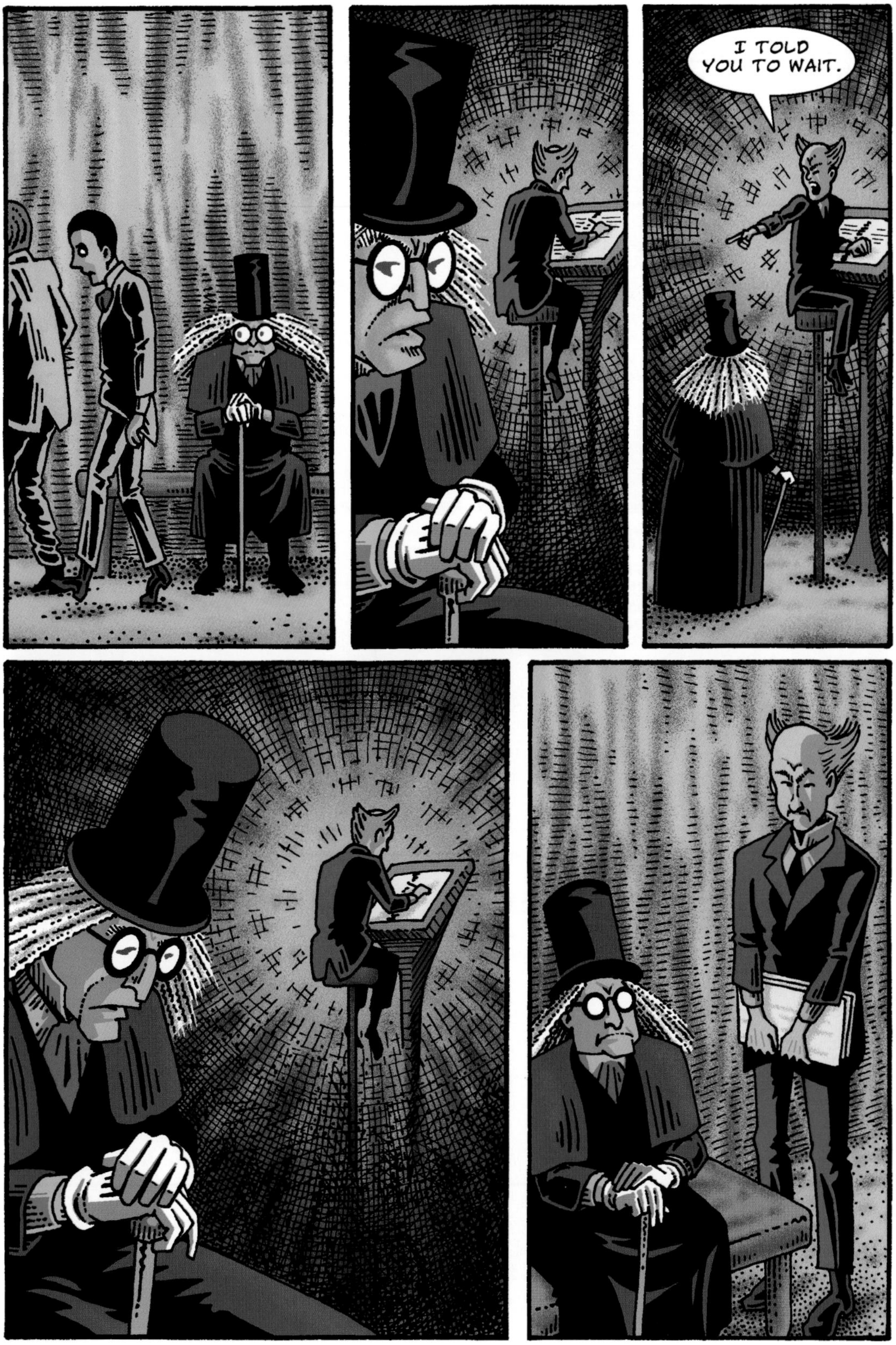
I TOLD YOU TO WAIT.

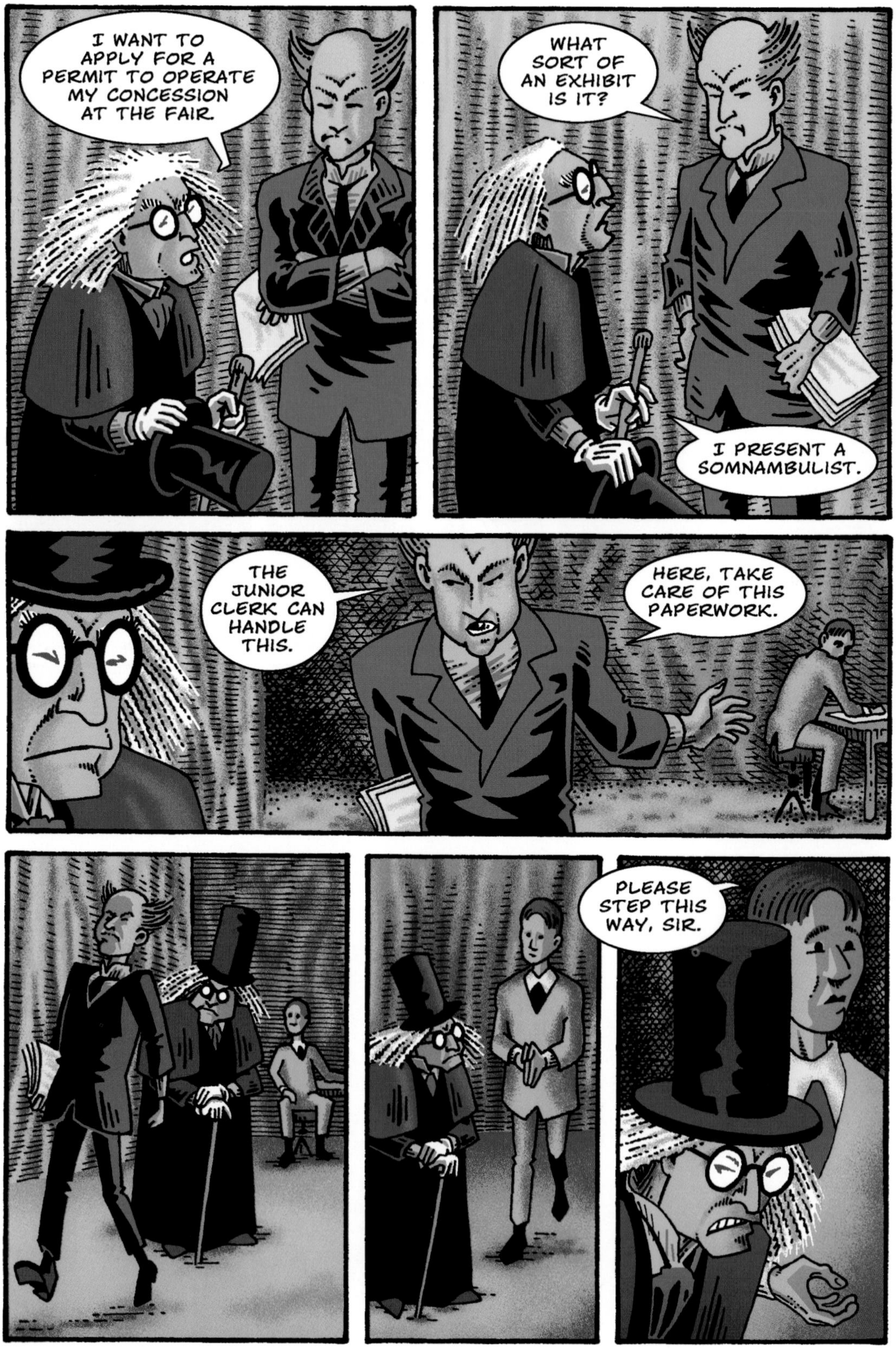
I WANT TO APPLY FOR A PERMIT TO OPERATE MY CONCESSION AT THE FAIR.
WHAT SORT OF AN EXHIBIT IS IT?
I PRESENT A SOMNAMBULIST.
THE JUNIOR CLERK CAN HANDLE THIS.
HERE, TAKE CARE OF THIS PAPERWORK.
PLEASE STEP THIS WAY, SIR.

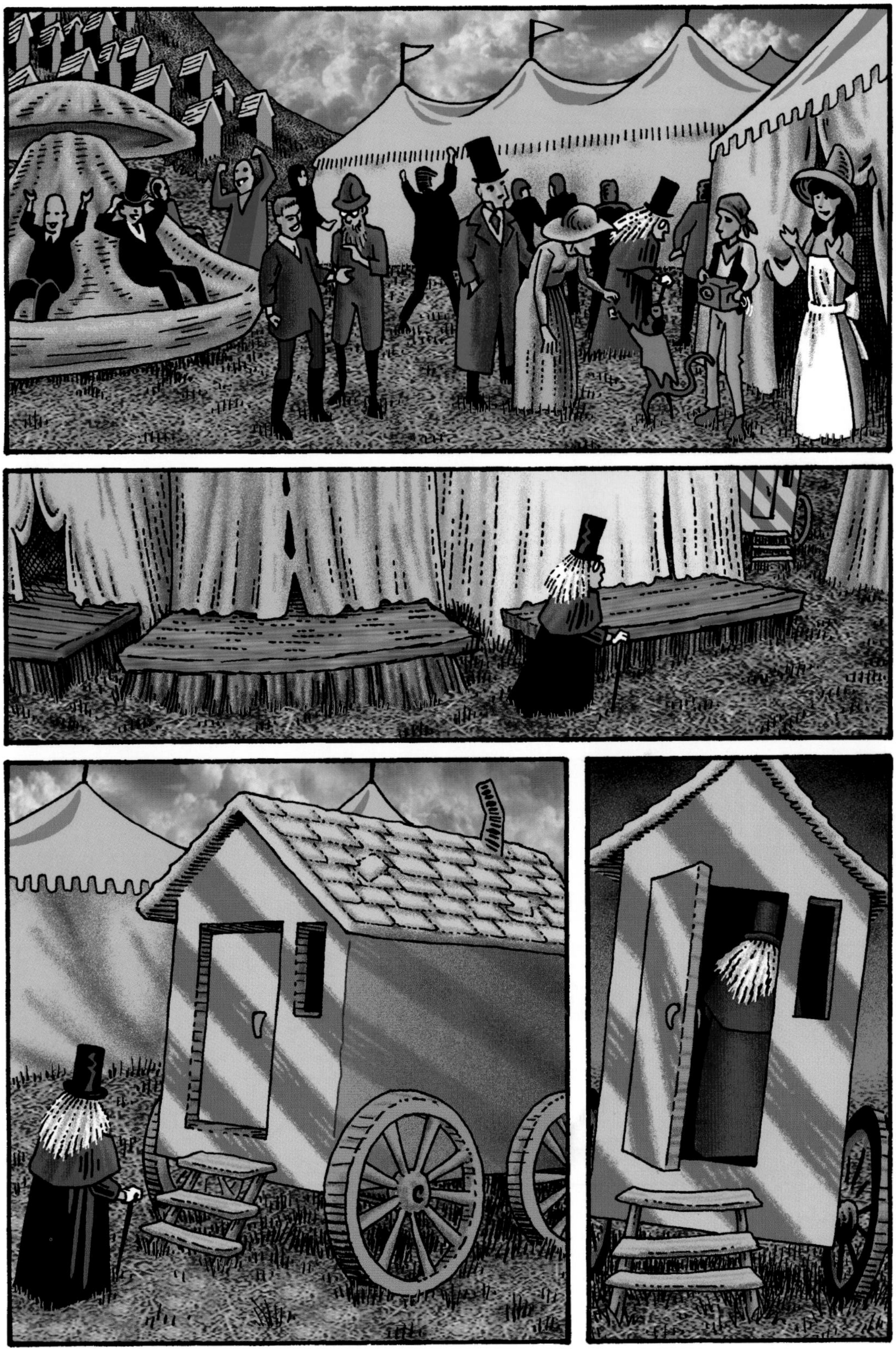

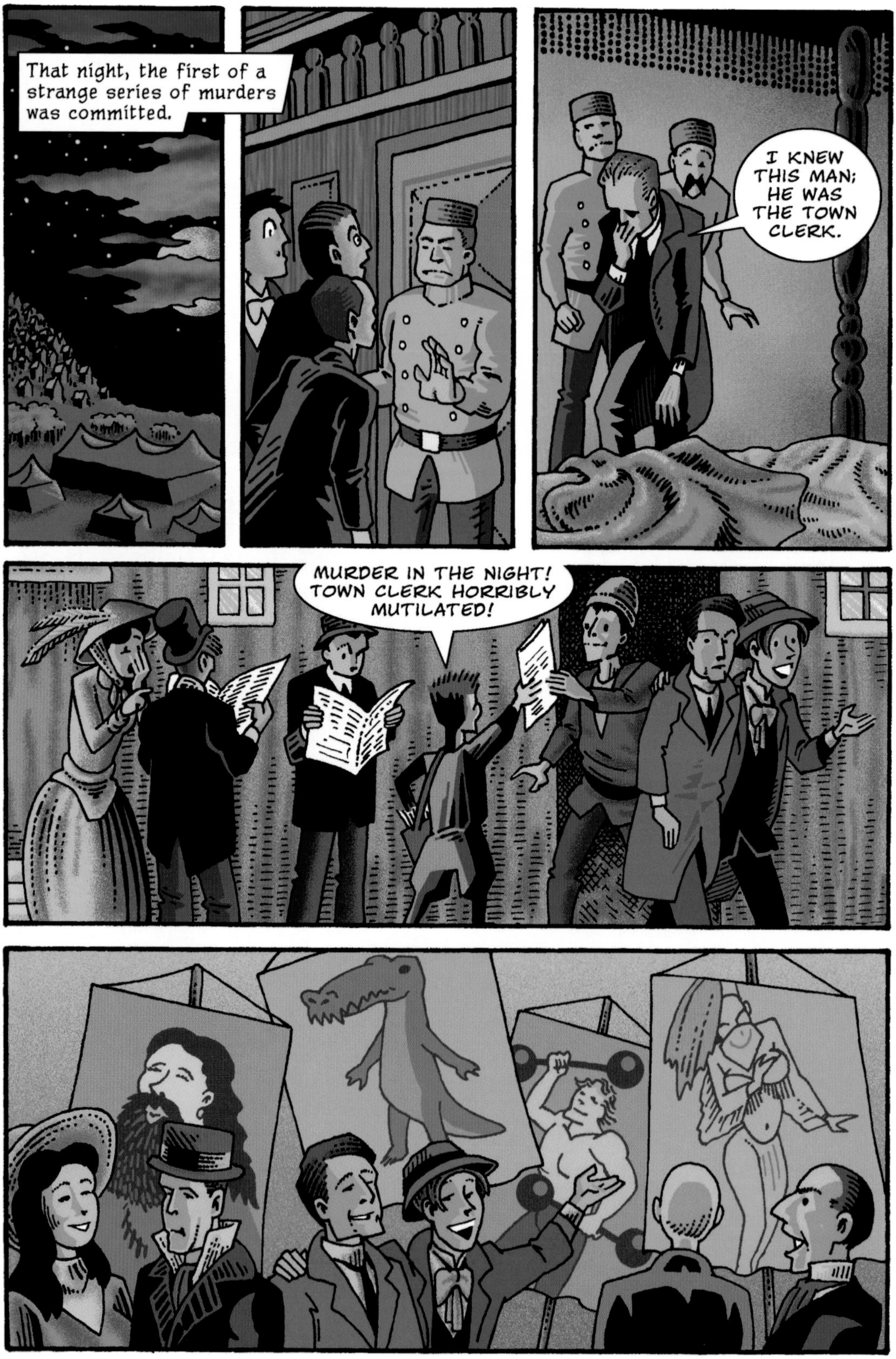
That night, the first of a strange series of murders was committed.
I KNEW THIS MAN; HE WAS THE TOWN CLERK.
MURDER IN THE NIGHT! TOWN CLERK HORRIBLY MUTILATED!

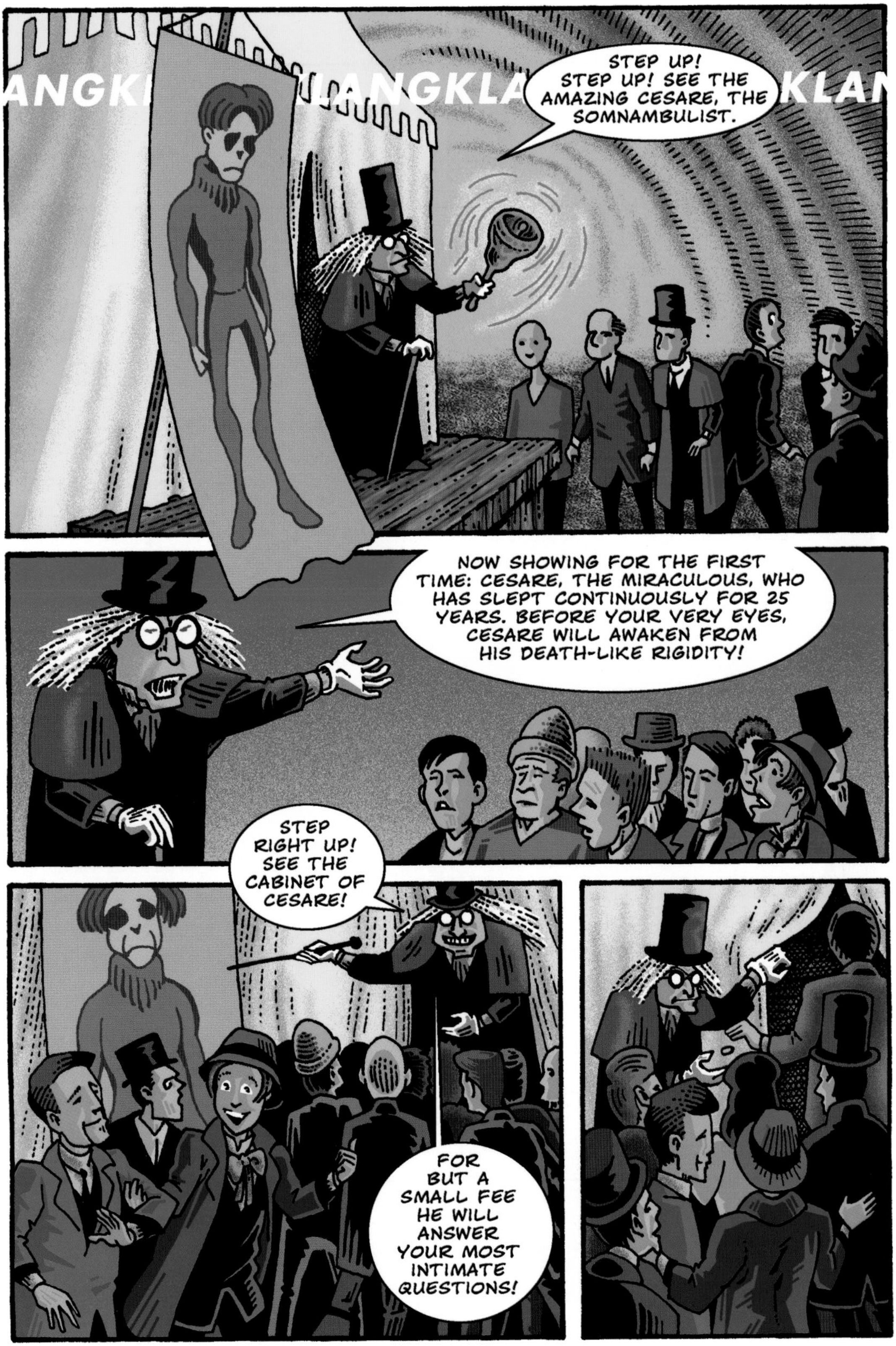
ANGK LANGKLA KLAN
STEP UP! STEP UP! SEE THE AMAZING CESARE, THE SOMNAMBULIST.
NOW SHOWING FOR THE FIRST TIME: CESARE, THE MIRACULOUS, WHO HAS SLEPT CONTINUOUSLY FOR 25 YEARS. BEFORE YOUR VERY EYES, CESARE WILL AWAKEN FROM HIS DEATH-LIKE RIGIDITY!
STEP RIGHT UP! SEE THE CABINET OF CESARE!
FOR BUT A SMALL FEE HE WILL ANSWER YOUR MOST INTIMATE QUESTIONS!

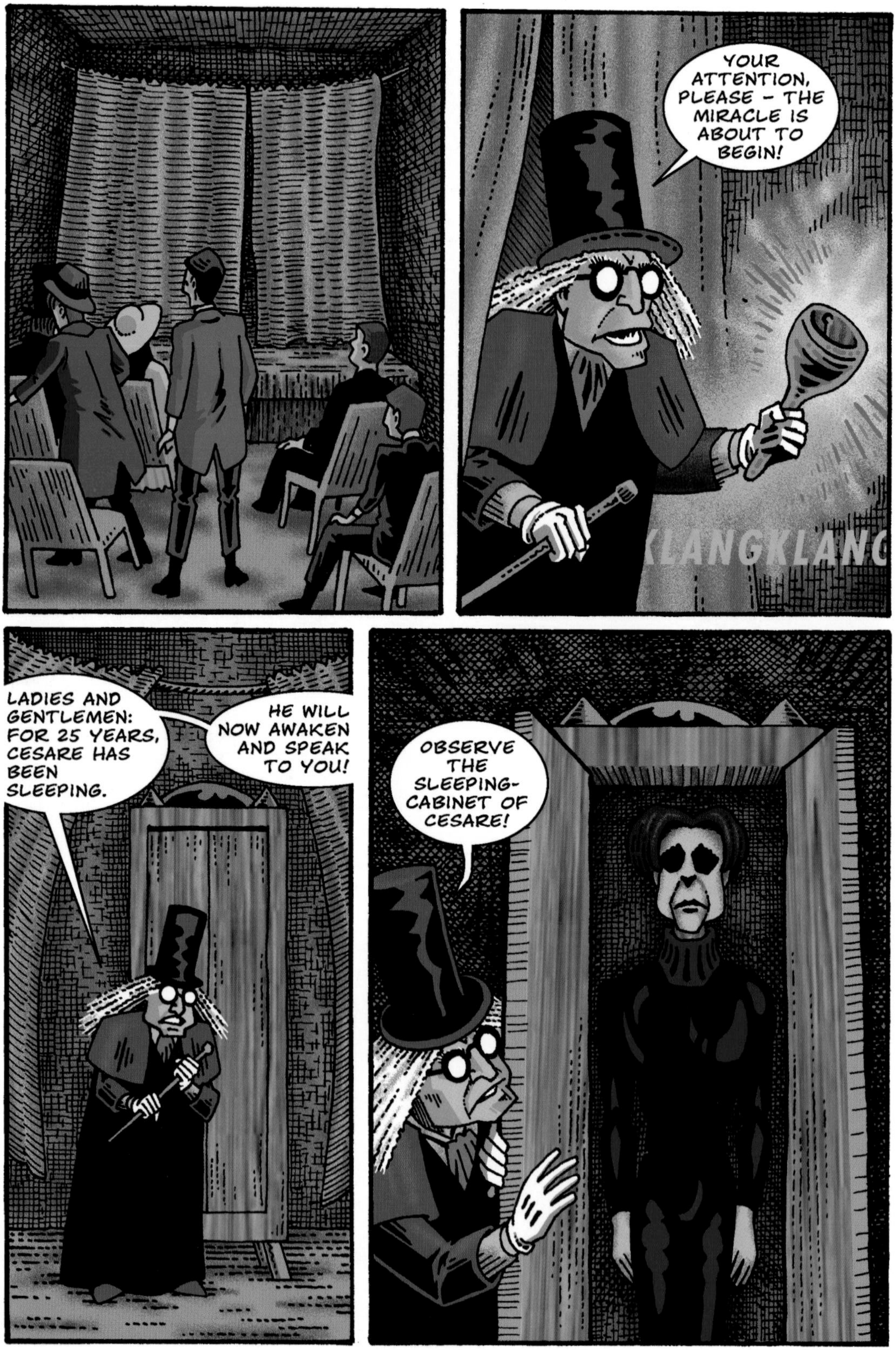
YOUR ATTENTION, PLEASE – THE MIRACLE IS ABOUT TO BEGIN!
KLANGKLANG
LADIES AND GENTLEMEN: FOR 25 YEARS, CESARE HAS BEEN SLEEPING.
HE WILL NOW AWAKEN AND SPEAK TO YOU!
OBSERVE THE SLEEPING-CABINET OF CESARE!

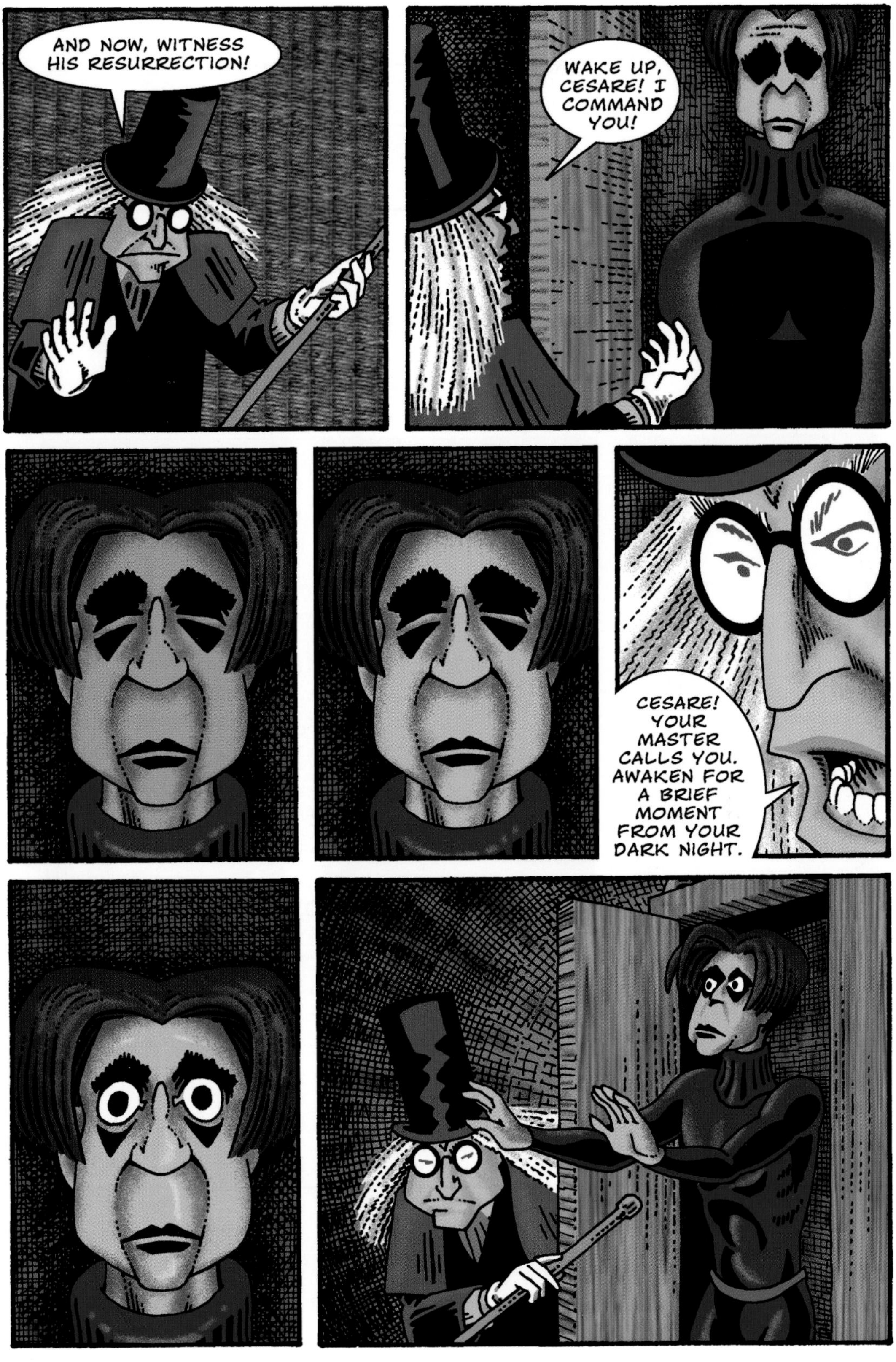
AND NOW, WITNESS HIS RESURRECTION!
WAKE UP, CESARE! I COMMAND YOU!
CESARE! YOUR MASTER CALLS YOU. AWAKEN FOR A BRIEF MOMENT FROM YOUR DARK NIGHT.

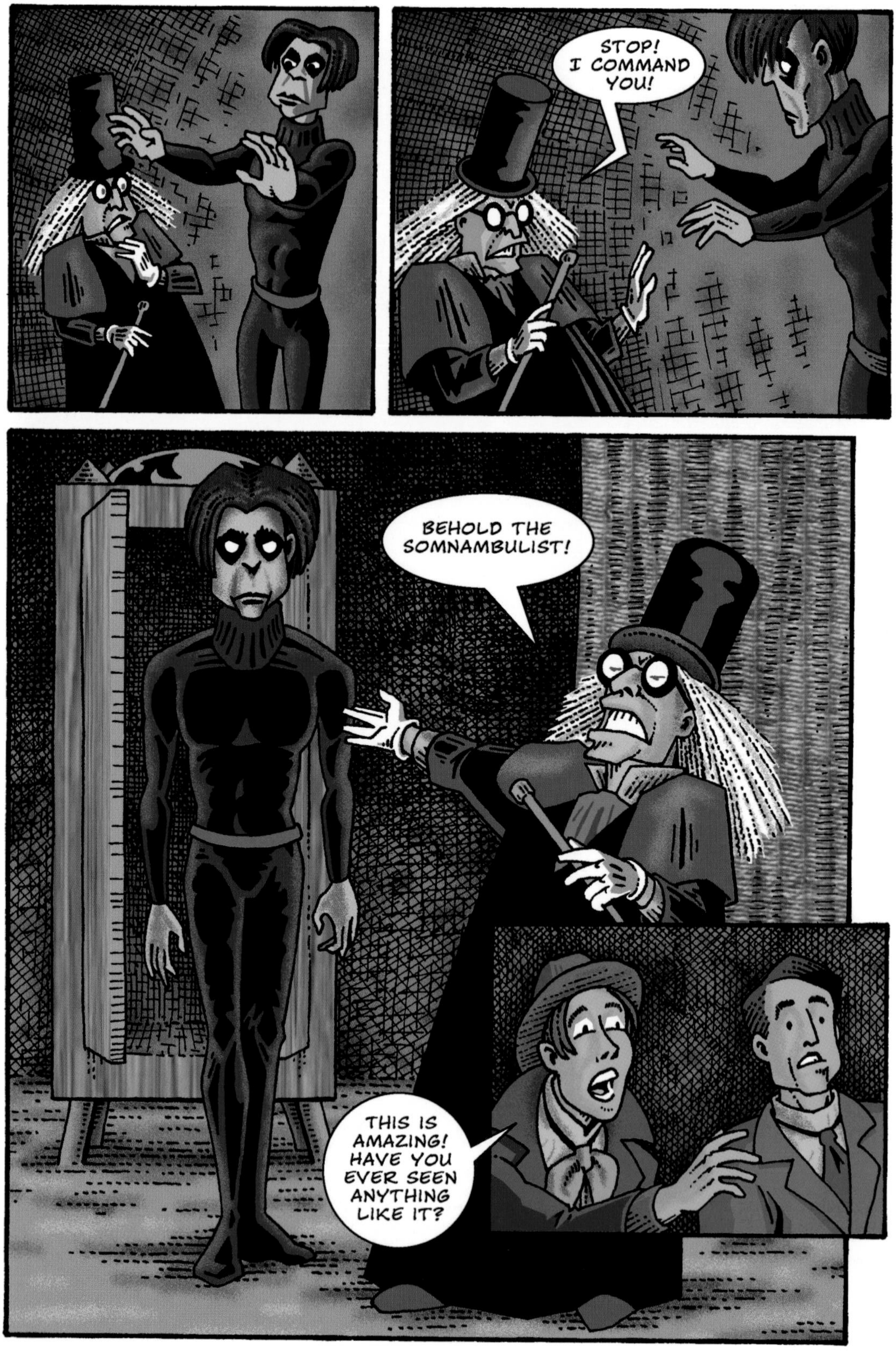
STOP! I COMMAND YOU!
BEHOLD THE SOMNAMBULIST!
THIS IS AMAZING! HAVE YOU EVER SEEN ANYTHING LIKE IT?

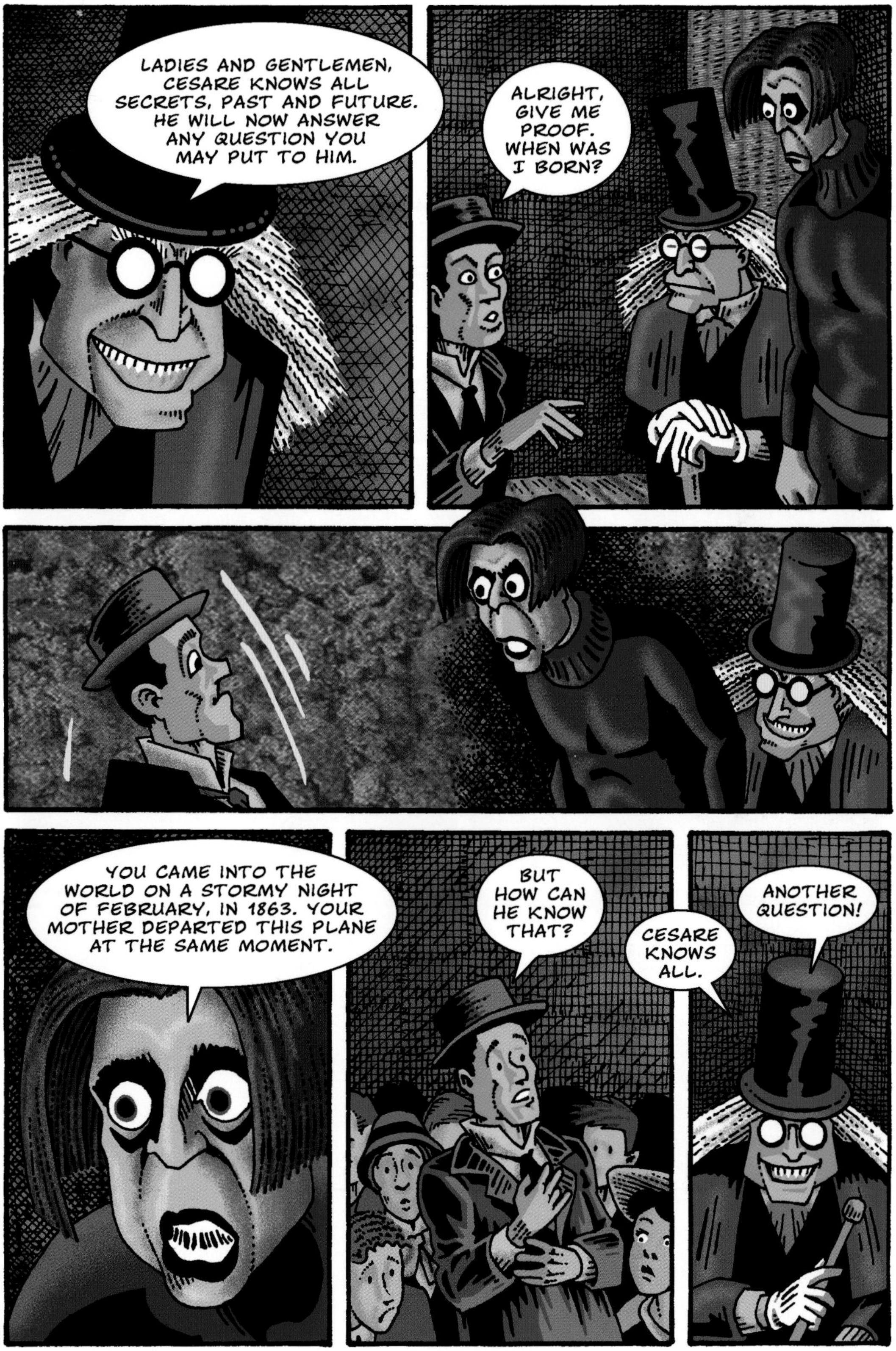
LADIES AND GENTLEMEN, CESARE KNOWS ALL SECRETS, PAST AND FUTURE. HE WILL NOW ANSWER ANY QUESTION YOU MAY PUT TO HIM.
ALRIGHT, GIVE ME PROOF. WHEN WAS I BORN?
YOU CAME INTO THE WORLD ON A STORMY NIGHT OF FEBRUARY, IN 1863. YOUR MOTHER DEPARTED THIS PLANE AT THE SAME MOMENT.
BUT HOW CAN HE KNOW THAT?
CESARE KNOWS ALL.
ANOTHER QUESTION!

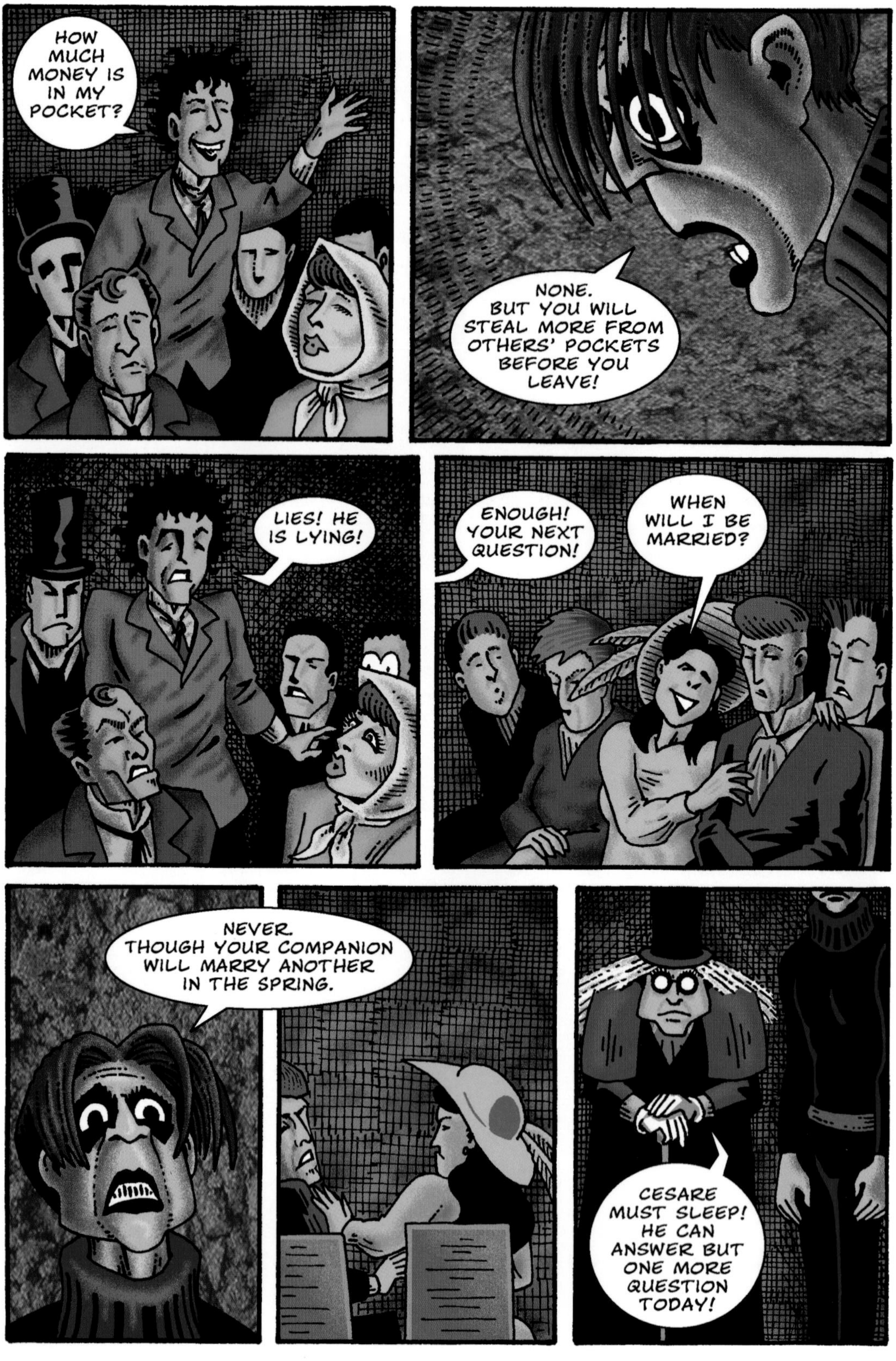
HOW MUCH MONEY IS IN MY POCKET?
NONE. BUT YOU WILL STEAL MORE FROM OTHERS' POCKETS BEFORE YOU LEAVE!
LIES! HE IS LYING!
ENOUGH! YOUR NEXT QUESTION!
WHEN WILL I BE MARRIED?
NEVER. THOUGH YOUR COMPANION WILL MARRY ANOTHER IN THE SPRING.
CESARE MUST SLEEP! HE CAN ANSWER BUT ONE MORE QUESTION TODAY!

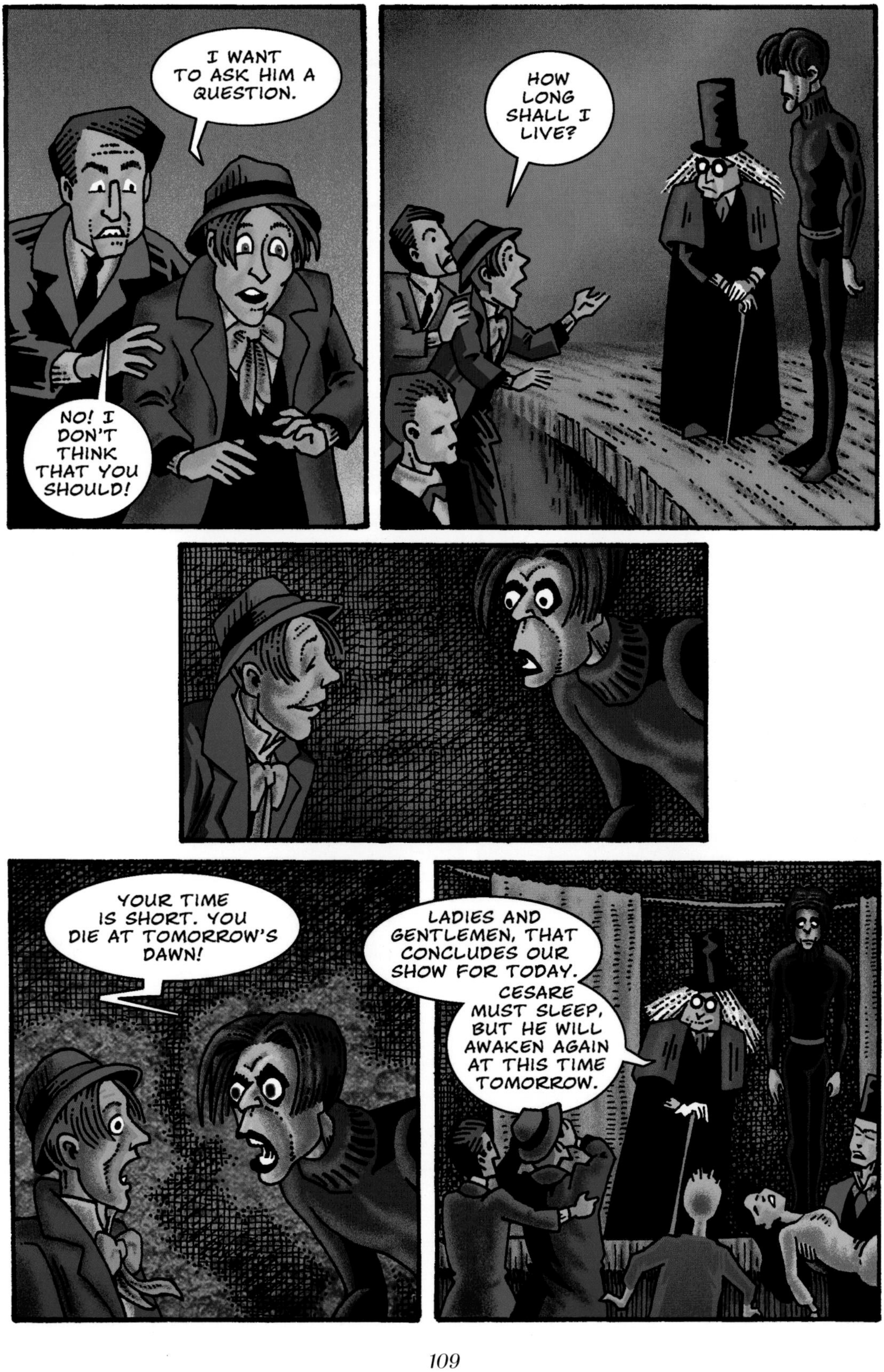
I WANT TO ASK HIM A QUESTION.
NO! I DON'T THINK THAT YOU SHOULD!
HOW LONG SHALL I LIVE?
YOUR TIME IS SHORT. YOU DIE AT TOMORROW'S DAWN!
LADIES AND GENTLEMEN, THAT CONCLUDES OUR SHOW FOR TODAY.
CESARE MUST SLEEP, BUT HE WILL AWAKEN AGAIN AT THIS TIME TOMORROW.

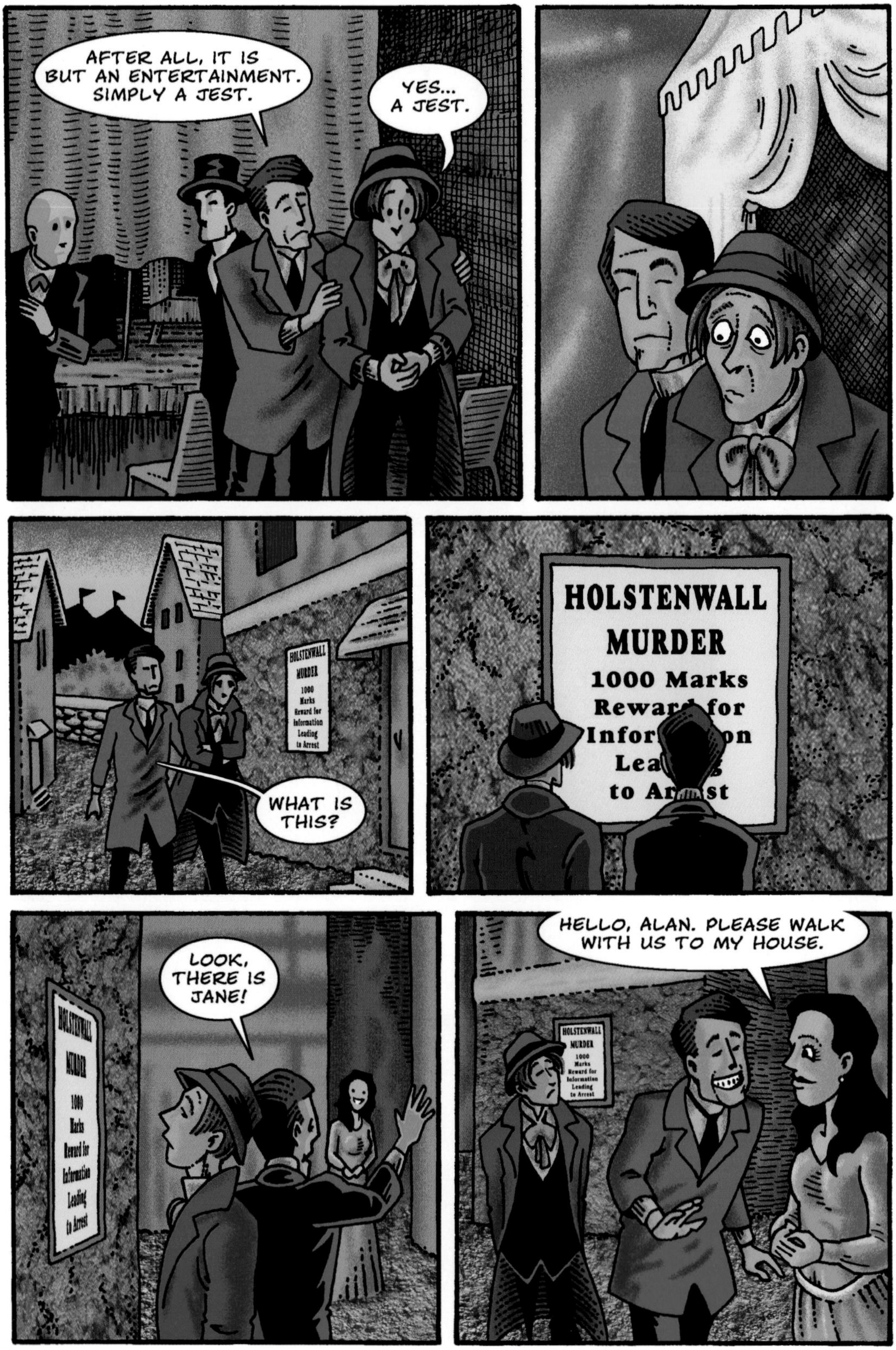
AFTER ALL, IT IS BUT AN ENTERTAINMENT. SIMPLY A JEST.
YES... A JEST.
HOLSTENWALL MURDER 1000 Reward for Information Leading to Arrest
WHAT IS THIS?
HOLSTENWALL MURDER
1000 Marks
LOOK, THERE IS JANE!
HOLSTENWALL MURDER 1000 Marks Reward for Information Leading to Arrest
HELLO, ALAN. PLEASE WALK WITH US TO MY HOUSE.
HOLSTENWALL MURDER 1000 Marks Reward for Information Leading to Arrest

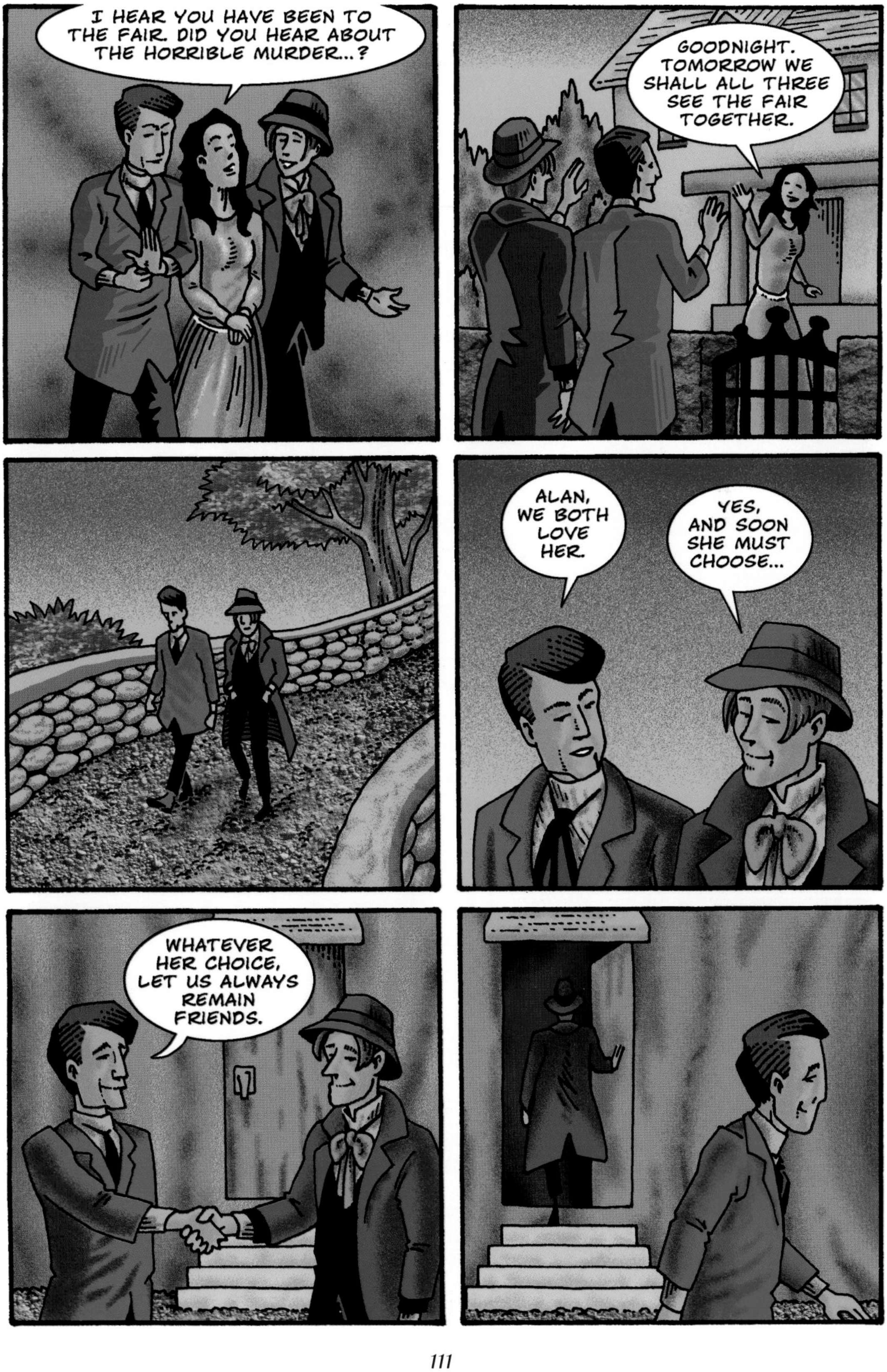
I HEAR YOU HAVE BEEN TO THE FAIR. DID YOU HEAR ABOUT THE HORRIBLE MURDER...?
GOODNIGHT. TOMORROW WE SHALL ALL THREE SEE THE FAIR TOGETHER.
ALAN, WE BOTH LOVE HER.
YES, AND SOON SHE MUST CHOOSE...
WHATEVER HER CHOICE, LET US ALWAYS REMAIN FRIENDS.

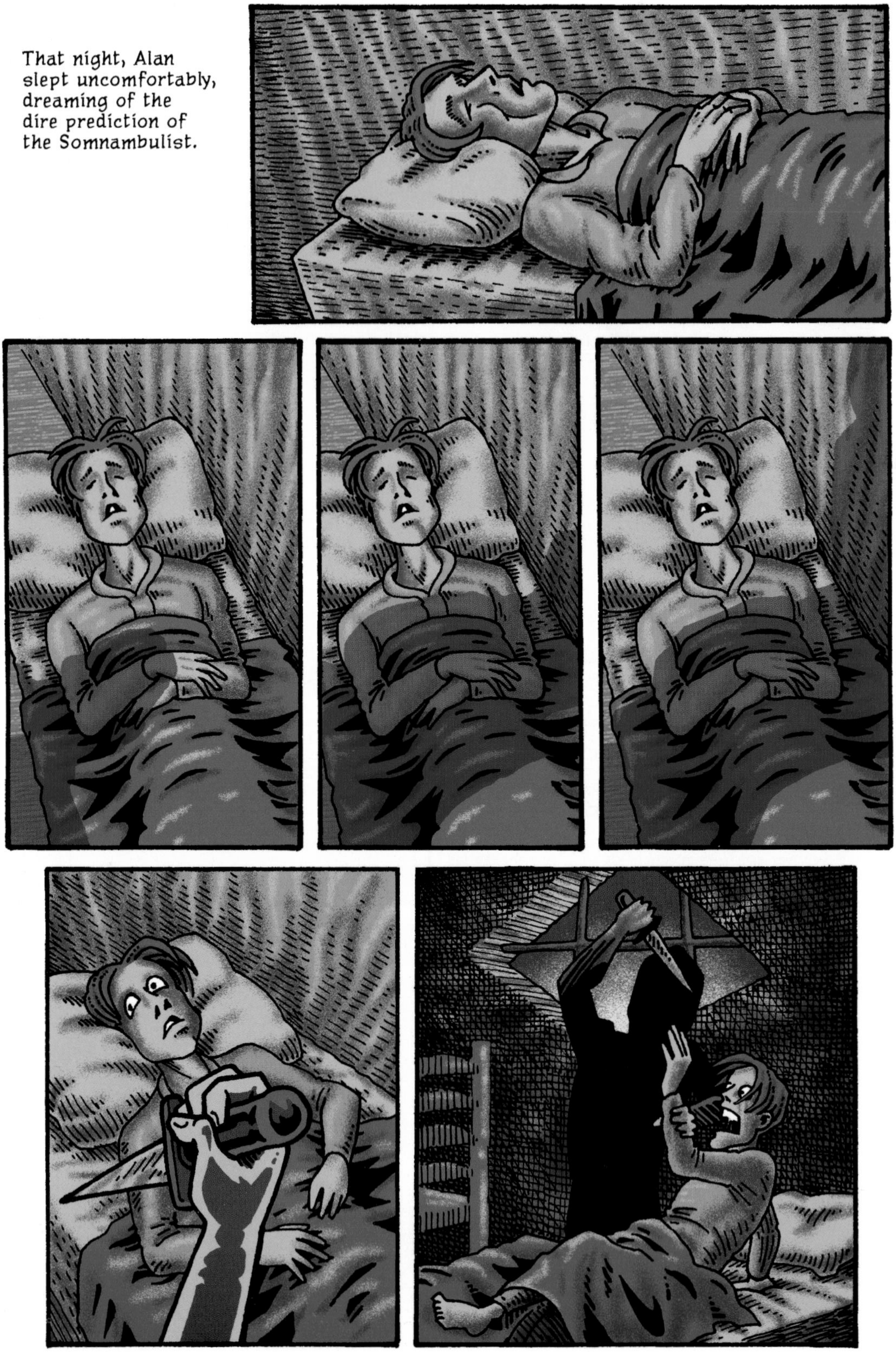
That night, Alan slept uncomfortably, dreaming of the dire prediction of the Somnambulist.

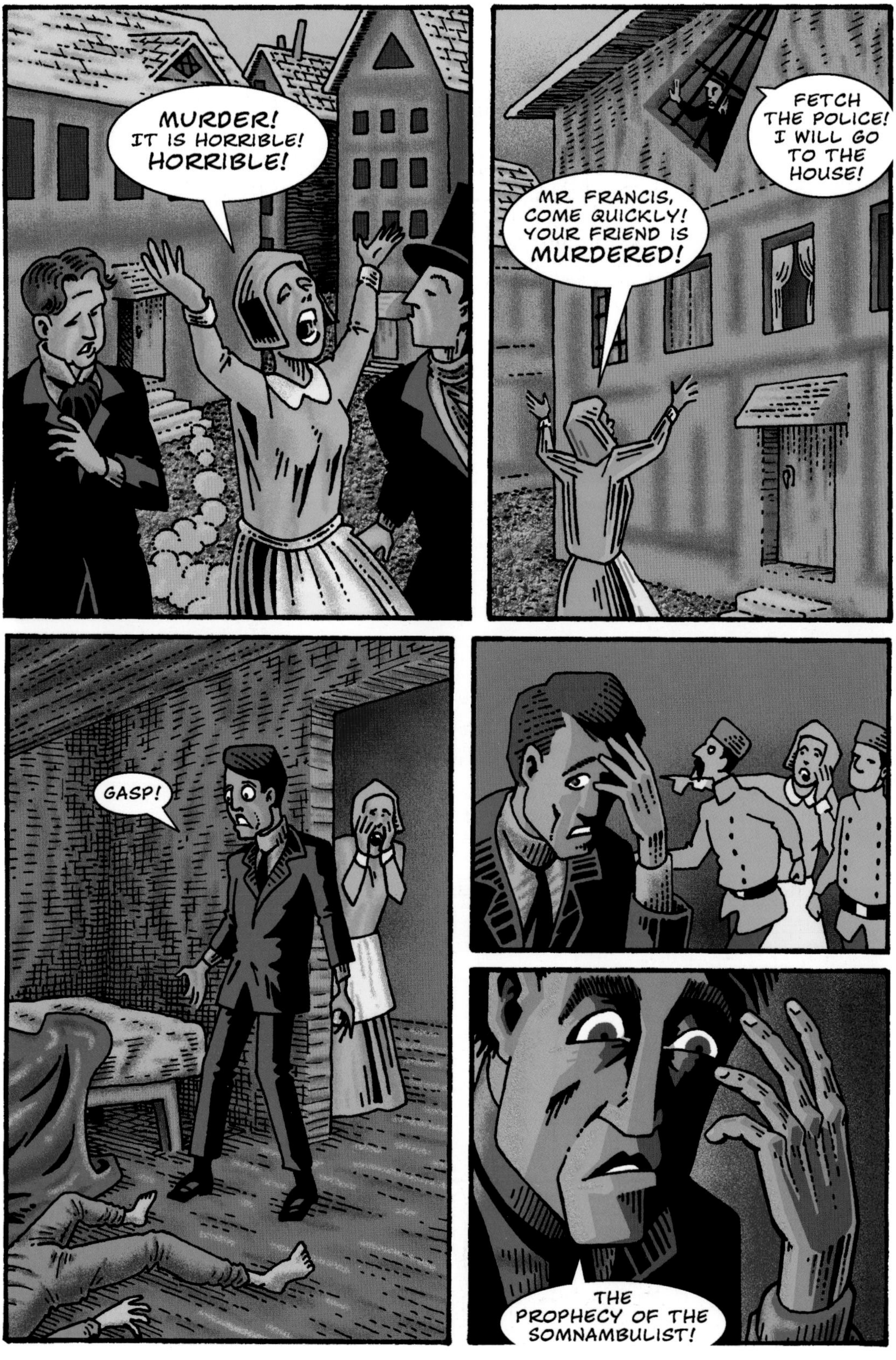
MURDER! IT IS HORRIBLE! HORRIBLE!
FETCH THE POLICE! I WILL GO TO THE HOUSE!
MR. FRANCIS, COME QUICKLY! YOUR FRIEND IS MURDERED!
GASP!
THE PROPHECY OF THE SOMNAMBULIST!

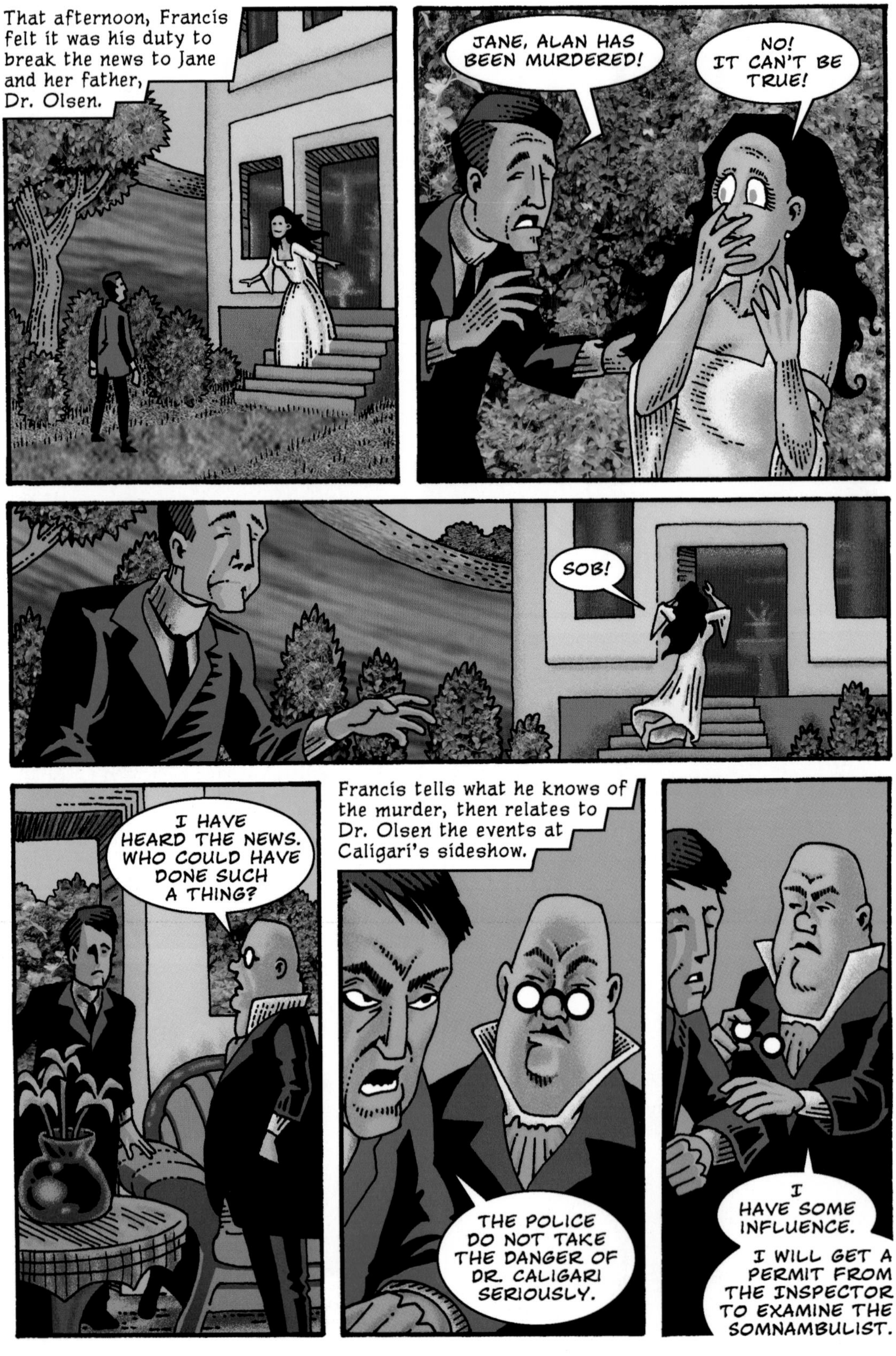
That afternoon, Francis felt it was his duty to break the news to Jane and her father, Dr. Olsen.
JANE, ALAN HAS BEEN MURDERED!
NO! IT CAN'T BE TRUE!
SOB!
I HAVE HEARD THE NEWS. WHO COULD HAVE DONE SUCH A THING?
Francis tells what he knows of the murder, then relates to Dr. Olsen the events at Caligari's sideshow.
THE POLICE DO NOT TAKE THE DANGER OF DR. CALIGARI SERIOUSLY.
I HAVE SOME INFLUENCE.
I WILL GET A PERMIT FROM THE INSPECTOR TO EXAMINE THE SOMNAMBULIST.

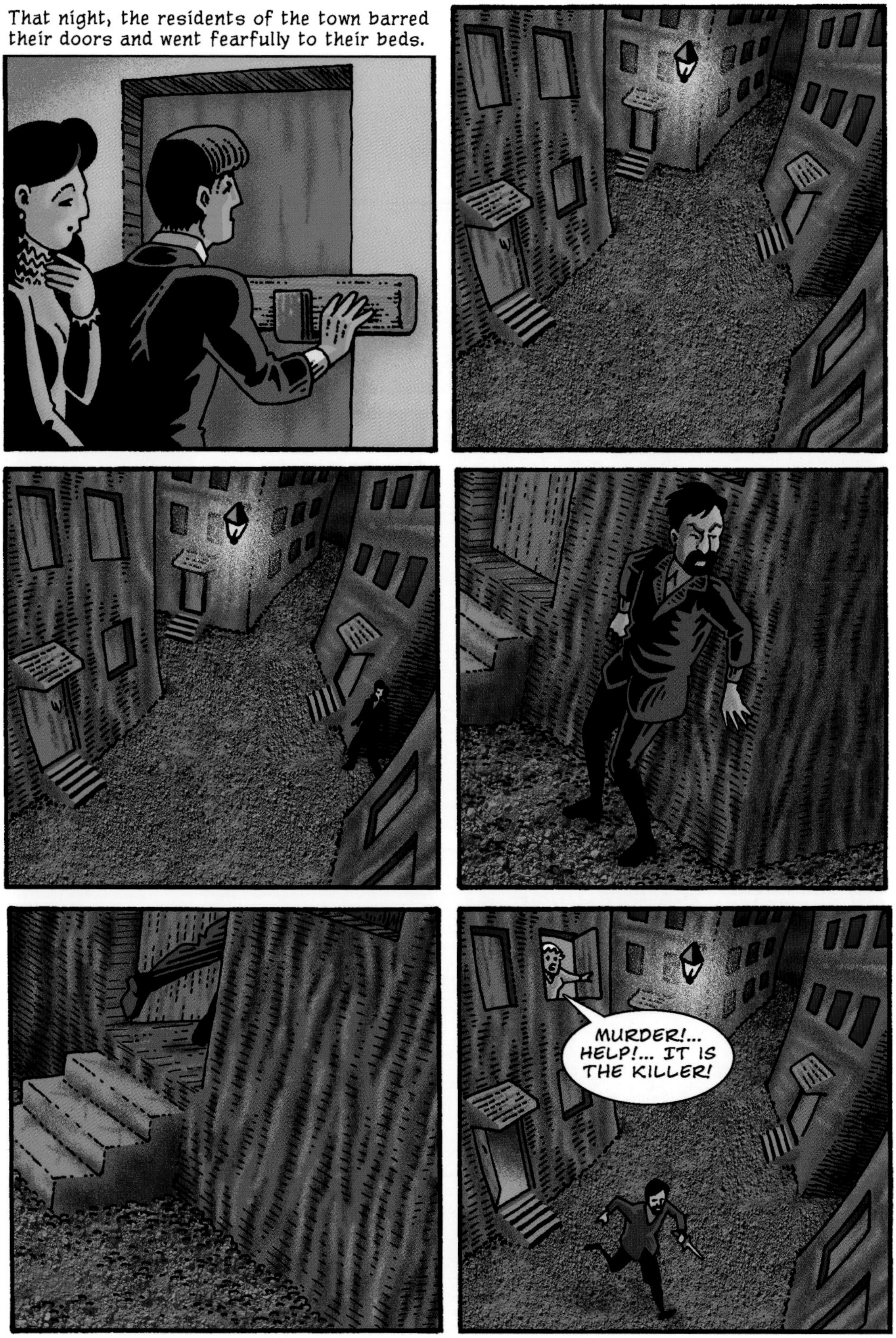
That night, the residents of the town barred their doors and went fearfully to their beds.
MURDER!... HELP!... IT IS THE KILLER!

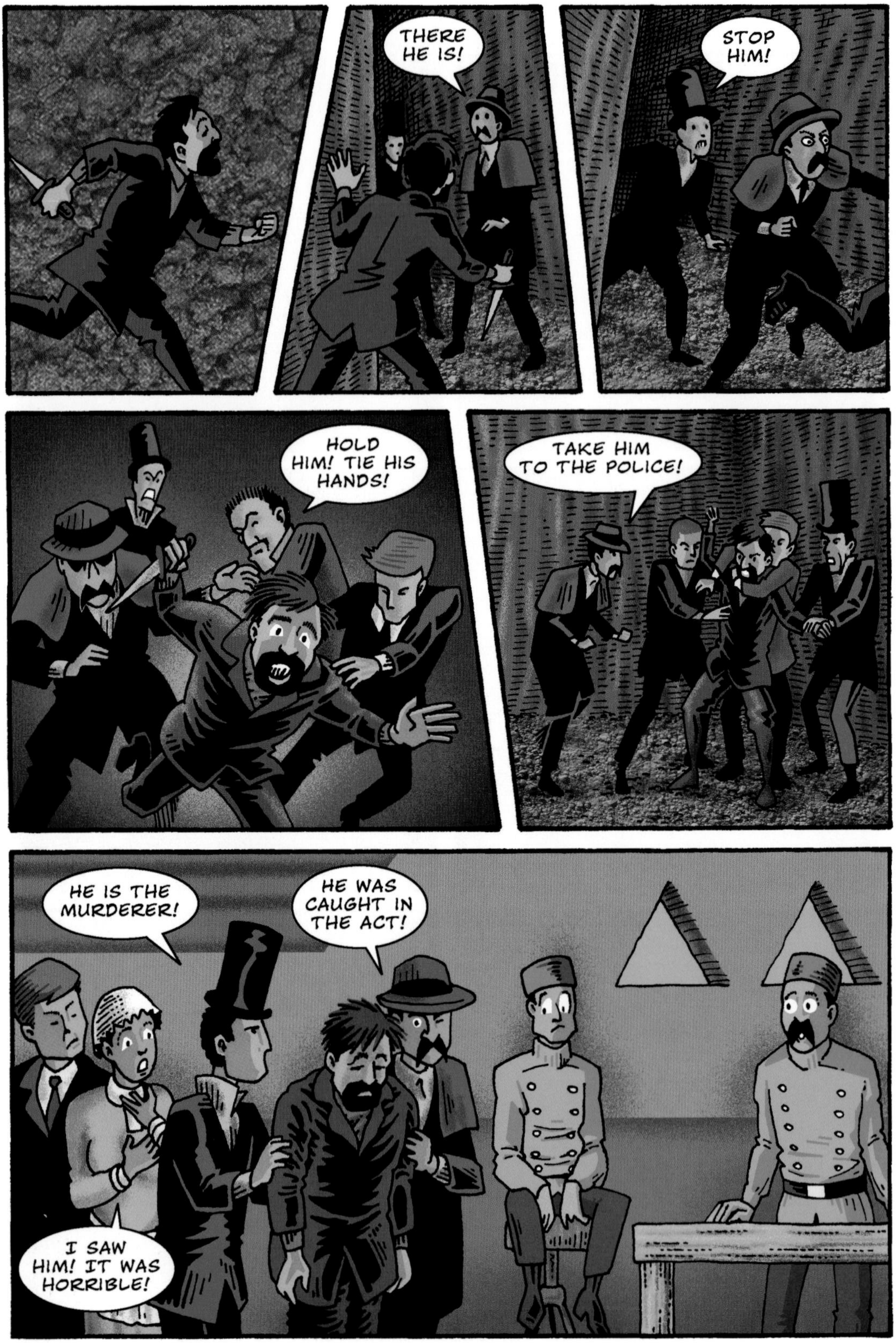
THERE HE IS!
STOP HIM!
HOLD HIM! TIE HIS HANDS!
TAKE HIM TO THE POLICE!
HE IS THE MURDERER!
HE WAS CAUGHT IN THE ACT!
I SAW HIM! IT WAS HORRIBLE!

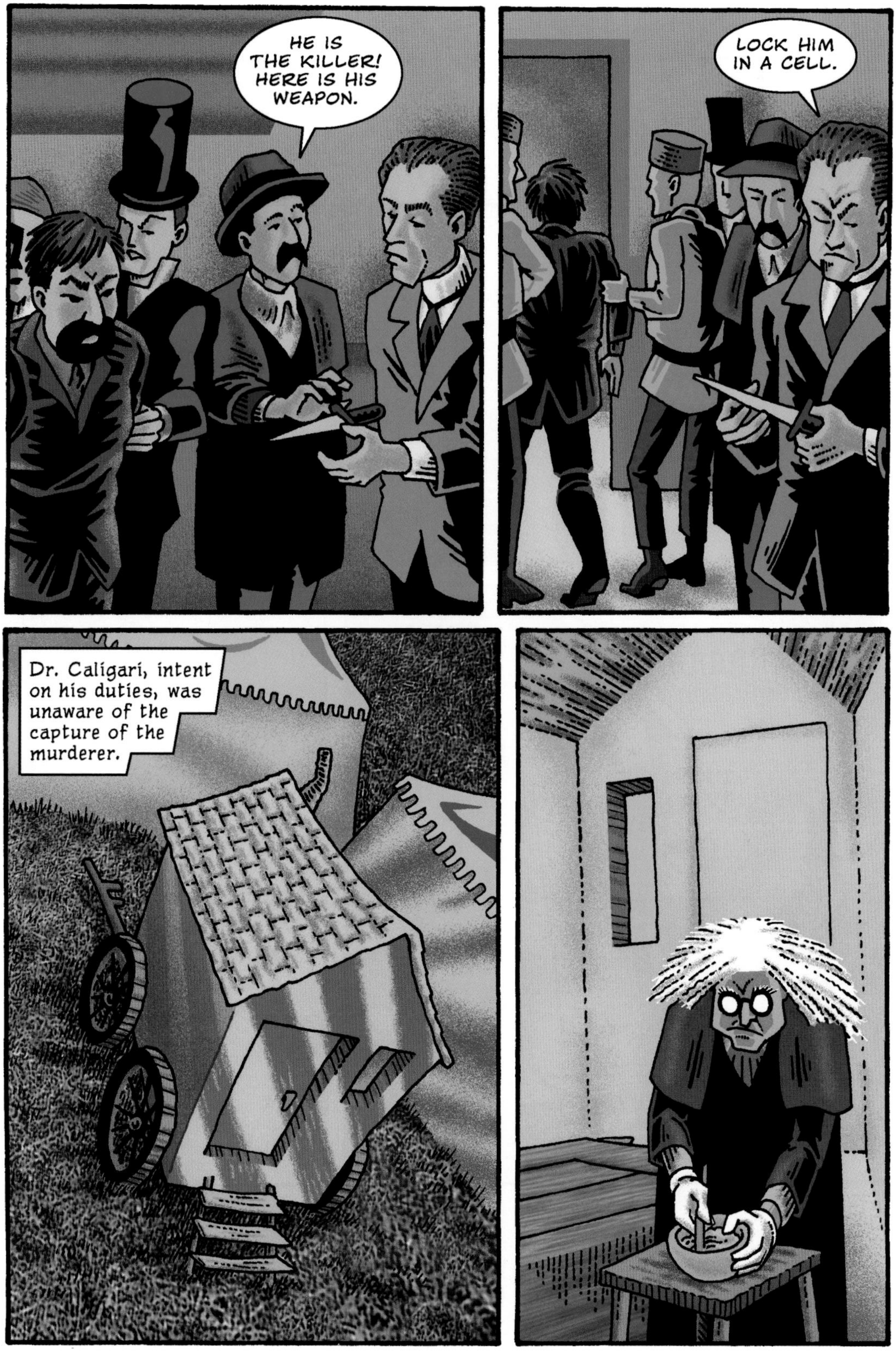
HE IS THE KILLER! HERE IS HIS WEAPON.
LOCK HIM IN A CELL.
Dr. Caligari, intent on his duties, was unaware of the capture of the murderer.

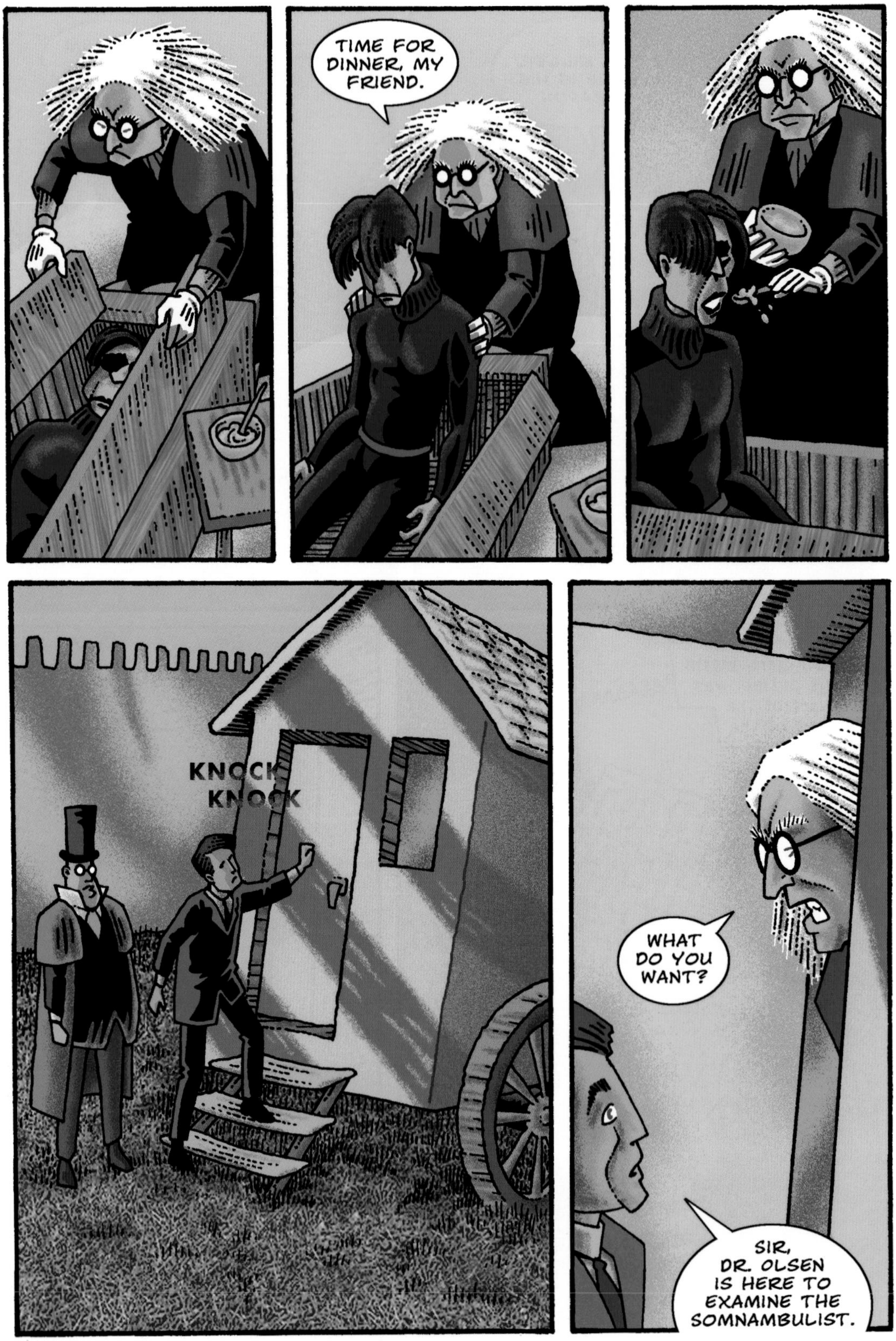
TIME FOR DINNER, MY FRIEND.
KNOCK KNOCK
WHAT DO YOU WANT?
SIR, DR. OLSEN IS HERE TO EXAMINE THE SOMNAMBULIST.

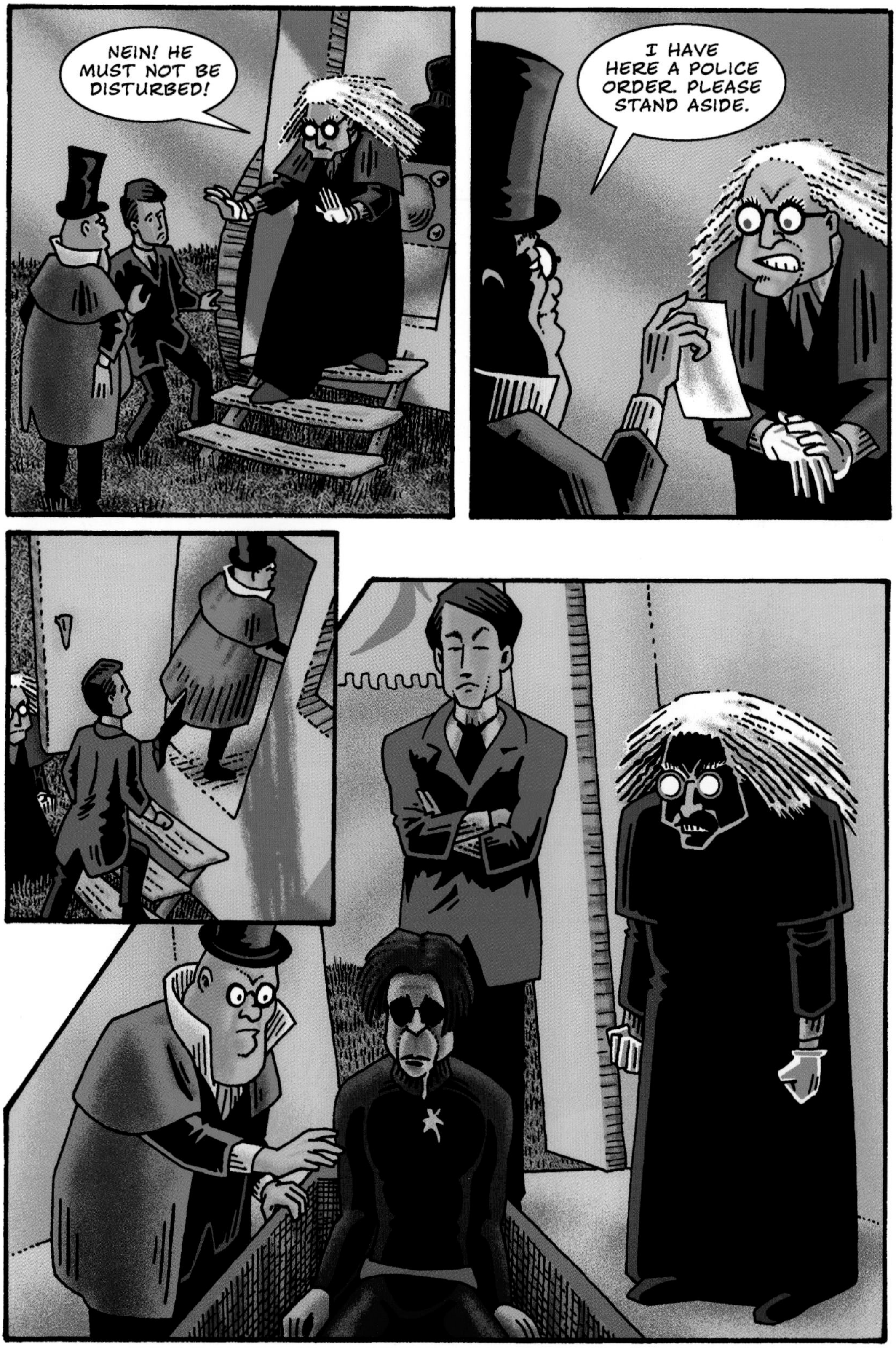
NEIN! HE MUST NOT BE DISTURBED!
I HAVE HERE A POLICE ORDER. PLEASE STAND ASIDE.

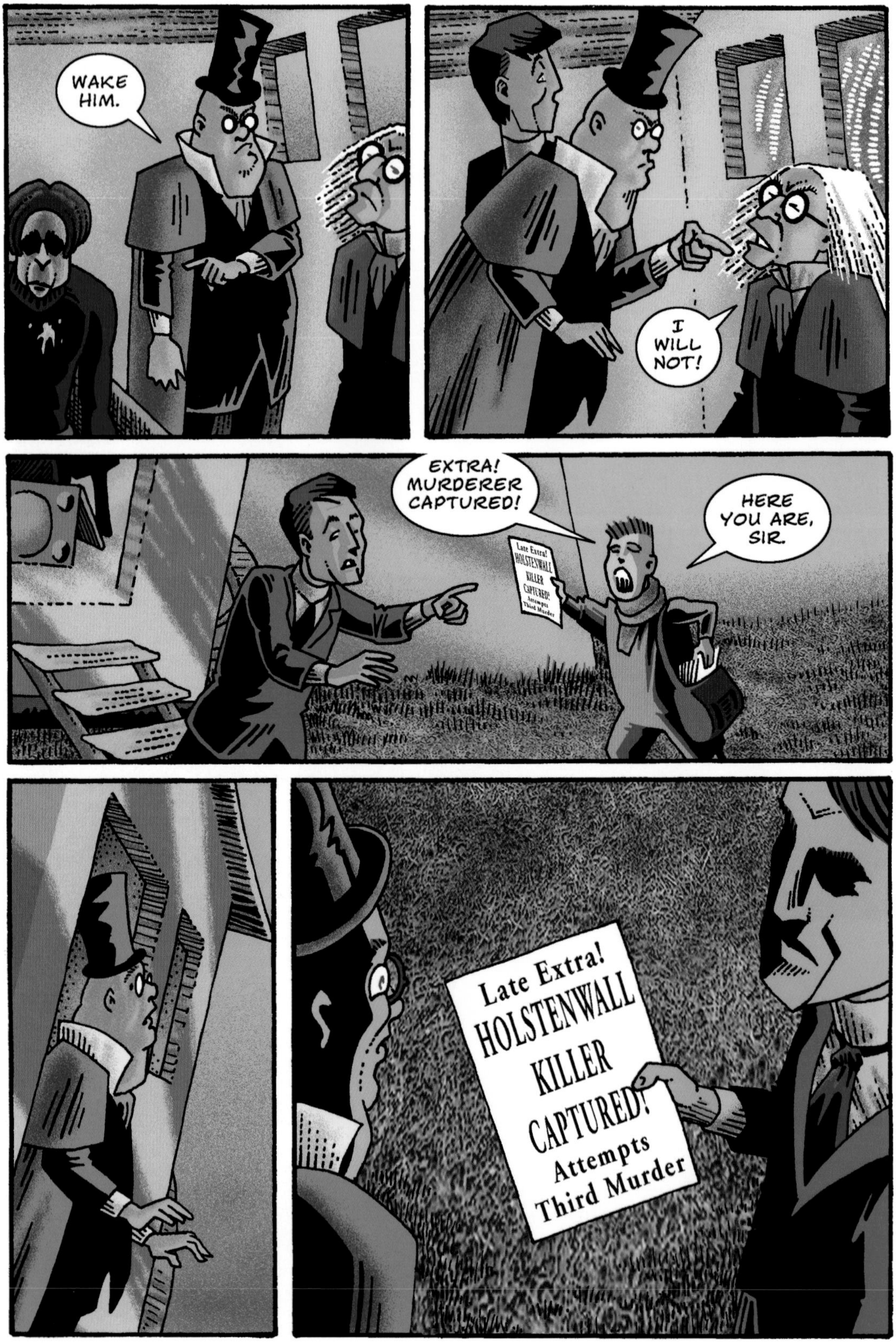
WAKE HIM.
I WILL NOT!
EXTRA! MURDERER CAPTURED!
Late Extra! HOLSTENWALL KILLER CAPTURED! Attempts Third Murder
HERE YOU ARE, SIR.
Late Extra!
HOLSTENWALL
KILLER
CAPTURED!
Attempts
Third Murder

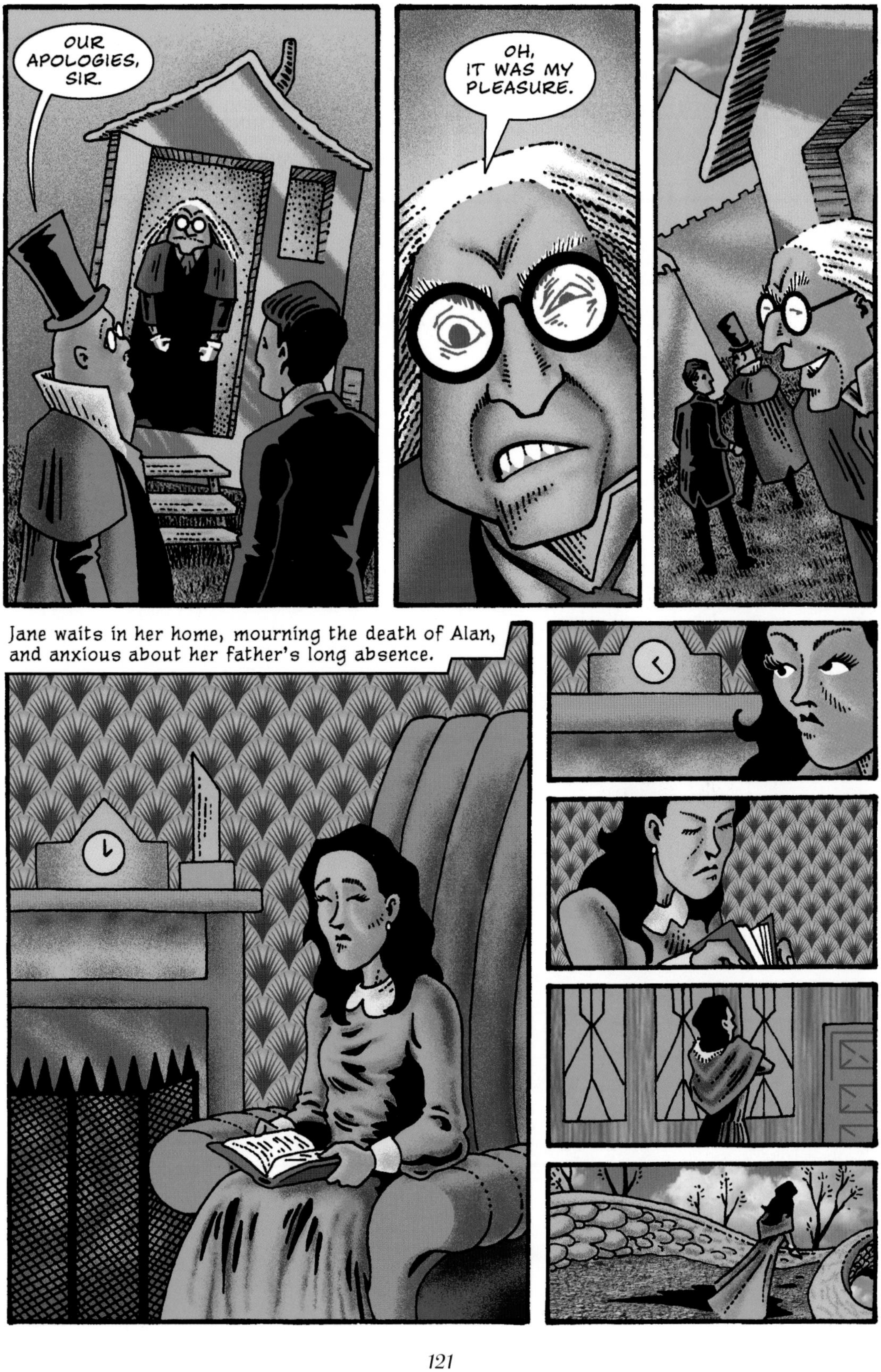
OUR APOLOGIES, SIR.
OH, IT WAS MY PLEASURE.
Jane waits in her home, mourning the death of Alan, and anxious about her father's long absence.

I AM HERE TO SEE THE INSPECTOR.

I ADMIT IT — I KILLED THE OLD WOMAN FOR HER MONEY. BUT I HAD NOTHING TO DO WITH THE FIRST TWO MURDERS, SO HELP ME GOD.

I HEAR YOU HAVE CAPTURED THE MURDERER.

YES, AND AFTER YOU NEARLY HAD ME CONVINCED IT WAS THAT SIDESHOW FREAK.

WOULD YOU LIKE TO SEE THE MAN?

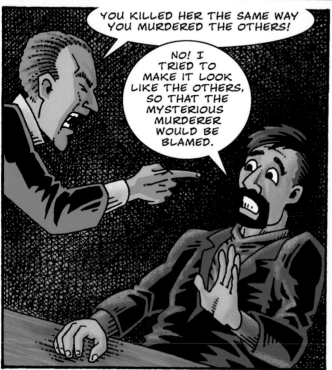

YOU KILLED HER THE SAME WAY YOU MURDERED THE OTHERS!

NO! I TRIED TO MAKE IT LOOK LIKE THE OTHERS, SO THAT THE MYSTERIOUS MURDERER WOULD BE BLAMED.

BAH! HE'S LYING! TAKE HIM AWAY!

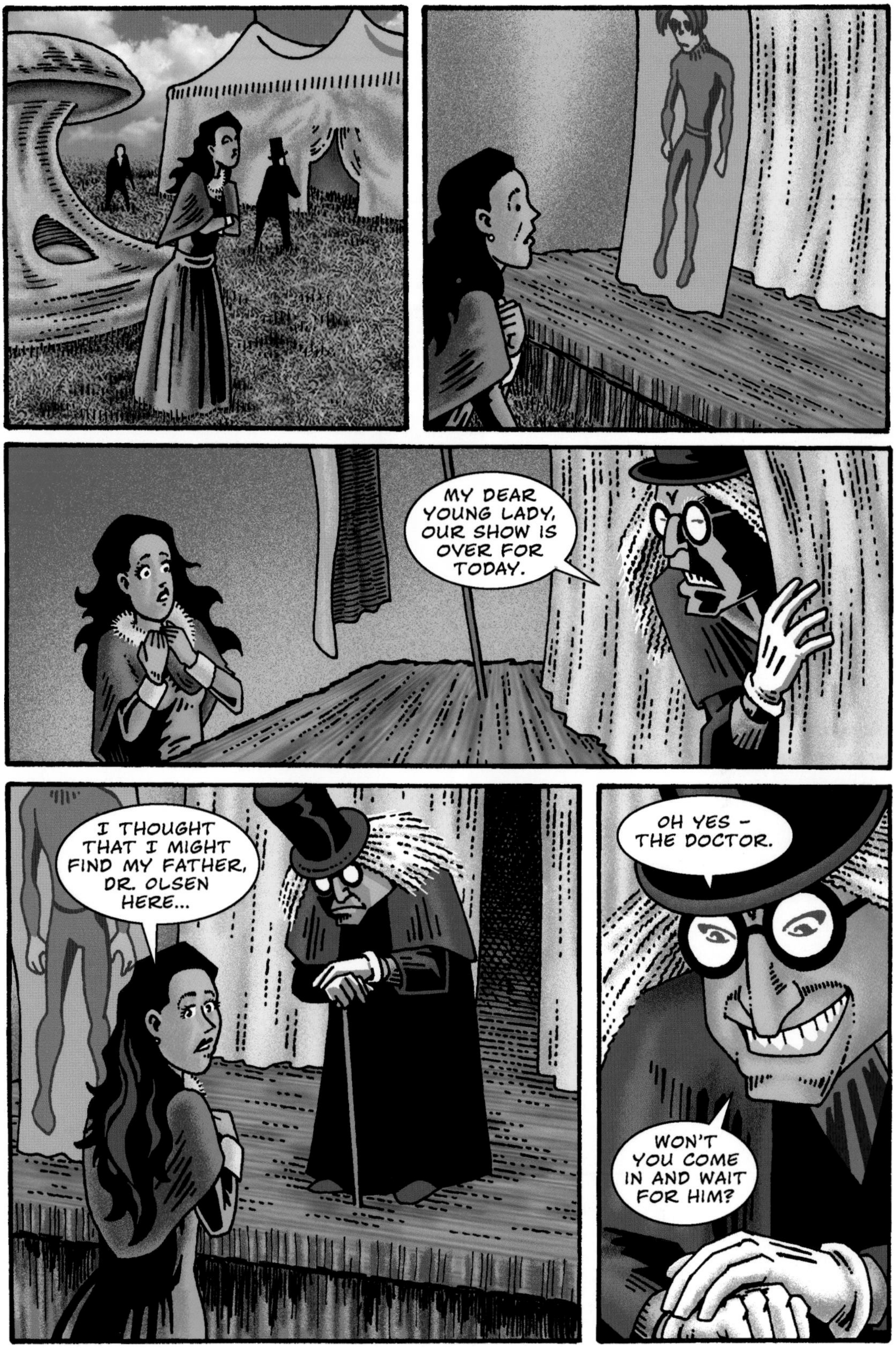
MY DEAR YOUNG LADY, OUR SHOW IS OVER FOR TODAY.
I THOUGHT THAT I MIGHT FIND MY FATHER, DR. OLSEN HERE...
OH YES - THE DOCTOR.
WON'T YOU COME IN AND WAIT FOR HIM?

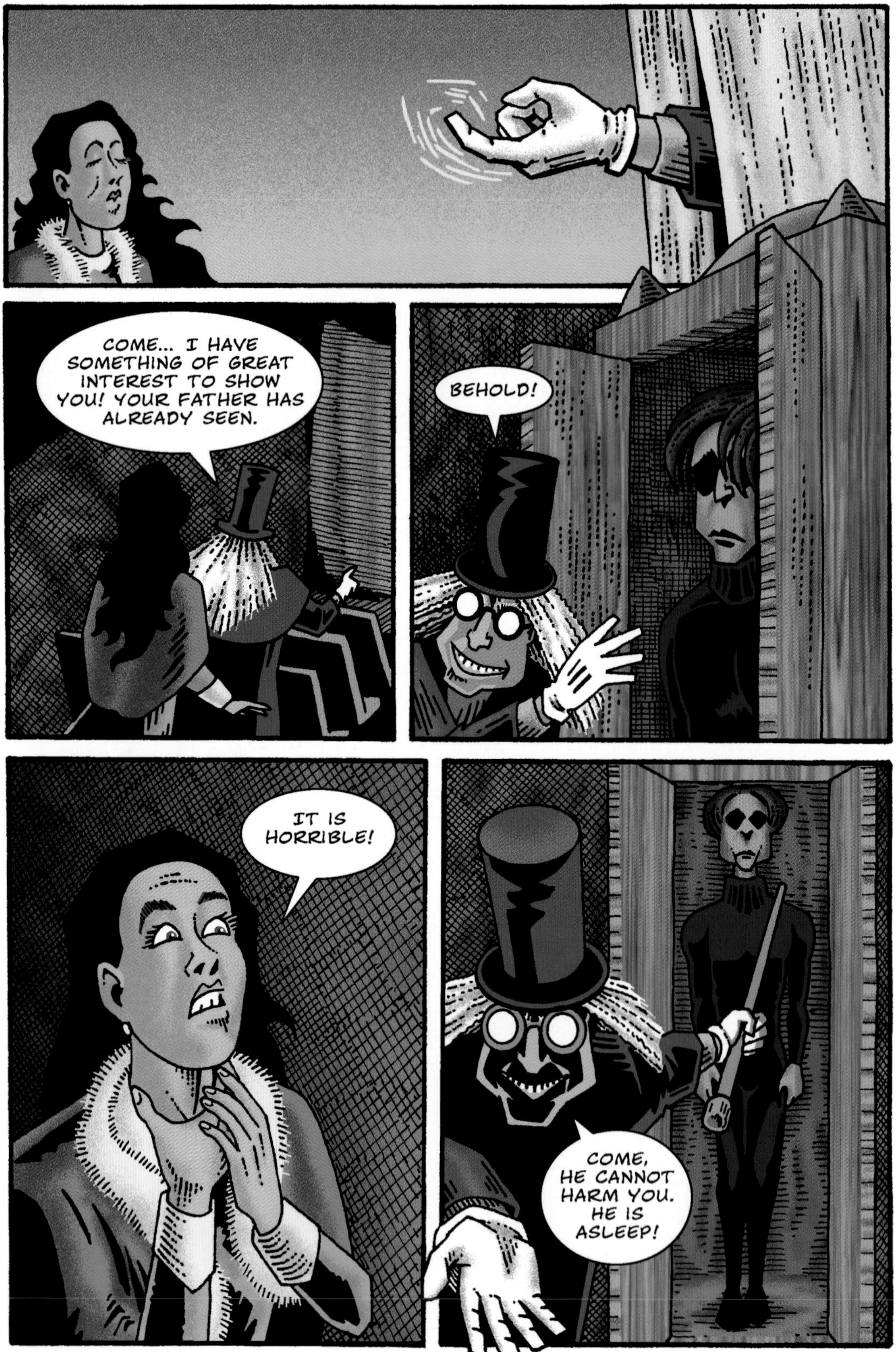
COME... I HAVE SOMETHING OF GREAT INTEREST TO SHOW YOU! YOUR FATHER HAS ALREADY SEEN.
BEHOLD!
IT IS HORRIBLE!
COME, HE CANNOT HARM YOU. HE IS ASLEEP!

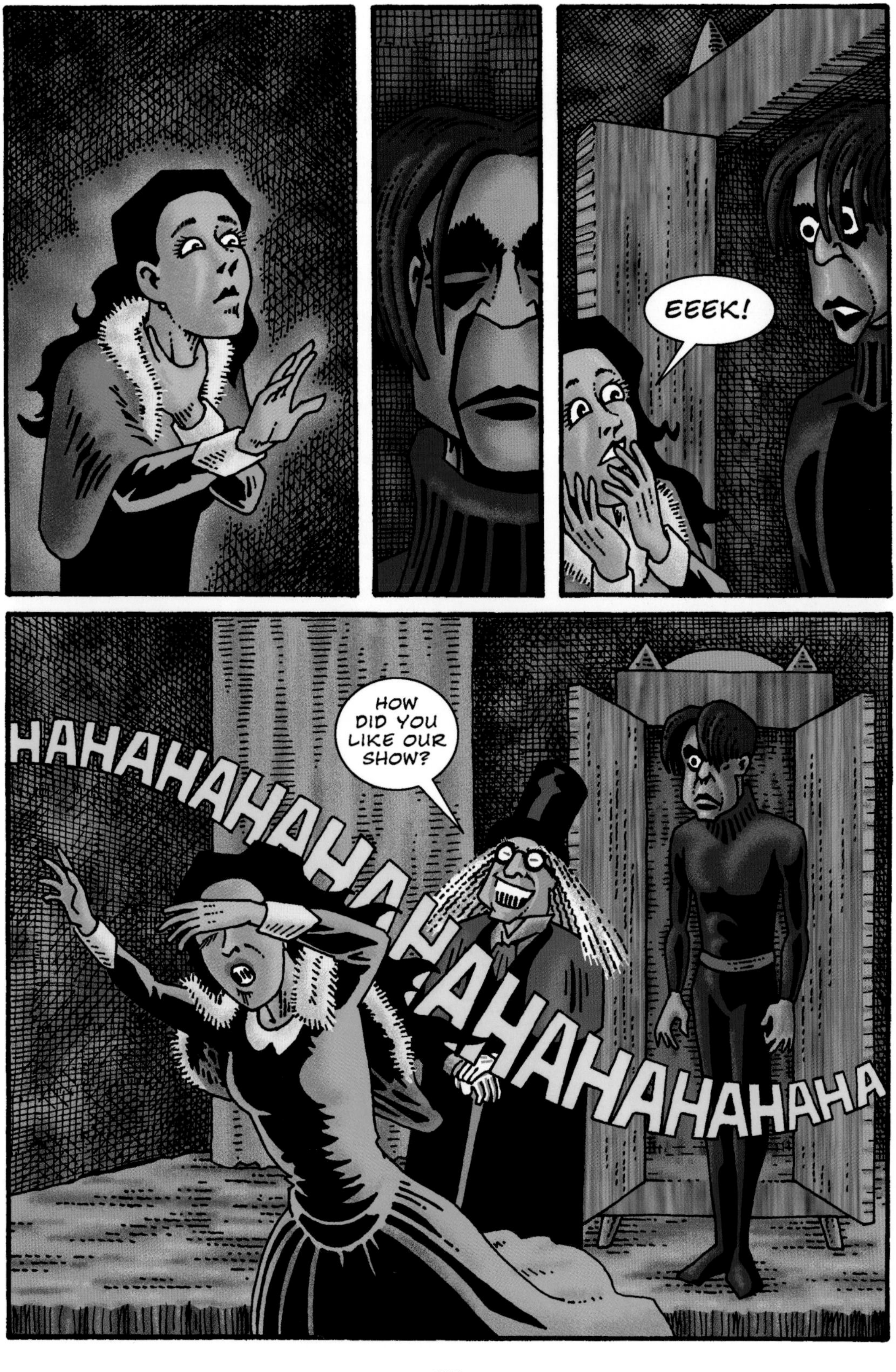
EEEK!
HOW DID YOU LIKE OUR SHOW?
HAHAHAHAHAHAHAHAHAHAHAHAHA

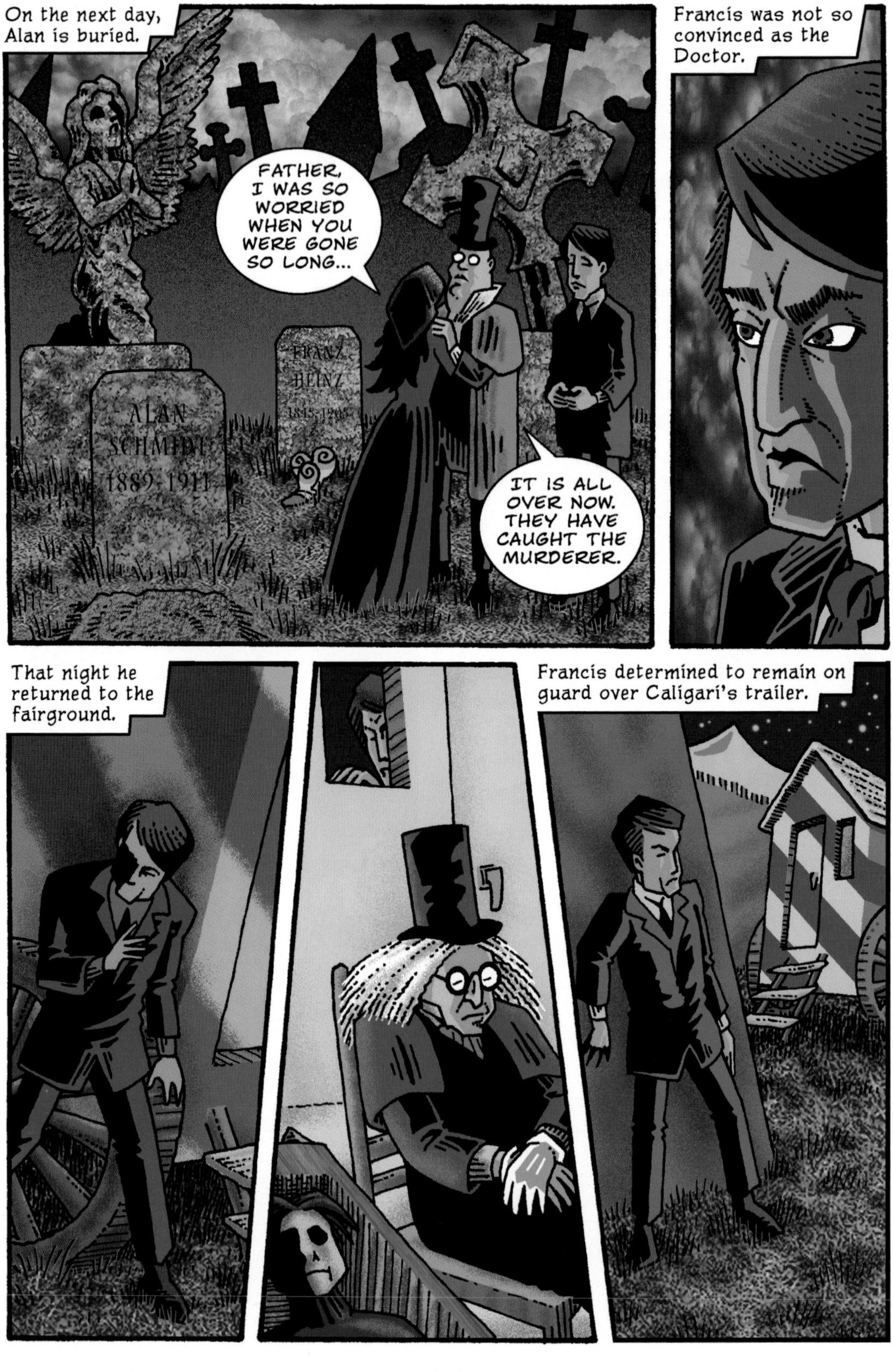
On the next day, Alan is buried.
FATHER, I WAS SO WORRIED WHEN YOU WERE GONE SO LONG...
IT IS ALL OVER NOW. THEY HAVE CAUGHT THE MURDERER.
ALAN SCHMIDT 1889-1911
FRANZ HEINZ 1845-1908
Francis was not so convinced as the Doctor.
That night he returned to the fairground.
Francis determined to remain on guard over Caligari's trailer.

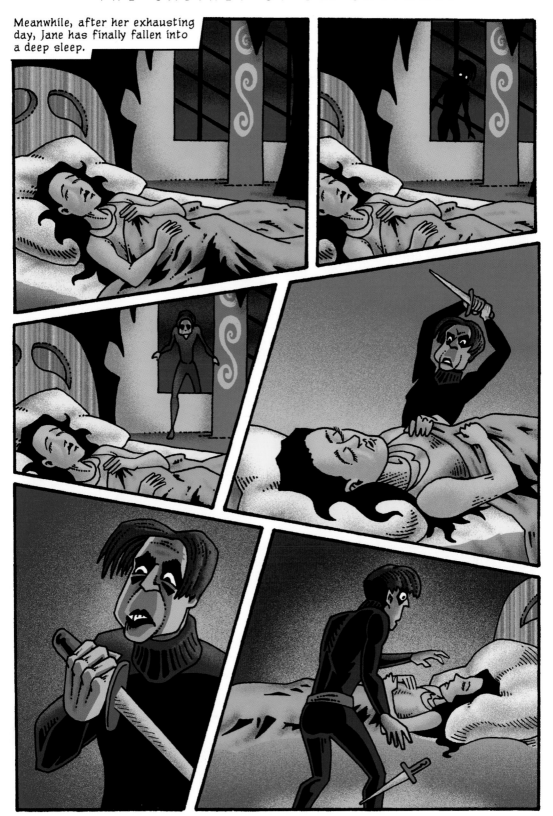

Meanwhile, after her exhausting day, Jane has finally fallen into a deep sleep.

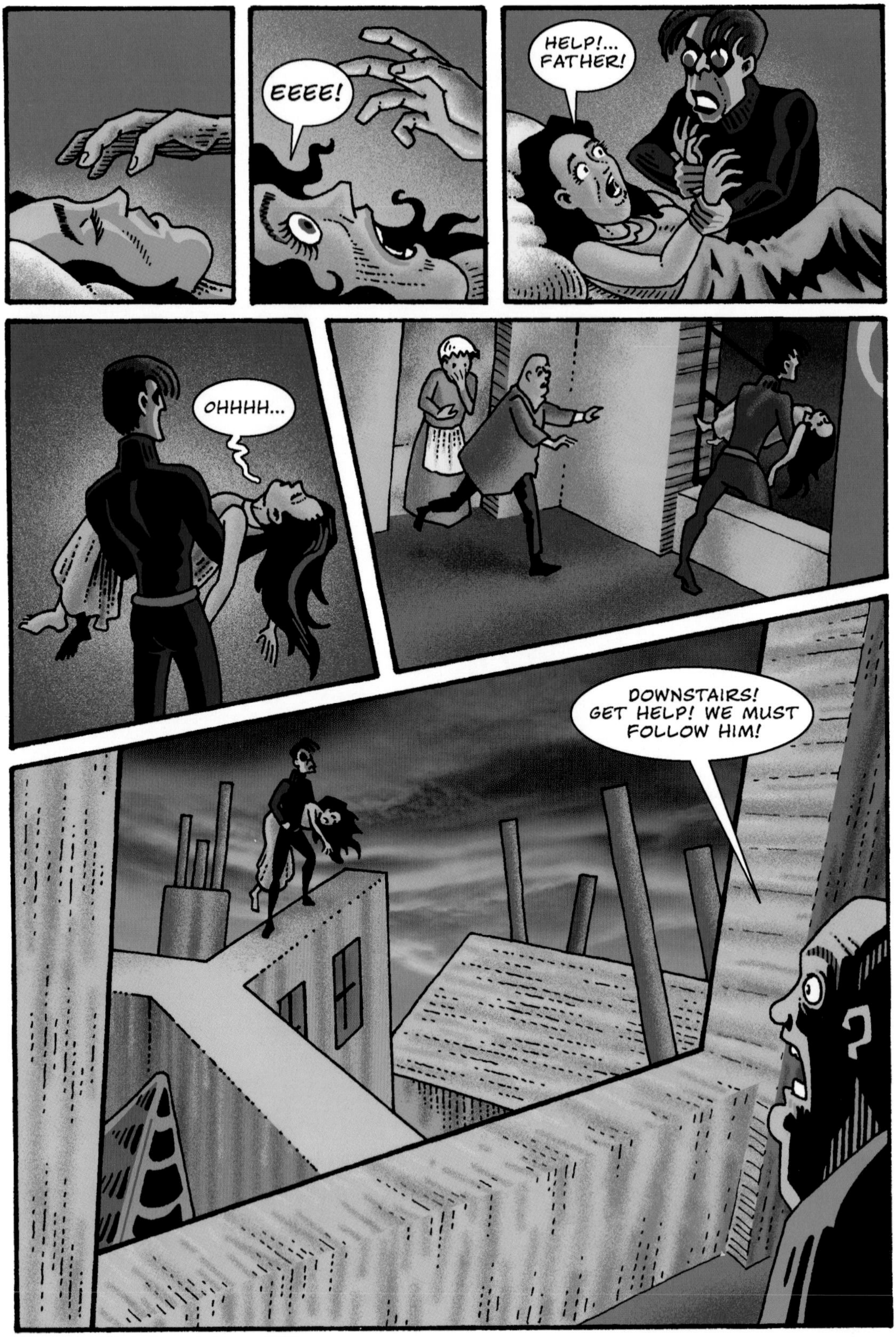
EEEE!
HELP!... FATHER!
OHHHH...
DOWNSTAIRS! GET HELP! WE MUST FOLLOW HIM!

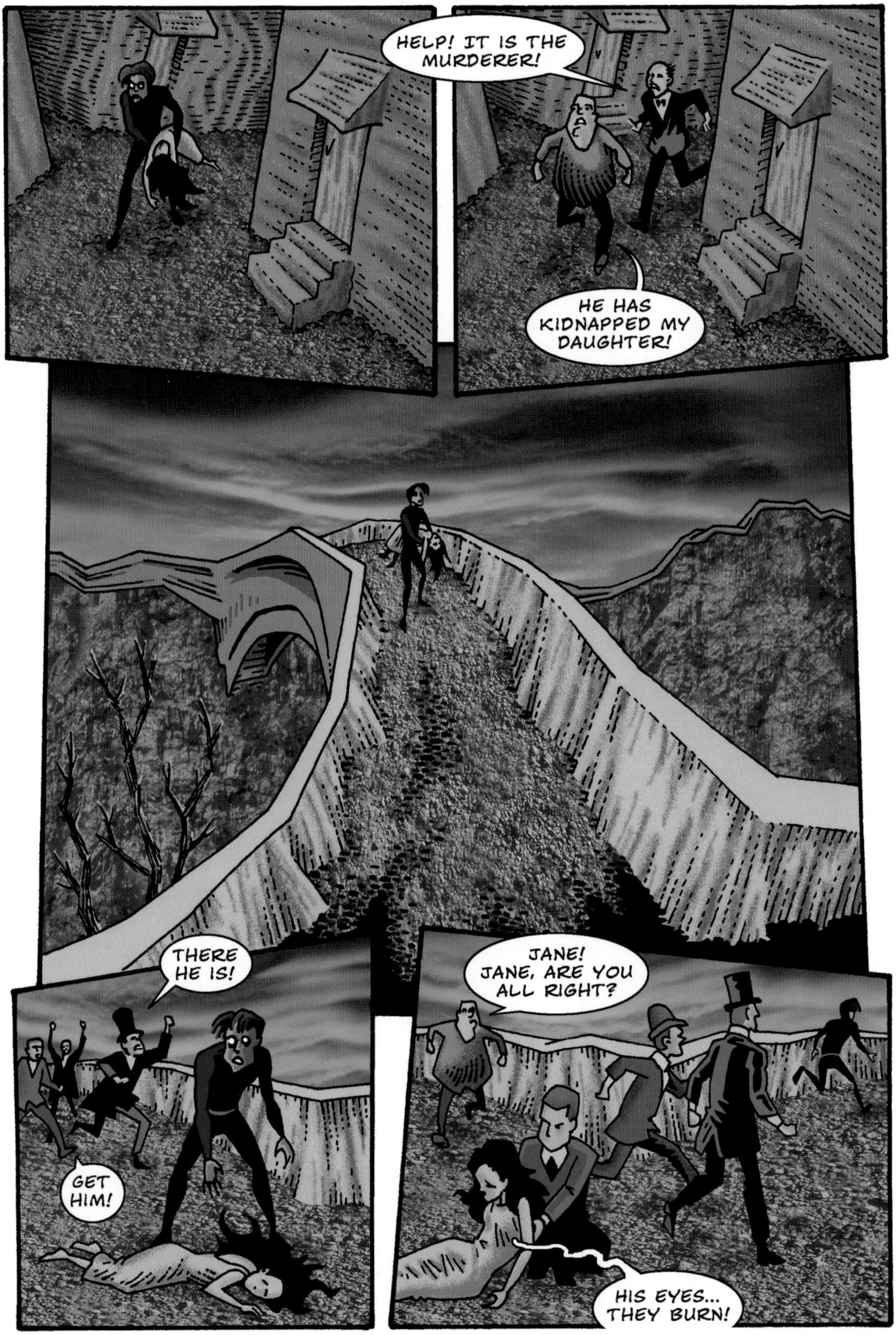
HELP! IT IS THE MURDERER!
HE HAS KIDNAPPED MY DAUGHTER!
THERE HE IS!
GET HIM!
JANE! JANE, ARE YOU ALL RIGHT?
HIS EYES... THEY BURN!

DON'T LET HIM GET AWAY!
HE IS TRAPPED!
THAT'S THE END OF HIM, THANK THE LORD!

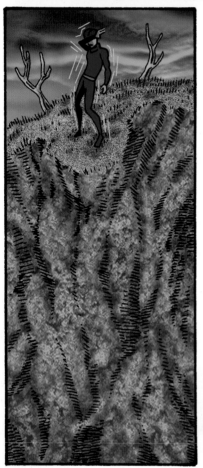

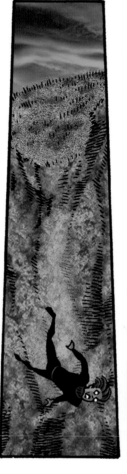

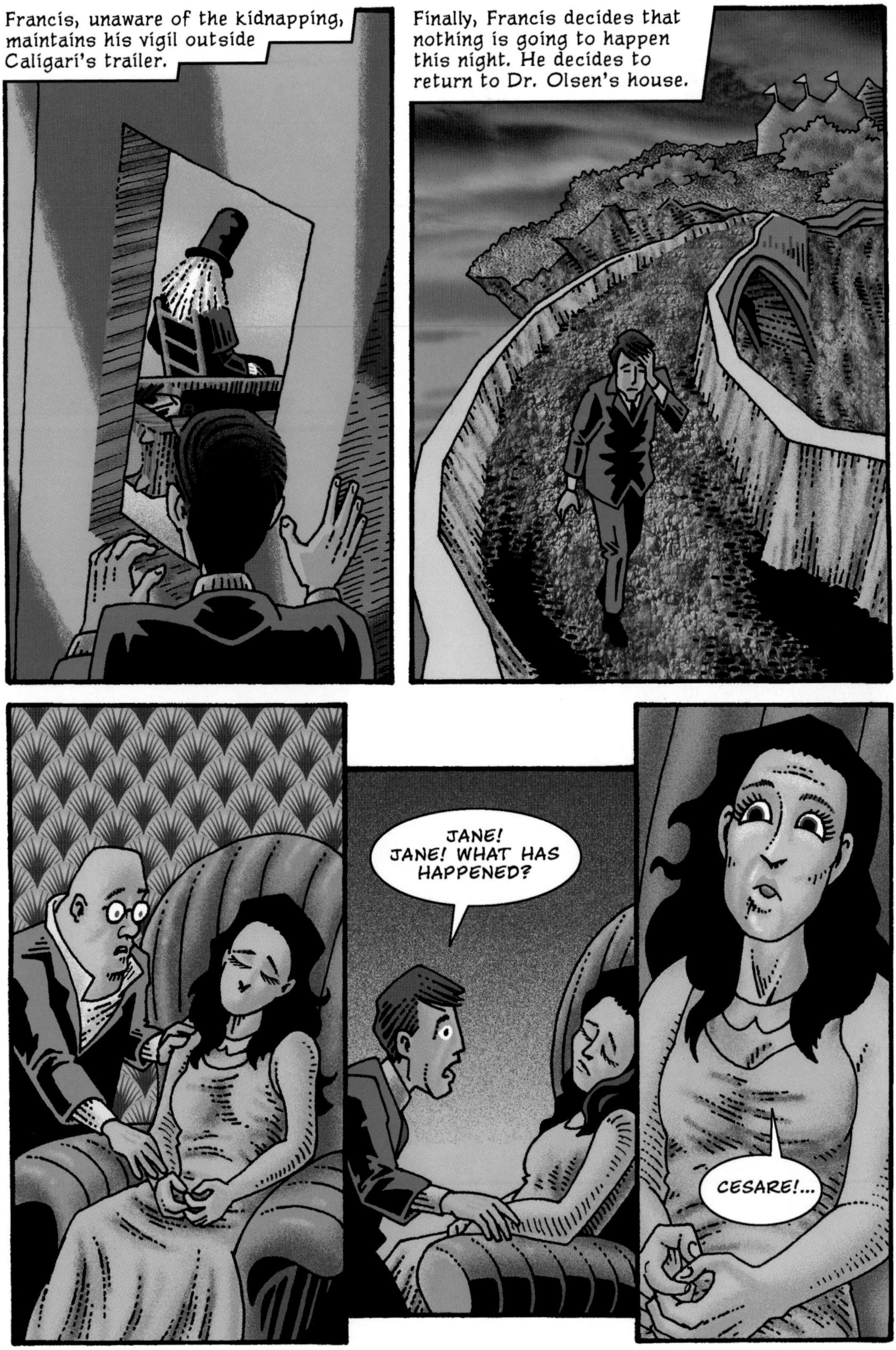
Francis, unaware of the kidnapping, maintains his vigil outside Caligari's trailer.
Finally, Francis decides that nothing is going to happen this night. He decides to return to Dr. Olsen's house.
JANE! JANE! WHAT HAS HAPPENED?
CESARE!...

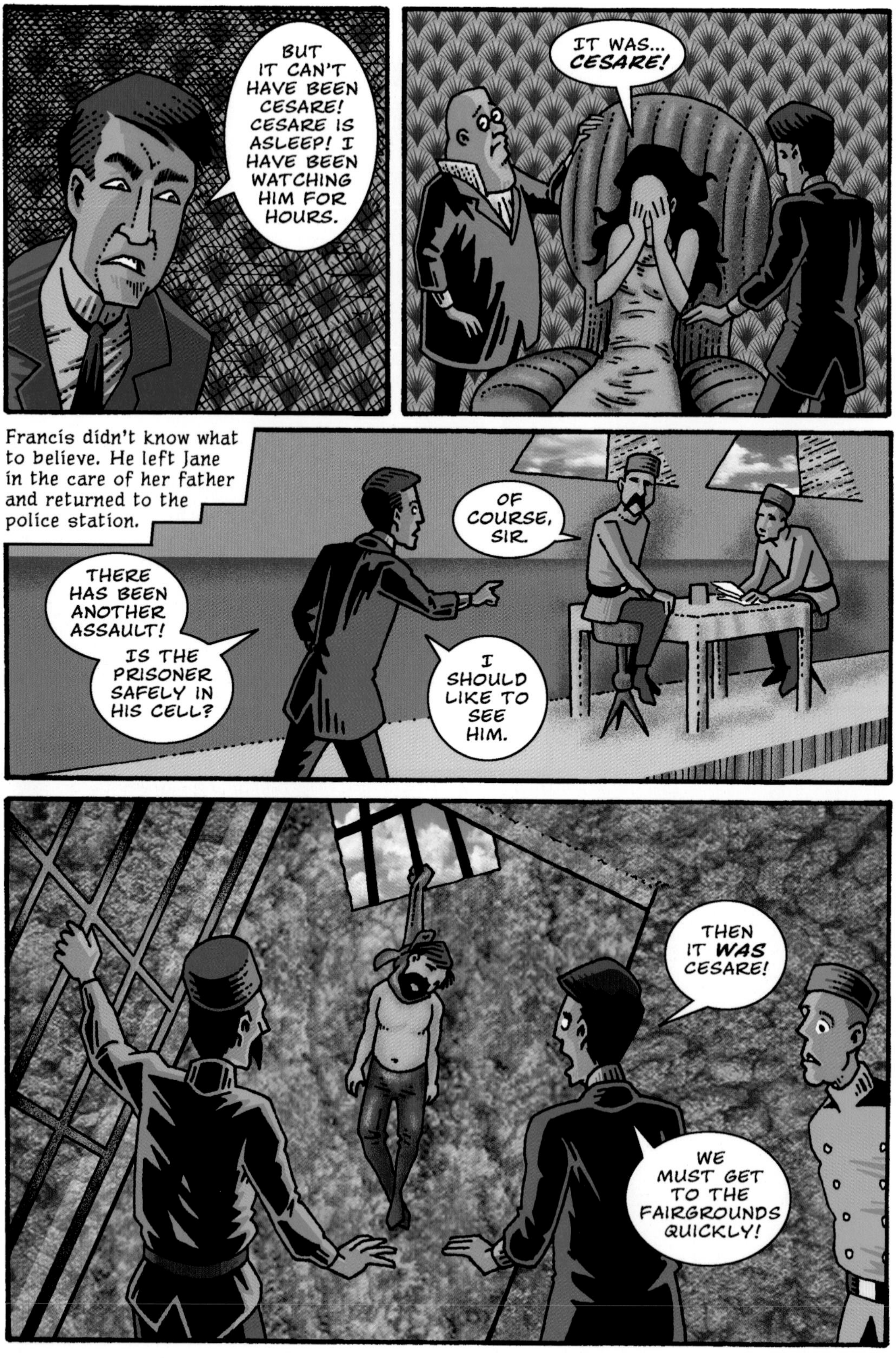
BUT IT CAN'T HAVE BEEN CESARE! CESARE IS ASLEEP! I HAVE BEEN WATCHING HIM FOR HOURS.
IT WAS... ***CESARE!***
Francis didn't know what to believe. He left Jane in the care of her father and returned to the police station.
THERE HAS BEEN ANOTHER ASSAULT!
IS THE PRISONER SAFELY IN HIS CELL?
OF COURSE, SIR.
I SHOULD LIKE TO SEE HIM.
THEN IT ***WAS*** CESARE!
WE MUST GET TO THE FAIRGROUNDS QUICKLY!

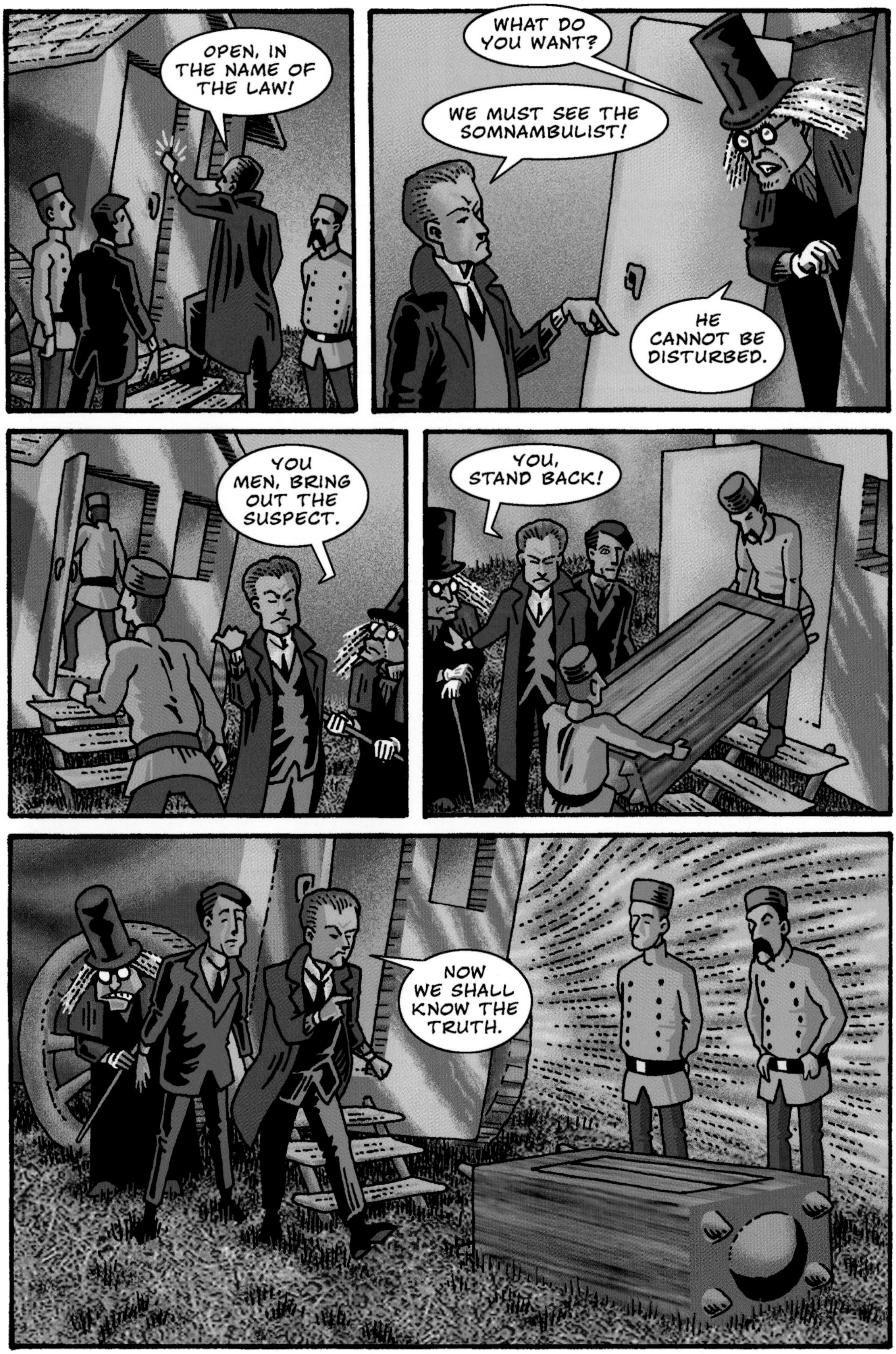
OPEN, IN THE NAME OF THE LAW!
WHAT DO YOU WANT?
WE MUST SEE THE SOMNAMBULIST!
HE CANNOT BE DISTURBED.
YOU MEN, BRING OUT THE SUSPECT.
YOU, STAND BACK!
NOW WE SHALL KNOW THE TRUTH.

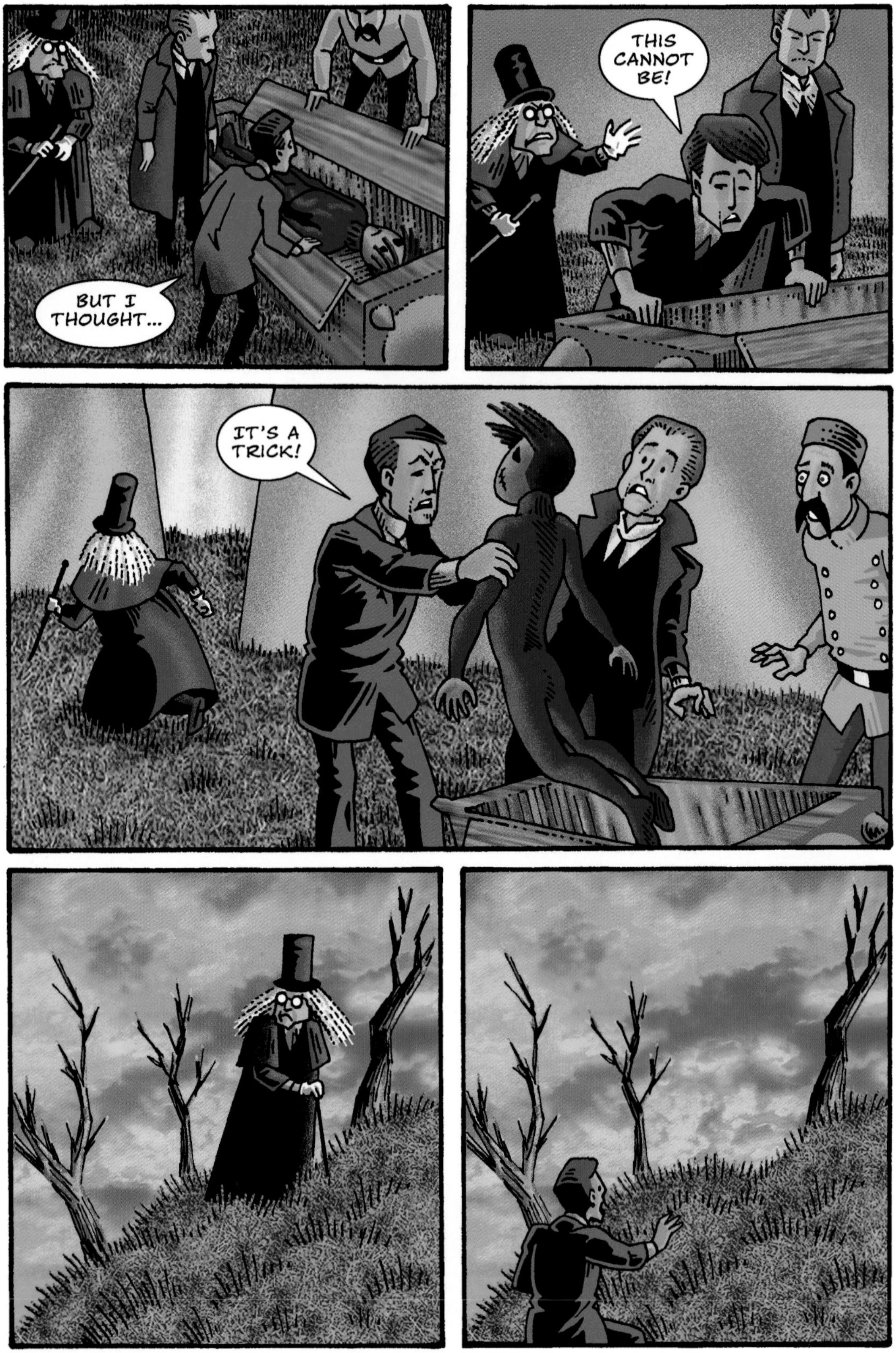
BUT I THOUGHT...
THIS CANNOT BE!
IT'S A TRICK!

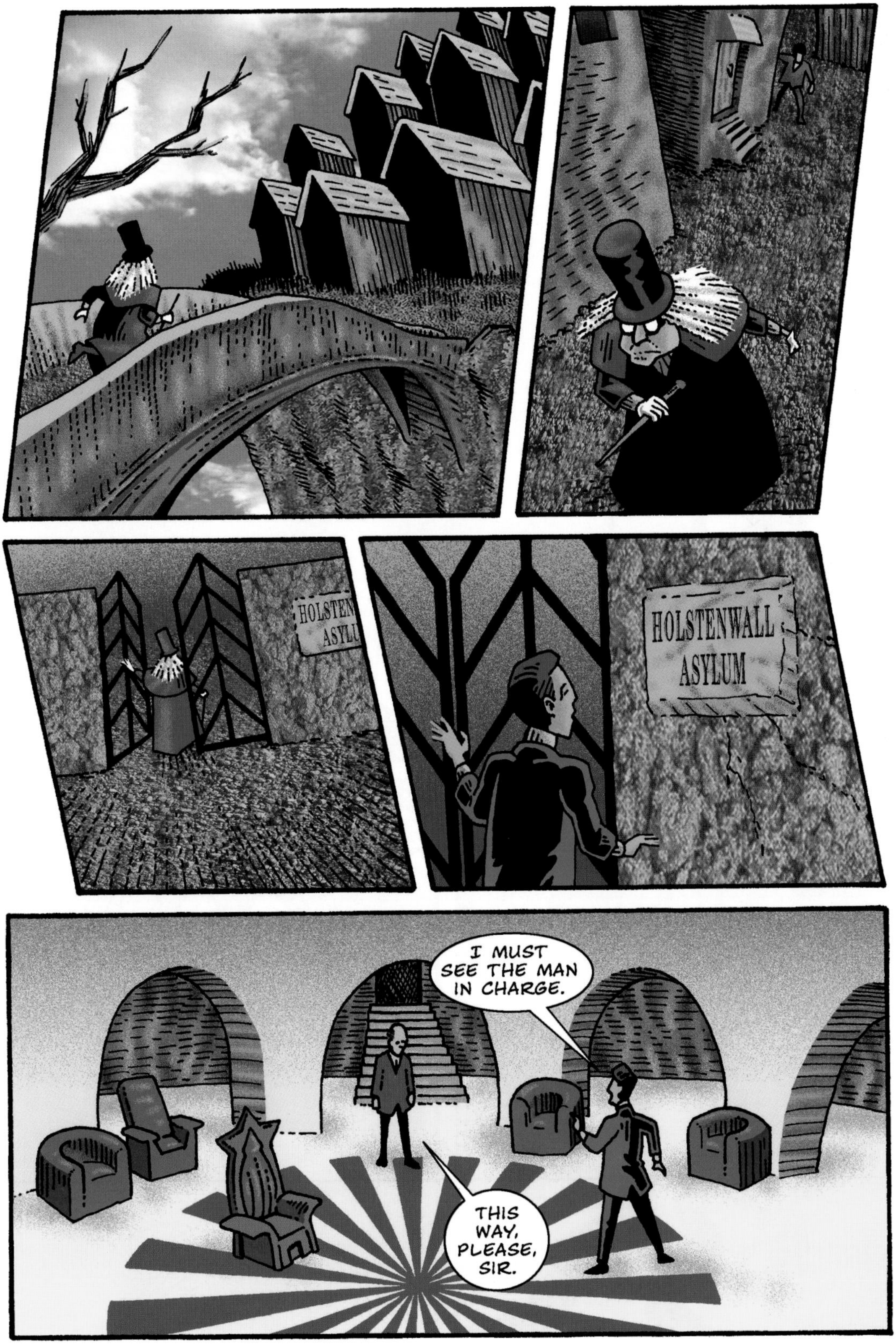
HOLSTEN
ASYLU
HOLSTENWALL
ASYLUM
I MUST SEE THE MAN IN CHARGE.
THIS WAY, PLEASE, SIR.

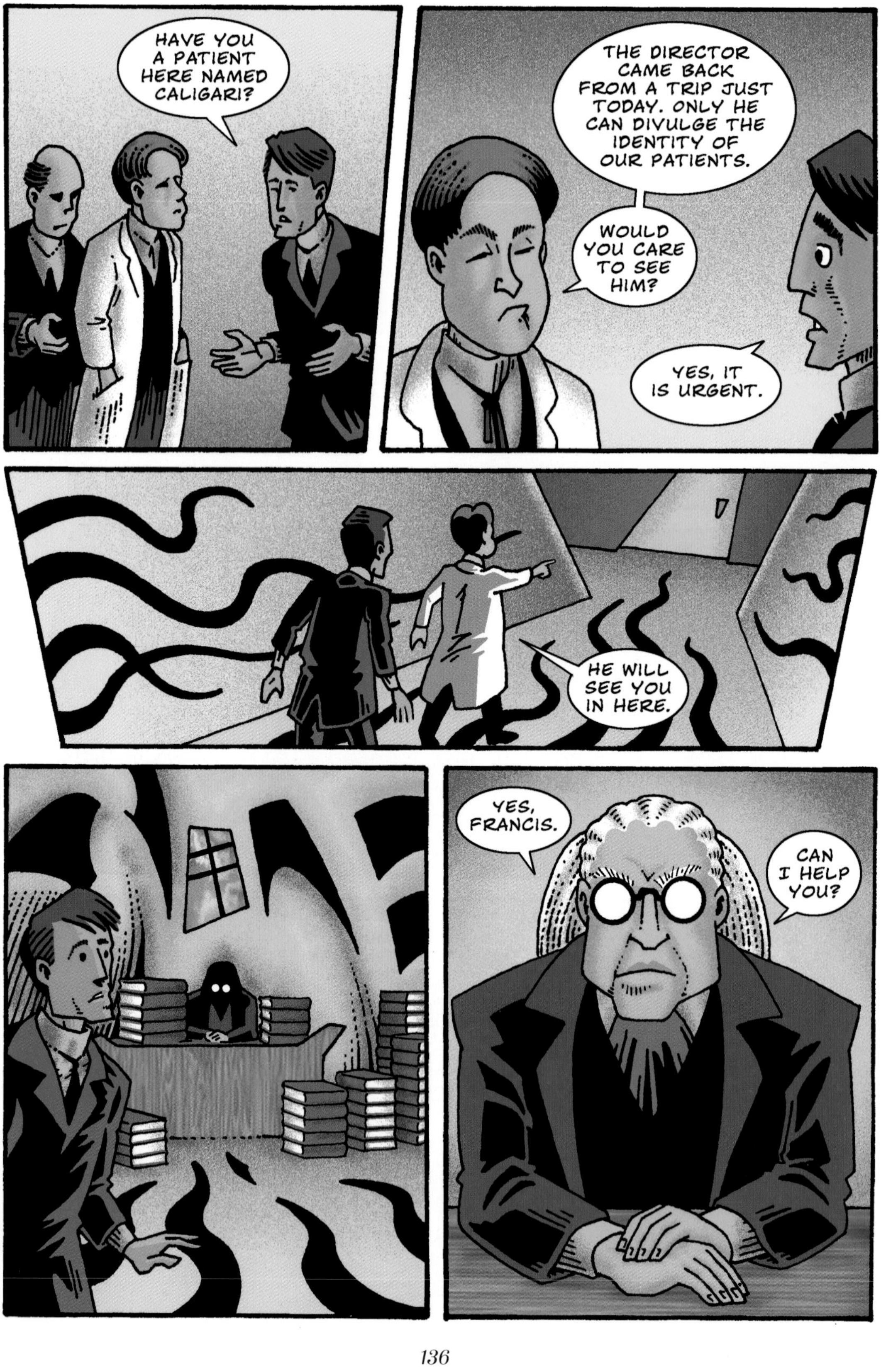
HAVE YOU A PATIENT HERE NAMED CALIGARI?
THE DIRECTOR CAME BACK FROM A TRIP JUST TODAY. ONLY HE CAN DIVULGE THE IDENTITY OF OUR PATIENTS.
WOULD YOU CARE TO SEE HIM?
YES, IT IS URGENT.
HE WILL SEE YOU IN HERE.
YES, FRANCIS.
CAN I HELP YOU?

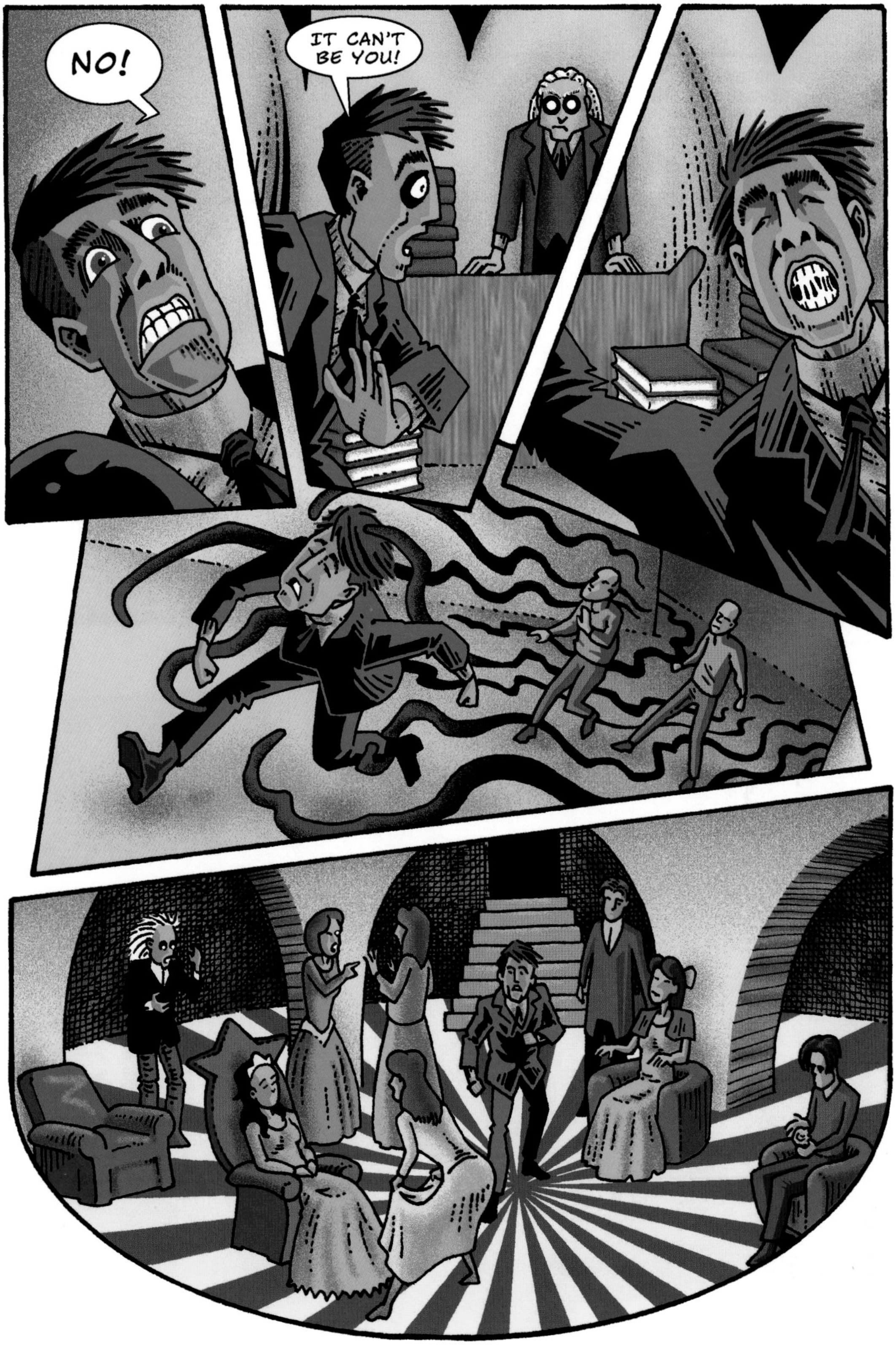
NO!
IT CAN'T BE YOU!

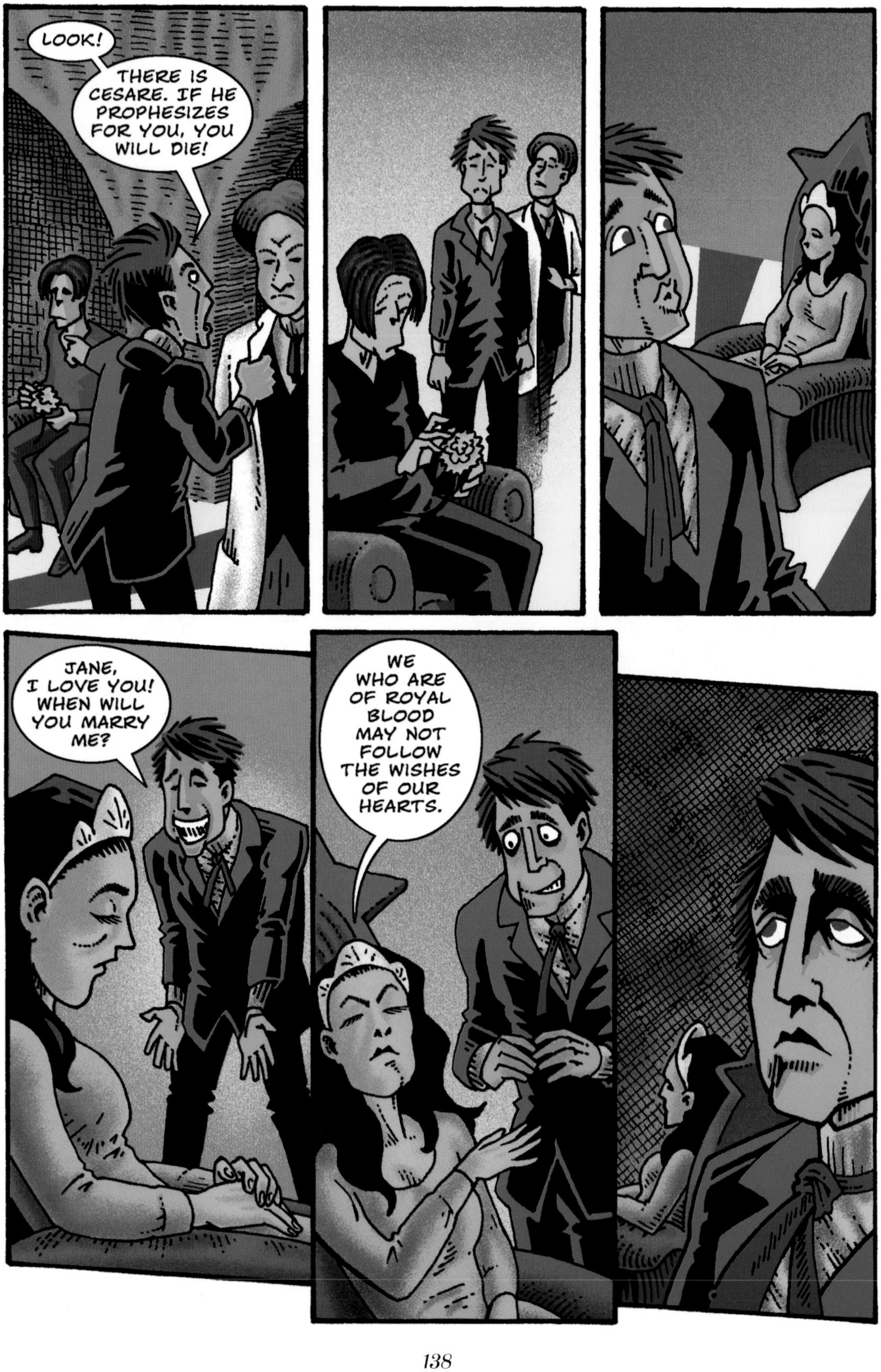
LOOK!
THERE IS CESARE. IF HE PROPHESIZES FOR YOU, YOU WILL DIE!
JANE, I LOVE YOU! WHEN WILL YOU MARRY ME?
WE WHO ARE OF ROYAL BLOOD MAY NOT FOLLOW THE WISHES OF OUR HEARTS.

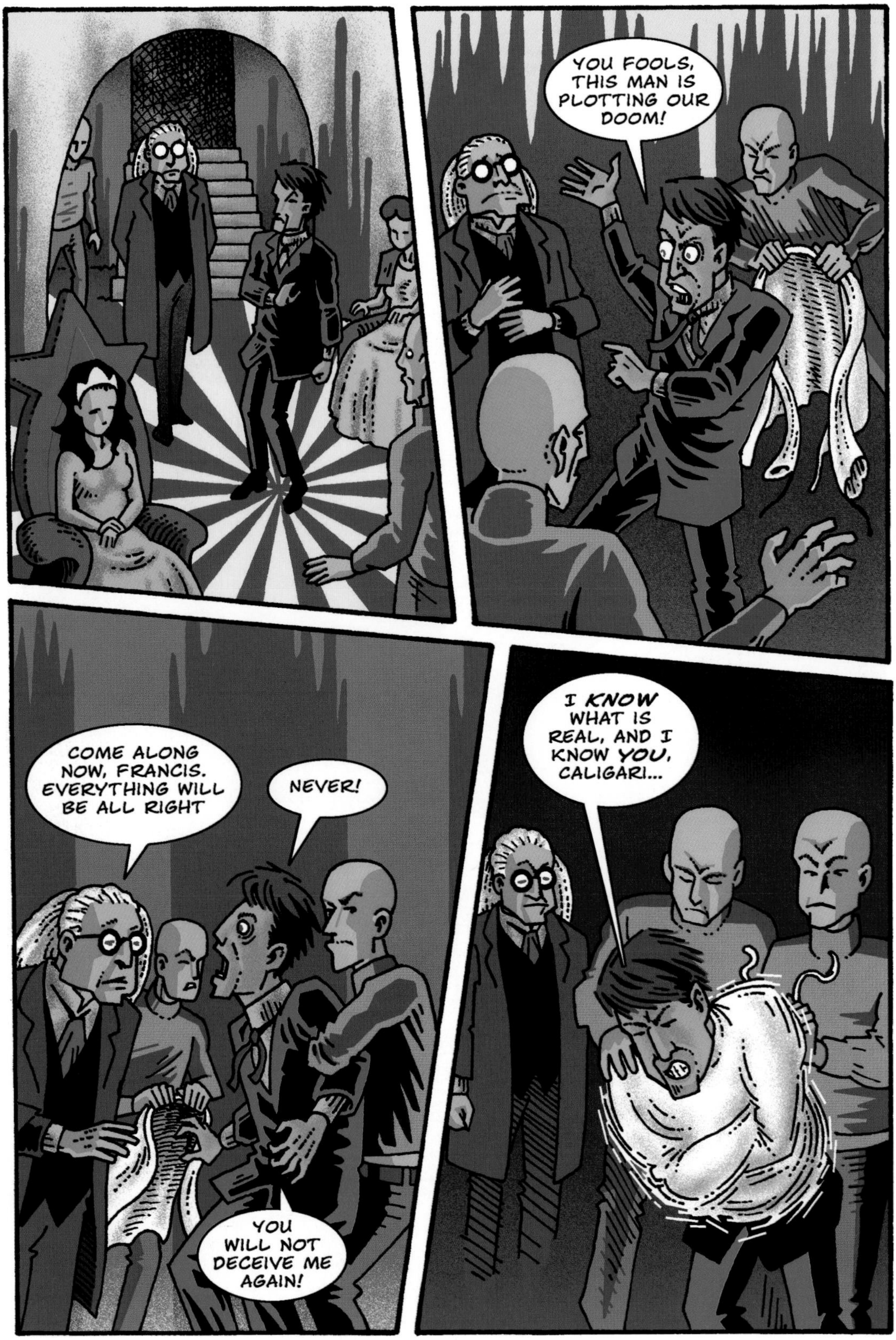
YOU FOOLS, THIS MAN IS PLOTTING OUR DOOM!
COME ALONG NOW, FRANCIS. EVERYTHING WILL BE ALL RIGHT
NEVER!
YOU WILL NOT DECEIVE ME AGAIN!
I *KNOW* WHAT IS REAL, AND I KNOW *YOU*, CALIGARI...

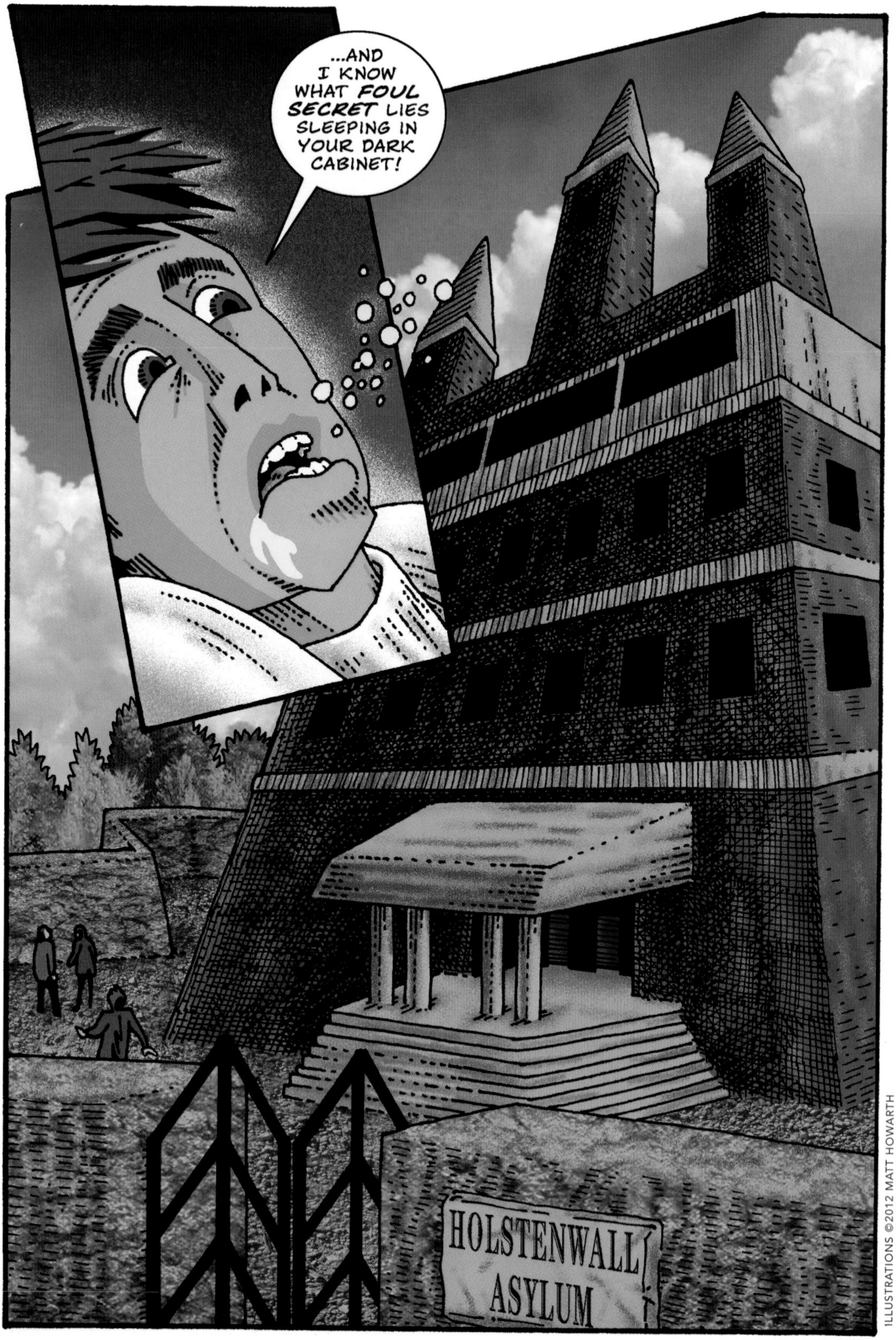
...AND I KNOW WHAT FOUL SECRET LIES SLEEPING IN YOUR DARK CABINET!
HOLSTENWALL ASYLUM

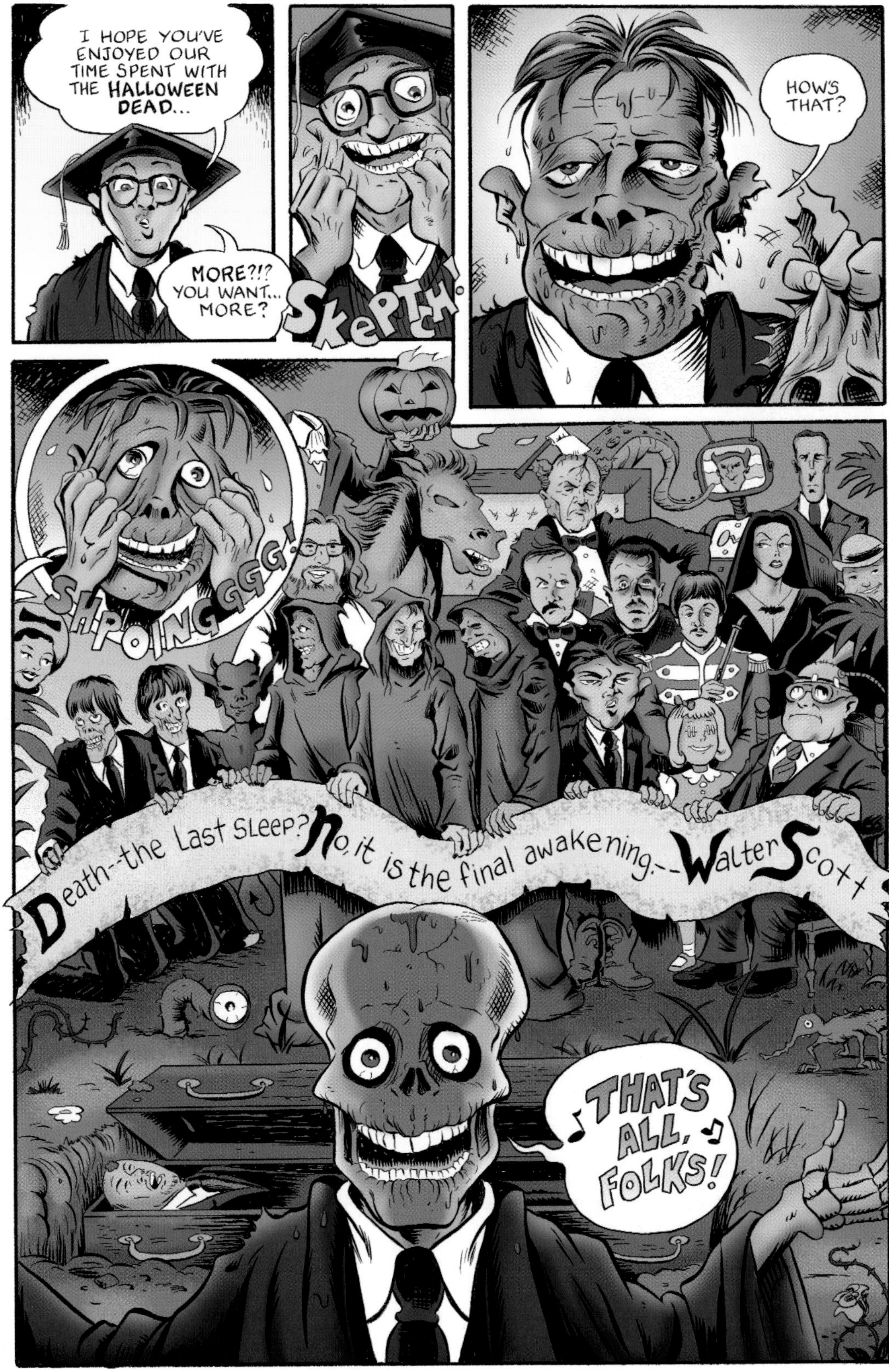
I HOPE YOU'VE ENJOYED OUR TIME SPENT WITH THE HALLOWEEN DEAD...
MORE?!? YOU WANT... MORE?
SKEPTCH!
HOW'S THAT?
SHPOINGGGG!
Death--the Last Sleep? No, it is the final awakening.--Walter Scott
THAT'S ALL, FOLKS!

TERROR
TALES
NO. 24
JUNE-JULY
FROM THE
10¢
CRYPT
FEATURING...
DANGER
QUICKSAND
KEEP AWAY!
THE CRYPT-KEEPER
THE OLD WITCH
THE VAULT-KEEPER

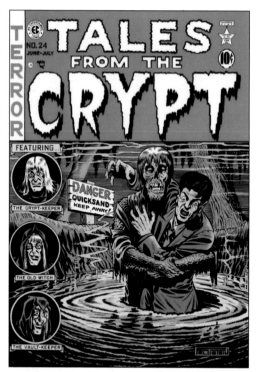

Tales from the Crypt #24 (1951), cover art by Al Feldstein

ABOUT EC COMICS

This volume is a tribute to the seminal EC Comics horror books of the 1950s. EC was founded as Educational Comics in 1944 by Max Gaines. After his death, his son, William Gaines, took over, and in 1949 he hired editors Harvey Kurtzman and Al Feldstein, who also illustrated covers and stories. They expanded the line to include horror, war, crime, science fiction, and humor titles. But the most notorious of these were the horror comics *Tales from the Crypt, Vault of Horror* and *Haunt of Fear*. The horror books were introduced by a trio of hosts, the Crypt Keeper, the Vault Keeper and the Old Witch. The books soon drew the wrath of Dr. Frederick Wertham in his 1954 book, *Seduction of the Innocent*, which spawned Congressional hearings accusing them of promoting juvenile delinquency. The resulting Comics Code Authority drove all of EC's titles out of business, with the exception of *Mad* magazine, which continues to this day. But the EC horror style spawned numerous imitators in comics including Warren's *Creepy* and *Eerie*, DC's *House of Mystery* and *House of Secrets*, and many of the underground comics of the 1960s and '70s. Their influence also extended to other popular media, including the movies, *Creepshow* and *Vault of Horror*, and the television show, *Tales from the Crypt*.

AL FELDSTEIN *(page 1)*

Al Feldstein served as artist, writer, and editor on EC's books, and illustrated many of their most distinctive covers. The illustration on our title page is a revised version of his 1952 cover for *Tales of Terror Annual*, featuring EC's trio of horror hosts. In 1956, Al took over as editor of *Mad* magazine, presiding over the most popular years of the publication, until his retirement from comics in 1984. Al moved to Wyoming, and later to Montana, where he began a second career as a painter of western life and landscapes. One of his fine western paintings appears in *Western Classics: Graphic Classics Volume 20*, and more examples can be viewed at www.alfeldstein.com.

SIMON GANE *(cover, page 49)*

British artist Simon Gane lives and works in Bath. His first published strips appeared in the self-produced punk fanzine *Arnie*, and more followed in numerous mini-comics. Other titles include *All Flee*, a comic about a "finishing school for monsters" and *Paris*, penned by Andi Watson and released by SLG Publishing. His most recent works are the DC/Vertigo series *Vinyl Underground* and the graphic novel *Dark Rain*, written by Mat Johnson. Examples of Simon's work can be found at simongane.blogspot.com and in:

Graphic Classics: Arthur Conan Doyle
Graphic Classics: H.G. Wells
Graphic Classics: H.P. Lovecraft
Graphic Classics: Ambrose Bierce
Graphic Classics: Mark Twain
Graphic Classics: Robert Louis Stevenson
Christmas Classics: Graphic Classics Volume 19
Graphic Classics: Special Edition

H.P. LOVECRAFT *(pages 2, 78)*

Howard Phillips Lovecraft was born in Providence, Rhode Island in 1890. His father died in 1898, and his mother suffered from mental instability until her death in 1921. Poor health and his neurotic, overprotective mother combined to make something of a recluse of Lovecraft. Growing up, he had little contact with other children, and as an adult maintained his many long-distance relationships through voluminous correspondence. He was obsessed with dreams, and wrote most of his stories and poems around a central theme of ancient gods who once ruled the earth and are merely awaiting a return to power. His writings appeared mostly in the "pulp" magazines of his time and received little critical attention outside of the horror genre. Since Lovecraft's death in 1937, his stories have grown in popularity and have spawned a huge cult of both fans and professional writers who continue to expand Lovecraft's themes through stories set in the "Cthulhu Mythos." More stories by Lovecraft appear in:

Graphic Classics: H.P. Lovecraft
Horror Classics: Graphic Classics Volume 10
Fantasy Classics: Graphic Classics Volume 15

JEFFREY JOHANNES *(page 2)*

Jeffrey Johannes, from Port Edwards, Wisconsin, is an artist, poet, and cartoonist. His writing and art have been published in journals, including *Modern Haiku* and the *Wisconsin Academy Review*, and he has won awards, including the Best New Poet and Poets' Choice categories of the Triad contest sponsored by the Wisconsin Fellowship of Poets. His art has also won awards, been featured in juried shows, and appeared in publications including *Rosebud 26*. Jeffrey is currently drawing comic strips from his poems, which he calls "pometoons," after Walt Whitman's pronunciation of 'poem.' He co-edited the 2012 Wisconsin Poets' Calendar with his wife, Joan, and his first book of poetry was published in 2011.

MORT CASTLE *(page 4)*

A writing teacher and author specializing in the horror genre, Mort Castle has written and edited fourteen books and around 500 short stories and articles. His novels and collections include *Cursed Be the Child, The Strangers, Moon on the Water* and *Nations of the Living, Nations of* the Dead, and he recently edited Shadow Show: All New Stories in Celebration of Ray Bradbury. He has produced an audio CD of one of his stories, Buckeye Jim in Egypt, and is the author of the essential reference work for aspiring horror writers, On Writing Horror. Mort has won numerous writing awards, and has had several dozen stories cited in "year's best" compilations in the horror, suspense, fantasy, and literary fields. He has been a writer and editor for several comics publishers, and is a frequent keynote speaker at writing conferences. Mort's comics stories also can be found in:

Graphic Classics: Jack London
Graphic Classics: Ambrose Bierce
Graphic Classics: Bram Stoker
Graphic Classics: Robert Louis Stevenson
Graphic Classics: O. Henry

KEVIN ATKINSON (page 4)

"I've lived in Texas my whole life with the exception of 1985–1988, when I went to New Jersey to study with [famed comics artist and teacher] Joe Kubert," says Kevin. Since then he has created short stories and full-length comics for various publishers. He wrote and drew two series, Snarl and Planet 29, and collaborated on another, Rogue Satellite Comics. He's also inked The Tick comics, and illustrated Drew Edward's Halloween Man. Visit eatenbyplanet29.tumblr.com or co2comics.com to see Kevin's online comic Eaten by Planet 29. He has illustrated stories in:

Graphic Classics: H.P. Lovecraft
Graphic Classics: Mark Twain
Graphic Classics: Rafael Sabatini
Horror Classics: Graphic Classics Volume 10
Adventure Classics: Graphic Classics Volume 12
Science Fiction Classics: Graphic Classics Volume 17

WASHINGTON IRVING (page 7)

Washington Irving (1783-1859), a prolific author of both fiction and nonfiction, was one of the first American writers to be acclaimed in Europe during his lifetime. In 1842 he was appointed ambassador to Spain, where he served until 1846. Irving wrote numerous short stories, novels, biographies, histories, and travelogues, but his most enduring legacies are the tales Rip Van Winkle and The Legend of Sleepy Hollow, both first published in his short story collection, The Sketch Book of Geoffrey Crayon, Gent. in 1819. These stories have been adapted numerous times in modern movies, plays, and cartoons. Batman fans may note that Irving coined the term "Gotham" for New York City, and he was an early popularizer of the Christmas holiday, including the invention of St. Nicholas' flying sled.

BEN AVERY (page 7)

Ben Avery adapted the script of the critically acclaimed graphic novel, The Hedge Knight and its sequel, The Sworn Sword, published by Marvel and based on the novellas by New York Times bestselling fantasy author George R.R. Martin. Ben wrote the Oz/Wonderland Chronicles from BuyMeToys.com, based on the beloved fantasy characters. He has worked on Image Comics' Lullaby and The Imaginaries and his own all-ages series TimeFlyz (about time-traveling flies). Ben lives in Indiana with his wife and four kids, but wishes he lived in a northern Ontario cabin (with his wife and four kids, of course). His adaptations also appear in:

Fantasy Classics: Graphic Classics Volume 15
Science Fiction Classics: Graphic Classics Volume 17
Western Classics: Graphic Classics Volume 20

SHEPHERD HENDRIX (page 7)

Shepherd Hendrix began his comics career in 1991 as an inker on DC Comics' Swamp Thing. He also penciled and inked Restaurant at the End of the Universe with Steve Leialoha. In the late 1990s, he left the industry and began working as a storyboard artist, background designer, and concept artist, using both traditional and digital mediums, collaborating with LucasArts and EA Games. In 2006, he returned to comics, illustrating the Eisner Award-nominated Stagger Lee, written by Derek McCulloch, for Image Comics. You can find pages from Stagger Lee in Black Comix: African American Independent Comics, Art & Culture, and examples of Shepherd's art at www.shepko.com. His adaptation of a Charles W. Chesnutt story appears in African-American Classics: Graphic Classics Volume 22.

MARK TWAIN (page 37)

Born in Missouri in 1835, Samuel Langhorne Clemens took his pen name from the alert common among steamboat crews on his beloved Mississippi River for water "two fathoms deep." As a boy, he wanted to be a riverboat pilot, and became one, until the advent of the Civil War caused him, with his brother, to move to the Nevada Territory in 1861. He started as a newspaper reporter in Virginia City, and there wrote his first successful story, The Celebrated Jumping Frog of Calaveras County. He went on to become one of the most popular authors and humorists in American history. While today best known for what are taken as children's novels, The Adventures of Tom Sawyer and The Adventures of Huckleberry Finn as well as the lesser-known sequel, Tom Sawyer Abroad, Mark Twain also authored a vast range of novels, short stories, travel books, articles, essays, and satirical sketches. Failed investments and the early deaths of his wife and daughters led to an increasingly cynical view in his later writings, including The Mysterious Stranger. He died at his home in Connecticut at age 75. Stories by Mark Twain are adapted in:

Graphic Classics: Mark Twain
Christmas Classics: Graphic Classics Volume 19

ANTONELLA CAPUTO (page 37)

Antonella Caputo was born and raised in Rome, Italy, and now lives in Lancaster, England. She has been an architect, archaeologist, art restorer, photographer, calligrapher, interior designer, theater designer, actress, and theater director. Her first published work was Casa Montesi, a fortnightly comic strip which appeared in the national magazine Il Giornalino. She has since written comedies for children and scripts for comics and magazines in the U.K., Europe and the U.S. Antonella works with Nick Miller as the writer for Team Sputnik, and has collaborated with Nick and others in:

Graphic Classics: Arthur Conan Doyle
Graphic Classics: H.G. Wells
Graphic Classics: Jack London
Graphic Classics: Ambrose Bierce
Graphic Classics: Mark Twain
Graphic Classics: O. Henry
Graphic Classics: Rafael Sabatini
Graphic Classics: Oscar Wilde
Graphic Classics: Louisa May Alcott
Horror Classics: Graphic Classics Volume 10
Adventure Classics: Graphic Classics Volume 12
Gothic Classics: Graphic Classics Volume 14
Fantasy Classics: Graphic Classics Volume 15
Poe's Tales of Mystery: Graphic Classics Volume 21
Graphic Classics: Special Edition

NICK MILLER *(page 37)*

Nick grew up in the depths of rural England, and now lives in Lancaster with his partner, Antonella Caputo. The son of two artists, he learned to draw at an early age. After leaving art school he worked as a graphic designer before switching to cartooning and illustration full-time in the early '90s. Since then his work has appeared in many comics and magazines in the U.K., U.S. and Europe, as well as in comic anthologies, websites and in advertising. Nick's weekly comic strip, *The Really Heavy Greatcoat*, is online at www.lancasterukonline.net. He works as part of Team Sputnik with Antonella Caputo, and also independently with other writers including John Freeman, Tony Husband, Mark Rogers, and Tim Quinn. Nick's stories have appeared in:

Graphic Classics: Arthur Conan Doyle
Graphic Classics: H.G. Wells
Graphic Classics: Jack London
Graphic Classics: Ambrose Bierce
Graphic Classics: Mark Twain
Graphic Classics: Oscar Wilde
Horror Classics: Graphic Classics Volume 10
Adventure Classics: Graphic Classics Volume 12

ARTHUR CONAN DOYLE *(page 49)*

Arthur Conan Doyle, born in 1859, studied in England and Germany and became a Doctor of Medicine at the University of Edinburgh. He built a successful medical practice, but also wrote, and created his most famous character, Sherlock Holmes, in 1887. Following a less-successful practice as an oculist, Doyle concentrated on his writing career. He was proudest of his historical novels, such as *The White Company*, and in 1894 introduced his second popular character, Brigadier Gerard. In 1912, he created Professor Challenger, who appeared in a series of science fiction-themed stories. But Holmes continued to be his most famous creation. Doyle felt that Holmes was a distraction and kept him from writing the "better things" that would make him a "lasting name in English literature." He killed his detective in 1893 in *The Final Problem*, only to resurrect him in 1903 due to public demand. Doyle wrote an astonishing range of fiction including medical stories, sports stories, historical fiction, science fiction, contemporary drama, and verse. He also wrote nonfiction, including the six-volume *The British Campaign in France and Flanders*. His defense of British colonialism in South Africa led to his being knighted in 1902. By 1916 Doyle's investigations into Spiritualism had convinced him that he should devote the rest of his life to the advancement of the belief. He wrote and lectured on the Spiritualist cause until his death in 1930. More stories by Arthur Conan Doyle are adapted in:

Graphic Classics: Arthur Conan Doyle
Adventure Classics: Graphic Classics Volume 12
Science Fiction Classics: Graphic Classics Volume 17
Christmas Classics: Graphic Classics Volume 19
Graphic Classics: Special Edition

ROD LOTT *(page 78)*

Oklahoma City resident Rod Lott is a corporate managing editor for a media company. He is the founder and editor of *Bookgasm*, a daily book review and news site at www.bookgasm.com, and for twelve years he published the magazine *Hitch: The Journal of Pop Culture Absurdity*. Rod's humorous essays have been published in several anthologies, including **May Contain Nuts** and **101 Damnations**. You can find more comics adaptations by Rod in:

Graphic Classics: Edgar Allan Poe
Graphic Classics: Arthur Conan Doyle
Graphic Classics: H.G. Wells
Graphic Classics: H.P. Lovecraft
Graphic Classics: Jack London
Graphic Classics: Ambrose Bierce
Graphic Classics: O. Henry
Graphic Classics: Rafael Sabatini
Graphic Classics: Louisa May Alcott
Horror Classics: Graphic Classics Volume 10
Adventure Classics: Graphic Classics Volume 12
Gothic Classics: Graphic Classics Volume 14
Fantasy Classics: Graphic Classics Volume 15
Western Classics: Graphic Classics Volume 20
Poe's Tales of Mystery: Graphic Classics Volume 21

CRAIG WILSON *(page 78)*

A director/storyboard artist of animation, as well as an illustrator, Craig Wilson has been pushing a pencil professionally for over twenty years. He's received two Emmy nominations for his direction of *Where in the World is Carmen Sandiego*, and a Leo Awards nomination for *Dragons: Fire and Ice*. A resident of Vancouver, Canada, you can see more of Craig's work on his blog at www.money-shotz.blogspot.com or his website at www.boardguy.ca. He illustrated *The Oval Portrait* for *Poe's Tales of Mystery: Graphic Classics Volume 21*.

HANS JANOWITZ & CARL MAYER *(page 93)*

German author Hans Janowitz and Austrian screenwriter Carl Mayer, both famous for their later work with director F.W. Murnau, first joined forces in 1920, on the screenplay for the great silent film, *The Cabinet of Dr. Caligari*, directed by Robert Wiene. They based their story for the then-new medium of film on their experiences of the first World War and their joint visit to a post-war fair and sideshow. The film today is most noted for its pioneering Expressionist style, and has inspired numerous remakes and adaptations to this day.

MATT HOWARTH *(page 93)*

Best known for his *Those Annoying Post Bros.* series, Matt has spent his career mixing the genres of science fiction, comic books, and alternative music into a unique and entertaining gestalt. His twisted talents have spawned innumerable comic books, several novels, and nearly 100 digital publications. He has collaborated with a variety of international musicians to create a revival of the "concept album" in the 21st century, mixing music and graphic storytelling, and musicians have "guest starred" in many of his comics. His weekly music review column can be found at www.soniccuriosity.com since 2001. He has drawn graphic adaptations of works by Greg Bear, Hal Clement, Warren Ellis, Chinese poet Pu Songling, and Vernor Vinge, and recently released his Lovecraftian science fiction novel, *The Eden Retrieval* (2011, Merry Blackmith Press). You are invited to visit www.matthowarth.com, and to see Matt's work in:

Graphic Classics: Edgar Allan Poe
Graphic Classics: H.P. Lovecraft

TOM POMPLUN

The designer, editor, and publisher of *Graphic Classics*, Tom also designed *Rosebud*, a journal of fiction, poetry and illustration, from 1993 to 2003, and in 2001 he founded the *Graphic Classics* series. Tom is currently working on *Native American Classics: Graphic Classics Volume 24*, scheduled for February 2013 release, with associate editors John E. Smelcer and Joseph Bruchac.